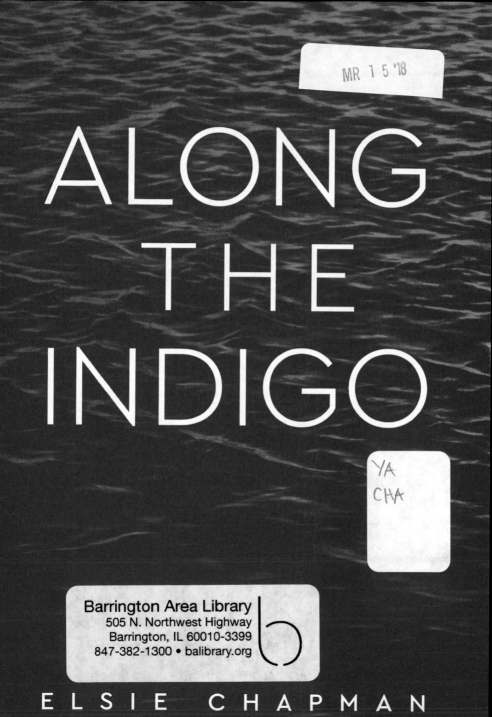

ALONG THE INDIGO

ELSIE CHAPMAN

ALONG THE INDIGO

ELSIE CHAPMAN

Amulet Books
New York

Cataloging-in-Publication Data has been applied for and may be obtained from the Library of Congress.

ISBN 978-1-4197-2531-9

Text copyright © 2018 Elsie Chapman
Cover design by Neil Swaab
Cover photography copyright © Ute Klaphake / Trevillion Images
Book design by Siobhán Gallagher

Printed and bound in U.S.A.
10 9 8 7 6 5 4 3 2 1

Amulet Books are available at special discounts when purchased in quantity for premiums and promotions as well as fundraising or educational use. Special editions can also be created to specification. For details, contact specialsales@abramsbooks.com or the address below.

ABRAMS The Art of Books
195 Broadway, New York, NY 10007
abramsbooks.com

To Jesse, Matthew, and Gillian. Once more.

one.

THIS EARLY IN THE SUMMER, MARSDEN HADN'T YET REMEM-
BERED HOW FAR SOUND COULD CARRY COMING FROM AN
OPEN WINDOW.

She half scowled as she looked back at the boardinghouse, the
lights from the exposed bedrooms blazing into the near dusk like eyes
from the shadows. Echoes of Nina's brisk instructions—*softer lipstick,
bolder eyebrows, heels should be taller than four inches*—swirled out into
the air from behind mesh screens. Low murmurs as the girls fixed one
another's hair, as they chose between dresses, as they wondered who
would be the unlucky one that night, the one to end up with the oldest
john or the ugliest. The cheapskate. The fetishist.

Her mother, she knew, mostly dreaded the old ones. Shine feared
age as though it were contagious, the weakness she said it was.

"Marsden, you're tipping the bucket! We're losing berries!"

"What? I'm not."

"You *are*."

She glanced down at the ice-cream bucket in her hand, saw that
her little sister was right, and tilted it back to save the rest of the berries

they'd just picked. Saskatoon ones, purple as night, hard as gems—they would still be more tart than sweet. Marsden knew they could have used more time on the bush, but when Wynn had suddenly wanted to get her hair done with the girls, offering to take her out into the half-dark to pick berries for homemade strudels had been the first thing to pop into Marsden's head. Bribery: She would never be above it if it meant saving Wynn from the truth.

Still, she hadn't missed her sister's occasional glances back toward Nina's girls and the boardinghouse as they moved toward the berry bushes at the edge of the covert—wistful, still longing. She'd understood it, even, despite not wanting to—that strange wish to get to know them well enough to call them friends, the ache to be surrounded by their sheer number, to let herself be cradled and wanted and accepted.

Wynn tugged at more branches. Berries fell into the bucket, plunks like rain on a roof. Marsden sucked at her thumb, still pricked from when it'd met a thorn, and blood ran into the tastes of dinner—salmon with dill and cream, grilled tomatoes—still lingering on her tongue. As one of two cooks for the boardinghouse, she'd made the dish dozens of times before. It was one of Nina's favorites to serve guests.

Suddenly, her sister froze, her gaze locked on something past the line of berry bushes, and dread rolled into Marsden's stomach. Because she knew, even before her eyes chased Wynn's and saw what they saw deeper in the covert, lit up by the falling sun like a piece of shiny foil among all that dark green forest.

The body was a pale slash, and Marsden sighed—too late to try to hide it from Wynn. She'd checked the covert just that morning as always. But she'd been in a hurry—now that school was out, she had less time to comb the grounds before her sister was awake and up, wanting to play. She cursed herself for not being more careful, summer for existing, and Nina for wanting Wynn out of the boardinghouse in the mornings while johns were still slipping away.

"I bet she used a gun," Wynn finally said, no longer frozen but contemplative—nearly clinically so—as she analyzed the presence of one more dead person found in the covert. Seeing her like that dismayed Marsden, though she wasn't surprised. Wynn had grown up with the covert's secrets and not-so-secrets. This was all normal to her. "It's what I would use," her sister continued.

"Don't say that. It's morbid."

"What do *you* think she used?"

Marsden sighed again. "Probably a gun."

"It wouldn't have hurt, right?" Wynn grabbed Marsden's hand. In the dim light, Marsden saw that berry juice had turned the tips of their fingers the shade of new bruises. The taste of blood on her tongue seemed to surge. "However that person died?"

Love flooded Marsden. In that moment, her sister was such the ultimate *kid*—choppy black hair askew all over her head like upturned paintbrushes dried wrong from inside a jar. How she hadn't bothered changing her outfit from yesterday: a Jem and the Holograms T-shirt spotted with grass stains, a pair of baggy cutoffs, a striped rainbow belt with a drooping tail. She was even wrapped up in kid smells: sweat,

3

cheap strawberry-marshmallow candy, the dusty outdoor burn of early July heat.

"Right, Mars?" Wynn pressed, needing to know, her fingers squeezing. Her bones felt as fine as a sparrow's. At eight, her sister was tiny for her age, as Marsden herself had been—and still was, at sixteen—both of them sparse and stunted and wiry. Like plants grown beneath strange light, the town sometimes still said. "It would have been quick?"

Marsden nodded, though she had no real clue. Wynn knew she had no clue. She wasn't really asking about *how*, anyway—more *why*. And that was a question they could never really answer for sure. Suicide notes, if they were found, had little meaning but for the person they'd been written for.

Marsden got a glimpse of pale skin through the trees, of blond hair splotched with the telltale darkness of blood. "It wouldn't have hurt, no. Out like a light. Totally painless."

"You're guessing."

"Why ask if you're not going to believe me, runt?" She flicked a crumb from Wynn's nest of hair—buttermilk waffle. Her sister had brought one along with her, a leftover from breakfast that she had crumbled into the grass to feed the squirrels.

"I do believe you." Wynn chewed the plum-tinged thumb of her free hand; a sliver of nail coiled out from between her teeth like apple skin off a peeler. Bodies changed her covert, made it dangerous. She was never scared of the land, though sometimes Marsden wished she *were*, just a bit—it would make life that much easier, her sister not wanting to play there. Wynn's expression was thoughtful as she looked up at Marsden. "But I bet Grandma wouldn't have had to guess. I bet she would have known for sure."

Wynn had never known their grandmother on their mother's side, who'd died before she was born. But she'd heard all the stories and was familiar with the legend Star Liu had been in town. How she could hear the dead. How she could connect with them as a service.

"If *Theola* were here, maybe she could tell, too," her sister continued.

Marsden snorted. She pictured their dead grandmother's old friend: gaudy floral dresses, oversize feathered hats, a probing stare that tried to unearth all kinds of foul, shameful things from your mind. Old Theola Finney dressed bigger than the town, but her advertised psychic abilities said she fit Glory just fine.

"Theola tells *fortunes* down at her café, Wynn. Looks deep into your eyes and tells you your future."

Wynn pulled her hand free. "I like her, even if you think she's a liar."

"I never said she was a liar. I just don't think she tells the truth. It's not the same thing."

"How come we can't hear the dead talk if Grandma could?" Her sister was staring at the body again. "Mom used to be able to, too, she says. So why can't we? Don't you wish we could?"

The summer heat—which was always bad in Glory, where it built into a thick shimmering wall that wouldn't tumble down until nearly October—suddenly seemed cold. "Not really, no," Marsden said.

"But—"

A laugh wafted out from the boardinghouse—a soft trill, perfectly crafted to appeal, their mother's when she was working—and Marsden found herself scowling again. Still, it meant that all of Nina's girls would soon be in their rooms for the night, and she could stop worrying about Wynn accidentally seeing what she didn't need to see.

"Listen, you know the deal, if we ever see anything in the covert . . ." She dug a dollar bill from the pocket of her shorts. "It's still light enough out, and the corner store won't be closed yet." Gwen carried Wynn's greatest weaknesses, Kraft caramels and elasticized candy bracelets. "Go eat some sugar. I'll come get you when I'm done checking."

Wynn eyed the money and moved on from chewing her thumb to her pinky. Her expression was torn. Marsden knew that look. It said her sister wanted to be old enough to face the ugliest parts of the covert. It *also* said she wanted to pretend she didn't come from a family whose name had long become synonymous with death.

Finally, Wynn shrugged, spitting out another sliver of nail. "Want me to bring the berries to the kitchen first?"

Marsden shook her head. "No, we'll just grab them on the way back." Another day bought. Still, her relief at saving Wynn from one more body in the covert was already fizzling away. Wynn saw Glory's businesses during the day and assumed appearances were everything. Her sister had no clue that home—her beloved boardinghouse and the town's best-rated overnight lodging among tourists—was also the town's most popular brothel. She had no idea that Nina was more their captor than their savior. How much longer before she got old enough to decide Nina's girls were more fun than her dull, worried sister?

Wynn began to head down the path toward the shed for her bike. "Want me to buy licorice for you, Mars?"

"Sure. Black."

"Barf."

"Not the rope kind, either"—she grinned for her sister's sake—"but the kind that comes in big, fat chunks."

"*Double* barf."

"And don't bother Rupert at the back of the store, even if Gwen says it's fine." Gwen's brother-in-law ran his bookie side business out of the staff room. "See you in a few minutes, runt."

She watched Wynn disappear from sight as she followed the wooden fence that separated the covert from the rest of the town, her family's property from the rest of Glory. Hewn and nailed together by the bare hands of their long-dead great-grandfather, the snaking chain of timber seemed as old as the earth. The *For Sale* sign that was nailed to it was nearly so, the words on it faded away to nothingness. No one wanted land whose soil would always bleed red, that crawled with ghosts and strange stories and decades-old myths. The town itself had no reason to buy it from her mother when the covert—as morbid as it was—was nearly as much a tourist draw as the midnight casinos and gambling houses. Shine had long ago declared the place unnatural and unbearable; Marsden couldn't remember the last time her mother had set foot in it.

If there had been potential buyers for the covert, then none offered the price Shine wanted for the only thing she truly owned. This, Marsden could understand—the setting of a price for freedom was something she still did every day, calculating, wondering which corners could be cut.

She turned into the covert, toward the body, and hoped there would be cash for her to steal.

Cash: the one thing that would get them out of the terrible, death-ridden town they called Glory.

two.

MARSDEN'S SNEAKERS BROKE THROUGH THE GINGER PLANTS THAT CARPETED THE COVERT, TURNING THE DUSK AIR PUNGENT WITH THEIR SCENT. Their heart-shaped leaves ran rampant in the space, thriving beneath the cool shade thrown by the trees. Only in the covert, away from the simmering heat of town, would they not wither and die.

Once the groundcover had been nothing but crabgrass and clover and thistle. It would have been like that when her great-great-uncle had walked over it nearly a hundred years ago, when Duncan Kirby first came to this part of the world looking for gold. The stuff was first discovered in the banks of the Indigo River back in 1890, with the most generous amounts in the deepest, most crooked bend that eventually became the town of Glory.

When the gold began to disappear, so did most of the townsfolk who had come west for it. But Duncan stayed, waiting for the gold to come back. He built a cabin for his young family in the town's west end on land he won in an epic game of poker. And when the gold refused to show again, his sanity ended up lost with it, and he went on to shoot his wife and kids before turning the rifle on himself.

Glory decided to burn the cabin—and the bodies still within it—to the ground afterward. A cleansing fire, the townsfolk nervously called it as they stoked the flames until nothing remained but the gray and salty ash of bone. It would change the covert from a cursed place to one that was blessed, the place where sins could be left behind before going to heaven. Dying after touching its purified soil meant salvation—just a handful of the covert's dirt needed to be stuffed into a pocket or smeared onto skin.

Marsden decided long ago Glory's first settlers had no idea what they were doing, because her family's land still felt cursed. And all the fire did was turn the town into a spectacle. Nearly a century later, and still people came. Like the thirstiest of bees, the most vulnerable of them, the ones looking for understanding of some kind, were drawn in by the covert. The *Private Property* and *Keep Out* signs nailed along the outer fence might as well have been blank. Each body Marsden found was just another person fooled, lured by a promise that redemption could be found in its bloodstained and now ginger-scented dirt.

At least the sanctity of the covert's myth was strong enough that no murder had been committed there since those at the hands of Duncan. Or had yet to be caught, anyway.

She saw the gun a second before she would have stepped on it. It had fallen to the side of the body. In the covert's shadowed light, the black of it was harsh against the soft green needles, the pale gray stones.

The woman had aimed for her mouth.

Marsden had to fall into a crouch at the sight, dizzy as the covert spun. Not since her first body—a man hanging from a tree by his midnight-blue tie, his name had been Caleb Silas, he'd had ten dollars in his wallet—had she thrown up.

But she had to hurry to finish.

Private property or not, she wasn't the only skimmer in town.

She took a deep breath and moved over to the body. She pulled out the thin gardening gloves she always carried for just this purpose. There were ghosts everywhere in the covert—her own ancestors were but a few of them—and she felt their eyes on her as she ran her hands over the woman, searching for her own kind of gold.

There was a necklace, as delicate as spider webbing, its hue that of wheat in falling sunlight. A ring studded with gems.

Both were useless to her. She'd learned that the hard way when she brought a pair of cuff links she'd taken from Caleb Silas's body to Seconds, the town's biggest pawnshop. His widow had reported them missing, but the pawnshop owner at the time had already sold them for a nice profit to a tourist passing through—the only reason Marsden escaped. Forever scared into thinking the owner would remember her face, she never went near Seconds again.

She took the five-dollar bill she found in the woman's wallet, then placed the slip of cheap red vinyl back in the pocket. It wasn't much, but it brought her that much closer to the two thousand dollars she wanted to have before she could even think about taking Wynn and leaving Glory. It would be enough for two bus tickets to Seattle, a few months rent for a cheap apartment, and food while she looked for a job.

She had just over a grand and a half saved up, hidden in a pair of old boots in her closet. All of it from skimming—tens and twenties most of the time, the very occasional fifty—and from working in the kitchen in the boardinghouse, which never amounted to more than a few hours a week during school months. Summers were when she tried to make up for the rest of the year, to save the fastest. But summers were short; she could not add hours to the clock just as she couldn't add bodies to the covert. Some months saw a dozen if not more; some saw only one or two—the only thing she could count on for sure was never knowing.

She readjusted the fall of the woman's blond hair and fixed the patches of dirt still carefully scrubbed into the backs of her hands. Marsden made sure it looked like the body had never been touched. Glory police would be there not long after she called in the discovery. The department was small given that the town was also small—outside of tourists—so it wasn't hard for Nina to pay all the cops well to only patrol the area when they had to, and discreetly. It didn't make for good business, having cop cars driving around the boardinghouse all the time. And while dead bodies in the covert were worse, they didn't make any noise; their names printed in the paper the next day were easily missed, the print fine, the column small. The police would barely give the body a glance—head cop Hadley might even skim it himself—before taking it away, but Marsden had learned to always cover her tracks anyway. The covert was her best chance at escaping from Glory; she could never risk it.

Marsden tucked away the cash and her gloves and got to her feet. She was brushing off her hands and knees when the sound of a branch snapping nearby made her freeze. Her eyes went everywhere and nowhere, and her breath caught in her ribs like a fork clanging off teeth.

She saw Hadley coming over the dusk-dimmed rise, shouting at her to empty her pockets.

She saw Nina telling her that she belonged to her now, that she would always work for her, in whatever way Nina decided best.

She saw her mother, crying to never leave her alone, that their debt was Marsden's, too.

And then she saw Wynn, her black hair as messy as ever, her face full of fear as she slowly approached, and she knew her sister was the one who was real.

Wynn's gaze darted to the body, and through the gloom she paled, came to a stop. "I . . . the store was closed, there was a sign—"

Marsden darted forward and spun Wynn around by her frail shoulders. "You should have waited for me by the fence." She heard the fury in her voice, the fear, and tried to soften. And failed, because most of that fury was for herself. "Let's go."

They marched in silence, her mind racing, her eyes threatening to fill. Here she was, determined to keep her sister safe from who they were, what the town had determined them to be. But how to run from your own shadow? Your own name?

"Mars?" Wynn was working ginger leaves between her palms—crushed, their scent was strong enough to make Marsden's nose tingle.

"Yeah?"

"Can we go see Dad's grave?"

• • •

Their mother had had him buried on the west side of the covert, where the trees were thinner and sparser, their canopy less protective. As such, the one that marked his grave was about as expected, its branches wispy, almost fragile in the gray light.

Marsden wished Shine had chosen a more mature tree to watch over the man she'd met and fallen in love with when they'd both still been kids—one sturdier, more remarkable. She wondered again if it had been a final dig at him, his being buried in the covert. How it wasn't because it was family land, or because he'd died by suicide—and suicide and the covert went hand in hand—but because it was Shine's way to finally corral her useless, restless husband.

Wynn let her crushed ginger leaves fall to the ground and plucked clover blossoms from a nearby patch. She tucked them beneath a small rock at the base of the wimpy tree. After a long moment of silence: "I don't hear him like Grandma would have. Do you think it's because I never met him?"

Like their grandmother, Grant Eldridge was a stranger to Marsden's sister, too, having walked into the Indigo six months before Wynn was born. Shine had always told Wynn this was a blessing—memories could also be curses.

"Well, I have definitely met him, and I don't hear him, either." Marsden shifted on her feet. "Why are we here again?"

"It's Daddy—we should visit when we can."

"We do. But now it's getting dark."

Wynn decorated the rock with more blossoms. Her hand and arm glowed a ghostly gray against the murk of the forest. "Do you think Mom could hear them again, if she only tried?"

"You know she won't. And it's been too long since she's heard anything, not since she was a kid." Or so Shine claimed. Her mother had gotten good at talking without actually saying much at all. It came with her job, Marsden knew. Like a final polish that, over time, became hard to remove. "Grandma told me once that the ability's just like any living creature—it needs air, or it dies."

Her sister was watching her. "Do you ever still try to hear the dead?"

Marsden's face stiffened with embarrassment, heat along her ears, and she was glad for the thin dark so she could hide.

She *did* try, but she didn't think she could ever admit to Wynn her reasons. That she sometimes sat in the covert in front of a body, eyes shut tight against the quiet and the trees and the ginger, trying to extract from all of it the voices of the dead. Telling her how they came to be there, who they'd once been. Because she thought if those she stole from could be bothered to talk to her, then it couldn't be long before the voice she heard next was that of her father. Explaining to her why he did what he did. Assuring her he didn't leave because of *her*. That he hadn't hated life because of *her*.

Always, though, she heard nothing. From anyone.

"The dead are dead, Wynn," she said quietly now. "They came here to find some kind of peace. And I think, sometimes, we might be wrong in demanding they still be here, just for us."

Her sister poked in a final blossom and stepped back. "I still wish I'd known him, even for just a bit."

"Me, too."

"But you *did* know him, Mars."

Had she, though?

She'd been eight when they found him drowned in the shallows of the Indigo. No explanation, no note left anywhere. It'd been classified an accident.

Marsden couldn't remember him well enough to still hate him for it. Memories of him were like cards in a deck, slowly shuffled away as time passed, moments of her childhood falling through some metaphorical hole in the pocket that was her brain. He'd spun in and out of her and Shine's lives like a shifty alley cat, unsure if it lived indoors or out, if he belonged to them, or no one, or just himself.

She recalled him once playing tea party with her, patient enough to sip pretend tea and eat pretend sandwiches. His aftershave had smelled of the outdoors, had made her think of cool, gray flannel and winter mornings. He liked loud movies and songs heavy with guitar. His hair had been Crayola chestnut brown, his eyes a tint lighter than midnight black. He'd been tall. His laugh had come from somewhere deep.

Of that last day, though, she remembered him and Shine arguing explosively. His one retort that had stuck—ravaged, with a desperation so bleak her own chest went hollow with it—about being trapped. *I never wanted this life!* He'd looked right at Marsden as the words had ground from him. She remembered the sound of the flimsy screen door slapping back against the house as he slammed his way out, and how the smell of that evening's terrible spring storm had rushed inward seconds later.

"A squirrel!"

Marsden squinted, saw a fat black shape rustle free from a nearby bush and run toward the last of the sun.

Wynn clambered off after it, clucking her tongue as she made her way toward the entrance. "I'll meet you at the fence, okay?" she called over her shoulder. Her voice was muffled from the density of the trees, what had proven thick enough to swallow up the sounds of gunshots.

"Don't head off anywhere else," Marsden called back.

"I won't!"

She followed in her sister's wake, the scent of ginger freshened again from their steps. She wasn't exactly reluctant to go, but sometimes it was being out in the open that made her feel trapped. Dread packed itself into the corners of her heart and filled her head with the most miserable of thoughts.

The boardinghouse, where Nina's girls—including her own mother—wore clothes and makeup as colorful as candy, so they appeared just as delectable.

The town, bleached pale from the summer sun.

The future, laid out for her as surely as though it were already set in stone.

three.

THE NEXT MORNING.

Dawn was still edging over into day—the sky from navy to lavender to the shade of robins' eggs, the air from cool to an inferno—when Marsden crept back into the kitchen from checking the covert. She yawned as she tossed off her shoes, a cloud of ginger wafting from her bare arms and hair. It'd already been proven that she couldn't hide the covert from Wynn forever, but Marsden was never going to accept it. That would be like choosing to sink into the quicksand that was the whole town.

When it wasn't summer, her job meant helping cook dinners, to be served in the common dining room, for the boardinghouse staff and its guests every weekend. When it *was* summer, she worked every day and had to cook and serve breakfasts, too. The one thing that never changed during the year was the johns who stayed overnight. Unlike official guests, it was an unspoken rule that they never saw the inside of the dining room. Neither were they served food in the bedrooms with Nina's girls. Instead, they slunk out of the boardinghouse through a side entrance while breakfast was served to everyone else.

Marsden never felt bad that the johns had to leave the boarding-house hungry. They hadn't come for the food anyway.

She was stirring eggs and milk and laying down sausages on the grill when footsteps sounded overhead. They were stealthy, secretive, and Marsden steeled herself. It wouldn't be the first time she'd had to make breakfast with some of the girls Nina employed right there in the kitchen with her, tired of listening to the snoring of the johns still taking up space in their beds.

It was never easy when they tried making conversation with her. Usually, all she could think about were the secrets she held and the way her hands still recalled the feel of cold, stiff limbs as she tucked away stolen cash. She'd gotten used to being lonely, she supposed; the town had long ago painted her with certain brushes and into too many inescapable corners. Letting Nina's girls get close was a waste of time, and dangerous—for her, for Wynn.

It was the main reason why Marsden minded them being in her space. But loneliness lingered, an echo that seemed without end—which meant she also didn't mind.

They descended the stairs and swarmed into the kitchen like butterflies—if the insects came in pairs, wore flimsy silk robes, and smelled more of perfume and old makeup instead of the outdoors.

Peaches puffed on a cigarette as she leaned over Marsden's shoulder to watch her cook. "Why do you even bother?" The other girl's voice was husky from smoke. Marsden heard the pointed sneer in it, the clear impatience. "*Cooking*, I mean."

Early twenties, curves like the women had in one of those old-fashioned paintings and which Peaches wielded like weapons. Wild auburn curls, skin like porcelain. Her hazel eyes were always hungry, her smiles slow and wide—johns loved her, and she knew it. Originally a college student from North Dakota—or maybe it was South, Marsden could never remember—she decided one day she was tired of classrooms and dropped out of college. Meandering across the country in the name of alternate education had somehow ended up with her in Glory.

Of all of Nina's girls, Peaches was the one most comfortable in her skin. Marsden sometimes liked her but usually feared her—and always she wondered what it would be like to have even a bit of that confidence. Would it have already led her from Glory, or would she simply already be working for Nina?

"It's my job," she finally said. And she was good at it. Glory's best bed-and-breakfast—simply named The Boardinghouse—prided itself on its breakfasts and dinners, and guests always rated them as one of the best parts of their stay.

"Just give it back to Dany," Peaches said.

Marsden would never. Couldn't. "I like it."

"Slaving away over a stove—over *eggs*—when your face alone is enough to save you from this?" Peaches laughed, shaking her head. Her messy updo bobbed along. "Just how much is Nina paying you, anyway?"

So little it felt like she would be saving up forever to get herself and Wynn out of town. Especially since Nina made her own deductions: a cut for how much it cost for Shine and her daughters to live there, a bit toward the debt they still owed her for paying off the loans Grant Eldridge had died with. The two women had once been friends in high school, and Nina had offered Shine a job when no one else in town would. But Nina was, more than anything else, a businessperson.

Marsden had been fourteen the first time a john had asked about her. It was then that Nina had begun to eye her like property instead of the pseudo daughter Marsden had convinced herself she was.

That was when she wormed her way into the kitchen as staff, convincing Nina to be satisfied with owning her in that way, at least. The town's businesses had already decided she was off-limits; hiring her themselves would mean risking Nina's wrath as one of Glory's wealthiest, most ruthless businesspeople. Nina, with her rose-tipped thumbs jabbed in pies all over the place.

Fourteen was also when Marsden began skimming in earnest, with the goal of escape in mind.

"The eggs are going to taste like your cigarette smoke," Marsden said to Peaches, continuing to stir so she wouldn't have to look at her. "You can be the one to tell Nina that when the guests complain."

"Always so worried." Peaches blew out a thick stream of smoke. She took the spatula and poked at the sausages. "It's going to age you if you're not careful."

"Oh, leave her alone, Peaches." Lucy leaned in from Marsden's other side, peering closely at the eggs through her large tortoiseshell glasses. They were the same ones Nina had detested until she realized they held an appeal of their own. "Marsden covering the kitchen just leaves Dany more time for the rest of the house."

Despite being a couple, Lucy couldn't have been more different from Peaches, a subtle carnation to a heady orchid. She had long, blond Alice in Wonderland hair, complete with hairband; along with the glasses, there was a sense of innocence about her that kept johns coming back. A runaway, Lucy had hitched her way north from Florida five years ago. She had arrived at Glory with sad eyes and a quiet voice she rarely used. Both gave away nothing about why she'd run in the first place. She wasn't so quiet anymore, and her eyes weren't so sad, but Wynn had once whispered to Marsden that she didn't agree. *Lucy just hides the sadness better. And we've forgotten to look.*

Peaches rolled sausages with the spatula's edge and smirked. "I guess Marsden *is* the better cook."

"Don't ever tell Dany that, you'd break her heart." Lucy took a wooden spoon from the drawer and began to stir the eggs, yawning behind a hand.

"And risk having to do my own laundry? Never." Peaches squinted against smoke. "Hey, aren't these sausages done?"

Marsden felt hemmed in by how closely the girls stood around her, the easy way they spoke to each other. "Give them another couple minutes."

"You got a timer going?"

"I don't use one—cook enough of anything, you just know."

Life as a kid with her parents in their old duplex had been little more than a string of broken images—her father placing money on the kitchen table before leaving again; her mother screaming into the phone about late bills and not having enough, then smiling with empty eyes as she tucked Marsden into bed. By contrast, she remembered her grandmother's visits like entire shows.

She'd been the one to teach Marsden all about food.

And those times Shine was out of the house, Star had been the one to cook what Shine had declared too strange, too Chinese.

Your mother, always wanting to pretend you two look the same as everyone else in this town, Star would mutter over setting chicken to steam as she stir-fried. *Pretending her grandfather didn't go on to marry a Chinese woman, that I didn't go on to marry a Chinese man. Don't be ashamed of looking different, Marsden. Don't be afraid of hearing what others might not.*

Her grandmother's dying led to two things:

First, Shine decided that the covert—and the family ability to hear the dead—would no longer be subjects she was interested in talking about. Second, Shine became a housekeeper for Nina in exchange for room and board, a job that lasted until Wynn's birth six months later. When she took on another kind of work, as soon as she was able to.

Peaches gave the sausages another jab with the spatula. "I can't wait until my guy finally leaves. Older than Methuselah, swear to God.

And he wanted to play teacher, because he found out this place used to be a boarding school."

The school had gone up after the state bought half an acre of land from Marsden's great-grandfather. Nina's family then bought it in turn, keeping bits of the original structure intact as they converted the school into the boardinghouse-slash-brothel it was today—pine-framed windows, gray velvet flocked wallpaper, navy tiled floors. The heart of the covert remained untouched, a swath of forest west of the place.

Lucy moved to Peaches's other side and kissed her. "Well, my guy smells."

They both laughed against each other's mouths, and Marsden, her face on fire, turned down the grill's heat so it only warmed.

How did that work, anyway? To love someone knowing that, at times, they were someone else's? To touch them knowing it would soon be someone else's turn? She wondered if such questions ever crossed their minds anymore, or if they just didn't let them because they were too hard to answer.

Down in the staff wing, a radio began to play. A song from that week's Top 40.

Marsden was sure Wynn had set it. Her sister had discovered that most of Nina's girls listened to the radio as they got ready in the morning. Which meant she would, too.

Peaches and Lucy danced their way back upstairs, and Marsden found herself moving in a rush now, struggling to finish before Nina stormed into the kitchen, demanding to know why breakfast wasn't in the dining room yet.

It left Marsden annoyed, being in a hurry. She should have known better than to let Peaches and Lucy distract her. It would never be worth it to risk Nina cutting her pay.

four.

"MARS, CAN YOU MAKE WAFFLES FOR THE SQUIRRELS
AGAIN?"

Wynn was sitting at the kitchen table with a bowl of cereal, her
usual place for meals when Nina wanted Wynn to stay quiet and out
of the way. From the dining room just off to the side, there came the
clanging of cutlery, the low chatter of guests as they ate the breakfast
Marsden had just finished bringing out.

"Not today, since I've already made breakfast." Marsden scrubbed
at the grill. "See, I'm cleaning now. You're going to have to make friends
with the wild fur balls some other way."

"They don't like cereal."

"There might be leftover eggs coming back from the dining room,
if you want to wait."

"Squirrels don't like eggs."

"*You* don't like eggs."

"I'm serious."

"It's food." Marsden began to wipe at cold grease. "Of course they'll
like it."

"I think they're vegetarian."

"Eggs aren't meat."

"But they come from chickens."

Marsden turned the stove back on and dropped a slice of bread onto the grill. The cold grease started to melt around it. "Toast will have to do, all right?"

"Can we check for more berries this morning? In the covert? We didn't pick enough yesterday to make strudels."

Marsden pushed the bread along the grease. It was going to be a long summer if Wynn wanted to go to the covert every chance she got. "Wouldn't you rather hang out with your friends? Where's Caitlyn today? Or Ella? I can try to bike you over later to meet them if you want." Both girls were her sister's best friends, and during the school year, they often played at one another's houses. More accurately, Wynn played at theirs, since neither of the girls were allowed near the covert.

"Caitlyn and her family are camping somewhere," Wynn said, "and Ella's cat is sick. She has to bring it to the vet."

Marsden bit back a sigh. "I think the berries need to ripen a bit more. Besides, the covert isn't going anywhere—and there are other places to play."

"Nothing that's like a whole forest to myself. I saw a whole family of mice in there the other day. And it's the only place where the trees and plants aren't all dried up from the sun."

"You know what happens in there."

"No one comes during the day." Wynn spooned Lucky Charms into her mouth. "And it's part of the family, so we're supposed to take care of it. How can you be scared of family?"

Marsden nearly smiled at how many ways she could pick apart the last of Wynn's words. "It's *not* family," she said instead. "It's just land—that's all."

"Grandma wouldn't have said that. The covert is a part of us. Or we're a part of it—like it's in our blood."

Kirby and his crimes popped into Marsden's head. The covert would be forever stained with what he'd done, its soil and trees and air sown from it. More than one person in town believed some of that raging madness still flowed through his descendants.

Her sister picked out marshmallows from her bowl with her fingers. Watching her, Marsden saw the resemblance to their mother, though it was nothing compared to how she herself resembled Shine. While Wynn's hair and skin and eyes were all a shade softer than Marsden's—a kitty cat at the side of a lioness, Dany had once said about the two of them—they'd both inherited their mother's jawline, the broad sweep of her cheekbones, the slope of her nose, and her thick black hair. But the shape of Wynn's eyes, the slightly clefted chin, her paler skin must have been from their father.

"Don't you ever wonder if it's us making the dead talk or them thinking we should hear?" Wynn asked. "Because of our ability?"

Marsden flipped the grilling bread. "We've never heard anyone."

"We might one day. So don't you wonder?"

29

"People aren't parts of places," she tried again. "And I only go to the covert for a good reason."

"Death," her sister whispered, the suddenly ominous tone in her voice lifting up goose bumps on Marsden's arms. "So you can call Hadley as soon as possible if you see someone."

"Exactly. So finish eating, will you, runt? You know Nina will want you outside while guests check out or head for town."

"It's hot outside. And if I hide in here long enough, I'll get to see the others before they're busy for the day."

The others. Wynn meant their mother and Nina's girls.

"You'll see everyone enough later."

Wynn shook her head. "Not enough if we're leaving soon like you want. Can't we stay here longer?"

Marsden glanced over, dismayed. Her sister's hair was a crown of midnight cowlicks. Just a slip of an undersized girl who loved the covert despite its horrors, who had no clue what her mother did for work most nights.

She wasn't ready to lose this Wynn yet. She wanted her to remain unchanged for as long as possible, young and blind and trusting. Not like her, dealt, at eight, a dead father, a forest full of death and tainted riches, a mother's desperate decision. Then that one overly tall guest, his gaze crawling—*Is Shine's girl available yet?*

"Glory's small," she said. "Just because we won't be living in the boardinghouse doesn't mean you still won't see everyone in town." Of course if they left town altogether, they *wouldn't* see them (which

Marsden wasn't sure she was really sorry about), and it was what she was still secretly planning. She'd brought up the idea with Wynn once but her sister had only shaken her head and refused to consider it. So Marsden had retreated and Wynn believed what she wanted to believe. When the time came to finally leave, Marsden would tell her the truth.

"I *like* living in the boardinghouse, though." Wynn stirred her cereal milk—turned chunky and blue—with her finger. "There's Mom, and Dany, and the girls. Even Nina isn't always so bad—she said Peaches and Lucy can show me how to do my hair and makeup. So I can look as nice as I want, whenever I like."

Marsden stabbed and gouged at the toast, something bitter on the back of her tongue. Nina had known exactly what she was doing, saying that to Wynn. "Seriously, you don't need to do any of that."

"But I *want*—"

"You don't! And if you think Nina's that nice, you're just being stupid."

Wynn's mouth trembled, and tears sprang to her eyes. Her finger went stock-still in her bowl of milk.

Marsden could have kicked herself. Had she ever called Wynn stupid before, in a way that sounded like she meant it?

"Hey now, what's all this?" Dany swept into the kitchen, maternal and capable, a cozy blanket of a woman. Even her voice was comforting, big and warm enough that it seemed to wrap around you as she spoke. After Marsden, she was the person Wynn sought out in the boardinghouse—never Shine.

"Just blue cereal for breakfast, sweetie?" she said to Wynn, giving Marsden a sideways look. "I'd be upset, too. How about I go grab you some of the food from the dining room?"

"It's eggs on the menu today," Marsden said quietly, turning off the grill. "She doesn't like them."

"Ah. Well, let me go check what else there might be." Dany ruffled Wynn's uncombed hair and swept away, her expression expectant as she looked back at Marsden. *Don't forget which of you is the big sister.*

"Sorry, Wynn," Marsden said as soon as they were alone. "You know I didn't mean it."

Her sister began to stir her blue milk again and Marsden was stiff with guilt, unsure of how to fix things.

Then Dany was back, bearing nothing but a stack of dirty plates. "Too late, as everything's been eaten. But Wynn, I have an idea for us this morning—go around back to the outer shed and get the old manual ice-cream maker? Jack is bringing by a delivery of fresh rhubarb from the store. Be careful, though—one of the attachments doesn't stay on so great. Meanwhile, your sister and I will start cleaning up from breakfast."

Not needing to hear any more beyond the words *ice* and *cream*, Wynn was up like a shot and out the door without a single look back.

"You two all right now?" Dany poured coffee from the pot on the counter. "You don't often snap at Wynn like that."

Marsden began to scrub at the grill, working around the toast still on it. "Nina needs to stop putting ideas in her head about needing to dress up—she's eight. And Peaches and Lucy—" She felt nearly betrayed at how oblivious they seemed to be to her problems. But what did they owe Marsden when none of them were really friends? When Nina was the one whose roof they slept under? "They need to remember she's just a kid. And not like them."

"They're simply being nice, that's all."

She could argue with Dany all morning, but she knew the woman would never say a bad word about Nina. Same way she could never turn on her or Wynn or any of the girls. Her loyalty to the house was unshakeable. It was what made her so lovable. But it also made her no help at all.

"Nina wasn't just being nice when she promoted my mom from housekeeper to whore," she muttered as she scrubbed. "What's an old friend's reputation when it comes to her business bringing in money, right?"

"*Hush*, Marsden." Dany's voice was low as she began to fill the sink. "She helped your mother when no one else in Glory would, when no job offers came despite the promises. And then Grant's loans . . . Listen, she was not a child when she agreed. She knew she'd make good money."

"She could have just said no to Nina. She could have left. She—" Marsden bit off the rest of whatever she was going to say. They would have been words she'd already said dozens of times before, and they still wouldn't change what her mother ended up doing.

And Shine *had* left. Once. Or started to. Marsden had been ten and

Wynn just a baby. Shine had gathered them one winter morning and they had taken the bus to the bus depot. Then they had sat on one of the benches inside for hours, waiting. Marsden had asked her mother over and over again where they were going, and her mother had simply sat there, staring up at the ticket board, her face pale and her hands clenched around her purse in her lap.

They had brought almost nothing with them, since all they really had was clothing anyway. Tucked into her carrier, Wynn had slept nearly the whole time. Marsden remembered how her excitement had slowly disappeared, the bus depot around her emptying of people and then filling back up and then emptying again. When she got hungry, Shine gave her five dollars for candy bars from the little kiosk by the ticket booth. By the time the sky was starting to go dark, she was no longer asking about where they were going but instead when were they going home. Eventually, Shine gathered up Marsden and Wynn and they took the bus back to the boardinghouse.

Nina had been cold to Shine for a few days, but then everything went back to the way it had been. Her mother wouldn't talk about it when Marsden asked, and soon enough, Marsden was no longer asking about it at all. Bits of that day still came back to her at times, but they seemed almost unreal, as if the whole thing had happened to someone else. A different ten-year-old girl with a sleeping baby sister and a mother who forgot how to speak, one who was heading out to a different city for real.

Dany slid dishes into the sink, her expression carefully patient.

"Skill-less, with two little girls to take care of, and saddled with a bloodline and a skin color the people in this town were afraid of. Yes, she could have tried leaving again, but as bad as it was for her here, she came back because at least she knew Glory. Better the devil she knew than the one she didn't, was her thinking. Now, I'm going to go finish clearing, if you want to start washing."

"Sure." Guilt deflated Marsden's anger, and she watched Dany stride away. She picked up the cooled toast and tucked it into the front pocket of her shirt. The covert should still be empty from her check that morning, and she knew Wynn would want to feed the squirrels.

Then her mother walked into the kitchen, and Marsden braced herself.

five.

SHE HAD ALWAYS BEEN TOLD THEY LOOKED ALIKE, AND IT WAS FACT. Both of them had olive skin that darkened to a gold by the end of the summer, the shades rooted in their Chinese blood. And while Marsden's straight black hair was usually down to her waist because she was often too lazy to get it cut, her mother always kept hers nearly as long because she said it made her look younger. *No matter how much certain men might want me for the shape of my eyes, it's youth that keeps them around.*

Marsden's eyes were the same shape, too, but she liked that hers were even darker. So deep a brown they never altered, whatever the light—unreadable, hidden, a warning for others to not bother. Her being a skimmer would remain a secret, as long as she stayed careful.

Shine unhooked a coffee mug from the tree on the counter and filled it. Dressed casually because it was day, her makeup faint in the morning sun, she appeared too young to have a teenage daughter. Marsden had been unplanned, her parents both sixteen when she'd been born. As much as her coming along had derailed whatever plans they might have had, it had also forced them to stay together when

36

maybe they wouldn't have, until it all ended with the river. That had been worse.

"Did I just see you hide toast in your pocket?" Shine asked.

Marsden wondered if her mother had overheard any of her conversation with Dany. "I'm supposed to go feed a squirrel."

"No pets." Her mother's reply was instant and automatic. "Nina's rules."

"Not in the house, Mom. Out in the covert."

"*Shine*, not *Mom*." Her mother took a long sip of coffee and stared out through the window at the ever-muddy Indigo. "Not *Mom*, not *Mother*, and, Lord"—a shudder, as though her coffee had suddenly turned repulsive—"never *Ma*."

"Sorry." Marsden still remembered when she'd been allowed. Those words sometimes felt foreign on her tongue, and sometimes completely natural—she missed saying them, as much as she resented them for what they stood for. Wynn, though, rarely needed reminding. "Shine."

"I really wish you would stop going out to the covert so much." Her mother set her mug down, lit up a cigarette, and looked at her daughter. "You go there every day. You even let Wynn go with you sometimes, letting her see God knows what. The girls tell me you do."

The girls. Aside from Peaches and Lucy, the bulk of Nina's prostitutes—including Shine Eldridge—were starting to slide into what Marsden had once heard johns call "well-done" territory.

The light switches in the bedrooms having dimmers was no happy accident. Suddenly, the sun flowing in was more revealing than kind, and Shine's face, beneath the careful makeup, showed the truth with each line.

Her mother did not know she skimmed. She did not know why Marsden would have any reason to make more money than she already did working in the kitchen. She might decide she didn't know about skimmers at all, if she really did choose to ignore talk of the covert.

She also didn't know that even as Marsden was on the lookout for bodies, her daughter strived to hear the dead. The sight of blood-splattered, heart-shaped leaves was easier to live with, it turned out, than the memory of a father saying he regretted her.

"I go there because it's quiet, Mom—Shine. That's all."

"Do you know how unhealthy that is? *Enjoying* being in a place where people go to kill themselves?" Her mother blew out smoke, more anxious than angry. "Please, Marsden."

Guilt—familiar, hateful, Shine's most effective weapon against her—began to grind its way home, and Marsden sighed. She knew her mother had once actually mothered, that she would be better off simply forgetting most of that time. But Shine continued to try despite everything, and it only made it harder. Because crumbs still went toward hunger, still forced off starvation, even if that kind of mercy wasn't necessarily kind.

"I don't enjoy it," she said. "I could never. But I have to find them."

"Let the place be," her mother pleaded. "Whatever happens in there is Hadley's problem, not yours. You should be spending more time with your girlfriends, ones from school."

She could not tell her mother that most girls talked *about* her, not *with* her. It'd been that way for nearly as long as she could remember. By the time they moved into the boardinghouse, Marsden had already been struggling to keep the few friends she had, each of them deciding hanging out with her would be dooming her own reputation at school. She recalled them the way she did favorite toys she once played with, before they broke and she could no longer play with them. Jessica, who liked Barbies, Jillian, who preferred Hot Wheels. Mattea, who had a tree house.

Marsden stopped fighting their withdrawal after a while. How do you fight fact? Her family *did* own the creepiest place in Glory, after all, had made it that way in the first place. What if whatever evil was in their blood could spread? She was the descendant of a madman, the protector of cursed land. She was one of the "Orientals" in town. Her mother becoming one of Nina's girls—simply one more of Glory's not-so-secrets—was, she supposed, the icing on a very ugly cake.

"It's summer," she said now. "People do stuff."

"Fine. I mean when it's *not* summer."

"So ask me in the fall."

"Don't be glib. It's not an appealing trait."

Marsden's hand squeezed the piece of toast in her pocket. Compulsively, like a muscle cramp. "To johns? Then oh well."

Shine drew hard enough on her cigarette that it shook in her fingers. Her unending need for security filled her eyes, turning her expression both childlike and calculating. Marsden's father had put that look there, Marsden knew, had taught his wife to fear being left alone as she dealt with his recklessness and inability to be responsible. His leaving had pushed her toward Nina and the boardinghouse, too. For that, she saw how her mother could be unforgiving. Just as she saw how it made her mother need too much protection to ever be able to protect anyone else.

"Those johns are what keep us fed, Marsden." Ash fluttered to the ground from Shine's trembling cigarette. Her voice trembled along with it. "But soon I'll be too old for them. You know Nina knows this. And Nina . . . she's asked me to come talk to you. She says it's time you stop hiding in this kitchen."

Marsden's skin went icy, chilled with the revulsion of a touch she could already imagine. She'd known, but it was another thing hearing Shine say it out loud. "I won't."

"I know you don't want to, but we owe Nina. She's a business-person when it comes to this, not a friend. She covered those loans of your father's that we're still paying her back for."

"Then go back to housekeeping. I'll get another job somewhere else, on top of cooking here."

Shine tried to smile then, of all things, and it was even shakier than her fingers around the cigarette. Her eyes simmered with panic. They said she was trapped and that she knew she was trapping Mars-den along with her.

Something too close to pity flooded Marsden. An image of her

40

mother at the window of their old duplex, watching for signs of her husband, flashed behind her eyes. One of her carefully counting bills before triumphantly declaring to Marsden that she could pick out ice cream.

She knew some of her mother had become an act, but not all of her, and it was terrifying how she blurred. Just how much could she let Shine need her? How much could her mother beg of her and still let her believe it came from love, not resentment? Her own selfishness?

"Housekeeping doesn't pay as much," Shine said. "And no one else in Glory would hire you. We're not one of them, despite how long we've been here. Also, they know you're already Nina's; they won't risk her coming after them. I'm sorry, but please, you need to consider—"

"I'm not Nina's, and I'm not you. How can you not hate her for this?"

"Because we can't afford to. And this place is still home for Wynn. Think of her when you tell yourself you're too good for this town, when you're out there with no money and nowhere to go."

"I *am* thinking of Wynn. And I *have* money," she blurted in a low rush. Surprise flooded her mother's face. Marsden wondered if she would regret her slip; she'd never talked to Shine about her money before. But then she supposed it made no difference in the end— whatever her mother knew of her plans wouldn't convince her and Wynn to stay. "You don't think I've been saving as much as I can?"

"I just . . . I assumed you only *wanted* to leave," her mother said faintly. "Not that you really could."

"Well, now you know."

Shine's eyes glistened. Cigarette smoke haloed her head. Her despair made her stunning. "Then think of *me*. How could you make Nina wonder if I'm getting so useless I can't even ask you to do this? How could you leave me when I was the one who stayed?"

Barely able to breathe, Marsden stepped back from the vortex that was her mother, the insecurity that turned her desperate. She didn't need someone's loneliness. And her mother was boxed into a corner of her own, forced there by her blood, her dead husband, her daughters.

"I don't care if you don't tell Nina no for me, then," Marsden whispered, "as long as you don't say yes. Can you at least do that? Until I think of something?"

Shine's arm continued to shake as she reached for her mug of coffee. It would be close to cold by now. She took a sip and showed no reaction. Her face had gone pale. She set down the cup again. "I'll see if . . . I will try—"

"Mars! Mars!"

Wynn's bellow broke into the kitchen like a riptide as she burst in through the back entrance. Cradled in her arms was the old ice-cream maker—Marsden could tell with one glance that an attachment was missing. The observation felt vague, coming from a distance, as though she were merely watching the unfolding of a scene from someone else's life. Her conversation with her mother still rang in her ears— her own plea, Shine's struggle to remember her daughter.

"What is it?" she asked Wynn, the sister that she loved too much and wanted to protect more than anything. Who, because of that, was now being used against her.

"The covert!" From the corner of her eye, Marsden saw Shine go stiff. "There's someone there!"

"You didn't touch it, did you?" *How much did you see? How much will you not be able to forget?* "The body."

"It's not a body—it's a boy!"

A boy. The two words seemed alien in the room, coming from another universe. "What?"

"And, Mars?" Wynn was frowning, her expression thoughtful as she absentmindedly cranked the handle of the ice-cream maker. "He looks kind of mean."

six.

WYNN HADN'T BEEN ENTIRELY RIGHT. It was more of a pissed-off, frustrated look than outright meanness on the boy's face.

Jude Ambrose.

Marsden knew him in an instant.

Not just because they'd gone to school together since they were little kids, making him a part of her life in Glory, no matter how small, but also because nearly three weeks ago, she'd been the one to discover the body of his older brother in the covert.

Rigby had been twenty-one. He'd left a note folded into the cash she'd stolen from his wallet. It'd been more than cryptic, was still hidden in her room even now, tucked away between books. She was stuck with it—to throw it away was unthinkable, but to give it back to Jude would be telling him she was a skimmer, the only explanation of how she'd come to have it. Even mailing it anonymously was too risky when only so many people saw a body after death by suicide in her family's covert.

As it was with most of the kids in school, she couldn't call Jude a friend. He was a senior and she was a junior; the times they passed each other in the hall were only occasional. If they'd ever spoken, she had no recollection of it. But she still *knew* him, if only because they lived in the same town, had grown up within the same boundaries. So it was all too easy for her to picture him at his older brother's funeral, to imagine the events of the terrible day unfolding after reading the brief obituary in the local paper.

Seventeen years old, tall and lithe, his dark eyes both burning and hollow as he stood in a neat slate-gray suit next to Rigby's coffin. Beside him would be his closest friends from school, other guys she'd known since elementary and each of them just as much a non-friend to her as Jude. The school counselor would be there, wishing he could do more. Other mourners from town, as defeated as they were grieving, forever helpless in the face of the covert's strange, twisted lure. The promise of dark magic in its soil.

It would already be hot out, the late-spring sun a blistering yellow coin in the sky. The air would smell of fresh grass, bitter and sharp, of a coming summer already destroyed.

The service would be closed casket.

Marsden knew this. Had seen Rigby herself. Knew an open service could never be an option.

And she hadn't been wrong about Jude wearing a gray suit, though by the time she saw him outside the covert the day of the funeral, his tie was little more than a twist of mangled fabric, his dark pants dulled with road dust, his white shirt sleeves messily shoved up past his elbows. He hadn't seen her watching him from within the line of trees, but she'd seen *him*, leaning back against his family truck parked on the shoulder of the highway, his eyes turned toward the covert's entrance. It came off him in waves, a thick grief and confusion that was layered into the June heat blanketing the entire town. She could sense it even from where she'd been standing, barely daring to breathe. From the time on her watch and what she remembered reading of the obituary, Marsden realized he must have walked out during the middle of the wake. She was still wondering what might have driven him to do so when he'd turned abruptly, climbed into his truck, and sped off down the highway.

He wasn't, she supposed, classically handsome, but he was infinitely memorable, made up of parts crafted with driven, relentless motions. His face, all sharp angles and wary, deep brown eyes. A mouth that looked like it hurt to smile.

How hard would those eyes go, how brittle that mouth, if he ever found out what she was hiding? Something she could never give up without giving herself up?

Jude wore a stretched-out black tee with a chest pocket, baggy olive shorts, sandals that were starting to fall apart. She'd always heard his family had money, but if so, he didn't make it obvious. He had some kind of booklet shoved into one of his side pockets. The sun was already in full force, making the outline of his figure shimmer in the heat. He was tall and broad-shouldered, slim but still muscular, his big hands the kind sketch artists live for—full of jutting bones and deep hollows, stories in every long swoop and arc.

He didn't belong here.

That was the thought that kept popping up in Marsden's head as she moved toward him. He met her stare head-on, something he'd never done in the halls whenever she saw him.

Well, that was more her own doing than his. It'd become habit a long time ago, the way she never really met anyone's eyes at school anymore. It came from too many years of being stared at, whispered about, snickered about.

Still, his gaze was steady on hers, intense, the cool eye of a storm. Different from she remembered it being, the ways she'd seen it before. In school, surrounded by his friends, his eyes had been warm, lit up; by himself, they turned unwelcoming, nearly hostile. And that was even before Rigby.

What could Jude Ambrose want with her now? When they'd been strangers for years and years? The last thing she needed was one more problem to deal with when her whole entire *life* was a problem. A mess. A dead end.

She decided he was too tall. She also decided that his dark hair was way too thick and pretty, with its black-gold shine, its soft-looking waves. It half covered his eyes, was tossed all over his forehead, in desperate need of a cut. His skin was all coppers and bronzes, going a deeper hue along the top of his cheekbones, the slope of his nose—wherever the sun touched it. He wore a fat ladder of friendship bracelets—blacks, whites, neons—around one wrist. Their weave was careful and intricate and somehow feminine, and Marsden wondered who had made them for him.

From behind where he stood, past the fence her great-grandfather had built with his own hands, the smell of the covert bled loose and free, a roaming cloud of ginger. It drifted out and surrounded them, thick with spice and heat and other mysterious things.

She hadn't expected his eyes to be so dark. Which was stupid, because hers were just as dark, and Jude was as mixed as she was, except black to her Chinese.

It was another reason why Marsden had stayed aware of him in school. So that she couldn't help but glance over and imagine what it was like for *him*, growing up in Glory half-black, while nearly everyone else was white, white, white. She wondered if he ever got paranoid over a lengthy stare, at a laugh that came from behind as soon as he moved past, whenever someone else got chosen for something with no real explanation. If he was sometimes confused about why the white half of him *didn't* make him belong.

She also wondered why, just as she pretended she didn't care what anyone thought, Jude acted as though he wouldn't mind if someone did have a problem. Like he would welcome a confrontation.

Maybe that was the difference between them, she thought—hurt or be hurt. Maybe he'd learned something she hadn't yet.

"Hi." She didn't bother with a smile as she reached him. "Were you looking for something?"

"You're Marsden Eldridge." His voice was rough and rusty, like he hadn't spoken in a while. "From school."

She waited a beat, but he said nothing else. "And you're Jude Ambrose. From school."

His eyes narrowed as she said his name, a muscle along his neck jumped, and Marsden tried not to be irritated. He was on *her* property—why was he acting like she were the intruder?

But then an image of Rigby popped into her head—grisly, scattered, still too fresh—and she decided to start over.

"I'm really sorry about your brother." Already, Jude seemed like a puzzle. The same way Shine was a puzzle, full of hidden doors, tricky passageways, dangerous traps. "Rigby."

"It was—you were the one who found him."

Marsden nodded. "The covert is family property. I try to check often enough that if someone goes in, they won't accidentally see something."

He shoved his wavy hair out of his eyes with one hand, his expression slightly less guarded now. "Thanks for not talking about it with anyone."

"I wouldn't do that." She couldn't stop her frown. "Why would I?"

"Sorry, I don't mean it that way. I just meant that I knew you kept it quiet because I never heard anything going around. And Glory—well, this place can talk. And it likes its stories. The covert has its share."

She tried to smile, hoped it looked even remotely close to natural. "Latest I've heard is that saying its name three times in a row, while standing beneath a true crescent moon with your eyes shut, means a year of bad luck."

There were other stories, of course, passing from ear to mouth, ear to mouth. Stepping foot over the property line at midnight meant dooming someone else to die that very same second. A breath breathed while walking past meant living one less year. Running through the place beneath a full moon bought three wishes—but only if you first outran the ghost of poor crazy Duncan Kirby. He with the still-smoking hunting rifle in hand, chasing after you in boots slick with blood and splattered with Indigo mud, bellowing the names of his wife, his kids, the river, the town.

Jude smiled in return, and it broke across his face slowly, carefully, like a newly formed wave shyly brushing over the shore. Marsden liked how it looked on him. She didn't know what to think about that.

"*Two* years of bad luck," he said, "if it's a weekday."

"And if you do it too close to the covert?"

"You'll open your eyes to see Duncan's ghost right in front of you."

She nearly shivered, despite already knowing the tale. "I guess my ancestors don't play around."

"Makes you wonder how they'd punish skimmers."

"'Skimmers.'" The word, clumsy and ugly in her mouth—she flushed. How could she have forgotten who she was talking to about the covert? His brother's body was still imprinted all over its ginger plants, its soil saturated with it, her hands shadowed. "What are those?"

He looked surprised at *her* surprise. "You know, grave robbers, tomb raiders. Looking for bodies to steal from before they're taken away."

"Steal what?"

"Money would be the first thing, most likely. Then jewelry, or whatever's valuable—Seconds pawnshop would resell it, even."

Marsden shoved her hands into the front pocket of her shirt to hide how they wanted to twist. The toast inside had gone soggy and cold—her fingers were colder. "People trespass, but you don't know they steal. Skimmers are likely just another story in town."

A hint of impatience played on his lips. "Because neither of us know any personally? Doesn't mean they're not around."

"The jewelry part makes no sense." Her nerves thrummed. She hoped she sounded steadier than she felt. "People would recognize pieces." But she knew that didn't mean much. Glory had long grown comfortable with death, and most wouldn't care where a good find came from.

"You can still steal money, though," he said.

"You can't prove it was stolen."

"Doesn't mean it doesn't happen."

"It doesn't mean it *does*." She knew she sounded defensive, but she couldn't help it. Whatever little ground they'd managed to gain together already seemed lost. "You can't believe everything you hear about the covert, you know. And this place is mine. I would know what was real or not, don't you think?"

Jude's gaze had cooled. His voice was raw again. "Look, I'm not here to accuse you or anything. Or to be told I'm stupid."

She saw his dead brother in his eyes and fresh guilt filled her.

Did he know? she wondered. That the anger she saw in him even before Rigby died was nearly all gone now, turned into grief? Was now something so bleak she felt it in her own chest just by looking at him?

From over his shoulder, the sudden piston of a small black form split apart the ground. The squirrel ran toward them, barely visible in the grass that rose up to cover her ankles, surrounding the covert's fence in a wide ring of pale green. Technically, this part of the property belonged to the township; it wasn't uncommon for Glory to let the grass grow unchecked for weeks before finally sending someone to cut it. More than once, Marsden had given in and mowed it herself, the grass bleached nearly white by the sun by then.

She took out the toast, recalling Wynn's pleas to go with her. *To talk to the boy with the angry face and ask him what was wrong.* Her little sister, with her weakness for things that she believed she could help— squirrels living with ghosts in the covert, boys with sad eyes and dead brothers. But Shine had said no, and only Marsden promising to feed the squirrels on her behalf appeased her sister enough to be satisfied with waiting with Dany for rhubarb and ice cream.

"You just pulled out a really disgusting-looking piece of toast from your shirt pocket," Jude said slowly, staring at her hands. Then he glanced back up to meet her gaze, lifted one brow, and asked with great care, "I'm guessing you must be hungry?"

A small laugh escaped before she'd even known it was there. "My sister's trying to bribe herself a pet. She's decided squirrels will do."

"Didn't know squirrels liked toast." His slow grin was back, making it hard to stay annoyed with him. Making him way too easy to look at.

"She says they prefer waffles, but I have to draw the line somewhere." She passed over half the toast. "Here—do you mind? I promised her."

Jude took it without hesitation, and Marsden sighed inwardly—how could she *not* think he was okay, considering how he wasn't even questioning being asked to feed toast to a rodent?

She led him a few feet along the outer curve of the wooden fence, and he followed silently, taking this so seriously she admitted she found it endearing.

If Wynn were there, she'd already be head over heels at seeing Jude smile the way he proved to be able to.

Sudden memories of a very young Jude began to fill Marsden's head as she walked. Each image turned over on itself until it was clearer than the last, just as though she were searching for gold along the Indigo, shaking her pan, tilting out water and mud and silt—the fog of time, the messiness of her own childhood—until only the precious metal remained, finally revealed in full.

seven.

HE'D BEEN A TINY SCRAP OF A KID, NOT YET GROWN INTO HIS BONES, SO SMALL AND VULNERABLE, THE WAY DELICATE BIRDS SEEMED VULNERABLE. His hair, nearly as messy as he wore it now, a chaos of dark brown spikes and waves. Huge eyes dimmed with anxiety and dread—before he'd learned to turn all of that into fury.

Because Dany had reminded Marsden about Jude's father, hadn't she, after the news of Rigby Ambrose had spread throughout Glory? How Leo Ambrose had moved his young family out West after he lost his job due to his drinking. How his wife died of cancer not long after. How his drinking spun even more out of control and his sons met his fists. All of it, leaking throughout the town like bad gas, borne on whispers and sly glances and the kind of boredom so deep it almost welcomed danger.

A clumsily bandaged wrist as Jude walked around outside during recess.

A split lip as he entered the classroom.

Then, one spring weekend in the public library. Marsden had been seven and Jude eight. His bronze-hued cheek had been red and puffed, his eyes wet and streaming, as she watched him run between towers of books toward an older boy. His flight had been desperate and terrorized, full of fear. She'd felt all of that crash into her own heart, so that it hurt for him, too, this schoolmate she only knew by name.

She'd been in the next aisle, browsing the cookbooks—Star had promised to bake cookies with her the next time she visited, Marsden's choice of recipe—when the pounding of sneakered feet came from behind the racks of books at her side. She heard muffled crying, comforting murmurs.

She'd walked to the end of the aisle and peeked over.

There was Jude, crying into the shoulder of an older boy. He seemed huge by comparison, this other boy, his shoulders and hands and feet all oversize—only his soft cheeks and long, messy limbs gave away how young he was still. Marsden saw how his skin was the exact same shade as Jude's, all ambers and sweet molasses. They had the same eyes, too, full of glints and hidden hues that only peeked out depending. Her own eyes were like that, not wanting to give things away.

That older boy would have been Rigby, she knew now. Doing his best to protect his little brother from their father, even if Jude's swollen cheek told her Rigby had been too slow that day. And seeing Rigby's expression, the tears in his own eyes as he struggled to convince Jude he would be fine, she saw how he hated himself for it.

She knew that feeling now, too, didn't she? How each time she failed Wynn, it ate at her like a strange hunger, the kind that no food could fix? How it made her realize all over again that she was not good enough to make up for all the bad, not strong enough to save anything?

If she ever heard Rigby in the covert, she'd tell him she understood all of it. How lonely it was to save someone. How his leaving had left Jude hollow, but that his brother was still here, and alive, and so he hadn't failed at all.

And, maybe, then she'd ask something of him.

If he knew of her father. If somewhere in the covert, Grant Eldridge still had a voice.

Then Jude was grabbing her hand, jolting her back to the present and the covert, stopping her from walking any farther.

"The squirrel's right at our feet." His face was amused, wanting to laugh. And his voice was still husky, but no longer scraped or painful sounding, just full of valleys and low, soft slopes. He dropped her hand. "Hidden in the grass."

The ghost of his touch lingered like the long, measured stroke of a sure brush on paper. Marsden ignored the sensation and ripped up the rest of her half of the piece of toast, dropping the pieces onto the ground near where they stood.

Jude started to do the same. "Captivity for toast. Seems fair enough to me."

It didn't escape her, the way it was both strange yet completely normal to be standing there with him, just outside the place where his brother had shot himself weeks ago. In that moment, more than anything, she wanted to ask him if it really had been his dad who used to hurt him. If he was still being hurt. If that was why he always looked ready to hurt someone back.

"So you live at the boardinghouse with your family?" He tossed the last of his toast into the grass. "And work there as a cook? Your mom's a housekeeper there, right?"

Marsden's mind raced, trying to decipher if he was being sarcastic in pretending to not know. If unspoken facts were simply lies to him, or stories, or rumors.

"Who told you we lived there?" she finally managed.

"That girl who found me here outside the covert. I'm guessing she's your sister?"

She nodded. "Her name's Wynn." Who was now going to be served eggs every day for breakfast for the rest of the summer—for the rest of the entire *year*.

"I asked her where I could find you, so she told me you were still at home. Then she pointed to the boardinghouse."

Surprise wiped away all further thoughts of punishment for Wynn. She realized now that he never did say why he came to be there, waiting outside her woods as though he were guarding it. Or spying. "You were actually looking for me?"

A second of hesitation, then Jude pulled out the book he'd tucked into his shorts pocket. He unrolled it, showing her the front.

Putting Together the Perfect Time Capsule. The cover was worn and scratched up. He handed it to her, his expression uncertain again, vulnerable. "Open it, please."

Marsden did, even though she was lost. Why was he showing her a kids' book?

The pages inside were laminated, protection from sticky and careless fingers. Someone had written on them, the handwriting that of a child's. There were lists and arrows and charts.

She flipped more pages and dried blooms whirled free.

Leaves, palm-size, in the shape of a heart.

The familiar scent of wild ginger filled her nose as the leaves danced around them to land at their feet. It was the covert, leaving traces of itself on their skin, in the breaths they breathed.

She should have instantly thought of death, of sad, lonely things. And she did. But standing there with Jude, some of her thoughts also stayed with him—with the book he'd brought for her—so that she was curious, confused.

The grim expression had crept back into his eyes. It was now laced with a painful kind of hope, and she braced herself for anything and everything.

"Rigby had a time capsule, and it's buried somewhere in the covert," he said. "I need to find it. I need to dig it up."

eight.

MARSDEN TURNED FROM HIM SO FAST, HER HAIR SPUN OUT IN A WILD ARC, AS THOUGH TO CUT AWAY HIS REQUEST. Her heart skated in circles in her chest, pounding.

She had to get away.

Jude's hand shot out and grasped at her arm. There was desperation in his grip, a panic of his own that nearly touched hers. She barely had time to consider that: the puzzle of why he'd be feeling something close to scared when he was only supposed to be mourning his beloved big brother. When he said her name, it sounded raw.

"Marsden. Please. Just hear me out for a second."

"No." Fury was the only thing that could contain her fear. "You've lost your mind to ask me that. And you need to leave." Each word had to be a hammer blow to his hopes, no matter how cruel each might be. She stared down at his hand, still on her arm, and grimaced. *Let go.*

Jude did, quickly, as though her skin had burned him. He flushed, and for a second, she was ashamed for making him feel he'd done something wrong when, between the two of them, she was the only guilty one.

"Don't you understand why I need to do this?" His voice was a rasp. "It's my brother I'm talking about here. *My brother.* I need answers, and—" He stopped, his mouth snapping shut, his expression torn.

"Digging up the covert won't bring him back." Guiltily, she thought of Rigby's note. How it fell from the thin wad of folded-up bills when she was back in her bedroom, creased by her fingers as she shoved it away, hiding it.

"Look, it's not going to be me digging up the covert like I'm laying out the works for some new building," he said. "It's me looking for something he left behind."

"By digging up the covert."

"For a time capsule. Nothing like excavating, I swear. Rig would have done it as a little kid. We're talking about something the size of a shoebox, or one of those Kraft mayo jars. Small like that."

Something inside her wanted to give—she needed to fight it. How would she keep skimming? How could she not want to get her and Wynn out as soon as possible? "The smaller it is, the harder it would be to find. It would mean *more* digging."

"He left notes." He opened the book and pointed to a scrawl on one of the pages. Now that she knew whose writing it was, she couldn't see how she'd missed seeing it the first time around. It'd changed a lot since he was a kid, but Marsden saw hints of future Rigby's handwriting: the fat, gaping *O*s, the overly tall and loping *T*s. "He wrote down right here that he was going to use a cookie tin, a metal one. And his old metal detector from when he was a kid is still in the shed. It's going to be easy."

She shook her head. Jude was reaching, nearly painfully, and his acute need for his brother to not be dead was warping reality. She knew how that was—didn't she still do the same with her own father?

"You don't know for sure that he ended up using that," she said. "He might have changed his mind."

"Maybe. And maybe he didn't."

"You're basing all of this on a book you happened to find in his room. On notes he could have written down for any reason." Marsden needed him to realize on his own just how far-fetched his assumptions were, to walk away on his own—she didn't need the guilt of having to say no on top of what she already carried. He'd apologize for disturbing her, tell her to have a good summer, that he might or might not see her in the halls at school, and then he'd leave.

Except he wasn't interested in playing along.

"If you'd known Rig," he pressed, "you'd know he never did anything half-assed. He was weird that way, okay? He spent one whole spring break doing nothing but watch Kurosawa films. Last summer was dead male author reading—nothing but books by guys like Faulkner, Steinbeck, Wells. Two years ago, he studied disco as hard as he'd ever studied for any school subject. *Disco.* Its rise and fall in the seventies. I had to listen to the Shindiggs for *weeks*."

"I don't mind the Shindiggs," she said mildly. Dany still had a soft spot for *Burn Out*. Whenever she played it from her room, the sound would come drifting down the staff wing—she was pretty sure Wynn knew the entire soundtrack by heart.

"Okay, but—" A smile flickered on his lips, then he grew serious again. He scrubbed at his thick hair, thinking. Rigby was etched in his eyes, a ghost lingering on. "Well, anyway, that was Rig, always looking for something to disappear into. Because the reality of home really sucked."

His misery was so plaintive, the ache of it lay in her own throat. Again, she heard the echoes of people whispering about his father's drinking. Dany had told her Leo had seemed to get better a few years ago, had apparently stopped hitting Rigby and Jude, but who really knew the truth, outside of the family? Outside of Jude, with his perpetually hard eyes; of Rigby, who was dead; of Leo, who would never have reason to talk about any of it?

"And then the dried leaves inside the book," he went on, "the ginger. You know that stuff only grows freely here in the covert. Nowhere else in town."

"Because of the shade inside."

He nodded. "The rest of Glory just burns."

She saw how he'd connected the dots—a book about capsules, containing physical evidence of only one possible location.

"Where would you even start, Jude? The covert is bigger than it looks."

"What, maybe the size of a basketball court?"

Marsden shut her eyes. Shine had papers with the actual measurements, but he wasn't really asking about numbers. He just wanted her to agree.

In her head, she walked through the space, measuring the distance between the trees, how far the smell of wild ginger traveled with her, the way the sun fell through branches and leaves and bounced off the ground. She sensed death in the echo of her footsteps, in the call of the animals as they skittered through the forest alongside her, but she wasn't all scared. She knew the covert, just as it knew her, and she could either fight that terrible connection or accept it for what it was.

Last summer, in the middle of a heat wave so intense the air was on fire, Marsden had lain awake one night, unable to sleep. She'd thought of the river and decided to sneak out, suddenly wanting more than anything to slip into its cool waters. It was past midnight, and the sound of cars along the highway was a distant, insignificant whoosh in her ears. The gravel beneath her bare feet had hurt; she smelled mud and silt and dampened rock in the air. Beneath the moonless sky, the surface of the river was an unbroken ribbon of darkness, its bottom on the other side of the earth. And in the instant before she hit the water, it'd been like leaping into a crevasse with no end, dooming her to fall nonstop. But then she'd splashed through, the terror fled as though it'd never been, and the relief of being cool was visceral, whole. She could have swam forever that night. Could have kept diving, again and again.

The covert was like that for her. The same way it embraced her even as it screamed a warning. The same way a fever had to climb in order to break.

"Try *two* basketball courts." She opened her eyes. "And people *die* in there. To go and start hacking through—"

"You make it sound as bad as if I were going in as a skimmer." Jude's eyes glinted. "I'm not an asshole."

It was true she already sensed he would be respectful. Nothing like Red and Coop and other skimmers. It was the place where Rigby died. Where parts of his brother were still soaked into the ground of the covert, were still coursing through the tissues of its plants and trees.

"My father is buried in there," Marsden said quietly.

He stilled. "I didn't know that. I'm sorry. Though I should have realized because—" His voice broke off. "Because it's family property."

"Because it was suicide, you mean."

"The papers said it was an accident."

"I know what the papers said." She crossed her arms in front of herself, like they could act as armor.

He twisted the book in his hands. "Look, I know this tin won't bring Rig back. But whatever made him do it, it's like a piece of him that's gone missing, and I want it back. Even if it's just Hot Wheels or hockey cards or marbles—they're still his, right? I always thought I knew him so well, but now I think there are parts of him he kept from me. And however it might end up, maybe I'm meant to try to find them."

"Or maybe not."

"Or maybe not."

Marsden gave in before she even knew she'd stopped fighting. Because she saw herself, and the need for answers, in his eyes. And if she was deluded enough to think they could come in the form of dead people's voices, then having them be buried in old cookie tins waiting to be dug up wasn't any stranger.

And that tin . . . It was a direct connection to Rigby.

If she found it, she might be able to hear him, talk to him, just as Star could, what people in Glory had gone to her for. Marsden could tell him what she wished she'd known to tell him all those years ago as she watched him cry over having failed: that he hadn't failed at saving Jude. Then maybe she would know, somehow, that she wasn't going to fail in saving Wynn. And maybe once she heard Rigby, she could finally hear her father.

"You'd be here every day?" She still had her arms wrapped around herself.

"I'll stay out of your face when you're in there checking for bodies, if that's what you're worried about."

"Checking for bodies?" Her skin was cold, and panic rose in her throat. What exactly had she given away?

"Yeah, so you can call Hadley and report them."

She exhaled. "Right." Then she realized why the image of him simply waiting outside of the covert had been so striking—because no one ever waited. "Can I ask why you didn't just walk into the covert on your own? The signs have never stopped anyone from going in. You could have started digging without me even knowing about it."

"I admit I thought of it. But then if I got caught, you'd be too pissed to hear me out for a second chance." He gave a small smile. She found her eyes falling to his mouth, circling back to his eyes, liking his face more and more. "And like I said, I'm not an asshole."

"I would have been too busy kicking you out to believe you."

Jude laughed, then glanced back at the covert. "You know, all that wild ginger in there—I never would have guessed it hadn't always been that way."

"How did you know that?" Outside of family, she didn't think the covert having changed was talked about much. It appeared on the town's timeline as stealthily as summer's heat snuck in each year—slowly, then so unrelenting it didn't seem possible to have ever been banked.

"I work part-time at Evergreen, the garden center downtown. Roadie—the owner, my boss—he pretty much watched Rig and me grow up since our mom took the two of us to his shop so often. She had a thing for filling up the house with flowers. Rig said living in Glory made her hungry for them."

Marsden liked that. Being hungry for flowers instead of things like answers, or escape, or a parent's love.

"Roadie used to drive along the highway right here as a teen—his nickname, right?—chasing down the squirrels. The smell gave it away, he said, because there never used to be a trace of ginger."

She nodded slowly, still feeling strange talking about the covert to anyone other than Wynn. She tried to imagine Jude at work, surrounded by flowers and delicate blooms, and couldn't. "He's right. It never used to grow in the covert. I don't know when it started."

"Anyway, finding those leaves in Rig's book . . . I had to come here."

"I'll make a deal with you." She kept her eyes on his to gauge his reaction. If he even suspected she was a skimmer, she would tell him to leave and never come back. "The mornings here are mine, alone. And once the sun's gone down, the place is off limits—you wouldn't be able to see anything without flashlights, anyway, and if my mom or her boss saw you moving around in there, they'd be upset. But you can have the afternoons and evenings, if you still want them. And I'll have to be in there with you. I can't leave you alone in the covert."

"Because you don't trust me."

"No, because it's not easy being alone with the dead. You'll see."

His gaze narrowed. "The trust thing sounds easier."

"Am I *supposed* to trust you?"

"Maybe." His smile was nearly playful. "One day."

"Fair enough." Wind whistled through the trees in the covert, there was the slightest hum in the air, and the scent of wild ginger wafted out and stained them all over. "Okay, so those are my conditions."

Jude nodded. "You've got yourself a deal, Marsden Eldridge."

nine.

HOWEVER MARSDEN FELT ABOUT WHAT TOOK PLACE IN THE BOARDINGHOUSE—WITHIN ITS WALLS, BELOW ITS ROOF— SHE'D ALWAYS LOVED HOW IT LOOKED. She knew she was growing up in the prettiest place in all of Glory.

By comparison, the town's lone public library—plain brown concrete shell, pitted concrete front walk, nonexistent windows—was a hopeless cause.

She would have preferred to live there if she could.

Wynn yanked open the heavy front doors and was already running toward the kids' section before Marsden had fully stepped inside. "Come find me when you're done!" she called out.

"Runt, remember where we are again, right? You can't yell in here."

"*Sorry!*" A hiss of a whisper, and her little sister disappeared, swallowed up by old steel racks, by tens of thousands of pages. Her hair was everywhere, the butterfly clip she'd stuck in it that morning already lost.

Marsden went upstairs. It was where the library stored its research materials. Where she could read up on Glory's history. The nicest parts of it and the ugliest.

It was summer, so the study cubicles were mostly empty, the few scattered tables unoccupied. But the air-conditioning in the place was strong, which likely explained why it wasn't entirely deserted.

Yesterday's conversation with Jude was what brought Marsden to the library in the first place, and she found herself walking over to where she once saw Rigby try to right the world for his brother. The aisle was empty now, but standing there, the memory sharpened, got clearer. She remembered how there'd been books scattered all over the floor, in piles at Rigby's elbows. How all those cream-colored pages came together to form a pair of giant paper wings, ready to fly him away.

Jude would have seen them the second he came running, those wings at Rigby's side.

Would he have thought the same thing? That if he waited long enough, those giant paper wings would fly his brother far away from him, leaving him alone with their drunken father?

Marsden turned away and headed for the library's newspaper collection.

Rigby's death was just one more in a long, long line of suicides in Glory, but his father had been someone, once, out East. Maybe enough of a someone that his son dying meant an article, talking again about Leo Ambrose. She could have asked almost anyone in town, and they probably could have filled her in on Jude's father, but then her asking would become news itself. The last thing she needed was more talk about her.

Thumbing through back issues from three weeks ago, she picked out ones for the local and East Coast–based papers—the second of which always arrived in Glory a few days late—and carried them over to a free cubicle. She was more than curious about the history of the boy she was bringing into *her* history. *Jude, meet the covert. But first, what are your family secrets, before you learn mine?*

The local write-up and obituary—she still remembered both from the first time she'd read. When both had been fresh, when the town had still been rumbling with news of Rigby.

But that was before Jude, a boy who could barely say his dead brother's name without sounding like it hurt, had come to her. Before she'd said yes to his being a daily distraction, to the possible unmaking of all her plans, to not being able to skim as freely or as quickly with him around. When she had yet to consider how his being in the covert—and connected to his own dead—could prove another way for her to reach her father, since she'd already failed on her own.

Reading it again, she felt a sense of purpose she hadn't the first time. Before, she'd felt nothing but the dull sadness she always felt reading about deaths in the covert. It was also how she felt whenever she skimmed, whenever she stilled over a body and listened to the covert and heard nothing. Her helping Jude—she could be something other than what the town already decided she was.

In the East Coast papers, only one mentioned Rigby, and it was a finance one—the tiniest, briefest note that the son of a former CEO of a stock company had suddenly and tragically passed.

Marsden returned the newspapers and went to the microfiche cards. She located the cabinet that stored the data for out-of-state papers, flipped through cards until she found East Coast ones, and then narrowed *those* down to the time right before Leo Ambrose headed west.

She carried the cards to the microfiche reader.

Leo Ambrose hadn't merely lost his cushy job when the market turned, it turned out, but also the entire family fortune, which had been deeply invested in stock. His firm set up a satellite position for him on the West Coast, and so the Ambrose family moved.

That was all. But Marsden had heard enough from Dany and the town to fill in the rest. How Glory was close enough to Seattle and the firm's West Coast office that Leo would still feel important but far away enough that his drinking wouldn't be an embarrassment. How the death of his young wife on top of all that had turned his sons into targets.

Marsden returned the cards back to the cabinet, thinking about Jude, knowing he would have wondered the same thing: How much did Leo's anger affect Rigby's choice that day?

She was about to go find Wynn to leave when she glimpsed the cabinet that held the cards for the local paper. Sorted by year, from the gold rush to town establishment to present day, Glory's entire history, if she were interested.

Most of it she already knew, had learned all the facts and folklore and legends.

After Duncan Kirby bled his family and himself all over the covert nearly a hundred years ago, his brother eventually came to Glory to claim the land. That had been Asa Kirby, her great-grandfather. He didn't build a cabin for himself in the covert like Duncan had, but instead built a fence around the entirety of the land before buying a small duplex right in town, where he lived out the rest of his life. He sold off bits and pieces of the family property over the years, like chunks of bitter chocolate broken off the bar, until the duplex and the fenced expanse of trees and soil and ghosts was all that remained in her mother's name—at least until Shine had to sell the home where Marsden had lived with her parents.

Just as the covert's reputation as a place of redemption grew—Duncan's waiting ghost, taking your hand and leading you deep—the rest of the town grew, too. First as a humble tourist town, its folk—stubbornly sure gold would return to their river's shores—serving travelers drinks and snacks from stands along the highway while selling handmade protective charms meant to ward off spirits lost and wandering free of the covert. (The first time Marsden saw these charms—a stand of little Duncan dolls on key chains, their tiny fabric boots dyed red, thin rolls of black felt for their guns—she'd been with her mother, and Shine's face had blanched, her mouth had gone a bloodless, lipless line, and she'd led Marsden to the corner store and bought her dollars' worth of penny candy.)

But honest money came slow to the town, and still no gold showed. So casinos and game parlors opened, though the highest risk machines only came out at night. Card and gambling houses operated as car re-pair bays during the day. Pharmacies cooked up more than prescribed medicines between dusk and dawn.

Marsden's skin chilled from the suddenly too-strong air-conditioning. Her hand riffled through the stack of cards until she came to 1980: the year of the mysterious death of Grant Eldridge. Officially classified as an accident, but the town quietly believed it to be a suicide despite there being no covert soil on him.

Her heart thumping, Marsden fed the cards into the microfiche reader, and she was eight years old again, struggling to read about her father never coming back.

She scrolled over magnified black text, feeling sick as the words painted images of that night in her head:

Her parents' argument inside their duplex home.

The building spring storm outside as she and Shine waited for him to come back. And waited.

The Indigo finally giving him back up the next morning.

But she'd misread the news, it seemed, that first time eight years ago. Or not read enough. Or Shine had revealed more than a little girl needed to know, and Marsden had never even realized it.

She sat up abruptly from the reader, the walls of the library spinning just as her brain whirled with microfiche words. Her stomach clenched the way it always did when she'd failed with Wynn, when her sister saw real glimpses of a body or when she asked one of Nina's girls to do her hair instead of Marsden.

The articles she'd just read—they were bare bones, only the facts, dry as dust. What was one more death in a death-ridden town, after all?

Her father, more drunk than not after a night of blackjack at his favorite card house, making his way down the highway in the direction of the covert, the direction of home. Reports from other players at Decks that night had said he'd had a winning night. His pockets being empty when they pulled his body from the Indigo meant little, considering it was Grant Eldridge. Likely he'd stumbled somewhere else after Decks, made an impromptu bet, and then lost it all. Or, just as likely, that the tide had taken it, the river's muddy, silt-filled fingers greedy.

But years ago, before she refused to speak about her dead husband anymore, her smoke trembling between her whitened fingers as she whispered it was time to let go, Shine had told Marsden how he'd been with friends that night, all of them playing out the hours over games of blackjack. She hadn't been more specific than that—only *friends*—or if she had, then Marsden had forgotten. The articles made it sound like he'd gambled on his own.

How could she have forgotten Shine telling her about her father's winning night? So that the knowledge had then slipped away from her as easily as he himself had? It didn't seem possible that her mother wouldn't have said anything, given that most of Shine's everyday life back then had revolved around money, or the lack of it.

Unnamed friends, whom the police hadn't felt necessary to report.

Missing winnings, which her mother might never have spoken about.

Marsden's skin rippled—and not just from the air-conditioning.

"Excuse me? Are you done with the reader?"

Marsden blinked, saw a boy standing in front of her, a stack of microfiche cards in his hand. Waiting for a turn.

"Oh, sorry. Yes, I'm done." She gathered her own cards and walked them back over to the cabinet, filing them away with fingers gone cold.

Her pulse was too fast and dread had lodged in her chest as she headed downstairs, looking for Wynn.

Because she knew what she needed to do.

She had to ask her mother—who'd become nothing more than an act—to tell her, all over again, exactly what happened the night her father died.

ten.

IT WAS LATE AFTERNOON BY THE TIME MARSDEN AND WYNN LEFT THE LIBRARY. The sun remained blistering, pounding the dusty pavement with waves of heat. Marsden didn't welcome it, even after a solid hour of overpowering air-conditioning—and even though she was still chilled from the inside out after uncovering the unknown about her father's death.

She'd always had questions for him, but not for anyone else. Why would she when the truth was obvious, regardless of what the papers had to say?

Death by suicide, nothing else.

Her hand shook as she unlocked Wynn's bike, then her own, from the rack on the sidewalk.

"You ready to go?" She hoped she sounded normal, though her mind was racing. All these years of living with the covert nestled into her heart like another hollow chamber, the idea of death, whatever its form, should be something she was used to. "I have to stop at the post office on the way back."

"Who are you writing to?" Wynn leaned over and squished the

books that wouldn't fit into her own bike basket into Marsden's. Her eyes lit up with curiosity. "Like a pen pal? Where are they from?"

I'm writing to the dead. They come from places all over, just to see the covert.

She kept her smile casual as she hopped onto her bike and headed down the road. "Not a pen pal, no. Just a payment I have to mail for Dany." A white lie, boring enough that Wynn wouldn't think twice about it. Through the gaps of the houses along the highway, the Indigo was visible. Marsden caught flashes of the setting sun, winking off the river like bits of lightning. The faint metallic smell of the water floated through the air and tingled her nose. And though it was getting close to dark, there were still rental boats and canoes out, their shapes black wedges of shadow cutting close to the shore. She heard distant hollers and laughter and the splashing of water.

"It'd be neat if you did have a pen pal, don't you think?" Wynn asked.

"Sure."

"Because you don't like the kids from your school very much."

Marsden was surprised enough that it took her a few seconds to respond. She showed a sudden prolonged interest in the buildings they biked past, the same tourist-friendly ones she'd seen all her life: Poseidon, where you could order takeout fish and chips *and* rent fishing equipment by the day; Spokes, for bikes if you wanted to explore the town and the long Indigo coast; the Glory Heritage Museum, where they did slideshows of the town's historic gold rush four times a day, carefully edited to end before Duncan Kirby lost his mind. "Who says I don't like them, runt?"

"No one." Riding along on their bikes, there was the slightest of breezes, and Wynn's nest of hair was only getting messier, clip still missing. "But I can tell. You're never on the phone with anyone like I am with Caitlyn and Ella. And you're always home, working."

Her sister was shades of Shine, lecturing her, and it would have struck Marsden as amusing if she weren't already on edge. Wynn never seemed bothered by stares and slights, was still mostly oblivious—but that would slowly change with time, with age. When she knew the truth and began to view Glory through it. When the friends she had now learned to see her through that same truth, too.

"I'm always home because that's where I work," Marsden said carefully. "And just because you don't see me on the phone making plans to hang out with anyone doesn't mean I'm not, right?"

"I guess there *was* that boy looking for you outside the covert yesterday." Wynn's earlier curiosity was back tenfold. "Does *he* go to your school? What did he want?"

"Just—oh, there's the post office. Let's go."

Marsden was greatly relieved to bike a bit ahead, to avoid having to answer her sister's questions. Jude was more dangerous than not, his sudden presence in her life like the key to a change she wasn't ready for.

"Uh-oh, it's closed," Wynn said, coming up alongside her. "The windows are all dark."

"Dany had stamps at the house, so I just need the box anyway," Marsden said. "Wait here for me, okay?"

But her sister was no longer listening, was already reading one of her library books pulled from her basket as Marsden swung off her bike, leaving it standing alongside the curb.

She'd been prepared for the post office to be closed when they'd left for it. In fact, she'd planned it that way. For as long as she'd been mailing away bits of her guilt—and it'd been years now—she'd always used the after-hours box outside the entrance. She already stuck out in the town—she didn't need her letters to be remembered, too.

She slipped an envelope from her purse.

After skimming the woman's body in the covert yesterday, she'd taken the five-dollar bill to the boardinghouse's front desk and changed it for singles at the till. After the newspaper had been delivered that morning, she'd scanned the small column hidden deep in the local news section that was dedicated to covert updates, searching for the woman's name, then looked for her address in one of the phone books in the lobby (Dany kept both local and state ones for boardinghouse guests to use; beyond that, Marsden was sometimes forced to call the operator to ask for an address). She'd addressed a plain white envelope, slipped in a dollar bill—it was always a dollar whether she skimmed five or fifty—stamped it, and sealed it shut.

Where there should have been a return address, she'd left the envelope blank. As she always did.

Now Marsden dropped it into the mail slot, heard the shimmy of it as it slid down.

It'd started with Caleb Silas, of course, the first body that she'd skimmed. Her guilt, the letters.

She'd known skimming was wrong, just as she'd known she was going to keep doing it. At first, because it was rebellion—against her new home, her father being gone, her new life. Then it became a weapon, a means to an eventual escape. And soon, a compulsion, the only way she could ever understand why her father left. The only way how, given her blood and its dark magic, she could hear from him, be told that his death had nothing to do with her. How, as long as she kept going, she could also hear from those she skimmed, be assured they understood why she did what she did.

But he didn't speak to her. No one in the covert ever did.

So she talked to them with these letters, this money. An apology of sorts, sending back a portion of what was rightfully theirs. Or, even more than an apology, the absolution she would never earn. She would always owe a debt.

The problem was Wynn might end up being the one to pay it. Marsden's guilt was slowing down her saving, keeping them in Glory even longer.

Jude Ambrose. He might end up paying, too. Jude, with his hard slash of a mouth and so much fiery sadness in his eyes.

Away from him right then, safe from the spell of his face, she was nearly sure she was making a mistake agreeing to his searching the covert. She was risking him finding out she was a skimmer, after all. What if she couldn't make herself lie about stealing from Rigby? What if she had no choice but to show Jude what she was still hiding? Had to then make him see firsthand the proof and depths of his brother's misery?

The note. A simple and terrible handful of scrawled lines in Rigby's now-recognizable handwriting—those Os, the Ts:

I'm sorry, Jude, I never wanted you to know.
I told myself it was Dad.
I didn't want to stop.
But I didn't mean to do it.

They were nearly out of downtown when Wynn caught sight of the pop-up kiosk on the sidewalk. Marsden saw the cheap souvenirs on display as she biked past—magnets, mugs, key chains, most emblazoned with some kind of symbol representing the Indigo. All false—blue instead of mud.

Wynn turned her bike toward it before Marsden could stop her.

"Hey, it's getting late, I've got to get started on dinner," Marsden called after her sister, exasperated. She'd already taken a look at the menu, knew exactly how much time she needed. She would be cutting it close—the library had taken longer than she'd thought it would. To be fair, she'd only planned on looking up one death, not two. Running late also meant she'd have to wait until tomorrow to talk to Shine about her dead husband. As with all of Nina's girls, her mother's evenings and nights were taken.

"But I need another hair clip, remember?" Wynn got off her bike and walked over to the kiosk. The vendor was busy talking up a group of tourists, leaving Marsden to roll her eyes more freely over the merchandise. No hair clips as far as she could tell, but stuff she hadn't seen from afar—snow globes, bottle openers, postcards.

And a row of protective charms suspended from display hooks. Little Duncan dolls, complete with blood-splattered legs and miniature guns.

Marsden drew back, both annoyed and flustered. She remembered Shine's humiliation at seeing the things, and felt touches of it herself, hating that it was one of the few things she still shared with her mother.

She wanted to get away before the vendor saw them. He might recognize them and back away himself. Even worse, though, was that he might not know who they were. Would then try to sell them charms. Would tell them all about the legend of mad Duncan Kirby. "We really should go, Wynn. No hair clips. And if dinner's late, Nina's going to cut some of my pay."

"These charms are so stupid," her sister whispered loudly, leaning in closer to the display to examine. She wrinkled her nose, as though they even smelled bad. "The covert's just a place. And how would having dolls of our great-great-uncle protect someone from his ghost, anyway?"

Marsden had to grin. She'd known Wynn had seen the charms

82

for sale before—everyone in Glory had—but had never thought to ask how she felt about them. Disdain, her sister's not caring yet, was about as good of a reaction as she could ask for. Caring too much about anything, that was how traps happened.

"Well, they can't even get the color of the river right—we all know it's not the least bit blue." She shrugged. "Ready to leave for real now, runt?"

eleven.

SHE WAS STILL PULLING THE PORK CHOPS OFF THE GRILL WHEN DANY FOUND HER.

"Marsden, have you seen Wynn? Has she eaten?"

"She has, and she's outside collecting ants in a pickle jar. I know, don't ask—and don't tell Nina, okay?"

"Don't tell me what?"

Her mother's boss strode into the kitchen. As usual, she was dressed as though she were going to high tea instead of dinner with sunburned guests who smelled of the river. A long slim dress the shade of pale lemons. Hair, a shimmer of a brown bob. Rose-tipped nails—claws in disguise, Marsden had realized long ago.

She pretended to check the doneness of the pork chops so she wouldn't have to look up. Her mother hadn't exactly been excited at the idea of telling Nina that Marsden wasn't going to become one of her girls, but she still said she would do it. Marsden wasn't sure she was ready to see if Shine had failed her.

From the corner of her eye, she saw Dany pick up the bread basket full of still-steaming rolls. "Dinner's going out right now, Nina—coming along?"

"Hmm, shortly. I actually came in search of aspirin. The bottle in the medicine cabinet is empty and a headache is starting."

"Extra supplies are in the basket in the pantry, top shelf."

Nina disappeared through the pantry's wooden doors.

Marsden began to move the meat over again. Her face was hot, and it wasn't all from the stove. Nina's voice said Shine hadn't talked to her at all. Marsden would have been angrier if she hadn't been grateful for one thing—from what she could tell, Shine hadn't told Nina yes, either.

Suddenly, Dany stepped close and spoke into her ear. The steam from the bread basket wafted up against Marsden's arm, warming her skin.

"For your information, one of the dinner guests is a longtime client, all right?" Dany kept her voice low. "So when you go in there, please don't react."

Marsden piled more meat onto the platter next to the grill, chilled despite the steam against her skin, the heat of the stove. "Shine's."

"Yes. But just do your job. Don't look over if it bothers you, and then you are free for the whole rest of the evening, all right?" Dany squeezed Marsden's arm and left the kitchen for the dining room, bread basket tucked beneath an arm.

Marsden turned off the stove and finished stacking the sizzling meat on the platter. She didn't want to think about Dany's news, which meant she could think of nothing else.

Johns were only ever around the boardinghouse from post-dinner onward, when they slunk in, did their thing, and slunk back out before breakfast. Anything to do with Nina's day business was free of their presence, and this included official meals in the dining room. It worked out for everyone—johns could go live their safe lives, and boardinghouse guests who had no clue they were staying in a brothel could stay happily ignorant.

Only the johns Nina called "clients" were welcome to eat with her girls. Clients were the repeat customers, the ones who kept coming back over the months, if not years, usually requesting the same girl each time.

Shine, despite being far from a young girl, had her share of them.

Nina emerged from the pantry, a new bottle of aspirin in her hand, and came to stand next to the stove. This close, Marsden smelled her perfume, the light and inoffensive floral that did nothing to soften Nina's ruthless heart. Nor did it mix well with the scent of meat that still lay heavy in the kitchen, and Marsden's stomach rolled.

"Before you bring that food out, I need to speak with you," Nina said. "Something that's been on my mind lately."

Marsden knew what it was, of course. Shine had already told her. "No, Nina, I don't think so."

"I'm merely asking you to consider it—*really* consider it." Nina's voice was mild, as though she were discussing items for a new menu.

She squeezed Marsden's arm, right were Dany had, but instead of feeling motherly, it was like a warning. "You and I both know you're only making a fraction of what you could be, choosing to stay here in this kitchen the way you have."

"That's because you've cut my wages so they're next to nothing."

Nina dropped her hand from Marsden's arm. "Your keep has to come from somewhere, as does your share of repaying my having settled your father's loans."

"Then talk to Shine about that—she works for you *because* of those things."

"And your mother works hard. But she's only getting older, and she's simply not bringing in as much as she once did."

She couldn't meet Nina's gaze, which burned the side of her face. "So I'll take over more of Dany's shifts here. It should be enough to make up the difference."

Nina sighed. "What can I say to persuade you? Make you come to your senses? For your own sake."

"Nothing." Marsden carefully set the meat tongs down, untied her apron, and dropped it onto the counter in a heap. She was, at the very least, glad her hands weren't shaking.

"All these years, you've had a place to live, call home. The collection agency no longer after your mother, her actually having a job. Wynn, safe. There is a debt."

Marsden's hands did shake now as she lifted the platter. "Like I said, I'll take more of Dany's hours." How she would do this, she had no clue. How to create time out of nothing? "I'll work it out."

The small tight smile that Nina eventually offered did not reach her eyes, and it left Marsden far more uneasy than relieved.

"Fine," Nina said. "I'll speak to Dany about rearranging the schedule. It's just . . . such a shame, the opportunity you're passing up."

Marsden nodded, thought fleetingly of the money she'd sent away to the dead over the years, and wished the concept of guilt had never bothered her. "Sorry."

"We'll talk about this again soon, I think." Nina gave her arm another squeeze before letting go. "Your face, your youth—it won't last forever. And there's something to be said about having a certain kind of look, for those with a certain kind of taste."

Something sour crawled up Marsden's throat. "I'm going to bring out this meat now."

"Thank you, dear."

She followed Nina out to the dining room. Dany was finishing arranging vases of flowers on the tables, guests were milling about with glasses and plates full of tiny food in their hands, and Nina immediately began her rounds, her greetings full of welcome.

And her girls, they seemed everywhere, laughing and smiling and being attractive—part of *their* job. Their filmy summer dresses floated. Their jewelry winked beneath the lights like stars. Their faces were those of dolls—lips glossy, cheeks ashimmer, eyes like paintings.

Vibrant hothouse flowers to her plain old weed, Marsden thought, standing there in her worn Heart shirt and sloppy cutoffs, food clutched in her arms, feeling as out of place as she almost always did. Her gaze sought and found Peaches and Lucy, and she could barely recall the rumpled girls who'd been in her kitchen just yesterday, kissing each other over the heat of a stove and through cigarette smoke, talking to her as easily as if she were one of them.

Shine's pleas to not be left alone came back to echo in her ears along with Nina's thinly veiled threat from just moments ago. The scent of ginger—of the covert—drifted in from the open windows, and the walls of the room suddenly pressed inward. She wanted to run—to the kitchen, to the covert, all the way across town lines, in whatever direction. It didn't matter, as long as it meant being elsewhere.

"Whoops, watch out, your tray's tipping." It was Lucy, swirling close, smiling and smelling of honey. But her celery eyes were watchful behind her glasses, the hint of quiet sadness she always carried also there in their green depths. She reached for the platter of meat to help steady it. "You want a drink? It's hot in here, even with the windows open—you look pale."

Walking over to the buffet table, Marsden waved her away. What had Lucy seen on her face? Fear? Desperation? Nina was in the room. If she saw Lucy acting like kitchen help, both of them would hear it. Marsden set the pork chops down and scanned to make sure everything was there—salad, quiche, dessert—so she could leave.

Peaches came up, her lips slicked in red, her auburn curls shining.

She was scowling at her drink. "Tell Dany she can't make the sangria anymore. She forgot there's supposed to be booze in it."

Nina had asked them to cut back—*I want my girls sparkling, not tipsy.* "It's a new recipe, Peaches."

"Then use a different new one."

"Nina would still have to okay it."

Peached sighed. "I need a smoke." She scowled again. "*Nina* needs a smoke."

Marsden let a half grin slip free. "Well, maybe the new recipe somehow gets lost and we have no choice but to use the old one."

"Thank God. I'll love you forever." With a wink, Peaches left in a cloud of musk, earth, and a kind of confidence Marsden knew she would never have.

A man laughed, low and appreciative, and she turned.

Her mother's *client.*

It took her only a second to recognize him, standing at Shine's elbow, his face smiling down at hers.

Brom Innes. He'd been coming to the boardinghouse for years, from the very beginning of Shine's time as one of Nina's girls. Every few months, he'd stay for a week or two before leaving again. She had no clue what he did, had no desire to know, had never even talked to Shine about him. With his average height, pale-blue eyes, and light-brown hair, he was like the oatmeal of johns, as placid as plain white bread. Dull, agreeable, and safe enough, she supposed—for a john.

A tug at her arm, and she was completely stupefied to glance down and see Wynn, jar full of roaming ants in her hand.

Her little sister, exactly where Nina asked her not to be during meals—and within spitting distance of their mother's steadiest john.

"You're supposed to wait for me outside," Marsden whispered.

"I wanted more dessert." Her sister's eyes weren't on her, though. Instead, they roamed the room, drinking in all the details. Wynn's gaze caught on each of Nina's girls, studying the art of their carefully powdered and curled hair, their pretty, glistening mouths. Her eyes traced the swing of their dresses, learned the studied, deliberate movements of their limbs.

Marsden grabbed a bowl from a table, heaved two scoops of pudding into it, and dragged Wynn toward the kitchen by one arm. "C'mon, runt. Before Nina bans you from the dining room for the whole entire summer."

"Where are we going?"

"Somewhere else. Anywhere else."

twelve.

THE SKY WAS NEARLY FULLY DARK, THE AIR CLOSE TO COOL ON HER BARE ARMS. An owl hooted from within the covert.

They could have gone back inside long ago.

Any johns checking in for the night would have long done so. Just as Nina's girls would already be tucked away with them in their bedrooms, ready to get to work.

The common areas would be mostly empty, guests off to enjoy the shady offerings of downtown Glory that came with sundown.

Dany would be in her room, probably watching *Dallas* or *The Golden Girls* or *Miami Vice* on television, and who wouldn't mind at all if Wynn or Marsden wanted to watch with her.

Still, Marsden didn't move. She leaned back against the fence of the covert—the sunburned dying grass was nearly up to her elbows, she would have to cut it soon—and tasted the wild ginger that filled the air. It billowed from the woods, its fragrant fingers reaching out and stroking her hair, her skin.

She shivered. The covert was no sanctuary from the boardinghouse, either. Not from her mother, not from Glory as a whole. It grew a

92

darkness of its own, its yield the regular harvest of bodies and the subsequent ghosts and legends that would forever chase her name, forever linger in her blood.

Beside her, Wynn, humming a pop song from the radio, was dribbling the last of her pudding onto the ground. Freed ants teemed over the pink rivulets, gorged on the pool of sugar, grew drunk on her sister's generosity.

"That's gross, you know," Marsden said. A part of her envied her sister's carefreeness around the covert, even as she saw exactly how it had worked out to be that way. Wynn had never seen more than a glimpse of a body there, had no dead to try to listen for, had never spoken of ever experiencing anything weird about their woods—for all the stories and tales she knew about the place, she was much more easily frightened by a scary movie or book. Duncan Kirby had been her great-great-uncle, too, but he was no more real to her than any dead historical person she might learn about in school. Given all that, why *would* Wynn be scared of the covert?

"Ants need love, too," Wynn said as she watched her feasting insects wobble all over one another.

"How are you going to get them back into the pickle jar?"

Wynn shrugged. "I'm not. They look so much happier out of it, don't you think?"

"They do. See-through glass or not, that jar was still a prison."

"Mars, I need a dress."

Startled, Marsden looked more closely at her sister. It wasn't

Wynn's topic hopping that made her suddenly uncomfortable—that she was used to—but where their conversation had turned.

She scrambled for an argument, even a bad one. "Dresses are kind of impractical—how would you climb trees? Hop fences?"

"And I wish I had curly hair." Wynn grabbed at a chunk of her thick black locks. "Mine's so boring."

"I like your hair just fine the way it is."

"That's because it looks like yours, except messier."

"Exactly." Marsden stood up. "Let's go in. It's getting late, and I'm thirsty. We can check if there's any juice in the fridge."

"Do you think if I asked Peaches and Lucy, they'd take me shopping? I have allowance saved up." Wynn laid her jar on its side, a makeshift shelter for any ants that felt like it. Marsden thought of telling her it'd be an oven come morning, baking any unaware occupants, but she was frazzled, a touch panicked. "I'd ask Mom, but she usually just says to wait for Dany."

"*I'll* take you shopping, all right? We'll go to the bookstore and then get ice cream from Big Chill."

"Okay, but a dress first, one with—"

"I hear you, and we'll talk about it tomorrow," Marsden lied as she led the way back toward the house. Wynn chattered incessantly as she followed—about silks, curls, eyelashes. Marsden's mouth pulled into a grimace, concealed under dusk's thick light.

A low muffled giggle—barely trickling through from between the near-constant flow of her sister's ramblings—came from the side bushes.

Marsden took in the sound, the time of day, and that she and Wynn happened to be leaving the covert. And she exhaled to hide her irritation.

"Wynn, I . . . dropped my gardening gloves back at the fence, where we were sitting. Go on ahead and look for that juice, okay?"

Her sister raced past. "Hurry up, then, or I'll drink it all!"

"I'll just be a minute."

The second Wynn disappeared around the bend, Marsden turned and marched over to where she heard the giggle.

"Red and Coop," she said to the straggly bushes that were now starting to shake, "get out from there before I tell Nina you're on her property."

Both boys tumbled out onto the crisp grass, faces dirty and resentful as they got to their feet, eyes narrowed in humiliation at being caught. Their BB guns hung at their sides, and for a second, real fear filled Marsden's chest. The covert was the part of town that knew guns best, knew them most, but it didn't mean the rest of Glory was free of them. And BB guns, while toys, were still dangerous.

The brothers were fledgling skimmers, their mother a sufferer of early-onset arthritis, their father working the graveyard shift at one of the gas stations. Red was thirteen, Coop was fourteen, and both were on the low end of the brains scale. When they weren't failing classes at school, they spent their days shooting at birds, stealing penny candy from Gwen's corner store, or trying to trespass the covert to search for bodies to skim. Most of the time, they knew to wait until Marsden was actually in the boardinghouse before attempting, but only most.

"Who cares about Nina," Red muttered. His unwashed blond hair was thick with dirt. "This part is common land, owned by the town."

"Close enough that she won't care, and you know it." Marsden gestured toward the highway, unseen in the distance and through the dark. "Now leave."

Coop smiled—he needed braces, would never be able to get them—and it was somehow sly. She had to remind herself he was just a kid. "Maybe if you tattle on us to your mom, we'll leave, since it's her covert—and yours. Nina can't do anything at all. "

She thought of the brothers' sick mom, their work-beaten dad, tried to drum up some sympathy for them being as hardened as they were. She still couldn't. "Hadley's just a phone call away."

An empty threat, but she wasn't sure if Red and Coop knew as much about the corrupt cop as she did. Both brothers were already terrible, were on their way to being even worse, but they didn't live and breathe the covert like she did. Would maybe never even come close to what she was, BB guns and bird hunting or not.

Hadley, though.

She supposed it was only fitting that Glory's head cop was more crooked than the elbow along the Indigo the town called home. Lazy and greedy, too, a caricature of a villain she would find easier to laugh about if she didn't have so many dangerous secrets.

He skimmed, too. She'd seen it herself, silently watching him from behind the trees. Not just cash, either, but jewelry, leather wallets—anything he thought worth enough to take. Who would question a cop? Not Fitz, the guy who now ran Seconds after buying out the previous owner, who didn't bother asking Hadley where he got the pieces he was trying to unload. Not shoppers, who recognized them on the shelves and whose reports to Glory's police department ended up nowhere. Not families of the dead, who were told nothing else was found with their bodies.

After those times Marsden saw him in the covert, she'd hear of him hanging out at Decks' card tables playing blackjack, or at Prince's, where poker was played from sundown to sunup.

Worse, much worse, was him showing up at Nina's, his eyes greasy and eager.

"Hadley?" Red's mouth gaped open. He dared to seem betrayed. "You'd really call him on us? He'd talk to our folks, and we'd be grounded for weeks."

"Then he'd be doing his job." For once.

"Man, we were just hanging out, but fine." He gestured toward his brother. "Seriously, let's go."

Coop's eyes narrowed as he watched her, looked her up and down slowly enough that she wanted to cross her arms over herself. Again, he seemed much older than fourteen. Seemed much smarter than she knew him to be. And much too aware.

"Tell your mom we said hi," he said. "Sure must be tiring, doing all that cleaning, having to bend over all those beds. Hope you're picking up tricks of the trade. Because one day, you won't be telling me to leave, right?"

Long after they were gone, Marsden was still in the dark, her heart racing, winter in her blood.

● ● ●

She kicked off her covers, squinting at the clock.

Two in the morning.

Her skin still crawled with Coop's words. With what he didn't have to say.

Peeking over at Wynn to make sure she was still sleeping, Marsden crept down the stairs.

She flicked on the kitchen lights, the space still warm from the night's cooking, the day's collected summer heat. The air was fragrant with the scents of smoke, grilled meat, and the faint, perpetual hint of ginger.

Her hands moved surely—greasing and dusting pans, pouring and measuring and mixing. She melted chocolate, brought butter to a foam, dredged berries in flour. Shine and Nina and the secrets and shames of the covert—they all went away for a while. She baked them into oblivion, gone until her hands were done.

And when she sensed Star in the kitchen, Marsden knew her

grandmother wouldn't speak. She never did—just stayed silent, a kind of shifting warmth that did not scare Marsden at all.

It was the closest she ever got to hearing the dead, anywhere.

It was no longer enough.

thirteen.

SHE SAW HIS CAREFUL APPROACH THROUGH THE GRASS AND
THOUGHT OF WARY FERAL ANIMALS.

Marsden left the shade of the trees and headed toward the fence
that enclosed the covert. The tattered wood held together by rusty
nails had always marked the line between what was hers and not, what
was secret and not. Meeting Jude here and agreeing to him crossing
that line—well, that fence might as well have finally disintegrated into
nothing for the sense of safety it gave her now.

She'd wondered if he was even going to come that day. She'd mentally prepared herself for it and then she'd been anxious all morning, too
restless to do much more than walk back and forth between the house
and the covert. Being wired after being up half the night baking did nothing to help her nerves, either. Wynn had finally gotten bored enough to
agree to getting groceries and then go raspberry picking with Dany. Dany
herself seemed unaware of Marsden's mood, as had Nina and Shine.

So once noon hit, morning slowly becoming early afternoon, and
still there was no sign of Jude, she'd assumed he'd either been busy or
had simply come to his senses.

But it had bothered her—to be honest. To be counting time so carefully over him, the thoughtless carelessness of his absence after intruding on her life with his sharp-yet-lazy grin and eyes that hid less than she would have thought. She couldn't decide if she was relieved or resentful, and precisely because she couldn't decide, she'd gotten the pair of giant hedge clippers from the shed and spent more than a few minutes ferociously hacking away at the worst of the blackberry bushes overrunning parts of the covert. The scent of wild ginger mixed with ripening fruit bloomed like dust from her tracks as she worked, a tornado of things being crushed.

Last night, after she'd escaped Coop's too-adult eyes, she'd found Wynn in the kitchen, messily attempting to make punch. Marsden had broken a plate, then a glass, while finishing up the dishes, her hands so shaky that Dany had to finish. Then, at bedtime, Wynn had drifted to sleep while talking about dresses and makeup. And Marsden had lain there, absolutely wide awake, willing her sister to dream of child-like things such as puppies and ice cream and feeding toast to hungry, needy squirrels. She'd watched the moon shift shadows on the wall, listening to the clock tick away minutes of an endless dark, before finally getting up, needing to pretend things were different.

She was examining the worst of the blackberry scratches on her arm when she heard the growing roar of an engine from just outside the covert. It cut out with a deep rumble, and she walked over to look.

Through the trees, she saw Jude climb off a huge tank of a mower. The sight of his muscles working beneath his thin blue T-shirt had Marsden narrowing her eyes as something in her chest did a slow flip.

They met at the covert's fence.

"There's no real way to say this without it sounding wrong, but I'm here to mow your lawn," he said, smiling.

He looked tired and distracted, and that simmering anger he wore as an expression was a momentarily dampened fire. It made sense, though, his seeming on edge, perhaps even scared, considering where he was about to go. Maybe he hadn't even slept well the night before— the covert liked being a part of bad dreams.

She lifted a brow. "Not here to dig?"

"Afterward, I promise."

"You were supposed to be here by noon." She bit the inside of her cheek—she hadn't meant to reveal she'd noticed.

"I meant to be, but then a maintenance order came in from the town." He gestured to the area just outside the covert's fence, where the yellowing grass grew past the top of his work boots. "I had to put some gear together at work before I was able to leave." He frowned at the ground. "This area *is* overdue for a cut."

"You really work for Glory?"

"No, for Roadie, remember? Evergreen, the garden center, right downtown. We get contract work, though." He glanced down at her. "You sound surprised."

"That you work at a gardening center?"

His mouth lifted. "That I work."

"I just thought—never mind."

"That I didn't have to because my family is supposed to have money?" Jude shrugged. "Not really. Maybe once, kind of. A long time ago. Before we moved here."

She lifted her chin at the mower behind him. "Is that your summer, then?"

"And being here."

"I guess you haven't changed your mind?" Now that he was here, right in front of her—too immediate, too tall, too not angry—Marsden wasn't so sure she was ready. His being angry if he found out her secrets would be memorable, blistering.

Jude pointed to what she was still clutching in her hand. "Is that for me if I say I haven't?"

She looked down, saw that she was still holding the pair of huge clippers, their blades and the skin of her arms a sticky, sweet carnage, and laughed. "This doesn't look good, does it?"

"Have *you* changed your mind?" His voice was low and braced and not threatening, but she still shuddered. His desperation had slipped through, and it spoke to her in ways that smooth words and convincing arguments wouldn't have. She heard herself in it, an echo of her own need for answers.

"No, I haven't." She let her gaze slide from his—those slightly speckled eyes of his were too curious, demanding more than she could give. "I'll be back in a bit, if you don't mind waiting. I need to clean up back at the house."

"I have to finish this job first, anyhow, then get this thing back to

Roadie—the guy won't relax until his baby is back home and resting easy. Then I'll race back in the truck. Meet you back here?"

Marsden nodded. "Here, right at the fence." She touched it, the wood raw and scraping against her palm. Someone had scratched a new row of crosses into the wood, and their edges were still raised and splintery, fresh as a wound. "Wait for me before going in. That was the deal, remember?"

"Until you trust me." There was a glint in his eye that said he was joking. Still, she saw seriousness there, too. Had she ever seen him not serious at all? Completely free? She already knew she wanted to; her curiosity had awoken.

"Maybe one day," she said, daring a grin of her own. He made it easy to linger, to believe they were both typical kids without wounds still wide open, without ghosts to chase. "Unless I make you leave first."

"I'll behave. I promise."

She stepped past him to get to the house. He smelled of herbs and clean earth and sun. He touched her arm just before she moved out of reach.

"Marsden?"

"Yes?"

"Thanks." Jude's grin was like a finger on her heart, stirring her emotions. "For the 'maybe one day.'"

fourteen.

HE WASN'T PLAYING FAIR.

Jude Ambrose was supposed to be an ass, a guy who walked the school halls with either ice or fire in his eyes as he observed everyone, deciding if they were worth his time or not.

That version of Jude would have been a lot simpler to deal with, Marsden thought, a lot easier to just dismiss or ignore. The one who couldn't hide his devastation, the one arranging to meet her in the covert, was way too easy to understand.

She tugged on a T-shirt free of blackberry stains and left her bedroom. She was about to go into the kitchen for the back door when she heard her mother.

Shine's laugh, coming from the lobby, was light and silvery and declared she didn't have a care in the world.

Both fascinated and dumbfounded—her mother *never* laughed like that, not off duty—Marsden retraced her steps and peeked around the corner.

Shine and Brom, seated together on the love seat in the back of the lobby, half-shielded by a tall houseplant to offer a semblance of privacy. There was a pot of coffee and a plate of food on the table in front of them—two servings of the chocolate berry tart she'd baked just last night, she realized with a twinge of . . . what? Shock? Irony? Irritation? Brom kept talking, his hands moving animatedly from where he sat with his back to her, and Shine's face as she watched him was girlish, almost embarrassingly rapt.

If Marsden didn't know any better, she would have assumed they were a couple. An average, possibly even married, couple. Anger washed over her, a tidal wave of choppy ice.

Did her mother think what she did was merely a game? That she could set it aside and pretend she was anything but a whore whenever she felt like it? When her decision to be what she was still echoed in their lives every single day?

With no idea of what she meant to do or say, she walked over and simply stood there. Her mother looked up. Whatever was on Marsden's face made Shine stiffen. "Marsden."

Brom fell silent and turned toward her. His smile did nothing to make him less than repulsive to her. "Oh, hello."

Up close, his features were even blander than Marsden expected, an oval of oatmeal. Weak looking, his chin trembly and soft, and she wondered pettily how hard it was for her mother to work up such enthusiasm. Or if that blandness was actually his strong point—that he was, as far as anyone would say, easy to forget.

She couldn't work up anything close to politeness when she wanted him gone. "You're a john," she said to Brom. "This lobby is for guests. Unless you paid extra for day hours?"

"*Marsden.*" Her mother's whisper was properly shocked, unfailingly proper—Nina would be proud. "Please."

She remembered, then, what she'd meant to ask her mother since yesterday. If she hadn't been waylaid with dinner, with Red and Coop, with Wynn and Jude, the boundaries of her everyday life, drawn by the boardinghouse, by the covert.

She stared back at Shine. "I need to talk to you about Dad."

Her mother got up, circled the table, and grabbed Marsden by the arm. "Excuse me for a minute," she said to Brom. "I forgot cream for the coffee."

She marched Marsden to the lobby bathroom, locking the door behind them. Shine leaned back against it and lit up a cigarette. "That was extremely rude."

"None of it was a lie."

Her mother sighed tiredly. "What is it? What do you need now?"

"The night he died, Dad was at Decks, right? His favorite gambling house."

Shine's expression hardened for a heartbeat before slackening. "You already know he was. Why?"

"Who was he with?"

"What? I don't know. Whoever else was there that night, playing blackjack."

"No, you once said he was there with friends. The news said nothing, but I remember."

"The news? What are you—?" Shine's confusion, if it was an act, was more than convincing. Her eyes roamed Marsden's face. "There's been some news?"

"Not *new* news, no." Suddenly, she felt bad about not being more careful. Her mother's reaction surprised her, made her seem closer to the Shine she'd been, when she'd still been theirs and not yet Nina's. Where was the denial, the tears, the childlike pleading? "I meant from eight years ago. Sorry. I just . . . You said he was there with friends. Who?"

"Your father had a lot of friends—he was well liked in this town. It could have been anyone with him that night."

"But you must have known his best friends. Wouldn't they have likely been the ones with him?"

"Well, there was Eugene, but he's gone now, moved away." Her mother drew on her cigarette, recalling. "Casper, who's in jail. Quaid, who died of an overdose last year. And Fitz, down at Seconds."

Fitz. The pawnbroker who bought Hadley's skimmed pieces without question.

How much of that was because the corrupt cop gave him no choice? What if Fitz had been the one to suggest it to Hadley?

"Why didn't any of the newspapers mention they were there?" Marsden asked.

"They had no reason to, I suppose. He was never alone at places like Decks—that night was no different."

108

"Why didn't you ask his friends about what might have happened?"

"It was just one night out of hundreds, them gambling, all the same. I had nothing to ask. And if something *had* happened, they would have said something."

"Unless he didn't leave alone. What if they followed him and—"

"Stop, please." Ashes trembled free from her mother's hand. Her face was tired again, shaky looking. "Your father's friends wouldn't have hurt him. They adored him, thought he was cool and brilliant. Grant was like that, making people love him too easily. And it's not like the police didn't investigate."

"*Hadley* was the police."

"And he declared it an accident. I don't want to relive this. Let it go."

I can't. I need to know it wasn't me. "Did you ever tell me about him winning money that night? Why don't you care more about how it was missing?"

Her mother shut her eyes, and when she opened them—wet with tears, dark with the exhaustion of a daughter who wouldn't listen—she was again the Shine whom Marsden had come to know, her struggle everyone else's. "Don't you see? Your father *always* had a winning night. Even if he turned around and then lost it all, he'd still won that night, right? It was always what he told people, what he told himself—that it would always be a winning hand, eventually."

Marsden was frozen, hearing how her mother had hated her father as much as she'd loved him. "So you think he just . . . bet it away again. Before he died." She didn't want to believe it, but she also knew it made sense. Her father had gambled away their family long before that night, again and again—why would he stop then?

Her guilt over his death shifted then, just the slightest bit, and made room for anger. How could he have been so stupid when winning that money would have gone a long in way in saving them?

"Yes, I do think that." Shine stood up unsteadily and dropped her still-burning cigarette into the toilet. "When he could have used it to pay off his loans, or even just bills. Anything but bet it away. But I can also believe it was simply lost in the Indigo—that was our kind of luck, you see. Now, I have to get back to Brom—it's not polite that I've kept him waiting this long."

"You shouldn't be with him out there." Marsden's face burned as she recalled the image of them sitting together and laughing, as though he were a *suitor*. And her father was on her mind, clearer than he'd been for a long, long time—yes, she was angry with him, but her anger didn't change how he'd once been so alive, and it was somehow so wrong that he was no longer there. How could he not be on Shine's mind? How could anyone want to be with someone like Brom? "You're not even working right now, and he's a john. Can't you at least *pretend* you still plump pillows as a housekeeper instead of as a whore?"

Tears gathered and formed pools in the corners of Shine's eyes. "Let this town talk. You know it'll say what it wants, no matter what we do."

Marsden stared at their reflections in the oval mirror on the wall.

The pewter frame was ornate, full of scrolling curls, completely feminine. Inside it, her face was young and smooth, her mother's pale and strained.

"Wynn's around, and she has no clue what you do," she whispered, her chest tight. "What would you say if she saw you and asked about him? That he's your boyfriend?"

Shine came to stand behind her. She smoothed her daughter's hair back from her face and leaned close. She smelled like smoke and a perfume that Marsden didn't recognize, something Brom must have bought her. "Look at us. We look so alike, don't we? More like sisters than mother and daughter."

They did, it was true. Beneath her mother's fine lines and her own flushed youth, their bones were the same, their features nearly identical, Chinese in their skin and hair, all gold and black. But her own eyes were wide and alarmed, while her mother's were glittery with desperation.

"It scared me so much, those men asking Nina about you, and not me. Because I remember what it's like to worry where your next meal is coming from, or if you're going to wake up to no heat, no lights. And I swore to myself I'd never live without security again. I would never be alone. I would always be taken care of."

"So *Brom* is the answer?"

"He has a steady job."

"What does he even do? Where is he from?"

"He sells savings accounts for banks, for credit unions. He makes his own hours, which is why he can take a couple of weeks off every few months. He moved here from Seattle a long time ago. He enjoys me. And . . . I've known him a long time. From even before I started working for Nina. Your father knew him, too. They were friendly enough."

"And that's why he's been around for years." Marsden felt faint, and well-played—would she ever be as good as her mother at pretending? Did she want to be? "As soon as Dad was gone and you were free, he was there, waiting. He just paid his way."

More tears gleamed in Shine's eyes. "Do you want me to apologize? Would that help?"

"I don't know. I'm trying to not throw up." She knew how her father had barely been around, and how the family bank account never seemed to have enough. Shine had told her millions of times how he had promised to change, except he couldn't seem to give up Decks or any of the other card houses in town. *He wanted a different kind of reality, Marsden. We were just kids when we had you, and he wasn't ready to stop being one himself.* Marsden knew she was supposed to feel sorry for her mother, to say she understood. But how much longer could she be the reason for Shine's actions?

"It can't be shocking to you," her mother said, "that I needed someone after your father died. How I still do."

"And Brom's your way out." *From me and Wynn. How is that any different than Dad and his games of blackjack?*

Shine seemed to wilt. "What else am I supposed to do? I don't have a lot of options. I'm not getting any younger."

Marsden tensed. She kept her eyes on her mother's in the mirror. If Shine was still trying to trap her into her life, Marsden thought she might scream. "Don't put that on me again."

"I managed to speak to Nina for you," Shine whispered.

Marsden almost told her she shouldn't have bothered since Nina had already asked her again anyway. But she said nothing. Her mother had done something for her; she'd chosen her daughter over her boss. She blinked away tears—she had not really felt grateful to her mother since she was young. Since that futile trip to the bus depot, she supposed, when, for a day, Shine had managed to make the world seem bigger than Glory.

"Thank you," she said to her mother's reflection. "For trying."

Shine's fingers trembled just the slightest as she smoothed back Marsden's hair once more. "She was not . . . happy."

Relief washed over Marsden in a wave, and she nearly smiled. "No, she wouldn't be." And she didn't care. Nina could be as mad as she wanted, and it wouldn't make a difference at all.

"She said she wants to talk to you more about it before you make up your mind." Her mother lit a fresh cigarette; it shook like a leaf in a windstorm. "For my sake, can you at least pretend to consider it some more?"

Marsden got up, preparing to leave. She didn't miss the irony in her mother being the one to ask her to pretend. "She'll have to find me first, but okay, I can do that. And then let's not talk about this ever again."

fifteen.

THE BOARDINGHOUSE AND THE COVERT WERE ON THE OPPOSITE SIDE OF TOWN FROM WHERE JUDE LIVED AND WORKED, AT THE OTHER END OF THE CROOKED BEND OF THE INDIGO.

But the highway stayed faithful to the river's course as it hugged the length of Glory, and Marsden waited at the fence as the black truck approached. The shop name, Evergreen, had been painted on the dirt-filmed sides in an emerald hue that struggled to show. Road dust petered out from beneath the truck's wheels in puffy plumes the shade of wheat, lingering in the hot air, dry and smokelike.

Jude pulled onto the shoulder of the road, cut the engine, and climbed out.

He'd showered and changed while back at work—heather-gray T-shirt now, midnight-blue shorts, the same ladder of friendship bracelets—and his wavy hair was still wet, a deep black as he shoved it off his forehead. When he walked up to her, for a second, she smelled the Indigo on him, damp and marshy and metallic. And then it was all soap, all him, Ivory or Irish Spring or whatever it was he used.

Marsden forced herself to focus on what he was holding.

A metal detector, the length of it about the same as her arm, made of steel and plastic.

"I wanted one of those when I was little," she said.

Jude's smile was questioning. "Not so much into dolls?"

"Dolls weren't going to make me rich. I imagined walking along the riverbeds, finding buckets of change. I stopped believing in Santa the year I saw it in the Sears Christmas catalog and didn't get it."

He laughed. "I bet Rig had the same idea, but his wasn't a gift." He peered at the detector more closely, as though it was his first time seeing it, too. His expression switched between sadness and amusement, a leaf turning over and over as it whirled to the ground. "He found it behind the school field one day, just lying in the dirt. Still works, even now—I don't know why someone would abandon it."

She took note of the rust that bloomed at the screws, the dents that pinged their way along the handle, the warped sensor pad, and tried not to doubt.

"We're expecting a lot from an old toy, aren't we?" she asked as they walked toward the outer edge of the trees.

Jude smiled. "If I tell myself it's just an old cookie tin we're searching for, it doesn't seem so nuts."

Instead of a part of your dead brother, while I'm looking for a connection to finally hear the dead. "I'm just here for the ride."

"And it starts here?" Glancing around, his face was etched with uncertainty. They'd reached the fence, and wild ginger was already at their feet. It furled outward from its roots inside the covert, a roaming mass of green. "But we can still see the fence. You don't think he'd have gone deeper to bury the capsule, just to avoid being seen?"

Marsden shook her head. "I think it makes the most sense to start from the entrance and work our way in. Rigby would have been just a kid when he buried it, and somewhere he wasn't supposed to be—he probably didn't want to hang around any longer than he had to." She pictured a little boy trying to stay upright on a bike while holding something close, something he needed to keep safe. "Do you think one of those cookie tins would have fit in a backpack?"

Jude held out his hands so they were about a foot apart. "Maybe? But it doesn't matter if he used a backpack or not. I just think he left something behind, however he carried it over. And I think we'll find it in here."

Rigby *had* left something behind, of course. It'd been a note. The knowledge sat hot in her heart, uncomfortable. Well, whether or not he'd left more, they would soon find out.

Marsden watched Jude scan the part of the covert he could see and wondered what he was thinking, if he was aware of the fear that glimmered in his eyes like an odd light. If he could already tell that the farther they walked inside, the denser the trees grew, becoming nearly impenetrable in some spots. How soon the sky overhead would narrow into nothing more than thin slashes of blue. How sunlight would slide into shade, heat into a simmer. How once someone got past a certain point in the covert, it grew hard to remember the open vastness of a summer day.

He suddenly turned back to her. "Okay, what am I missing?"

"What do you mean?"

"You're more tense than I am, and you come in here in all the time. Should I be worried about something in there other than the given?"

"The given?"

"You know. Ghosts. Bodies. The police." One corner of his mouth twitched and his brows lifted. It nearly made her laugh, her nerves on edge as they were. "Your mom yelling at us to get out."

A laugh did slip free at that, but it didn't last. Marsden shook her head. *You forgot secrets, Jude. I'm so full of them in here, and I can't tell you any.* "I was just . . . seeing the covert through your eyes." This, at least, wasn't a total lie. "As if it were my first time, too."

"And?"

"I still think I'm right about Rigby staying close to the edge of the covert. Except maybe it wasn't because of the size or weight of whatever he was carrying that day."

"No?"

"I think it was because of fear of the covert. Same as what you're feeling now."

Jude nodded. "I'm about to walk into the place where my brother died. I thought I'd be mostly sad, or angry—which I am—but I'm definitely scared, too."

A few seconds of silence passed, and then he gave her an uneasy smile. "Also, you kind of have to admit this place has a distinct vibe."

Vibe. Like the covert was an energy field, something with its own life force. "That word nearly makes the covert seem cool instead of creepy."

"Nah, this place will never be anything but creepy to me." He pointed in the direction of the boardinghouse. "I was joking about your mom coming in, but can anyone really see us from there? What if she actually does? Or a guest?"

"Most guests are gone during the day, off fishing or boating, or walking around town. And my mom knows I come here." Marsden hesitated. "It's more after dark that we have to be sure to be gone. Being in the covert at night, it can be easy to lose your way. And—well, your imagination takes on a life of its own."

Jude swept the detector haphazardly over the ginger at his feet. "It doesn't even have to be at night for the impossible to get into your head. To try to convince you it's actually not impossible at all. Way too many times I've talked myself into believing that Rig was just going to walk out of this place, still alive, and tell me it's all been a mistake."

The presence of the hidden note fell from her heart and into the pit of her stomach. She said nothing. They continued to walk.

"Do you see skimmers moving in here at night?" he asked suddenly.

Marsden had to wait a few seconds to answer, smothered by the abrupt question, the quiet disgust she heard in his voice. She'd rather have been yelled at. "Trespassers, sure. Sometimes we see flashlights in here from the boardinghouse. Wynn says they must be like how fireflies move, darting throughout the trees."

"You make that sound nice."

She nudged at a dense bunch of ginger with the toe of her sneaker, not sure how to reply. She *had* made the covert at night sound nice—a charming image, completely harmless—and had no clue why she'd bothered. To make Jude feel better about where Rigby had died? So that if he ever found out that she was a skimmer, he'd remember that she wasn't wholly evil?

The harsh truth was, however nicely she or Wynn painted it, the reality of the covert wasn't about lights at all. Instead it was about the shadows that existed in there, those that took the shape of fallen humans. It was about the people who had died and the people who crouched over them, pawing at their bodies for money and jewelry. Reality was Rigby never coming back. Reality was her father, also gone forever.

"Hey, can I ask you something about finding his body?"

Marsden glanced over at him, praying he saw nothing close to guilt on her face. "Okay."

"Do you think—" Jude broke off. Swore softly. Tried again. "Do you think his body had already been skimmed? That someone else had gotten to him first and stolen whatever he might have had on him?"

Her heart skipped, tapped at her throat. The silence surrounding them was now pointed, the covert at attention. "I really don't think so."

"Why not?"

"I just don't."

A muscle moved along his neck. "If you see skimmers in here at night, why don't you guys stop them?"

She slowly shook her head. A part of her wanted to run; another, to explain, in whatever way she could. "Even if we did, there's always going to be more."

"What if you knew it wasn't a skimmer or a trespasser, but someone who's there because they mean to die? Shouldn't you try to stop *them* from doing what they came to do?"

She saw his dream unfolding in her mind as though he were asking for it to be her dream, too. And in this imaginary parallel world—made all the more painful because it couldn't exist—instead of walking out of their house in the middle of the night for the last time, Rigby was walking back into it. In this dream, he would still smell of wild ginger from the covert, but only a tiny bit, because the voices in the covert had refused to let him in. They had decided his sins, whatever they'd been, had to be fixed outside of it. In this dream, he would put the gun back in the kitchen drawer before shaking out the handful of covert soil he'd dumped into his pocket as his passage to peace. Then he'd go back to bed, and he would promise to try to get through another day once morning came.

"So?" Jude pressed. He emitted sadness like a warning, his grief acute—it hurt her to look him in the eye. "If you knew, would you try?"

Marsden thought of her father, of the insatiable pull of water, of a guy who liked games of blackjack more than having tea parties with his daughter, and said the only thing she could: "I think most people would try to stop them, if they knew, and if they could. The only thing is, sometimes we just don't know. And sometimes we just can't."

sixteen.

THEY WENT DEEPER.

Sunshine faded, fell weak in the air. The trees soared and their dusty, feathered tops turned spidery, full of traps and tangles. Patches of shade on the ground played tricks on their eyes, appearing as blood. The calls of crows overhead ballooned into shrieks. The scent of ginger was everywhere.

Marsden knew if Jude dreamed anything that night, it would be of the covert.

As they walked, a question stayed on the tip of her tongue, threatening to ask if *he* wanted to ask:

Where did you find Rig's body, Marsden?

But he didn't, and she was relieved. She knew he'd never unsee it once he knew. He'd replay what would have happened over and over again and would never stop questioning at what point his brother still could have been saved, at what point there could have been a change in angle or a turn of thought that Rig could put the gun down and still walk away.

A couple of hours in, taking turns with the detector, they'd finally settled into a rhythm on how to best use it—long sweeps across the ground, in wide, even arcs. Hold it too high and the sensor picked up nothing; hold it too low and it would catch on the brush.

The work was simple. And in between bouts of small talk, Jude fell silent and seemed utterly lost in thought. Marsden found her mind wandering, too, to this puzzle of a boy walking beside her, and the way he carried his tragic family around like a layer of invisible bruises set over being tough.

The dead of the covert remained silent, refusing to speak to her. Despite his brother being there with her, there was no hint of Rigby. No hint of her father, either.

Marsden wished it didn't bother her as much as it did, never being able to hear voices despite supposedly having the ability to. If anything, she should be happy—she was in the covert enough that the last thing she needed were ghosts trying to get her to pass on messages to the living. Or listening to them tell her just how wrong her skimming was.

And what if she did hear Rigby one day? And the things he wanted her to tell his brother only made Jude sadder? What if he wanted her to tell him about his note that she was hiding? What if she finally heard her father and he told her the thing she dreaded most was true? That he had hated being a father more than he wanted to be alive?

But all it took to make her keep trying was the single hope of hearing him tell her it really had been accident. And that he didn't regret her and hadn't meant to leave them.

She passed the detector over a stretch of dried-out dandelions, their blooms gone a mustard yellow, and tried to ignore how Jude stayed close enough that she could still smell his damn soap.

"Read any good books lately?" he asked, his tone deliberately flippant. It didn't make him appear any less tense. She knew he was imagining all the terrible things that would have happened around him, was seeing his brother in the covert's midnight corners and the depths of its strange foliage. "Or been to the movies? What do you do when you need a break from this place?"

Marsden kept her eyes on the ground. Dying dandelions disappeared as she and Jude moved on to crush a small patch of sweet woodruff. The detector rumbled in her hand, and she thought of trucks driving along the highway, shaking the beds of the Indigo (no signs of gold, though). "I don't. I'm here. I work. And summer means Wynn's home—I have to babysit a lot."

She couldn't tell him the rest. About having to fit in skimming, about juggling Wynn against the schedule of the boardinghouse. She didn't want to mention how going out for fun was the very opposite of how she liked to blend in. She dreaded running into groups of kids from school whose whispers to one another held echoes of Shine's name, who would cheerfully call out to her the same stupid questions about serial killers and people gone missing. Kids who only seemed whiter on account of her *own* whiteness, the side of her that did nothing but emphasize the part that wasn't. She thought about people staring at Jude and, if they did, whether it was for the color of his skin as much as it was for Rigby and his father.

"My best friends, Owen and Karey, drag me out as often as they can." Jude ran the detector in long arcs over a raised ridge of ground. "But reality just sits there in my brain, waiting to remind me as soon as the movie's over. *He's still gone. The credits will roll, the lights will come on, and he'll still be gone.*"

"They probably don't know what else to do." Marsden attached faces to the names of his friends, both of them white like nearly everyone else in Glory: Owen, tall and handsome, his face the kind made to gaze from magazine ads; Karey, with his long blond hair and drowsy drawl of a smile, America at its beachiest. She knew them, and yet she didn't, exactly as she'd known Jude before the forever absence of his brother drew them together.

"We've been to enough movies over the last couple of weeks that the food counter down at the Cineplex knows our popcorn orders by heart. There's an Eddie Murphy playing tonight."

"You like him?"

"Yeah, he's funny as hell. Bill Murray, Chevy Chase, Steve Martin—I'll watch them all, but Murphy's my favorite. Dude's black, and he's on the big screen—it's cool seeing that."

Marsden heard it in his voice, the simple acknowledgment that he knew he was different, and found herself nodding. She could count on one hand families like theirs in town, had always been able to. The quota was low in Glory.

"You're Chinese, right?" he asked. "Half?"

"Yes." She was surprised but not surprised that he knew enough to guess. For years, they'd never had real reason to connect, despite having shared lots of the same spaces at school. But they were also two of a very small club, noticing each other the same way shy new kids in class couldn't help but notice each other, united in their not belonging.

To keep Jude from asking anything else about her family, she asked first. "You moved here from out East?"

He nodded. "I still have family out there, my uncles—my mom's two younger brothers—and my aunts. A couple of cousins."

"All on your mom's side?"

Another nod.

She waited for him to add something about his father's side of the family, knowing that Leo Ambrose had also been born and bred out East. But he stayed silent, and she decided the omission was purposeful.

Marsden went along with it, and decided to ask him about safe things again.

"Your friends are Murphy fans, too?"

"Yeah, but not like me. And not like Rig was. We used to make a point of watching his movies whenever they came on television, or we'd rent a bunch and just play them on a loop. And Owen and Karey know that. Which is why they won't let me get out of going tonight. They're worried I'll be especially . . . I don't know, fragile, I guess. The thing is, I'm still too mad to be fragile." Jude's features were drawn beneath the burnished brown of his skin. His words seemed pulled from him. "Like you said, I might not have been able to stop him, no matter what. But I can still be angry at him for getting what he wanted."

Marsden stopped walking, dragged to a halt—not by the fury she heard, but the plea for answers she knew too well.

"There were no clues?" She sensed the ghostly weight of Rigby's letter, as heavy and dangerous as a bomb. "Your father. Maybe he knows?"

"My father?" Jude's smile was cold, bitter. "Whatever drove Rig to do what he did, who do you think played a part in it?" He began to walk again, staring only at the ground as he swept and swept. "Not only him, but me, too."

The echo of her father blaming her for his misery, for being a trap, pounded in her ears. She walked alongside Jude, her throat dry. "What do you mean you played a part?"

"I was nine, it was the science fair, and I had this project, and . . . something happened that night, and it made Rig change." His voice had gone choppy, full of tiny little breaks. "He just kind of . . . faded or something. He was there, but he also wasn't, like he'd run out of things to say. I joked with him once, about living with a ghost."

Her father, also only ever half there. "What did he say?" she asked, her lips stiff.

"He said everything was fine and that nothing was going on. That I needed to quit imagining things." Jude was still sweeping the detector, circling over fields of ginger. The plants grew thick, turning the ground springy. "A kid gets first prize at the science fair—it's supposed to be a good day, you know? And a lot of that day *was*. Dad didn't even crack his first beer until we got home from dinner. But then I remember leaving to get root beer floats and falling asleep in our truck somewhere along the way. I remember Rig carrying me back inside the house, feeling safe as I slept against his shoulder. Then he and my dad, talking in whispers—I dreamed their voices were like fish, darting around in the river. I still don't know what they were talking about."

"Why can't you ask your dad?" Marsden recalled the stories about Leo Ambrose's temper, how it and his fists had been fueled by alcohol.

"I did, once. He also had nothing to say about it, just like Rig didn't." Jude's gaze lasered into the ground, his hair falling back down over his forehead as he used the detector. It made a high, thin buzz as it worked. "He actually stopped drinking for a long time after that night. Maybe it was what he and Rig were whispering about after we got back, but I don't know." He shrugged. "And he's drinking again, now that Rig's gone. So I can't ask him."

Everything he left unsaid rang throughout the woods, came back at them like a boomerang. She saw an image of a little boy with wavy raven hair and a bruised cheek, huge eyes streaming as he ran past shelves of books toward the one person who would keep him safe.

"But, I'm confused," she admitted. "Your dad did stop for a while, you said. From when you were nine until now—so why would that make your brother *un*happy?"

"I don't know," he said. "Except . . . I remembered something else. It was when I first came here to ask you about the covert, and it happened while I was driving over."

The sudden gift of a memory, the crack of a seal—why did the air seem to chill? "What was it?"

"I passed by a broken-down car along the highway, so I pulled over to see if I could help or something. But the driver wasn't anywhere—he must have gone to call for a tow truck, I figured later—so I sat there in the truck waiting to see if he'd show, just looking around. I noticed how the part of the shore the car was on was really narrow, and how it seemed like the river could practically pull the car right in if it didn't get picked up soon. I thought about how the driver was lucky the car didn't break down at night, since being stuck on the highway in the dark isn't much fun. And how if there's a storm, it's even more dangerous." Jude let out a tight, humorless laugh. "I'd cranked the window open, and that metal stink of the Indigo rolled in, you know? I could taste it in the back of my throat, even. And hundreds of times I've driven past that point along the highway without . . . It came in flashes, Marsden. The memory. Science-fair night."

"Go on." She was rapt. Daylight had fallen away, the covert was gone, she was standing on a muddy beach watching a storm roll through the town.

"I was in the backseat of the truck, half-asleep. We were parked—from the smell in the air, I could tell we were close to the river. It was raining outside, coming down fast in sheets, I could hear it pounding on the truck's roof. Then Rig was there again, scrambling into the front seat, and we were racing down the highway toward home.

"He would have only been thirteen, but he was big for his age, and he'd learned to drive at Evergreen, spinning the shop trucks around the parking lot." Jude turned off the detector then, and the covert fell dead silent. When he spoke again, his voice was full of defeat. "Whatever happened that night, I was right there with Rig. And whatever happened, it took place out there along the highway, along the Indigo."

seventeen.

THE NEXT DAY, THE SUN ROSE AND ATTEMPTED TO BURN THE
WHOLE PLACE DOWN.

Townsfolk joked uneasily about Glory now being hell on earth for
real, before darting back indoors, away from a heat that made the sur-
faces of buildings and cars ripple like water.

But still the covert called, and still guests needed to be fed.

By dawn, Marsden had made her way back to the boardinghouse.
No bodies to report that morning, and she'd met this with her usual
mess of emotions—relief, frustration, panic, guilt. She tried not to
think about Jude just being there yesterday, how aside from a handful
of coins and various metal bits, they'd come up empty, too.

He would be back tomorrow afternoon, ready to keep looking.

She couldn't deny that she wanted to see him again.

Breakfast was served in the dining room—eggs, toast, Canadian
bacon, Bloody Marys—while she and Wynn ate in the kitchen. Not
Lucky Charms this time, but Cap'n Crunch and strawberry milk. They
ate like furtive mice, trying not to get caught. Like ghosts in the house,
there but not there.

"Can you come shopping with us today?" Wynn asked, blowing milk bubbles with her straw. The pink spheres climbed the inside of her glass, threatening to spill over. "It's Dany's turn to make lunch, not yours, right?"

"Hmm?" Marsden was distracted. She was still thinking about Jude and how he was different from what she'd expected. Nicer. Easier to talk to. More open. She wondered if he thought the same thing about her. If she was less closed off than the person he knew from school and heard about in town. She wondered if, outside of the covert, he thought about her at all.

"Are you okay?" Her sister was leaning in close, her expression more exasperated than concerned. "You look funny."

Because I'm thinking of funny things, Wynn. Waste-of-time funny things. She had to remember that Jude was a blip during this overly hot summer, a once-in-a-lifetime disturbance that would soon be dealt with and eventually forgotten. "Sorry, just watching your bubbles die a quick death. What's up?"

"Can you come shopping with us this morning? I like Peaches and Lucy, but I want to go with you, too."

A shard of ice formed in Marsden's stomach. "You're clothes shopping?" Shine had promised to take her younger daughter to the farmer's market. Wynn had been excited, her mother's time a rare thing. Marsden had intended to go down to Seconds, armed with questions for Fitz, her father's old friend. *I need you to tell me about that night.*

"Yes! For a dress! I want one just like the ones they wore last night to dinner. Mom said fine and gave me some money—I think she felt bad that she forgot she was busy. Peaches and Lucy also said that if there was time afterward, they'd treat me to the salon to get my hair and nails done." Wynn's grin was a beam of delight, huge and enveloping, and it left Marsden frozen.

"You already have a lot of nice clothes, you know," Marsden whispered through the hollow in her stomach. "Dany always finds them for you. And dresses—you won't be able to run around as easily, or climb—"

"Sure I can—why wouldn't I? So, will you please come with us? *Please?*"

Marsden silently willed Nina, Peaches, and Lucy into aging massively overnight. She prayed all the johns in town would lose every single cent down at Decks. Finally, she pictured Shine, and she wasn't sure what to feel at all.

"I'll come," she said, trying to sound normal, doing her best to hide the panic that welled. Seconds and Fitz and her questions would have to wait one more day. "I just need to do the dishes first, okay?"

Her little sister beamed again, slid off her chair, and began to clear the table. "I'll help you so we can leave earlier."

"And Wynn?"

"Yeah?"

"I don't think Peaches and Lucy would mind if we ask them to come along another time. Just you and me, okay?"

● ● ●

She knew it was sabotage, and she didn't care.

Being heartless came easily when the alternative was losing her little sister to the clutches of Nina, to the desperation of their mother, to the clueless but obviously good intentions of Peaches and Lucy.

Not that one, Wynn, the collar is too loose.

No, the material is too shiny.

The color is too bright

You'll get sick of the print.

It was close to noon, Marsden had seen enough dresses to last her for multiple lifetimes, and Wynn had gone mostly silent.

"We can look again when the stores get fall stock in." Marsden wheeled her bike along the sidewalk—beside her, Wynn pushed her own along, her face clouded. "But for now, how about some lunch? We have the money Dany gave us to buy coffee, remember? And if you don't care about saving the dress money, we can use that, too."

"We'll need that money for a dress the next time we go," her sister muttered. "And we're not supposed to spend kitchen money on our-selves, or Dany's going to stop trusting you with it."

"I'll tell her she can take it out of my pay." Marsden knew full well Dany wouldn't, not after she told her it was for lunch for Wynn. Dany was especially soft with her sister, indulgent when it came to making up for Shine as a mother. "The Burger Pit is right up the block—sound good?"

They rarely ate out, but when they did, and when it was up to Wynn to choose the place, it was always in the running. With its bottomless drinks bar, its long wooden tables covered with rolls of coloring paper, and the oversize cow jar at the front counter that mooed with the removal of each cookie from its belly, the Burger Pit was one of Glory's busiest restaurants with its locals if not its tourists.

What her sister didn't know was that each evening, halfway through dinner service, the Burger Pit's side entrance opened for business and the basement floor came to life.

Five dollars bought someone fifteen minutes with one of the viewing slots and his choice of peep video.

Ten meant a viewing slot and a live show.

A whole twenty meant a private booth and choice of live performer.

Marsden knew Nina's johns were frequent visitors of the place—they'd come crawling into the boardinghouse after they were done, smelling of fried cheese and the Pit's house beer, their eyes and hands especially friendly. On those evenings, she would drag Wynn even farther away from the premises and sit outside the covert, trying not to be horrified by the future while her sister played beside her, making houses of leaves and sticks for the bugs, for her much-longed-for pets. She would sit there and recall Shine sitting on a bench in the bus depot, frozen.

Now the sun was straight overheard, searing noon into their scalps—the Burger Pit would be safe for hours.

Wynn gave in, unable to sulk in the face of cheeseburgers and tater tots. "Can we get the bottomless sodas?"

"Fine, twist my arm."

Her sister scrambled onto her bike and took off down the sidewalk, weaving around other people on the sidewalk with a speed that had Marsden cringing.

"Hey, slow down," she called out, "you're going to—"

Too late. A group of guys stepped onto the sidewalk at exactly the wrong moment, and Wynn careened toward them like a rocket with too much fuel. There was a squealing of brakes and a muffled oath and Marsden blew out a sigh, climbed onto her bike, and rode over.

And she nearly turned right around when she saw who it was.

Jude.

He watched her approach with wide eyes, their dark depths flaring with surprise, and for a second, she thought of the boy she used to see in school, so good at warning everyone away even as he turned to his circle of friends with enough trust to seem another person. She'd learned to disappear in a different way, making herself small, shrinking into the crowd as much as possible.

Who was she to him now, after their time in the covert? Who was he to her?

Her heart pounded at she took in the scene: Wynn, her face red as she looked down at the blond boy still splayed on the ground; another boy, dark-haired and grinning, handsome as hell; and Jude—so tall, annoyingly magnetic, more unreadable than not.

"Don't worry about it." He gave her sister a half smile and smirked down at the blond boy. "Karey always walks around totally out of it. Bound to happen sometime."

"I'm sorry," Wynn strangled out. "I was going too fast."

"Nah." Karey waved from the ground and gave Wynn a smile so dimpled and charming it spread outward and had her sister smiling back. "I was just moving too slow."

Owen—the good-looking dark-haired boy—yanked him up by the hand. "Man, we keep finding ways to try to lose you, and you keep sticking around. What's it going to take?"

"I love you tons, too." Karey brushed off his board shorts, fishing for the sandal that had flown from his foot. Shaggy, bleach-bright blond hair; sky-blue eyes; and what appeared to be a fondness for actual beachwear—he really was California personified against the pale dust of Glory.

Jude was watching Marsden, apparently as uncertain as she was.

"Hi," he finally said.

Marsden lifted a stiff arm and waved. "How come you're not working?"

"I am, actually. Just getting Roadie and the others at work some takeout; I ran into these guys on the way." He glanced over at Wynn. "So your sister is also Evel Knievel?"

Wynn leaned toward him, her eyes widening in recognition. "You're the boy who—"

"I'm Jude, yeah." The panic that crossed his face came and went in a second, covered up by his smile. But Marsden still caught it.

So his friends had no clue about him going to the covert. She was still just another girl from school, instead of the girl helping their best friend find the last piece of his dead brother.

She looked over to see Owen and Karey both staring. They obviously had no clue how to take her. They'd all known of one another since they were five and started going to the same school, but out here in the open, she was brand-new to them.

"Hey, Marsden," Owen said, his voice careful but friendly. Beside him, Karey's expression was the same. "How's your summer going?"

She tensed as she waited for the rest, for him or Karey to hint that she wasn't fooling anyone by acting like her mother wasn't a prostitute. To ask her about being friends with ghosts. But when they just smiled, she made herself nod. "Good, thanks." Then she turned to Wynn, wanting to leave, sure it showed and unsure what to do about it.

Her sister was already pouncing, loving the idea of becoming friends with the boy who'd come all the way to their covert in search of her beloved older sister, of becoming friends with the friends of that same boy. "Can you eat lunch at the Burger Pit, too? With me and Mars? Jude, can't you stay and then just bring back takeout for your friends at work?"

Marsden's heart sank all the way to her toes.

If Jude and his friends agreed, there'd be no escape. She couldn't ruin this next part of Wynn's afternoon, given how she'd already fought—and won the battle—over buying a dress in imitation of Peaches and Lucy.

And her sister's eagerness to make friends with Jude and Owen and Karey was partially Marsden's doing—for years, she'd warned her to stay away from guys at the boardinghouse. Which meant *these* guys were safe, because they were from Marsden's school, were practically oozing with cool and nice and funny. *These* guys were friendly in ways that weren't frightening or wrong.

The deep clank of a large cowbell rang out, and the front door to the Burger Pit swung open.

A teenage girl, her face a just-as-attractive-but-in-a-different-way version of Owen's, stood in the doorway. She wore her black half apron and white *Burger Pit* work shirt with a nonchalance that nearly made the outfit stylish.

Abbot, Owen's twin.

Just as with her brother, Marsden knew her, yet didn't at all. The other girl was all pixie-cut black hair, watchful dark eyes, and sharp-edged humor stuffed into a human form that radiated fearlessness. Abbot seemed everything Marsden didn't know how to be.

"Wow, you guys actually managed to get out of bed before three in the afternoon." Abbot grinned. "What happened?"

Owen mock scowled at his sister. "You promised us a free lunch, and that's the only reason why I can deal with you this early."

"You're such the lesser half it's not even funny. I saved a table in the back, by the way." Owen and Karey headed inside, calling over their shoulders that they were starving and to hurry, and Abbot turned to look at Marsden, her expression slightly quizzical before recognition hit. "It's Marsden, right? How's it going?"

"Fine, thanks. You?"

"Everything's great. Just hanging out?"

Marsden's shoulders stiffened a tiny bit. "Yes."

"Cool." Abbot turned and gave Jude a huge grin. Marsden saw how it reached all the way to her eyes, came blasting through all her features to make her even prettier. She also knew then, without a doubt, who had taken the time and care to make him those friendship bracelets he wore so faithfully. Loops of string and a few hours of effort, but they reminded Marsden of who she was not.

Abbot reached out and pulled him into a hug. "Roadie sent you out *again*? Maybe he doesn't trust you around the inventory but can't say." She let him go and winked. "Unless it's just been too long since you've seen me."

Jude smiled back. Marsden might have let her eyes roll.

"Just the regular lunch order from the shop, thanks," he said. "I already called it in. And it's a double order of the cheese tater tots for Roadie this time—dude nearly cried when I forgot the last."

"It's all probably nearly ready, anyway; I'll go check the front counter for you. Too bad you can't stay to eat with us, though—I'm on my break and everything."

Jude glanced at Marsden, who had never been more uncomfortable in her life. Were she and Wynn included in the other girl's invite? Was it her way of saying to please leave? She didn't know Abbot well enough to read her the way she could Shine and Nina and the rest of the girls at the boardinghouse, the way she knew how to be slippery to avoid being with them.

She *wanted* to leave, and badly. But Wynn was still expecting lunch, not just with Marsden but also with everyone else—"everyone else" now including Abbot. Adding to the fun was the likelihood of Jude having to get back to Evergreen, leaving her to deal with his friends on her own.

Her sister was already locking her bike to the rack at the front of the restaurant, about to head inside.

And Marsden willed the Burger Pit's dried-up, sun-beaten sidewalk to crack open beneath her feet and swallow her whole.

"I don't have to take off right away, actually," Jude said. "Roadie got an emergency call about a shipment and had to go check it out—he's going to be delayed. I just figured it was already too late to call you guys and get you to hold off on the food."

"He won't care about a cold lunch?" Abbot slid her gaze to Marsden and then back to Jude again. Her expression gave away nothing.

Marsden couldn't decide if she was more relieved or skeptical or annoyed at Jude's rescue. Maybe she was all three.

Jude shrugged. *Well, what's the guy going to do about it?* Then he flashed Marsden a grin so sweet that it momentarily left her disarmed. In that single second, he was neither the angry boy from the school hallways nor the boy in the covert devastated by a ghost, but someone else entirely, and she felt a wave of pity for Rigby, for what he'd never know.

"So let's go," he said to her, "before your sister takes off running through the restaurant and mows down half the diners."

eighteen.

SITTING BESIDE HER IN THE BOOTH, MARSDEN WATCHED WYNN STRUGGLE HAPPILY WITH HER BURGER PIT CHEESEBIGGER AND GRUDGINGLY ACCEPTED THAT, OVER THE COURSE OF A SINGLE LUNCH, HER LITTLE SISTER HAD FALLEN HEAD OVER HEELS IN LOVE WITH A BUNCH OF TEENAGERS.

Marsden poked at the tray of chili tater tots on the table in front of her, sipped her Coke, and mentally reviewed what she'd learned about Jude's friends, cheat sheets that hung in her mind like bright white laundry from a line.

One thing she'd discovered: If she'd ever wondered how much he'd leaned on them in the immediate days after Rigby's death, or doubted exactly how much *they* needed *him*, she needn't have bothered.

They loved one another like family. A real and normal one.

Owen, all dark eyes and summer-tanned skin and a jawline that might as well have been chiseled from stone. Seventeen years old on the surface but ancient underneath, he was the worrier of the group, the one who tended the foundation of their friendship. He was so protective of those around him that he was often the one left in danger, a mother bear charging a hunter without pause to save her cubs.

Karey, with enough dimples to prove that life was, indeed, unfair. His smile was beatific and blameless, nearly as bottomless as the sea. Marsden would have thought him a goof, a misplaced beach bum stumbling happily from one foaming surf to another, if she hadn't caught glimpses of his cutting intelligence, a keen awareness he seemed to not mind hiding.

And Abbot, who insisted their lunches be on the house, who gave her sister brand-new boxes of crayons to use on the paper on the table, who teased her the same way Dany sometimes did. She was, for Wynn, fun and lighthearted in ways Marsden could never be, as confident with her looks as any of Nina's girls—again, nothing like her dull and plodding big sister.

And she was close to Jude in a way that left Marsden envious, left her chest shot full of small holes and tiny aches. She knew it was jealousy and hated herself for it, for wanting that same kind of closeness to a boy she barely knew and wouldn't even *want* to know, if she were being smart. And safe. And logical. She was hiding something from him that he would hate her for if he knew. Not that she had a choice about doing it.

And maybe she wasn't always those things.

Maybe, sometimes, she didn't really want to be.

Which bothered her—a lot.

She stuffed a tater tot into her mouth, relished the rude sting of chili pepper against her tongue, and prayed for Wynn to eat faster.

"By the way, Jude, listen." Karey burped behind a salt-dusted fist and poured more ketchup on his potatoes. "Langston is bugging me to get you to stay over for a couple of days. He says he's still waiting to beat you in that Atari tournament you guys started a while ago."

Jude stared at him, then lifted one brow. "Your little brother says he's still waiting to beat me at Atari? So I'm welcome to stay over at your place for a while?"

"Yeah."

"For a tournament. That we started. Last summer."

"Yeah."

"Don't," Jude said in a low voice. "It's fine."

"But he really—"

"You guys, just . . . drop it."

Just like that, the restaurant around their booth faded—the clang of silverware, the chatter from other diners at other tables, dialed to low—and a tension as thick as the river's mud swam in.

It carried with it the presence of Leo Ambrose. Marsden felt as if he were suddenly seated right there at the table with them.

Karey slowly shoved three tater tots into his mouth at once. She saw his eyes go to Owen—once, and quickly, as though unsure of what to do next—before going back to Jude. "C'mon. It's just Langston. And Atari." Beside him, Wynn drew another cat on the paper that covered the table, oblivious to the conversation.

"Except it's not," Jude said, sounding terse.

"I think it'd be nice for Langston to get to hang out with you."

Abbot stirred her Fanta Orange with her straw. "Think about the poor kid, with someone like Karey as his only role model."

Karey coasted a tater tot along the table so that it fell into her lap. "I can re-create the periodic table in my *sleep*. Langston is *blessed*, I tell you."

Jude picked up his burger and proceeded to not eat. "Tell Langston he wins by default."

"You'd get a break from your old man," Owen said quietly. "He'll have space to adjust."

The discomfort Jude couldn't hide . . . Marsden felt it herself. She hadn't known how much he hated being pitied. She wondered if her being there made it worse for him, or easier, or if it made any difference at all. If he would have walked out already, still bent on escape, if not for feeling bad about leaving her and Wynn behind.

"Home is fine," he muttered. "Leave it, you guys."

Suddenly, Wynn leaned forward, the hem of her Scooby-Doo T-shirt dragging through the mound of ketchup on her plate, and whispered loudly to Marsden: "I have to use the washroom, but I don't know where it is."

"I'll show you." Jude was up like a shot. His eyes met no one's. "Need a refill for my Coke anyway."

Wynn hopped down from the booth and followed Jude down the aisle.

"Hold up, dude, we're getting refills, too." Owen and Karey scrambled their way from the table to catch up. Their intentions—to corner Jude in another attempt to keep him safe from his father—were, to Marsden, as loud and clear as the clank of the Burger Pit's cowbell hanging over the front entrance.

"So, hey, I didn't know you and Jude were hanging out."

She turned and faced Abbot.

On Owen, the twins' shared beauty was a study in classic good looks, a painting where each stroke was preordained, made to flow only one way. Words like *handsome* and *elegant* and *smooth* suited Owen perfectly.

But on his sister, that same beauty turned sharp, its edges hard and precise and without give.

"We're not really." Marsden knew the best lies were half-truths. She picked up a fork and toyed with it, hating that she was nervous.

The other girl nodded, absentmindedly tracing one of the doodles on the table. It was one of Jude's, a bouquet of flowers he'd drawn for Wynn at her request. Their lines were messy, and not too sure of themselves, but there were tulips, daisies, lilies—Jude's world when he was at work.

"Do you guys just know each other from school?" Abbot asked. "Or something else?"

The question shouldn't have bothered Marsden, but it did. Especially if she admitted she'd been wondering the same things about Abbot.

And what about you two? Just how close are you guys? How close have you ever been?

"Just school," she finally said, reminding herself Abbot was only worried about Jude, was as protective of him as Owen and Karey were. It wasn't her fault that Marsden found her intimidating. That Marsden was also painfully aware of who she herself was in this town, who Shine was, and all the labels that came with those things.

How could Jude ever consider anyone like her?

"Can I say something without making you feel bad?" Abbot's gaze held none of the subtlety of her twin. "Because I really don't mean to. And normally I wouldn't say anything at all, because it's none of my business, what Jude does. . . ."

It was clear that Abbot *did* think it was her business. That she had a say in what Jude did.

And that Marsden did not.

But Abbot hadn't been there to see him that day in the library, when eight-year-old Jude had come running in to find Rigby, his cheek on fire. She wasn't the one he'd gone to see at the covert, his eyes miserable and vulnerable, needing something. She wasn't the one trying to hear the dead for him, even if her reasons for doing it weren't entirely selfless.

Marsden set her fork down. "It's not any of your business, no. But I know you're just worried about him, and that's why you're wondering how to tell me nicely to leave him alone."

The older girl's eyes went flinty and cold. "His brother just died. Jude doesn't need anything else to deal with right now."

It struck Marsden then, the particular construct of their group, the thing that made them work—if Owen was the foundation, Karey the brains, and Jude the heart, then Abbot was the fighter. The warrior.

She'd almost regretted figuring it out. Abbot being jealous was baseless; Abbot being protective was something else. Rigby's note, still hidden away in her room, was a grenade with a half-pulled pin.

"I know about Rigby," Marsden said. "Everyone does. Just like how I know *you* guys know about his dad drinking again. Why you're just as worried about that."

She'd caught Abbot by surprise, her knowing about Leo—the other girl's eyes widened, and she sat back in her seat—but the victory was hollow, sour.

"I never thought he'd ever tell anyone," Abbot said.

"Outside of you and your brother and Karey, you mean."

"He never had to. We've always known everything, right from the start."

Except about her, and their searching the covert—another meaningless victory.

"Jude's not weak or anything." Abbot's face was softer than Marsden had yet to see it, more like her worrier of a brother's than a warrior's. "Even with Rigby not here for him. But maybe he should be, for a while. Just . . . don't be someone else disappearing on him."

The moment was over. Wynn slid back into the booth, a cookie from the cow jar clutched in her hand. Owen and Karey were arguing in thin code over who they thought were regulars of the Burger Pit's side business. Jude—dark eyes apologetic for having left her at the mercy of his most ferocious friend—passed Marsden a fresh soda.

Later, biking home with Wynn as the Indigo curled its way alongside them and with Jude still at the edge of all her thoughts, she considered what she would have said to Abbot before they were no longer alone. How she would have defended herself against being the one to hurt him. To explain her confidence in him being fine after she walked away. That he would barely even notice, once he'd gotten what he needed from her and the covert.

The answer, when it came, hurt.

She already knew she was going to be sad to see him go, would start thinking of reasons for him to stay the day he was finally free to leave what had never been anything but temporary to him.

Abbot assumed Jude was the one at risk.

The truth was, Marsden was the one who was no longer safe.

Don't worry, Abbot.

This time it's Jude who gets to disappear on someone else first.

nineteen.

THE SHADOWS CAME IN THROUGH THE TREES AT A SLANT, HINTING THAT DAYLIGHT WAS LEAVING.

They would have to escape the covert soon, before dark arrived.

Marsden stepped over a gnarled, mossy root that stuck out from the ground like a finger from a grave. Likewise, Jude lifted the detector high enough to keep it from catching. Already, they'd mastered the odd dance the covert required for them to make it through while still being thorough—the contrived coordination of invading troops, the dogged determination of escaping ones.

It was their second search in three days, and it seemed as if they'd come to some kind of agreement with the covert. The anguished land agreed to let them in, but they would not be allowed to stop, nor go back, nor rush ahead. What happened, happened; the covert would decide what it would finally give to them, and when.

Time warped within that ancient wooden fence enclosing them from the world. Hours, like moments; moments, like days. It was like the story of Persephone, who was tricked into eating six pomegranate seeds, each seed cursing her to a month in the underworld. As the goddess ate those blood-red seeds, so Marsden's great-great-uncle had spilled his family's blood onto the covert's soil, and prisoners were born anew to them.

"Man, Rig coming in this deep?" Jude swung the detector over the wild ginger at their feet, the endless spools of spice. "As a kid? I bet most adults wouldn't come this far. Kind of amazing what you can convince yourself to do when you really want something."

Marsden thought of her mother convincing herself right out of her own ability. How Star had called her a coward for doing it. They'd argued about it once, and Marsden had been in the same room, the almond cookies her grandmother had brought for her gone tasteless on her tongue. *You're so full of fear there's no room for anything else*, Star had whispered harshly to her daughter. *Fear of this town, of yourself.*

"He was probably still really scared," she said to Jude. "He just wanted to bury that tin even more."

"It made him brave. Braver than I was at that age."

"You were just a kid. You shouldn't have *had* to be brave."

"Rig said Dad had a bad temper, even when my mom was still around," he muttered, swirling over a patch of clover. As usual, there were no bees in sight, the insects permanently shy of the covert. Their instincts had long ago warned them to stay away, to instead drink only from clover grown in light, grown from soil without traces of tragedy. "Later, having two kids to raise on his own didn't help it."

"Your mom died when you were just a baby, didn't she?" It'd been cancer that had taken Isabel Ambrose, its ugly pull stronger than any of that of the covert.

"When I was three. I can't remember much—I need pictures to see her face. Apparently, she hated it here—back East, she was Isabel Ambrose, but in Glory, she was the black lady married to the guy who used to have a good job, you know?" He shrugged. "My dad tried—small things, like he picked out the cherrywood flooring in the house to match what we had before—but that's just . . . surface stuff. Rig missed her all the time. I guess I got off easy, not remembering her."

Marsden held a tree branch to the side so it wouldn't smack him in the stomach as he followed her through a thick knot of pines. "I think we forget for a reason. If you remembered every single bad thing that ever happened to you, you'd never stop being sad."

Her words had been impulsive, almost embarrassingly revealing, and she wished she could take them back—they came too close to spelling out her secrets. How she was trying to hear the dead just to prove it wasn't her fault her father was gone. How that had made her say yes to Jude digging up the covert, but it'd been on top of feeling guilty about being a skimmer.

"When I think about Rig being brave for my sake, the worst part is it was because *he* didn't have a choice." Jude swept, the detector a slow arc of silver. "My being around meant he had to be brave, all the time. What a damn heavy load for a kid to have to carry, right?"

She took the detector from him, felt the high buzz of it in her bones as she took over. "It's—you don't question a load when you're the only one who can carry it." Wynn had always been hers, and only hers, to watch over—there'd been no one else. Only in her weakest moments, or her angriest, did Marsden sometimes let herself resent it. She wondered if it'd been the same way for Rigby. She saw the image of his eyes in the library again, how shuttered they'd been as he held Jude. *Rigby, can you hear me? Are you here with us, anywhere? You weren't evil for sometimes wanting to run away on your own, only real.*

"I asked Roadie once if he thought Rig was going to hell, handful of covert dirt dumped into his pocket or not." Jude plucked a vine of ivy off a trunk as he passed. "He said he didn't even believe in God, so how could he believe in hell?"

She didn't know what she believed. Because what kind of God would allow for a place like Glory, like the covert? "Do you agree with him?"

"I kind of have to, don't I?"

She led them over more patches of wild ginger, the plants' fragrance sitting on their tongues, the biggest component of their air. There was the occasional ping on the sensor that turned out to be coins or screws. And as they walked, her thoughts went from God to spirits. To the otherworldly. Special abilities had no place in reality now, not with technology what it was.

But her family owned the covert, in a town where most of its folk still believed in guaranteed passageways to the afterlife. She grew up listening to Star tell her stories about ghosts and mediums and the dead as though they were the most normal things in the world. She'd never talked to anyone outside of family about their ability to hear the dead. But most of Glory knew anyway, just as thinking of Leo Ambrose naturally led to thoughts of booze and a short temper. But unlike Jude's family's history, that of Marsden's was an older kind of knowledge, part of the town's very roots, from Duncan and his gun to Star Liu's death to Shine's shunning of her own dark magic.

Marsden slid Jude a sideways glance.

How much did he know? Or believe? If he ever guessed how often she stood in the covert, listening and trying not to fail again, would he ask her to listen for Rigby? What would he say if she told him she already was, but for her own reasons, too?

"Hey." He stepped up on a small outcrop of rocks, slid back down. He stuck his hands in his shorts pockets and looked nearly sheepish. "Yesterday, after the Burger Pit, I went to see Theola down at her café."

Marsden stopped walking, and he did, too. In her hands, the detector ran on and on.

Theola Finney. A reader of tea leaves and her grandmother's best friend when Star had been alive. Theola used to let Marsden pick out free muffins and juice from behind the counter of her café whenever Star dropped by with her.

Shine had kept her daughters away from the fortune-teller after her mother died. She warned them the old lady was full of strange stories, her head a nest of dangerous lies. That she would only try to fill their heads with those same lies if they weren't careful.

The tactic merely half worked. Wynn, by nature, was more curious

153

than scared—being warned off Theola so consistently only made her enjoy walking past the café whenever she could, eager for a chance to speak to her grandmother's mysterious friend. As for Marsden, who *did* do her best to stay away from Theola, her avoidance had nothing to do with Shine's reasons at all and everything to do with her own.

Her head was home to all her secrets.

She could never risk someone peeking inside.

"You went to see Theola Finney?" she finally said. "The town psychic?"

"Yes. Also the closest thing this town has to a resident witch, apparently." Jude stilled and then shifted his feet on ground made treacherous with its slippery layers of ginger plants. "I don't mean your grandmother was a witch, though. Since, you know, they hung out together."

Marsden wasn't surprised he knew about Glory's hearer of the dead and its psychic being friends. The fact was just one more piece of town history.

And do you think my mother is a witch, too? Me? Do you think me and Wynn can hear the dead, too? What else have you heard?

"I didn't know you were into the psychic scene," she said.

"I don't know if I am, to be honest—it all seems kind of ridiculous and pretty hokey most of the time." Fear flashed across Jude's features, before slowly fading. "But this is Glory—nothing's impossible."

Her grip tightened on the metal detector until her hands hurt. She swept low over weeds that were full of thorns. "You went to get your fortune read?"

His face flushed, obvious even in the falling light that turned his wavy hair a dense black. "No, I went because . . . I wanted to see if there was enough of Rig left in *me* that she could read him still. If she could look into my head and see him there, so she could tell me why he did what he did."

"But, Jude, I don't think—"

"I know, I know. I just figured I might as well ask. She told me right away she couldn't, so not to waste my money with a reading."

It *would* have been a waste. Theola was clairvoyant, her mind a tool that she used for a sixth sense, the same way one used a nose to smell. Reading leaves, or staring into someone's eyes, she could tell the future, dig into the past, figure out things in ways that defied logic and science.

But being clairvoyant didn't always mean one could do *all* these things. And as far as Marsden knew, Theola had never claimed to see into the past, or to be able to read still-living minds as a gateway into those of people already gone.

And that was what Jude so badly wanted.

His disappointment must have been crushing.

"But Marsden?"

"Yes?"

"Then Theola told me something anyway—and it made me run."

twenty.

They made *her* want to run—from his story, from the secrets the
covert held for him, from the danger that he held. She had enough
of her own secrets, didn't she? They filled her to spilling so she could
barely keep up with hiding them.

"She told me Rig had had an old soul." Jude's voice had gone cold,
floating out to touch her in an icy wave. "How he'd been haunted by
some load of guilt that she didn't need to read to have figured out. 'We
all have our brand of self-torment, Jude Ambrose,' she said, 'but your
brother Rigby had stopped being able to breathe through his.'"

"We should leave now." Marsden turned off the metal detector. A
cage-like silence fell around them. "The light in here—it's changed."

Jude ignored her. "She said she hoped people were being kind
about his death." He was little more than a smear of color against the
wavering gray of the trees, as much phantom as not. "Because Rig . . .
Everyone who knew him had liked him, you know?"

She knew she would have. And everyone had liked her father, too, before they found him floating in the Indigo. But not enough to embrace his widow—her blood was still too mad, her ancestry too foreign.

"*Have* they been kind?" she asked, suddenly needing to know, hoping Glory was mourning Rigby above anything when it came to how they were treating Jude and his father right now.

His laugh was low but real. "Lots of casseroles."

She had to laugh, too. "Did you leave the café, then?"

"I had to. Standing there, listening to Theola say all that about Rig like he'd actually told her stuff he couldn't have told me . . . I ran out of there like the place was on fire." Jude took the detector from her, fiddled with the knobs so he had reason to look away. "I was always supposed to know Rig best. But now, I wonder if I really knew him at all."

"You did know him. He was your brother."

"If I did, then it was only what he allowed me to see, and that's not the same thing."

"Don't we all do that?"

He pushed his hair back, watching her. Then: "I don't know. Do we?"

Marsden was sure she was sinking, the ground suddenly gone as soft as freshly tilled earth. What could have been kept from her when it came to her parents' relationship? Of her father and his demons and the moment of his death?

"Maybe, in this town"—a wind rippled through the covert and she rubbed goose bumps from her arms—"it really is only the dead who can tell you the truth."

"What?"

"Like with Rigby. Why you went to see Theola at all. And my dad."

"Your dad? It was an accident. In the Indigo."

She heard it in his voice, the town's doubt, how it had its own version of Grant Eldridge. "But I know what everyone really thinks. And it's what I think, too. You know why? Because the night he died, he looked right at me and said he'd never wanted the kind of life he was living."

In the dim, something brushed at her hand. It was Jude's, his fingers cool and sturdy, and they slowly wound their way through hers.

"Then your dad was a bastard for saying that." His tone was a slow burn.

Suddenly, there was a burst of sound—from behind, a sharp crack—and they both jumped a foot into the air before crashing back to earth. The detector flew free and landed on ginger with a soft thud.

"Christ!" Jude's fingers were still wrapped around hers. He leaned close. He smelled of sun and leaves and brisk evening air. "What was *that*?"

It took her a handful of seconds and a few deep breaths to unlock her throat so she could answer, to wipe away the scenarios that came to mind and know they weren't real. "A branch," she murmured. "And probably a squirrel. It's okay."

She was still holding his hand. Or he was holding hers. Whichever it was, Marsden knew she'd been right in deciding he had the kind of hands made for sketch artists. In her mind's eye, she painted slowly, languidly—the bumpy mountain ranges of his knuckles, the long plains of his bones, the deep lakes that were all recessed dips and smooth swoops.

Once she memorized him, she dropped his hand and took a careful step back. She couldn't tell if he was more relieved or disappointed, or if he cared at all. Then she decided not knowing was probably for the best, for the both of them.

"It's nearly dark in here"—she knew she sounded brusque, wanting to promise him he would be fine: *Don't worry, Jude, no one at school will ever have to know you touched me*—"which means we really do have to go." After leaving the covert's strange, haunted woods—its trees all tangled up, their shadows as dark as ink—time would go back to normal. It would go back to being late afternoon instead of feeling closer to midnight. Hours, rewound. Glory's summer sun, still blazing hot and true.

Jude nodded, the motion a blur. "For a second, I thought for sure it was a trespasser, maybe even a skimmer. And then I thought it was a gun, and . . . well . . ." His voice was small, young sounding.

Marsden bent down, picked up the detector, and knew what she had to do.

It was entirely wrong, considering what Jude had already trusted her with.

But she'd only ever agreed to let him into the covert. Letting him into her head, to peek past all her defenses and weapons and discover what she had to hide? None of that had been part of their deal.

"Jude, what I said about my dad a minute ago, can we forget it?

Because I've never talked about it, and I didn't mean to start now."

A long, long moment of utter silence, and then he finally said: "Okay."

She blinked. "That was . . . easy."

"Did you really think I would say no?"

"Not really, I guess."

"Because I'm not an asshole, remember?"

She laughed, making him laugh. And then his stomach growled, and they were both laughing again.

"Okay, you're right, we can barely see a thing and I'm starving," he said. "Let's get out of here."

Before Marsden could tell herself it was better to leave it alone— Hadn't she just decided they were a terrible idea? How she was doing him the bigger favor by giving him an out?—she shot out a hand and touched Jude's arm to stop him from moving past. Despite being in a place built solely on sad things, she couldn't keep from liking touching him. Her blood flowed heavy in her veins, her stomach fluttered. It made no sense. She was going to make things even more awkward for them.

In the half-dark, Jude had gone strangely motionless, an animal unsure of which way to turn. Which way was safe.

Still, he didn't pull away.

"I have to ask," she said. "What makes you so absolutely sure you're right about Rigby having a time capsule and burying it here? I mean, beyond that book. Because I know there's more than just you finding and reading it."

After so many hours of turning up nothing but junk, he only seemed more driven. She needed to know: Was pure faith really all it took, or was a touch of madness needed? How far could she let herself go in her own search for answers from the covert?

Jude sighed. "Beyond the facts?"

"Yes."

"You know how sometimes you just feel it in your gut? That it's something way beyond logic and probability yet somehow just *is*?"

Marsden nodded, wondered why she'd even questioned. Gut was why she couldn't stop skimming, why she kept Wynn close. Gut was what had her telling Jude Ambrose yes, despite logic and aside from her own selfish needs.

And gut was how she knew that however this summer ended, it was going to be hard to see him go.

"So has Wynn ever mentioned to you that I'm a pretty good cook?" she blurted out.

His surprise was whole, and then he grinned, his smile a flash in the dark. An ache flared to life in her chest, sharp and lovely and dangerous.

"She said you were terrible, actually. I think the cold, greasy toast for her squirrel pushed her over the edge."

Fumbling slightly, she let go of his arm and felt for his hand, not letting herself question her own motives or reasons. Why she was choosing a mistake for him.

"I'm going to make you dinner," she said. "C'mon."

twenty-one.

THROUGH THE SCREEN DOOR, MARSDEN COULD SMELL FOOD FROM THE KITCHEN, HEARD THE MUFFLED CLATTER OF CUTLERY. It was later than she thought, and dinner was starting. She wondered where Wynn had gone to wait for her. She'd been at Ella's all afternoon, but she'd be back for dinner now.

"Someone's already cooked and saved you the trouble." Jude peered through the dust-sheened mesh, trying to peek inside. She wondered what he was thinking. How much of the boardinghouse was simply the town's best lodging, the place where Marsden happened to live and work? Where her mother was supposedly still employed as a housekeeper? And how much more was it the brothel it became at night, well-known among those with reason to visit? Where her mother was a prostitute?

"It's Dany's turn to cook for the house tonight," she said, "but Wynn and I usually eat in the kitchen, away from everyone."

His hand was still in hers, and he squeezed it as she hesitated at the door. The press of his skin climbed all the way into her mind and lodged there. "Is this okay, my being here? I can go."

"No, I asked you." As long as they stayed in the kitchen, it would be fine. And she wanted him to see her in a place that wasn't the covert, for him to see past what the town had already decided she was. "Come in, really."

She saw Jude do his best to not wrinkle his nose at the smell—and fail—as soon as they stepped into the kitchen, and she had to grin. "Dany's on a health kick, which means her walnut cheddar loaf."

"What's that? Wait. Please don't tell me we're about to find out."

"I couldn't do that to us." The place was nothing but familiar, but she felt oddly adrift as she watched him look all around, just as he did in the covert, as though trying to connect what he saw to what he knew to be true. Boardinghouse, yet brothel; woods, yet death; the Marsden right then to the Marsden he knew from school, through the eyes of the town.

Other than its size, she thought the kitchen was a typical one. Touches of family, even.

Wynn's artwork taped to the front of the fridge.

The small potted geraniums and cacti lined up on the windowsill.

A cereal bowl full of rocks and wild ginger on the counter next to the phone.

"This is like the set of a television show," Jude said, walking farther into the room, "what kitchens are supposed to look like." His expression was carefully blank. She saw him comparing it to his own, how his own fell short.

"You guys don't cook?" she asked.

"My father does once in a while. Usually because he needs to assure himself he's good about spending time with us."

Us. A slip.

She made sure her face showed no sign she'd noticed.

Wynn was nowhere in the kitchen. Which meant her sister—growing bored as she'd waited for Marsden, getting hungrier and hungrier while listening to the sounds of a meal she'd been restricted from—had likely snuck her way to the dining room.

Marsden dropped Jude's hand, his fingers lingering on hers a second longer than necessary before letting go. What she'd wondered about earlier in the covert, then, when he'd touched her—he didn't regret it.

But would that change later, when the leaves fell and the heat went away and they were back in school? When he saw her in the halls and realized he'd forgotten who she was?

Then Wynn was barreling into the kitchen, braids flying, clutching a wadded-up napkin.

"Whoa, runt, hold up." Marsden went to block her way. "What are you up to?"

Her sister opened up the napkin, giggling now. "Peaches asked me to throw this out for her. She said she never puts anything gross in her mouth without getting paid."

Marsden sighed, avoiding Jude's eyes. "Of course Peaches said that."

"It *is* gross."

"I know. Wynn, you should have waited somewhere else for me—not in the dining room."

"I was just in the hall. Then Peaches called me over."

Jude came close, staring at the contents of the napkin. His expression made Wynn laugh again. "Is that the walnut cheddar loaf thing?"

"I told you I couldn't make us eat it," Marsden said.

"*Really* good call."

Wynn skipped over to the trash to throw it away, and when she came back, she was grinning widely, clearly delighted that Jude was there. "You're staying for dinner, right?"

"If that's okay."

"Yes. I guess you actually like hanging around Marsden?"

Jude laughed, a real laugh. Marsden was unable to look away as his face lit up, the way his eyes crinkled just a bit at the corners. "Your sister's been really nice."

"She is—most of the time."

He grinned. "I guess I've been lucky."

Marsden tugged one of her sister's braids. "Waffles tonight, remember?" She glanced at Jude, half-apologetic. "She picked this morning—sorry, I should have said something."

"As long as it's not cold toast, I'm good."

"Hey, that toast fed a squirrel." She plugged in a waffle iron to heat, took out the mixing bowls and measuring spoons, and placed bags of sugar and flour on the counter. From the bag of flour, a bloom of white puffed out through the seal and dusted the side of her cheek like a drift of snow.

● ● ●

Wynn dragged a chair over to the cabinet. She climbed up to stand on it to reach a stack of plates inside. "You should have let me go with you."

"Well, think of these as make-up waffles. And that was Mom's decision, not mine."

Jude reached over Wynn's head to help her grab the dishware. "Make up for what?"

"Mars wanted to feed them *eggs*." Her sister's expression said she was still disgusted.

He offered an exaggerated wince. "No way."

Marsden shrugged, enjoying that he bothered to banter with a little kid. She lifted a shoulder to wipe her face clean, knew she was making the mess worse. "You can also blame Jude for coming by when he did."

"Sorry about that—I've always had shitty timing." He reached over and slowly wiped the flour from her cheek with his thumb. His eyes danced. Her skin jumped. But whether he saw it on her face or it was simply his own survival instinct, he'd already dropped his thumb and backed off before she could warn him away. And then Wynn was talking again, letting them both escape, and Marsden was glad.

"You swore," her sister said happily. She began to set the small table, using oversize plates that made her appear even tinier than she already actually was. Marsden saw her own build there, the way she'd been at eight—skinny, with a shaky wisp of a frame, scabbed-over knees—and hoped her sister would take her time growing out of it. "But I won't tell."

"I did swear, didn't I?" Jude grabbed syrup from the fridge and placed it on the table. "My manners are also pretty crappy."

"If my mom heard you, she'd say swearing is only because you don't know a smarter word. And then you sound stupid when you have to talk to people."

"People people, like friends?"

"No, like guests at the boardinghouse. She says I'll have to get used to talking to them. Be entertaining."

Marsden, busy beating eggs and oil and milk to a froth in the mixing bowl, tightened her grip. She cursed her mother and Nina in turns, with each slap of the spoon. "Our mother is big on the art of proper . . . conversation." She heard how stiff her voice was and decided there was no point in hiding it. Whatever Jude picked up from it, whatever it might let him think, him knowing or not knowing didn't change Shine being a prostitute. "She says it helps make people feel important."

Wynn wasn't done explaining to Jude the finer points of decorum as dictated by the boardinghouse. "Now if *Nina* heard you swear, she'd say you have to go outside to do it." She placed napkins on the table, laid out cutlery on top of them just as Dany had taught her.

"Who's Nina again?" he asked.

"She owns the boardinghouse and is Mom's boss. Did you know our mom is a housekeeper here? She helps Dany clean the guest rooms."

Marsden poured chocolate chips into the waffle batter and stirred, her hands on cruise control. She was strung as tight as a wire, all her nerves electrified. A small and bitter part of her wanted to yell the truth at her sister, make her see the lie. But the bigger, defeated part of her remained grudgingly grateful to Shine and Nina for keeping Wynn in the dark. For sticking to the script she'd written for them.

"It sounds like hard work," Jude said.

Wynn poured lemonade into three glasses and stirred additional sugar into each one—Marsden heard Jude whistle under his breath, knew he was already feeling his teeth thud in anticipation of the excessive sweetness. "That's why we live here now," her sister said. "It was like a trade, after our dad died. Nina gave our mom her job. "

"And you get your own personal chef, too."

"Are you going to be coming here to eat all the time?" Wynn narrowed her eyes at him. "If you like Mars's waffles?"

Marsden poured batter onto the iron and closed the lid to let it cook, relieved that the conversation had turned—all her secrets, safe for one more night. "Everyone likes my waffles, Wynnifred Eldridge."

"Way to be *gross*, saying my full name out loud. You know I *hate* it."

"The real question is whether or not I would make them for him again."

"You mean you wouldn't?"

"Depends—I'll have to really think about it." She made a show of deep and deliberate consideration. "And it's your name, *Wynnifred*, so you shouldn't hate it. But fine, I'll save it for special occasions."

"Depends on what?"

"How many waffles he can eat."

"Because I like him." Wynn spoke as though Jude weren't right there, hearing every word she said. Her sister's childish earnestness made Marsden's throat ache with an odd kind of loneliness, at the inevitable passing of time. "Do you like him, Mars?"

"I like him," she managed, trying to ignore Jude—who'd gone absolutely motionless at her side—and the steady burn of his gaze that lit the side of her cheek on fire.

Wynn plunked straws into the glasses of lemonade. "And he's not old, like most of the guy guests around here. Peaches always complains to Lucy about the really old ones she has to spend time with. She usually doesn't know I'm listening, but she's also way louder than she thinks she is."

Marsden's pulse beat at her ears, and now her face was burning from the inside out. Jude still hadn't moved.

"That's . . . enough," she whispered. She'd been wrong to believe she didn't care how much he figured out, no matter how likely it was that he already knew.

Spending time with a guest.

Was that how Wynn deciphered seeing Nina's girls walk into their bedrooms with men? Did she imagine Peaches keeping them entertained with board games? With cat's cradle and thumb wars?

Marsden scrambled for escape from the moment. "Run out to the dining room for me, okay, Wynn? I bet most of the guests are done eating and have already gone out."

"Now you *want* me to go into the dining room?" Her sister was confused. Jude moved to close the bags of flour and sugar.

Marsden nodded and began to place dirty spoons into the sink. "See if you can sneak three slices of the fruit flan. I made an extra-large one for tonight—we had so many fresh berries—so there'll be leftovers."

"Her name's really Wynnifred?" Jude asked as soon as Wynn was gone, his voice light, nearly teasing.

Suddenly, she felt more defiant than humiliated. It was seeing him there, decidedly not judging, almost like a challenge of his own: *Why do you care so much about my caring, when I don't?*

She nodded, her hands clumsy as she lifted the lid of the waffle iron. She pried cooked waffles off the hot plates, piled them onto a baking sheet, and placed the whole thing in the stove to keep warm. "Wynn for short."

"The nickname suits her: *Win*." He poured more batter from the bowl onto the iron. He shut the lid and leaned back against the counter. "She doesn't seem like the kind of kid who likes to wait."

"She's not, so I like to keep her in check—hence torturing her with her full name." Marsden found Wynn being so headstrong maddening. Her little sister always charging ahead meant the risk of seeing too much, too fast. But if she wasn't just as she was—was fine being molded and guided by Shine or Nina—that terrified Marsden just as much.

She was watching Jude stir more chocolate chips into the batter, thinking about his name and wondering about asking if it'd been his mother or his father who had chosen it, when the answer clicked in her brain.

Her grin, she knew, was decidedly smug—she should have realized it a long time ago. "Speaking of names, I just figured out something about yours."

He answered with his own grin, even as he narrowed his eyes at her apparent glee. "You look way too pleased with yourself for me to like the sound of this."

"Your folks were Beatles fans, weren't they?" Her father had liked the Beatles, had blasted them throughout their old duplex on occasion—while fixing a loose floorboard, while adjusting the TV's antennae. Those particular images of Grant Eldridge were faint, hazy. But the notes of the songs? They'd been etched into her heart for life, were tiny little song cells in the makeup of her blood.

Jude softened, and his grin melted into a small smile. "My mom was."

"Because 'Hey Jude' and 'Eleanor Rigby.'"

"I know. It's kind of ridiculous."

She transferred more waffles, set more to cooking. "And if you'd been a girl?"

"Eleanor."

Her mouth twitched, and then she gave in and laughed. "No."

"I'm not kidding. Rig used to call me Eleanor whenever I really got in his face about something."

"He could have made it up just to tease you. I'd do the same thing to Wynn."

"Maybe. But . . . I don't want to stop believing it now. Know what I mean?"

Marsden nodded. Of course she did. The Beatles coming on the radio never failed to stop her in her tracks, to keep her drowned inside a past where her father was not yet dead. She'd lift her hand to hover over the dial, fully intending that *this* time she'd simply be able to turn it off and walk away. But she always ended up listening to the whole song, her heart feeling light, then going restless, then back again. For the rest of the day, she'd swear she could sense her father nearby, telling her she'd been mistaken about what she'd heard, how he hadn't said what he said.

Jude poured even more chocolate chips into the batter and began to stir lazily. "So, how did you get your name, then? With a grandmother named Star and a mother named Shine, I would have expected something different than Marsden."

"Such as?"

"Something . . . celestial, I guess. Astral, astronomical . . . *zodiacal.*"

She laughed. "Seems Wynn and I broke that trend."

"I guess she *does* call you Mars all the time. Planets count, right?"

"She's the only one who does. She never used to—I was always just Marsden before. But then last year, she got into my Roman mythology textbook from school and—" She stopped, unsure of how to say it out loud.

"Whoa, hold up, I think I get it." He dropped the mixing spoon into the bowl, where it sunk to the bottom, out of sight. "Roman mythology?"

She nodded, feeling absurdly and annoyingly tongue-tied. She reached over to the cutlery caddy on the counter and pulled out a fresh fork.

"Rig had had a book on mythology. Powerful gods and goddesses, tons of messed-up families. Fighting and blood. Lots of falling in love and then cheating. Misunderstandings and punishments that lasted for all eternity. Fun stuff."

"All of that, yes."

"Mars, the god of war." Jude's voice had gone gentle. "That's what Wynn calls you instead of Marsden."

She slid the baking sheet with its modest stack of waffles out from the oven, unable to face him, his unwavering stare and the curiosity in it almost too intense. "She said it was because if she ever needed someone to be on her side, it'd be me. That I'd fight for her no matter what, do everything I could to save her."

"Of course you would. She's your little sister."

Marsden nodded and opened the waffle iron. Steam hissed, warm against her cheek; melted chocolate chips clung to the lid, a crust of sweetness. She jabbed the fork into the cooked waffles, placed them on a fresh platter, and piled the ones from the baking sheet on top. She heard the sound of Wynn coming back down the hall. *But it freaks me out, too, her needing me. What if I was too busy saving myself and there was nothing left for her? What if I save her doing all I can and there is nothing left for me?*

She passed Jude the full platter and unplugged the iron. "These are the best chocolate-chip waffles you'll ever eat, I promise."

twenty-two.

INSIDE SECONDS, THE AIR OF THE PAWNSHOP WAS THE SAME
AS MOST OF ITS MERCHANDISE—USED, OLD, SAD.

Waiting impatiently for the one other customer in the place to leave, Marsden looked around, not even pretending to browse.

Late afternoon sun burned in through the cheap Roman shade that partially covered the front window, a mellow gold. The light had an old-time feel, but it was more washed-out than nostalgic, and it glided over the shelves full of things now in limbo. A clock with wooden animals inside, loaded on springs. Assorted porcelain tea sets with apparent certificates of authenticity. Small televisions, lamps, dartboards.

She knew each item was supposed to be worth something, to someone, somewhere. Maybe some of them were even on the rare side, were treasures in hiding.

But she was pretty sure most of it wouldn't compare to a piece of jewelry, whether its value lay in being brought in and sold or carried out, newly purchased. Hadley would know this, too. She wondered how many times he'd stood where she was standing, waiting for the store to clear to show Fitz his latest find.

The bell over the entrance rang, and the lone customer disappeared through the door, a bad replica of a Tiffany lamp in hand.

Marsden walked up to the counter, where the shop owner still stood counting cash into the till from the lamp purchase. A small and wiry kind of guy, he was surrounded by a wreath of smoke from the cigarette clamped between his lips. Hair worn in a severe buzz cut, a blond fringe of a crown over a narrowed hazel gaze.

Marsden rarely came into Seconds—had no reason to, with nothing to buy and no money to buy anything with—but she knew who Fitz was, even if she'd never spoken to him before. Glory was small enough that not many faces went unnoticed. But now she was seeing him through different eyes, knowing he'd been one of her father's best friends. She wanted to reach into his brain, take out his memories of Grant Eldridge, and have them be her own.

The counter was the kind with a glass top, its interior hollow to make room for display shelves. Marsden peered down and saw rows of jewelry, the gold of necklaces and the platinum of rings.

If Fitz asked, she could have told him the story behind too many of them, about the people Hadley had skimmed them from.

A necklace with a ruby pendant, its former owner a woman named Nicole Dremont. She'd lived three states over according to the tiny print of the covert column in the paper. She'd dumped a handful of soil into her purse.

A silver bracelet. Gina Laldeen, from California. She'd had a road map tucked into her pocket, directions to Glory indicated in bright red marker; covert dirt had darkened its folds.

A ring fat with inlaid stones had belonged to Sebastian Walsh, a local whose parking tickets, found in his wallet, revealed how much time he spent outside the casino. Needle tracks skewered the insides of both elbows, showing how often he was at the pharmacies. His palms had been coated with the covert—just as there was no way to tell if that had been intentional or he'd simply caught himself before falling, there was no way to tell if the overdose had been accidental or if some voice had drawn him to the land.

"What can I help you with?"

She glanced up, unsure of how to start. She had never seen a script on how to ask a stranger what they might be hiding about their old friend's death. "My name is—"

"Marsden." Fitz shut the till and met her gaze with his own, his expression curious. "Grant's daughter."

It shouldn't have surprised her that he would know her, but it did. What else did he know? "Yes, I—"

"Does Shine know you're here?" His expression was wary now, too.

Had her mother told her father's friends to stay away after he was dead? Was that the explanation behind Fitz's wariness? "No. Does it matter?"

"Not sure yet. If you're looking for something specific, I can tell you what's in the store. Is it a gift, or . . . ?"

"I have questions, actually—about my dad. So I guess what I'm looking for are answers."

Fitz leaned back against the wall, exhaled cigarette smoke. "Your mom probably wouldn't want you asking me. After your dad died, she was pretty clear she wanted us out of her life, which also meant out of yours. To Shine, we were just as bad as Grant's gambling."

"She doesn't have to know."

"Can't you ask her whatever you need?"

"I have. She can't help. Which is why I'm here."

He shrugged. "Okay. Makes no real difference to me."

"You guys were friends?"

"Sure, good ones. And Casper, and Eugene, and Quaid, too." At the mention of the dead Quaid, Fitz crossed himself clumsily. "The five of us would go to Decks and just hang out, playing blackjack or whatever."

"My dad always lost money."

"We all did. And then we'd win some. That's the game."

"The night he died, were you there? With him, at Decks?"

"Of course." Fitz's face clouded and turned unhappy. "The four of us were with him, as usual. Why?"

"The papers never said. They just said he'd been there, gambling, before he ended up in the Indigo."

"Well, we were there often enough that whoever the papers spoke to probably never thought to mention it. Like when you talk about the sky, you assume it's blue, unless you say otherwise."

"Did he leave alone?" Marsden watched him, this man her father would have trusted, and found herself hoping he hadn't been wrong to do so. Fitz didn't seem dangerous or even much of a liar. But he was also one of Glory's, a product of a town built on stories.

"That night? No, we all left together. Or, more accurately, the four of us stayed while your dad was the one who left. Me and Quaid and Casper and Eugene turned back after we said goodbye to Grant out in the parking lot. The place was hopping, more so than normal—your dad had gone on a roll, and people had stuck around to watch. Dash came out and called us back, said it was too early to leave. But Grant didn't change his mind, said he needed to leave."

"That wasn't in the papers, either. The part about Decks being especially full."

Fitz smiled, but it was wry. "Sky's blue, remember? This is Glory. There are gambling and card houses on every other block—there's always someone having a winning night somewhere. Not news. Just like it's not news when someone's losing a week's pay somewhere else."

Marsden knew her father had had those nights. She'd seen Shine cry over them. "Did he win a lot that night?"

"Four grand."

She was startled. Eight years ago, four grand would have gone a long way for a family of three with another baby coming. It would have done wonders toward appeasing a young mother who had more things to worry about than celebrate.

"Grant kept talking about how he couldn't wait to tell your mom. I hadn't seen him that happy in a long time. And you know, the guy didn't win any more often than us, but it was sure something to watch when he did. As though those cards were talking to him directly. Or everyone else's had turned transparent, just for him. So, yeah, no surprise that people gathered to watch. Just as it was never a surprise when some of those people decided they knew Grant like a friend, talking him up, wanting to absorb some of whatever luck he was having. That night was no different."

She thought of that four grand. Her father's empty pockets. "Who were they?"

"Just the same old guys who clung to everyone who had a winning hand. And the few out-of-towners who always end up drunk enough to do it too, forgetting they're not locals. That night, there was this one guy watching Grant play, and I thought he was just one of those drive-bys. But then I overheard him and your dad talking. Turned out they knew each other, seemed to go back a bit together, even though I'd never seen the guy before. But that was Grant. Everyone claimed to know him."

Shine had said the same thing, Marsden remembered. *Grant was like that, making people love him too easily.*

Shine had also said this of someone she'd known for a long time: *Your father knew him, too. They were friendly enough.*

Brom Innes.

The man she'd chosen to save her.

Marsden shuddered. Was it possible it'd been *Brom* there that night at Decks, watching those games of blackjack? Could he have waited for her father to leave, knowing he'd won big, then followed him along the darkened highway, the crash of the Indigo and the building storm keeping him faded, unnoticed in the background?

Brom, who had likely loved her mother in secret, because Grant Eldridge had been in the way?

The idea left her cold—robbery was one thing, murder something else entirely. She forced the ugly thought, the chance that for eight years she'd considered all the wrong things, away. "That guy, was his name Brom Innes?"

The shop owner lit a fresh cigarette. "Never asked, and he never told."

"What did he look like? Average height, light-brown hair, pale-blue eyes?" Even her description was bland and forgettable, the way she would describe a bowl of oatmeal. Just the way Brom was.

Fitz scratched his head. "I can't remember. I don't know. Maybe?"

"If I brought a photo, could you recognize him, do you think?" Peaches had an instant camera she could borrow.

"Yeah, maybe." He sounded doubtful. She didn't blame him. Eight years, and she was asking him to recall oatmeal.

"You look a lot like Grant, you know," Fitz continued. "He used to keep a photo of you in his wallet. Showed it around once in a while, like we all hadn't seen it before."

"He did?" It was such a normal thing to do, when their family hadn't seemed very normal at all, and Marsden's throat went tight.

"I mean, he never really talked about you or your mom all that much. It always left him moody or quiet. Everyone's got their fair share of demons, right? With Grant, they were all to do with fami-ly." Ash dropped from Fitz's cigarette onto the glass counter, a gray snowstorm. His face turned embarrassed. "Sorry. But it was what it was."

"No, it's . . . fine." And it was, though it was odd to hear someone talk about her father with more admiration than anger.

"They were his weakness, you know? Cards. Each time he walked out of Decks with less than he'd gone in with, he knew he'd failed you guys. He could go from feeling on top of the world to lower than dirt, all in the span of a game, and you'd just see his eyes change."

"You don't think it was an accident, him dying." She knew Fitz would hear it as an accusation, but she blamed herself, too, for also believing what the town believed—that her father had walked into the Indigo all on his own.

"I don't know what to believe. Just like we can never be sure what happened to all that money he'd won. Taken by the tide after the storm forced him into the river? Lost at some other gambling house that he stopped at on the way home, not knowing the blackjack gods had already turned their backs on him?" The heart of Fitz's cigarette flamed volcano red, then white hot, and over it, the pity in his gaze was nearly as searing. "The thing is, those gods might have blessed Grant that night, him winning what he did, but they still weren't a match for the demons your dad had living in his head."

Outside the pawnshop, the sun had fallen low, a wide, hazy band of yellow slung across rooftops. The dust that filled the air was now road dust, the dust of summer heat, instead of the dust of the used, the old.

Marsden biked home, thinking of this mysterious man she now had to find, so she could blame him for everything. Even if that man turned out to be the one her mother had decided she needed, the man her father had believed a friend.

twenty-three.

STARING OUT OF HER BEDROOM WINDOW, MARSDEN RUBBED HER EYES HARD TO MAKE SURE SHE WASN'T SEEING THINGS. Most people driving to her family's land were careful to leave their cars parked farther up along the highway, so it wasn't obvious right away where their owners had gone. Only once the covert revealed a body did a car get towed, the puzzle of the abandoned vehicle solved.

The brown sedan—sides filmed over with road dust, rust peeking out in spots—was parked only feet away from the gaping mouth of the covert.

She scrambled out of bed and into shorts and a T-shirt. After racing around to find them, she shoved her gardening gloves into her pocket. Wynn had stayed over Caitlyn's house last night, now that her friend's family was back from camping. It was why Marsden had let herself sleep in, delaying her dawn check of the covert, and now wished she hadn't. Because Nina would know, too, as soon as she saw the sedan, what it meant. She would call Hadley. He'd beat Marsden to the body.

Her breath came in gasps by the time she reached the wooden

fence of the covert. Sweat dotted her forehead. The air was already blazing despite the early hour, singeing the town.

It took her only minutes.

She rounded a stand of pine trees and stumbled right over him. Her gloved hands landed on his front, her fingers sinking into the fabric of his shirt. An older man, with a lined face. Beneath the dappled sunlight, the covert's supposedly holy soil lay in a streak across his forehead.

Her hands worked quickly as she searched his pants pockets.

One held a handful of soil; the other, a wallet and two one-hundred-dollar bills. She tucked the bills into her own pocket with shaking hands. It was the most cash she'd ever skimmed from a single body.

The jewelry that he wore—a fancy-enough watch, a nice-looking gold ring—was likely worth something and yet completely useless to her.

For a moment, Marsden was furious that Hadley would profit. That Fitz would, too, however he might feel about it. She reminded herself that she only stole out of necessity, but her fury simply changed to a kind of queasiness that filled her throat.

And there was no gun in sight. No clear sign of injury. However he died would remain a secret, unless they revealed it in the paper or on the radio. They didn't always do so, but sometimes it was included with the reports of his name, something she still needed.

She figured out a long time ago that a lack of answers could be just as hard to think about as finality. Because uncertainty always made her thoughts circle back to Grant Eldridge.

In an alternate world, this man might have been her father, the meaning of his death always to be a question.

In yet another, his cash might have been Rigby's note.

I'm sorry, Jude, I never wanted you to know.

Those were Rigby's words, what he'd scrawled on that small piece of paper.

Marsden could recite them by heart by now, so deeply were they burned into her memory from reading his note over and over again. She'd hadn't known him, had never even spoken to him. But in her mind, he was another version of Jude, with the same lightly speckled eyes that hid secrets, except he'd be less angry and more sad and doing all he could to keep his little brother from hurting any more than he was.

I told myself it was Dad.

I didn't want to stop.

But I didn't mean to do it.

Jude reading those words might change him forever. Might make him think the way she thought. Might fill him as full of shadows as she was, so that he was as warped by the covert as she was. Because he would read those words about death and, instead of thinking about loss as anyone else might, he'd think of something darker, something closer to violence. It was what leaped into her mind—against her will, almost subconsciously—reading them.

It was also what convinced her that Rigby had never really meant for his brother to find his note, not deep down. He would have been distraught when he wrote it and then stuck it in his wallet, folded into bills like the secret it had been. He would have been confused and vulnerable, not thinking straight.

And what if someone else had found that note even before Jude or she had? Like another skimmer, who would have found it and discarded it.

She didn't think Rigby would overlook that chance. Him writing that note, it'd been as though he'd confessed to a priest and that priest had then sworn to silence forever. Rigby had intended to die as thoroughly as though he'd disappeared into thin air.

So, fine, I'll be your priest, then, Rigby, Marsden thought as she finally got to her feet. *And I will not judge.*

Making sure the scene was as she'd found it, she tucked her gloves away and walked back to the boardinghouse, thinking of what came next.

First, she would call Hadley and tell him the news. He would come to the boardinghouse and talk to Nina about the tragedy of yet another body. He would go to the covert, more likely than not to skim the watch and ring, and she wouldn't be able to stop him.

Then she would find Peaches. She still needed to borrow her camera to take a photo of Brom . . . somehow. Marsden again heard Fitz's recalling the night her father drowned, his report of a faceless man who'd been her father's friend. The chill that ran its finger down her neck made her wish, for once, that the sun in Glory would burn even hotter.

She would make breakfast for the guests and then eat by herself—Wynn wouldn't be back until late afternoon.

And then Jude would be over.

Just the other day, she'd blurted out that she lived crippled with guilt and that her little sister called her by a name she could never live up to. She'd held his hand and pretended to not know a thing about skimmers. And then she'd brought him home and made him waffles.

Waffles.

When she could cook a freaking fantastic meal for more than a dozen people on any given day and barely break a sweat.

But he hadn't seemed to mind the meal in the least—or having Wynn around the whole time. And he'd been clear about not wanting to leave afterward. When they had finished eating and her sister had taken off to watch television to escape cleanup, she'd expected him to take off, too—Wouldn't his father be wondering where he was? she thought. But he hadn't, instead staying to help do the dishes. She remembered the shape and movements of his large hands as he washed and she dried, how nice his voice sounded in the wide depths of the kitchen, the laser beam of his eyes on her as she walked around, putting dishes away. And when Dany had come to tell him it was time for him to go home, his gaze—somehow devilish and soft and a bit perplexed all at once—locked on Marsden's as he'd said goodbye, his smile painting itself onto her brain as he finally turned at the last minute and disappeared into the night.

As soon as the door shut behind him, Dany had come over to where

Marsden was standing by the sink, squeezed her arm, and smiled so knowingly that the skin on Marsden's arms prickled to life with goose bumps.

"Ever see a forest fire when it's just on the cusp of really catching?" Dany had asked. "Right before it takes on a life of its own and it's beautiful to watch but also frightening?"

Marsden shook her head and felt her heart twist.

"Watch Jude Ambrose's eyes the next time he looks at you, and you'll know what I mean."

twenty-four.

NINA WAS IN THE KITCHEN, DRESSED AS SHE ALWAYS DRESSED, CAREFULLY AND FOR COMPANY.

Sometimes Marsden forgot that the boardinghouse owner and Shine were the same age, each seeming older than the other for different reasons. They'd gone to school together, had been semi-friends as teens. Then her mother had gotten pregnant and left school, while Nina graduated and went to college; having once been friends must have seemed like another lifetime. It wasn't until her mother became a widow with nothing to her name but a piece of land no one wanted to buy, and Nina took over as manager of her family's boardinghouse that sat next door to that land, that they reconnected in the strangest of ways.

She was at the table with a cup of coffee at her elbow and a half dozen mini blueberry pies on a plate in front of her—more of what Marsden had baked that night when she'd been too full of dread to sleep.

The coffee in the cup would be, she knew, as black and unforgiving as tar, unsullied by even a single grain of sugar. The sweet, fragrant pies, which Nina would have pulled from the freezer, would be merely lusted after and breathed upon.

189

As slim as a willow, her mother's boss had begun to worry lately about losing her figure.

Marsden could have assumed Nina was sitting at the table waiting for her, knowing that she wanted to talk to her again about becoming one of her girls. So far, Marsden had managed to avoid running into her alone.

But she wasn't the company Nina was looking for that morning, because seated across from her at the table was Hadley.

Marsden had missed seeing the cop's car parked outside the boardinghouse. She'd been distracted and thinking of cameras and drownings and Jude.

"*There* you are." Nina pressed a rose-tipped hand to her front, the nails like gems against the paler pink of her blouse. Her brown bob swung as she shook her head, concern all over her face. "Please tell me you weren't in the covert this morning—I know you like to take walks there, even now."

Even now.

Marsden tried not to roll her eyes.

Nina's show of distress over Marsden having found Rigby's body— someone so close to her age, with people in common—was for appearance's sake. Her mother's boss knew she was more effective as a cut-throat businessperson by being selective about when she showed her claws; bodies in the covert bothered her only because it was bad for the boardinghouse, and a nuisance to deal with.

More than the bodies that bothered her, though, were Marsden's reactions to them. Marsden knew it unsettled Nina, the way she was able to report a body and then go about her day. But Nina didn't know she needed those bodies more than she could ever be scared of them.

"No, I was walking along the river," she said, trying not to fidget, feeling stained by the covert. How much did she smell of ginger when what she needed was the scent of the mud from the Indigo? "Why?"

"Did you see a car parked along the highway out there?" Hadley asked. He took a sip of coffee, slurping just the slightest. His coffee would be thick with cream and sugar and lazy indulgence. "A brown Buick?"

"Yes, it's still out there now." She couldn't lie about that. There was no way she could have missed seeing that car if she'd been where she said she was.

"It appears to have been abandoned. The owner . . . Well, unfortunately, we think he went into the covert. You understand what that means."

She nodded. "Suicide."

"Most likely." The note of sadness in Hadley's voice almost sounded authentic. "People don't go there for much else, as you know. It's a terrible state of affairs—not just for your family, but for Glory as a whole. We're not sensationalized in the news much anymore, but people still know, and they still talk. Unfortunately, we can't just block off the entire west end of town from the world."

"If you want to do something, patrol the area more. Get Glory to pay for a proper fence. Cement over the covert so people have no dirt to touch." It was a mistake to goad the cop, but the shame she lived with—actually needing the covert the way it was for her own purposes—was suddenly suffocating. She wanted Hadley with his too-sweet coffee to feel some of that shame, too. Nina paid the cops well to do as little as they did, at both their conveniences.

The money stuffed into her pocket seemed to grow heavier.

The head cop stared at her with flinty eyes. "Yeah, well, too bad we can't change town history."

Marsden fought to keep her expression neutral at the dig at her great-great-uncle. It stung being blamed, but it wasn't wrong. And she'd half expected it, knowing Hadley would recognize her own dig.

"I called the police as soon as I saw that car out there." Nina's bob shimmied again. "And I'm glad Shine's in town, as she'd be distressed to see this. She always is, each time this happens, considering it's her property—as you're affected, too, Marsden. I was so very worried of what you might see."

"Where is she?" Marsden asked. "Do you know when she'll be back?" She wondered if Brom was with her. If Hadley weren't there, she might have asked Nina, but she didn't want the corrupt cop to know any more than he had to.

"She's at the mall," Nina answered, "with plans to be back after lunch."

The revelation at Seconds—the possibility that Brom had been there with her father that night—had stuck deep, like something caught in her teeth, so she'd decided she would take more notice of her mother's lover. Until now, she'd never had reason to watch him, to even want to acknowledge his presence. But things had changed. She wanted to know all about his days (she already knew too much about his nights). Shine had said his time at the boardinghouse was when he had weeks off from his job. So where did he go during the days? What was he doing to fill his hours when he wasn't busy "courting" her mother, trying to be who her father had been? Or was he simply with her all the time?

Hadley lumbered to his feet, tugged his hat back on. "I'll tell Shine myself if I find anything."

Marsden eased away, her skin crawling as Nina saw the cop out. Of course he would tell Shine himself. He took three of the mini blueberry pies on his way, his hands soft and white and absurdly delicate as he slid them off the plate. She could imagine his fingers on the body in the covert, not being careful at all as he skimmed from it before walking back to his car.

In the bedroom she shared with Wynn, Marsden dug out the pair of old boots from the closet and slipped in the money—she would change the bills for smaller ones from the till later. She used to store her cash in between the pages of books, but then Wynn started wanting to read what she read. She considered putting all of into the bank, but the owner liked to gossip on top of being friends with too many people in Glory. So she'd bought the used boots from a garage sale a couple of years ago, realizing they were just ugly enough that no one else in the boardinghouse would even think about touching them. Beneath the pair of socks she kept pushed down into them, the boots held all the money she'd saved over the years. They held her and Wynn's escape from Glory.

She left her room and went upstairs. It was still morning, but late enough that Peaches would be alone in her bedroom, her john gone. Marsden needed to ask to borrow her camera.

She silently named the girls as she passed their rooms: Kim, early thirties, whose boyfriend lived overseas; Wendy, late twenties, who used to teach Spanish part-time; Bridget, mid-thirties, who talked about one day going to fashion school. Shine. Marsden remembered how once, when she was too young to know that her mother was no longer employed as just the housekeeper, she'd heard a man's voice come from behind her door. She'd thought absolutely nothing of it until later that night when she fell asleep wondering if her mother had actually met someone else and was going to get remarried. If he would ever be willing to drink pretend tea with her.

As she neared Peaches's room, she heard laughter from behind its closed door. Wynn's.

Marsden's heart sank as she knocked.

She really wasn't much different from her sister, wanting something from Nina's girls. But Wynn wanted to learn their secrets, while Marsden had too many to hide—she needed Peaches and Lucy and all the others to stay away.

twenty-five.

SHE SAID PEACHES AND LUCY CAN SHOW ME HOW TO DO MY HAIR AND MAKEUP. *So I can look as nice as I want.*

Lucy came to the door. The scent she brought with her was not her own, but the heavy musk Peaches liked to wear. "Marsden?"

"I was just looking for Wynn."

Lucy opened the door wider and motioned her inside. "Oh, she's with us, in here. She was wandering around the house bored."

Marsden had seen Peaches's room before, but only in flashes, and only when she was helping Dany the times she was running behind—to drop off laundry or ask about bedding, to double-check about a spot on a dress. Sometimes, though, when it was just Peaches, Marsden was tempted to linger, to study the older girl and see past what she worked as. To pretend her room was that of a typical twenty-somethings, that she and Peaches were typical, too, and something close to friends.

Pale pastel floral prints and framed mirrors covered nearly every inch of the gray-papered walls. The bed was a king-size patch of yellow, topped with blue throw pillows, its headboard a panel of cream corduroy. A crystal chandelier sprawled from the ceiling like an oversized flower. Instead of a vanity, Peaches used a long wooden table that spanned the entire length of the back wall, a long mirror propped up on it so that it reminded Marsden of a ballet studio. Shoes and perfume bottles and sparkling coils of jewelry were scattered on nearly every flat surface in the room.

Everything was cluttered, overwhelming; she couldn't help but contrast it with her half of the bedroom she shared with Wynn, where her most important things were tucked into places no one could even see. As one of Nina's girls, Peaches's strengths were her exaggerated good looks, the way she swaggered in her femininity, her desires never a secret. Once, Nina had called her a barracuda, and Peaches had taken it as a compliment. But here in her room, her being a woman felt soft, not like a skill set. It left Marsden confused.

Who was the real Peaches? Where did the lines blur between person and performance? How far did she have to go before pulling back?

"Hi, Mars!" Wynn was sitting in a chair in front of the long table that doubled as a vanity. Her reflection waved madly. "Caitlyn's mom had an appointment this morning, so she had to bring me back early. But look—I'm getting my hair done!"

Standing behind her sister, winding a black lock around the curling iron in her hand, Peaches met Marsden's eyes in the long mirror. The cool smile on her face said she knew Marsden's wariness and was amused. "A royal coming to visit the commoners?"

"If you say so."

Peaches snorted. "It's going to be a bit before I finish, so you might as well sit. Your sister's hair is even thicker than mine."

Marsden sat tentatively on the edge of the yellow bed. She tried not to think about how Dany had yet to change the bedding for any of the rooms. "Thanks for keeping her company." She knew she sounded stiff, maybe even insincere, when she was only feeling awkward. "I didn't know she was home, or I would have found her."

"I don't mind. I've been meaning to do this for months anyway. I know she's been asking." Peaches winked at Wynn in the mirror. "And we'll do our faces together afterward."

"She's eight," Marsden said.

"And?"

"And she's eight. Take her for ice cream if you want to spend time with her."

Peaches sighed, released the lock of hair from the iron, and wound another. "It's lip gloss, not a career choice."

Marsden stared at her in the mirror. "Maybe if we didn't live here," she said quietly, "in this house, or if Glory was any different. Maybe if Shine was anything else."

In the mirror, Wynn's gaze darted from Marsden to Peaches, confused.

Lucy sat down beside Marsden on the bed. "Can I try something new with your hair?" she asked. "You have the nicest hair, and I've been dying to experiment."

Marsden lifted a hand to it, felt the thick, familiar strands. Aside from a ponytail, she hated fussing with it. It was a waste of time, and watching herself try to style it, it was always Shine she saw in the mirror. "No, it's okay."

"Mars *never* styles her hair." Wynn bobbed her head despite the curling iron still attached to it. Her whole head was now covered with spiraling black curls. Marsden wouldn't have been able to do that for her, not in a million years. She would have burned both of them trying. "It'd be really pretty if she tried, I bet."

"Thanks, runt. Very sweet."

Lucy smiled at Wynn. "Your sister's hair is pretty as is."

"Prett*ier*, I mean."

"Nice save," Marsden said. She got up, tired of her hair being the center of attention. "Here, I'll do yours," she said to Lucy. "French braid. I haven't forgotten, I don't think."

Lucy slid into the chair next to Wynn, and Marsden stood next to Peaches. In the mirror, the four of them made for a disjointed image, all different colors and desires. Marsden thought their eyes best said who they were: Peaches's bright, sharp hazel; Lucy's quiet pools of pale green; Wynn's sparkling, curious brown; Marsden's the same brown but wary instead of sparkling, careful instead of curious. She saw the window of Peaches's room in the reflection, too, thrown there by a mirror on the opposite wall. The trees of the covert filled it like a smear of gray shadow. It seemed nearly like another eye in the mirror, watching them, and Marsden dropped her gaze back to her braiding.

"Who taught you how to do that?" Wynn asked, sounding almost hurt as she watched Marsden weave sections of Lucy's hair together, as though a secret had been kept from her.

"Nina, actually, years ago." She'd forgotten until just that moment, and now she wondered about the undertones of the gesture, of the remembered feel of rose-tipped fingers smoothing out her stubbornly thick hair. How much of that had been a gesture of comfort, how much an early mark of ownership?

"Can you do mine like that one day?" her sister asked as Marsden's hands worked. It was taking a bit for her fingers to remember, but soon they were doing well enough that the braid stopped trying to fall apart.

She had to grin at the awe in her sister's voice. For years, she'd been keeping her from seeing dead bodies in the covert, but it seemed Wynn was more impressed with her ability to twist hair together. "Sure." It surprised her that she half meant it. That maybe she actually would. For the moment, the world of the night brothel, the future Shine and Nina threatened, seemed far away.

Peaches tugged at some of Wynn's curls. "Hey, I'm starting to feel like a third wheel."

"I love my curls, Peaches!"

"Another nice save, and *fast*. Didn't even blink, either. I smell a future politician."

"What's that?"

"Someone who works in the government."

Wynn shook her head. "I only want to work here when I get older. In the boardinghouse."

Marsden's fingers slowed on Lucy's hair, listening for more and absolutely dreading it.

"Like a cook, same as your sister?" Peaches's gaze met Marsden's in the mirror, and Marsden saw how she knew exactly what terrified her and actually sympathized. "Or a housekeeper like your mom?"

Wynn shrugged. "I just want to live here, like you and Lucy and the other girls do. Like forever guests—so I never have to leave."

"You know, it was the same for me when I was a little girl," Lucy said. "I couldn't imagine ever wanting to leave Florida. But then I got older, and I realized home was just one tiny part of the world."

"Do you miss it?" Wynn's eyes were on Lucy's in the mirror, curious against sad. "Home, I mean?"

Distress flickered across Lucy's face. "I miss . . . parts of it."

"Do you ever want to go back?"

"I don't think so, no."

"You don't miss any—?"

"Talking about Florida is giving me a headache." Peaches unwound the last of Wynn's hair from the iron and unplugged the appliance from the wall with a yank. She glided her hand down the length of Lucy's arm—Marsden sensed the comfort in the gesture, the need to soothe—then turned to Wynn. "Come help me make punch?"

After they left, Lucy swept her braid over her shoulder. "Just a hairdo, but you see Wynn's possible future." Her voice was soft. "The idea scares you."

Marsden stiffened. "Nina does. My mother. This whole entire town."

"Do we disgust you? Me and Peaches? The other girls?"

"No, I never said that."

"But our work does."

Marsden flushed. "I'm trying to remember they're separate things. I'm not always able to. Glory makes it easy to keep things mixed up." She would know.

It was a few seconds before Lucy spoke again. "Wynn doesn't mean it, you know. About never wanting to leave. She'll change her mind once she finds out about the boardinghouse, about your mom."

"*You* chose to stay here," Marsden whispered, "and you didn't have to. You could have kept running."

Lucy smiled in the mirror. But her gaze was distant, as though she were already partially elsewhere. "Being here, I got used to it, I guess. And then I had Peaches. And Wynn has you, her big sister to watch out for her—how could she not be fine, right? How could you not make sure she escapes from this town?"

Marsden thought of the money she'd saved that still wasn't enough. She thought of what Nina wanted from her and of her mother begging her to stay.

She finally managed a smile in return, but she couldn't think of a single thing to say.

twenty-six.

MARSDEN DIDN'T CARE THAT THE MAYOR'S RELATIVES WERE IN TOWN, OR THAT THEY WERE FROM SOMEWHERE SOUTH OF GLORY AND IT WAS THEIR FIRST VISIT WEST.

She especially didn't care that out of all the hotels and motels in town, they'd chosen to stay at Nina's boardinghouse.

But Nina cared, which meant Dany had to care, which meant all of a sudden, nothing was good enough.

"Let's go over the dinner menu again." Dany pulled out a chair at the kitchen table and flipped pages in her binder.

At the sink, Marsden looked at the large assortment of mixing bowls still left on the counter, at the tiny dots of butter and sugar still sparkling on the backs of her hands. The entire room smelled of the lemon-berry pound cake that was now baking for that night's dessert. It was one of the kitchen's most popular summer desserts, and Nina had asked that Marsden make it specifically.

Marsden rolled her eyes and began to scrub dishes. "This is all because of the mayor's family, isn't it?"

"Yes." Dany sighed. "Sorry, but I'm now wondering about our

choice of salad. And it's early enough in the day that we have time yet to make adjustments."

"What's wrong with a Caesar?"

"It's pedestrian. I know Nina would prefer something more refined."

Nina, wanting refined for the dining room while her prostitutes would be seated in it, dressed to the nines. "How about we just get more of that rocket? It's spicy enough to be different."

"*Too* different, I think." Dany laughed, though she still looked slightly desperate. "What if they complain?"

"Okay, we keep the Caesar, but add avocados and grilled garlic shrimp, and then switch out the croutons for baked parmesan chips."

"That sounds perfect—mind heading out to town to get everything? I'll finish cleaning up here, and then I'm supposed to help supervise Wynn and her friends at a birthday party. I'm already feeling sorry for the poor mother who volunteered her house."

"Sure." And she would stop at Seconds afterward to ask Fitz about a certain photo.

After borrowing Peaches's instant camera yesterday, she'd gone into the dining room right before dinner and taken pictures of the food, telling anyone who asked that she was getting a mock-up for a new brochure for the boardinghouse. Brom hadn't even cared when she'd taken one of him, under the pretense of focusing on the table in the background—he'd been too busy telling Shine another story that had her mother laughing appealingly, appreciatively.

Marsden had hidden the photo inside a book in her room. She'd bring it today and show it to Fitz. *Was this him? The man who might have destroyed everything? Over money, over my mother?*

"Oh, one more thing." Dany wasn't done.

"Hmm?"

"Nina wants more flowers at the table tonight, and Evergreen has the best selection in town."

• • •

She locked her bike at the rack just outside of the garden center, double-checked that the paper bag of groceries stuffed whole into her backpack hadn't self-combusted on the short ride over, and pulled open the door to Evergreen.

Her heart was pounding a bit faster than normal, and it sat in her throat like a tiny, nervous drum. She knew Jude was working, and she had no intention of disturbing him, but still. She'd never been on his turf before. Lunch at the Burger Pit had come the closest, but that had really been Abbot's territory, and Marsden had walked away sure she'd held her own. She'd never really considered Abbot an enemy, though, or the person who would cause her the most grief for having known them.

That person would be, she was coming to believe more and more, Jude himself.

Every second of the day she regretted saying yes to him being in the covert, praying he'd find Rigby's time capsule right then so he could finally leave her alone—just as every second she wanted to ask him if they were going to be friends come fall, if he was feeling safer at home and how his father was, if thinking about his brother was beginning to hurt less.

Inside the store, Marsden faced a sun-washed space, its yellow light afloat with bits of pollen and slow-wheeling motes of dust. Storefront window as wide as the room, crossed with panes. Blooms everywhere, their colors a spectrum that covered all ends of the earth: arrangements of dove-gray pussy willows, baskets heaped with pink and purple and blue cottage garden plants, a stand overflowing with freshly potted geraniums exploding into bursts of oranges and reds.

Used to the intoxication of wild ginger, it took a moment for her nose to react to the presence of other plants, and when it did, Marsden was positively steamrolled with scent, breathing in miles of it— lavender's plushness, rose's tang, the bright nip of sweet peas.

Evergreen wasn't the only florist in town, but it was likely the most memorable—no other place seemed capable of being both so riotous and calming at the same time.

Unsure of what to buy—Dany had said something summery and casual—and wanting to leave before Jude saw her, she looked around and hurriedly decided on sunflowers. There was a huge table display of them off to the side of the room, generous handfuls of their oversize yellow blooms stuck into old-fashioned milk pitchers. They sang of picnics and lemonade and kites on the breeze, all kinds of summery things—they'd be perfect.

That Marsden had once heard Nina say snippily to Dany that she thought they were cheap looking only made them even more perfect for the job.

There were other customers at the display, a group of women swarming over the flowers like bees over honey, charmed by the burst of sunshine-hued petals. She decided to wait them out and moved over to poke at a nearby display of tall ornamental grasses, a fountain of blue-green plumes that went higher than her head. *Pampas Grass*, the label said, and Marsden wondered if it was Jude's handwriting. She could trace out Rigby's by heart, but she had never come across his brother's.

When the chattering women were gone, she turned back toward the table, determined to finally get Dany's flowers.

There was still another customer there, a tall, broad-shouldered man with a stern expression that was, at the moment, annoyed. Cool blue eyes, hair the shade of wheat, pale skin that had somehow escaped the sun. He wore a dress shirt and black pants and carried a briefcase, clearly about to head into an office somewhere. He looked at his watch and grimaced.

Leo Ambrose had never been a patient man.

Marsden's mind went blank, and before she could question what made her do it, she simply turned back around and ducked behind the stand of ornamental grasses.

Apparently, she didn't mind waiting him out, either.

Her bag with its ingredients for dinner was starting to pull at her shoulders, and over the scent of flowers that permeated the space, she could smell the garlic that coated the shrimp, the smokiness of parmesan.

Marsden nudged two fat, feathered plumes of grass apart and peeked through.

Jude's father, still surrounded by summer, was glancing at his watch again, his impatience now nearly a glower.

She could see Jude in the man's features. He'd gotten his tall, lanky build, his intricately sculptured hands, his easy-to-curl mouth from his father. From his mother, his dark skin and eyes and wavy near-black hair.

So it deeply confused Marsden how Leo could look at his sons, be reminded of his wife, and still be able to hurt them—as the story went in Glory, he'd been shattered when Isabel had died. She'd been everything to him—shouldn't his sons by her be just as important?

But maybe it wasn't so much about love as it was about hate—or, at least, trying to get over that love. After all, Shine looked at her daughters and was reminded of a man who'd left her in the worst position possible. Maybe it was just about survival.

"Roadie says you were looking for me?"

Through the blue-green grass, she watched Jude approach his father. His eyes were cold, letting Leo knew he wasn't welcome. Weeks rewound, spun back, and she was looking at the same boy who'd walked the halls at school.

"You've been making yourself scarce at home, so I had no choice but to come to your work. We'll talk here if we have to." Leo's voice was stiff, tinged with resentment for finding himself where he was. Still Marsden could hear the elegant clip of his accent beneath it, still hear its smooth, carefully cultivated tones. Leo, clinging to his East Coast roots despite more than a decade of living in Glory—or, perhaps, because of it.

Jude took off his work gloves and shoved them into his back pocket. "Well, I'm still on the clock, so what's up?"

"I admit I haven't been around as much as I could be, either, since your brother. But I think we should make more of an effort to spend time together as a family."

"I don't think so."

Leo sighed. "You're not going to make this easy, are you?"

"Am I supposed to?"

"Yes. Who else do you have left now?"

"I'm fine."

"You have to stop blaming me for Rigby."

Jude went still, the sudden silence heavy in Marsden's ears. Beneath it, she was vaguely aware of the rest of the shop, of customers continuing to linger over blossoms and blooms and other living things, their soft, approving murmurs a near chant. Her breath made the blue-green grass at her face shimmy and flutter.

"You beat the living hell out of him for years, Dad," Jude finally said. "Don't think you had nothing to do with it."

"I didn't pull the trigger."

"Then you held the gun."

"You'd have to be blind to believe him going to that damn covert with a gun wasn't a long time coming."

"*Eight years coming*—science fair when I was nine, remember? Are you finally going to tell me what you guys argued about that night?"

"No. It's over. Let it go."

Jude shook his head, his face hard. "I can't."

Marsden had had the same conversation with Shine about her father's death, why *she* couldn't let it go. The echo of that moment in the washroom of the boardinghouse lobby rang in her ears now, pushed right up alongside the echo of Jude's and Leo's words, until it all became hard to tell apart.

"*You need to.*" Leo's knuckles were white around the handle of his briefcase, and his words came in a sawing kind of rasp, their elegance shattered. "There are far worse things than choosing to see only what's good and ignoring the rest. Some things are meant to stay buried, and some people should not have to be changed. Trust me."

"I can't do that, either."

"Will you just—"

"Hey, Jude—sorry, but where are these supposed to go again?"

Jude and his father turned to look at the worker who'd come up behind them. He was pushing a wide dolly full of flats of herbs, the colors of the plants all greens and silvers. Marsden recognized mints and basils and thymes, their branches starting to sprawl out of their individual baskets.

"Um, by the bedding plants." Jude gestured with his thumb toward the back of the shop. "Cleared off some space on the display unit for you already."

The worker nodded his thanks, and he wheeled the dolly away, leaving Jude and Leo still gripped by silence and Marsden not daring to move as she peeked at them through grass.

"You know, your mother used to grow plants like those herbs," Leo said quietly. Marsden felt a twinge of pity for him—his attempts at healing things with his remaining son were more than awkward. She thought it was like watching someone try to reach shore in a leaky boat while turned halfway around, and then someone standing on that same shore yelling at them to not bother. "After she died, your brother did his best to save them all, even though she had dozens growing everywhere, scattered all over the house and yard. He even went and planted one out in the covert when he saw that it needed shade, not sun, to thrive."

Marsden's pulse leaped at the words, knew Jude's was doing the same by the stunned expression on his face.

With a slightly shaky hand, she pushed the blue-green grass at her face a bit farther apart, leaned in closer toward Jude and his father, and learned how a seven-year-old Rigby Ambrose, in the name of mourning, came to be the one who changed her family's covert forever.

twenty-seven.

AS THE FRONT DOOR SWUNG SHUT BEHIND LEO, MARSDEN CREPT FROM HER HIDING SPOT AND APPROACHED JUDE, WANTING TO SEE IF HE'D RECOVERED FROM THE DISCOVERY. Still thoroughly surrounded by a backdrop of golden sunflowers, the image of how he looked in that moment gained a surreal quality, like a painting from an era too innocent for the capacity for secrets.

He stared unblinkingly at the front door, as though he could reach through it and drag his father back and shake from him more facts, more details, more *Rigby*.

"Jude," she said.

His confusion at seeing her there was whole, his surprise making her feel bad for having hidden. "Marsden? When did you get here? You've been waiting?"

"I didn't want to interrupt you and your dad while you guys were talking, so I just . . . stayed out of sight. Behind the ornamental grass. The, um, pampas."

"Oh." He exhaled and shoved his hair off his face. His half smile said he was glad to see her, but it was also distracted, full of restlessness. "So you heard all of that, then. About Rig, our mom's plant."

She nodded. It had been his brother all along, the reason why her covert grew all its wild ginger. She pictured a little boy as he biked along the Indigo, how he would have felt the sun setting but kept pedaling anyway. He would have followed the curve of the river's crooked elbow to get to a place with way too little light and way too much darkness.

Rigby had been the beginning.

And fourteen years later, he would be back there again. Not with something to save, but instead with something to end.

Only one time had she known for certain that Rigby had gone to the covert, and it'd been with a gun. Whether he'd been there before that, with a cookie tin for a time capsule, she and Jude had ever only guessed. Now, knowing for sure that he *had* been there before, but with his dead mother's dying plant tucked beneath his arm—it was all too circular, a fated chain of events too close to impossible.

Just how far back did her past coincide with Jude's? From how deep did her family's roots start pulling at his, his at hers?

"You know what this means, don't you?" he asked. "About your covert and how everyone in town says it's cursed, even as they say it's not?"

Marsden rubbed at her arms, nearly cold. Images of the bodies she'd seen in the covert flashed through her mind. "It *is* cursed."

"But for one time, at least, it really wasn't. When Rig went out there right after our mom died to plant that ginger, to then come back and know he was ready to go on . . ."

She looked away, unable to face his need for his brother to have been anyone other than who he'd been. Because in the end, Rigby had thought the same as all the others who'd ever walked into her family's covert and not come back out.

That they were beyond saving.

She could blame them for having that hopelessness, for keeping the covert and its stories going the way they did, even as she was also sorry for them. But really she blamed the whole town of Glory and the scope of its misery. She blamed her great-great-uncle for his madness, her father for leaving, her mother for refusing to. The covert was built right into her, and she was no longer sure that escape was possible.

"Why do I smell garlic?" Jude was sniffing the air, confused again.

She had to smile. "That's me—or my garlic shrimp, anyway. I've got groceries in my bag, for tonight's dinner. Then I came here because I needed flowers for the table."

He glanced down at her empty hands. "Which you still don't have."

"I was just about to grab sunflowers."

"Are you in a hurry?" His gaze was intense, suddenly close to rushed. "I mean, garlic shrimp can wait, right?"

She *should* get back. Dany would panic if she got back to the boardinghouse after the dreaded birthday party and Marsden wasn't already in the kitchen, prepping for a very important dinner.

And she still had to stop at Seconds to show Fitz the photo of Brom, which she'd tucked into the back pocket of her shorts before leaving the boardinghouse.

But Dany could start prep.

And what was one more day of not knowing on top of eight years?

"Shrimp doesn't really keep," she said, "but exceptions can be made."

He reached over and grabbed a handful of sunflowers from one of the milk pitchers. Their stems were thick and sturdy, their heads—frilled with thick yellow petals, centers clotted with seeds, all of it smelling faintly of nuts—wider than her palm. In Jude's oversize hands, the blossoms looked nearly fragile.

He held out the bouquet. Water dripped from stems onto their sneakers, the concrete of the floor.

"My dad's not going to give me the answers I'm still looking for, which means I have to ask someone else. Will you come with me?"

twenty-eight.

FOR THE FIRST TIME IN A LONG TIME, SHE KNEW SHE WAS MAKING A MISTAKE BY NOT LISTENING TO HER MOTHER.

Stay away from Theola Finney, Marsden. Do you hear me? I don't care if your grandmother was friends with her. The woman is nothing but a fraud, twisting lies so they look like truth.

Shine's warnings and distaste for anything to do with their abilities came as regularly as the tide, relentlessly and without real break. They, along with time, wore away Marsden's simple memories of the psychic as a chain-smoking old woman, her laugh like a rusty trumpet, until she became someone with hidden layers, who might or might not wear masks. And after Marsden began to skim regularly, her head filling with more and more secrets, her mind stained with the unforgettable, she began to avoid Theola with true terror in her heart.

And now, here she was, standing in front of the Finneys' café, risking the unraveling of all her work over the past seven years so Jude wouldn't feel so alone.

He stared at the front door, still working himself up to go inside, his face pale beneath its natural brown-gold tones. The afternoon sun blazed down on them, nearly alive in its ferocity, but Marsden saw how the skin of his arms was puckered and riddled with goose bumps. It seemed his need for answers still warred against his fear of what Theola might reveal.

He probably wouldn't have asked Marsden to come if he'd known the truth—that she was, for her own reasons, just as scared of Theola as he was.

On the sidewalk, the café's sandwich board advertised that day's discounted special of a muffin, coffee, and fruit combo. A customer just leaving walked past, carrying a grease-stained paper bag so that Marsden got whiffs of bacon, bread, and cigarette smoke. A strolling couple neared—she didn't know their names, but she recognized them from school, graduates last year—and looked at her and Jude a beat too long, giving them a wide berth as they passed. Marsden would have been more flustered than the annoyed that she was, but for where they were, and that Jude hadn't noticed. She knew that pause. It said she and Jude were lesser, were not like them. But Theola was their choice of battle today.

"You think Oliver might be around for once?" Jude asked now. He nearly had his nose pressed to the window, gazing at the last booth that Theola reserved for her readings. The psychic had never advertised her services, and no one had ever pointed them out. They didn't need to when everyone in Glory already knew where to go.

Oliver Finney was Theola's long-time husband. He co-owned the café with his wife, but no one in town ever saw him or had clear memory of last speaking to him. Stories ranged from his wife having secretly killed and buried him long ago to Theola keeping him locked up somewhere. Others said that he had simply ran one day, as likely to be completely mad as he was to be completely sane and carefully hiding from his wife.

Marsden thought Theola didn't mind it one bit—the rumors of a murdered or trapped or escaped husband only added to her allure as Glory's famed psychic.

"Oliver?" She shook her head. "I wouldn't bet on it. Why?"

"Just that I'm looking for an excuse, any excuse, to tell myself I don't have to do this right now," Jude said. "The sudden appearance of a phantom would work."

"Or, I could ask you out to lunch, at some place far away from this café," she quipped, not minding stalling at all. "Would that work?"

He lifted a brow. "It's a date. Where are we going?"

She had to laugh. Her cheeks burned. "You almost sound serious about wanting to leave."

"I think . . . I almost am." Jude frowned. Then his face lit up. "We could go to the movies. A matinee. Like a comedy."

An Eddie Murphy movie. The one Jude would have seen with Rigby, which he'd let Owen and Karey take him to, because they understood.

"You'd see that with me?" she asked, a small, sweet ache uncurling in her chest. A part of her knew it was just a movie, while another knew it was so much more—Eddie Murphy like this, right now, was . . . Jude saying he trusted someone. Even when he was fragile.

He smiled. And his eyes *did* seem nearly serious, saying that she

217

only had to say yes to continue the game, and he would play along and take her to the movies. He would damn whatever it might mean for him if kids from school saw, and Theola and whatever secrets she still had for him would be set aside for another day. Dark waves fell across his forehead as he nodded, as Marsden's pulse danced despite it all being not real.

"Of course I'd take you," he said. "Popcorn's on me, too."

She wanted to reach out and brush his hair away, for the excuse to touch. She had to stop letting her mind wander to the impossible. Her covert and Rigby's death were why they were even talking at all. How could their normal ever be about things like movies and dates? How could he see her as anything but the girl whose family made Glory the death magnet it was? Even *she* couldn't see past that. The thought was bitter.

"I actually prefer candy at movies," she said, "and apparently the gross kind, according to Wynn."

"Candy also works." His smile was still there, still teasing, but his gaze was different now, more questioning, his eyes locked on hers. Was he feeling it, too? she wondered. Thinking about more, about what else there could be for them, when really they'd only come together to see about the dead? Thinking how once he found his answers, there'd be no reason to keep looking for her?

Marsden sighed and decided to save them from the moment. She did brush his hair back now, careful to do it briskly, with a purpose that said it was time. "Are you ready?"

He took a deep breath and pulled open the door to the café. "Probably not, but let's go."

It'd been years since she'd been inside, but little had changed—the same cracked, fake-leather booths; the black-and-white tiled floor; the chalkboard wall with the menu. She had vague memories of drawing on it while Star and Theola had gossiped, sketching out comically round moonlike faces with a fat stick of chalk—her mother, her father, their unsteady family of three.

The scents of the place were familiar, too, and they tangled in her nose—baked goods, cheese, coffee. The same kind of scents she knew from the kitchen of the boardinghouse, which tickled back to life the even fainter ones of the kitchen of their old duplex.

But there was also the zing of odd herbs, of fragrant tea with steeped leaves that told stories, secrets, truths. The smell of danger.

Theola was sitting at the booth in the back, doing a crossword puzzle and smoking. She looked absolutely harmless despite the eccentricity. An old lady with three cats at home, someone whose needlepoint was of swear words, whose collection of mugs had lots of Elvis ones. She wore what Marsden remembered as a typical Theola Finney outfit—oversize hat with feathers, a dress with a screamingly loud floral print, costume jewelry slabs of color around her neck and on her ears.

As a girl, Marsden had found her flamboyance amusing.

Now she found it deceptive, a disguise.

Theola Finney always had her finger on the pulse of the town—no one could read it as well as she could.

With dark eyes so sharp they seemed nearly shrewd, the town psychic watched Marsden and Jude as they slid into the booth across from her.

"You *did* tell me to come back when I was ready to talk," Jude said mildly. "Though I'm still trying to figure out the invite."

She winked at him. "And I like your face—can't that be reason enough?" Her voice was pitted, a smoky rasp.

"Nope."

She shoved a menu at them. "My treat—whatever you feel like."

Jude picked it up, began to look at it as if he really did mean to eat, and Marsden wanted to kick him under the table.

"And haven't you made yourself a stranger since your mother moved all of you out there to the boardinghouse on the other side of town, Marsden Eldridge."

Reluctantly, she met the gaze of her dead grandmother's old friend. "Hi, Theola."

Theola signaled to the worker at the order counter with a hand while continuing to squint at Marsden through a billow of smoke. "How is your family? How is life working for Nina?"

Marsden felt about as scrutinized as the crossword puzzle on the table. She averted her eyes, folded her palms away, out of sight from Theola's eyes. "Everyone's fine, thank you."

Jude must have sensed her unease. He slid the menu back abruptly. "It's okay, we're not here to eat. Tell me why you asked me to come back."

The psychic blew smoke in his direction. The feathers on her hat bobbed—three of them, white as a dove's, fake promises of peace. "Did I do that, or did I merely suggest you were welcome to come back when you were ready? It goes against my principles as a medium to solicit customers—it's very pushy."

"I think *you* want to tell *me* something."

The worker brought over a teapot shaped like an elephant along with three teacups. Marsden felt a flush break out along her hairline as Theola poured out tea the color of weak grass. She placed a cup in front of each of them. "Thirsty?"

Marsden watched leaves swirl into the bottom of her cup, dancing as they sought to spin a tale. Panic was bees in her head, a thick roar—she had to remember to not touch the cup. To keep hiding her palms. "No, not really."

"It was never about me, was it, the first time I was here," Jude said. "All that stuff you told me about Rig . . . He came to see you."

Theola took a slow sip of tea and set her cup down. "I have two confessions." She held up a finger. "One: Rigby came to ask me about something, and it wasn't for a reading. And two: I didn't have to do a reading to see what I saw—that my telling him out loud what he already felt in his heart wasn't going to change anything."

The words sent a shiver through Marsden. Jude's eyes were as black as jet.

She reached for his hand beneath the table before she let herself think twice. His fingers wove through hers, clamped tight.

"What did he ask you about?" he asked Theola.

The psychic let her gaze slide in Marsden's direction before sliding away again. "He came to ask if I could hear the dead."

Marsden's whole body tensed up. Every muscle strained. Her hand squeezed Jude's.

"Who was he wanting to hear?" His voice had turned fearful, a little boy alone in the dark.

"I didn't ask, because hearing the dead isn't what I do. Now, if he'd asked *you*, Marsden, then maybe he would have gotten the answers he needed so badly."

Marsden's breath was a knot in her chest. "I've never been able to hear the dead, even though I've tried. . . . A lot."

"Bless that stubborn mother of yours, but she didn't do you any favors, keeping you from using your ability when you were a child. Like pruning too early in the season, too aggressively—a plant might never recover."

"She just wanted to be normal, to not stick out."

"And yet she was born into a family whose main legacy is the covert." Theola's eyes flashed, reminding Marsden she was no harmless old lady. "Star was so disappointed that Shine wouldn't embrace her gift. How she was making sure you wouldn't, either."

Gift.

Or, Marsden thought, *curse.*

She would have done nearly anything to be able to walk into the covert and be given answers. To be told she was no more at fault for her father's death than she could have strode into the Indigo and pulled him out herself.

But what if the answers she got were the wrong ones? Ones she would never be able to unhear?

"What did you say to Rig, then?" Jude asked Theola. "Since you couldn't help him?"

"Do you think people come to see me because they are looking for help? To tell them which path to take?"

"Yes. They're scared of making mistakes."

"I think they come because they want to hear they are already right." Theola coughed her smoker's cough. "Because deep down, people already know what they're going to do. They just want me to tell them it's not wrong."

"Why couldn't you tell him he was wrong?" His fingers had become a vise around Marsden's, as though she'd become some kind of anchor. It paralyzed her, him thinking he could lean on her when she was as much of a fraud as Shine said Theola was, as much as Marsden said *Shine* was. "Because he was. He just needed to hear it from somebody."

"Do you believe in God, Jude?"

"No, I don't," he said instantly. Marsden flashed back to the covert when he'd said as much, that his disbelief wasn't a choice.

"I think we might be our own gods," Theola said. "Our own voices will always be the loudest in our heads, telling us what we believe we deserve, deep down. And your brother didn't come here looking to hear mine."

"Then he heard the covert," Marsden said softly, "if you believe what everyone in Glory believes. A hundred-year-old story, right? Touch its soil before you die, and you'll still end up saved."

"Whatever seed was planted," Theola said, "it only grew because it could."

"Did you know what he was going to do?" The question seemed yanked from Jude's core, costing bits and pieces of himself he would never get back. "Even if you didn't do a reading?"

Theola shook her head. "But neither was I surprised. I'm sorry."

For a wild second, Marsden wondered if her mother had thought to ask that of Theola after her husband washed ashore, if she'd known. And if the psychic's answer had anything to do with why Shine hated her afterward.

"So if he didn't tell you anything, and you didn't do a reading, I don't understand why you wanted me to come back." Jude's confusion was encompassing, his frustration raw, swarming the room the same way wild ginger choked out the covert.

"Because what I saw in your brother's eyes that day I also saw in yours that first time you came to see me." Smoke from Theola's cigarette curled around the three of them like vines. "What I still see in them now."

"And what do you see?"

"Guilt. Enough of it to drown anyone if they go out too far." And Marsden couldn't mistake the message she saw in Theola's gaze as it slid over to meet hers. *And I see it in you, too, the guilt over your father.*

But that was all she saw in the old lady's eyes, and she shuddered, relieved. If that was the only guilt she revealed, then she hadn't doomed Wynn—her being a skimmer was still a secret.

The psychic blew more smoke in Jude's direction. "So maybe I just want to tell you it's time you think about coming back in."

"I'm not my brother."

Theola's laugh was just as raspy as her cough. "Then, like I said, maybe I just wanted to see your handsome face again, Jude Ambrose."

twenty-nine.

MARSDEN DEBATED BETWEEN MAKING SANDWICHES AND
SERVING TAKE-OUT CHICKEN FOR LUNCH.

Because sandwiches were mostly harmless, without hidden meaning
and inferred messages. They were like vanilla ice cream instead of souf-
flé, completely unassuming. But she would still be making them, and that
said a lot. It said that she was happy enough to make food for Jude *again*.

Well, she hadn't cooked for him since that first dinner of waffles.
After leaving Theola and the café yesterday afternoon and then searching the covert for a few hours, Marsden had had to help Dany prepare
the house for the mayor's arrival. And so Jude had left, deciding he
would invite himself to dinner at Owen's or Karey's house.

While his parting smirk told her he'd much rather have stayed.

Marsden kept frowning at the contents of the fridge.

But would using takeout be almost *too* casual? She couldn't even
put in *some* kind of effort, especially after bragging about her cooking
skills with still only waffles to show for it?

"Oh my God, get a grip," she muttered to herself as she finally
reached inside for ingredients. "It's just a meal."

She'd already decided on the sandwiches—egg salad, she made amazing ones—when Nina stepped into the kitchen, a flow of pink, from painted fingernails to the blush-toned heels. Even her floral perfume smelled pink.

Marsden looked down at her own outfit of cutoffs and T-shirt, her hair loose and already a bit wild from the heat, and was immediately aware of how sloppy she looked in comparison. As if she didn't care about herself at all.

Other than Peaches, who brandished her femininity as her favorite accessory, and her mother, who clung to it as though it were her last remaining oxygen tank, it was Nina who constantly reminded Marsden of her own face and body. It made her think again about what she was, what she had on hand, how it had a best-if-used-by date.

Remembering now that Nina had been wanting to talk to her and why, her discomfort gained an edge. It sat in her stomach like a cold, greasy lump and her shoulders tensed. She took a deep breath. She'd promised her mother she would pretend. That she'd become an act at least as good as Shine was. To be better than even Nina.

"Marsden, you're alone," Nina said as she walked to the fridge. "I was wondering if Shine was making lunch for you." She pulled open the door.

The comment was unexpected enough that it left Marsden close to laughing. She didn't, but her shoulders relaxed a fraction as she shook her head. Was it possible Nina had forgotten? That she'd actually accepted her refusal to become one of her girls? "No, it's just me." Her mother had not cooked for her since she was a little girl. She remembered there being a lot of orange—semi-burned grilled cheeses, watery bowlfuls of boxed macaroni, tins of no-name mandarin orange slices steeped in thin syrup.

"That's right." Nina shut the fridge, though she'd taken nothing from it. "She was going out with Brom for the afternoon. And where's Wynn?"

"At a friend's house. Then the market, with Dany." Marsden put eggs into a pot to boil. The lump in her stomach melted away—Nina making small talk was convincing her the worst was over. She decided it was as good a time as any to find out if Nina knew anything about Brom's habits. "So when Shine's busy, does he just hang out around here?"

"Brom? No, he's either here with Shine or not at all." Nina seemed restless as she peered into a cupboard next. "I don't know where he goes otherwise."

Marsden frowned to herself, wishing Nina knew about Brom the way she knew about Glory. Wishing *she* knew more, about what she was doing, and why she was even doing it. She still needed to find out if it was Brom that night at Decks, looking to rob her father, or worse. Because if not him, who? The passage of eight years without fresh clues meant anything was possible, as much as it meant nothing was.

Nina moved to stand next to her at the counter, boxing her in as she reached across to lift the lid of the dessert keeper. Inside was the remaining half of a raspberry crumble Marsden had baked. "Suddenly,

I feel like something indulgent. Would you like some?" She reached for a plate from the cupboard and transferred a piece onto it.

"No, thanks." Marsden added enough water to cover the eggs and slowly placed the pot on the stove. As she watched Nina pick up a fork and take a single bite, the lump in her stomach came back, and her shoulders nearly hurt as they tensed again. Her mother's boss and keeper—*her* boss and keeper—did not believe in momentary lapses like eating unnecessary sugar, let alone asking to serve her own kitchen help. She was lingering for a reason, and it wasn't for raspberry crumble.

She had not forgotten about wanting to talk to her after all.

Nina leaned in close, trapping her against the counter again. And when she spoke next, Marsden's world splintered apart.

"I know what you do out there in the covert. I know you're a skimmer."

The air went thin, Marsden's throat, dry. "No."

"Well, yes." Nina pulled away an inch, slipped another bite of raspberry crumble past her glossy lips. "I've been watching you for months, wondering how I could finally convince you to work for me. Then I saw you changing bills at the front desk, hours after you found a body in the covert. Not too difficult to see a pattern once I had all the pieces."

Marsden thought wildly of the times she'd heard noises in the covert, each time concluding it was animals. Each time thinking she'd gotten away with it, had pulled another one over Hadley and other skimmers. And yesterday, so worried about the town witch.

When all along it'd been Nina she should have been worried about.

"Why are you only telling me now?" She forced the words out, knowing she sounded guilty and unable to help it. "If you've known for months?"

"Because now Brom's in the picture, and Shine's getting older. And because I found the money you've been hiding in your room." Nina took another bite. "In those old boots of yours."

Marsden backed up almost reflexively, trying to get away from Nina. Her money. Wynn's. *Their future.* "That's not yours to take," she strangled out. Her lungs hurt with trying to breathe.

"You owe me," Nina said. "What's yours is mine."

Another bite of crumble.

Marsden hoped desperately Nina would choke on it.

"And if I refuse to work for you, you're going to tell Hadley about my skimming," she whispered.

Nina's mouth formed a moue of displeasure at the head cop's name, the same one she used to make over Lucy's glasses. "I think the man is thoroughly incompetent, but yes, I'll have to. Please don't get me wrong, Marsden. You're Shine's daughter, and I've watched you grow up—the last thing I want to do is threaten you with the police, to see you punished. But I had no choice except to take your money. I need you here, working for me. You can even keep skimming if you like, and I won't say a word."

Marsden's pulse boomed in her ears, a destructive rush of despair. Glory turned endless, time winked out, Wynn grew older. "How did you know where to find my money?"

"I didn't. I didn't think you had any at all, considering your wages

230

here. But then Shine came and told me you wanted to leave instead of working for me. She said you had money saved up to go. And for me to catch you skimming on top of that? I knew then that you had to be hiding a good amount of cash somewhere."

Marsden's eyes burned. Her mother had told Nina. She might as well have given Nina the money herself.

Nina patted the corner of her mouth for crumbs with a slim finger before placing her empty plate in the sink. "I'll give you a few days before you have to start. Come find me when you're finally ready. And thank you for the dessert—it was exactly what I needed."

thirty.

SHE SHOULD HAVE KNOWN, THOUGH, DEEP DOWN.

Not that Nina had had her figured out long ago, or that her mother would fail her, but that she was never meant to escape Glory. She'd long been bound to town through circumstance, through the family blood Duncan Kirby had tragically and madly shed in the covert.

Her life was closing in around her. She felt its teeth. Felt its glee. Felt whatever had been keeping her together as well as it had—delusion, blind hope, the very last bit of her childishness—starting to fall apart.

An image of the john who had asked about her at fourteen flashed across her mind, and she felt sick. Where would his hands leave her once he'd paid and gone? Who would she be? How much could she give and still be herself?

She was about to run to her bedroom to check for the boots in her closet, her desperation a sharp ache in her throat even as she knew how hopeless it was to think the money was still there—*Nina was only warning you*, she lied to herself, *she would never take away all you'd worked for over the years, she's cold but not cruel, she helped* raise *you!*—when there was a knock at the door.

She looked up to see Jude standing on the back porch. Through the screen door, his face was blurred, softened, completely safe. He held a take-out bag from the deli downtown in one hand. "Hey," he said, smiling.

"Jude." Marsden blinked, trying to adjust from the fresh destruction Nina had just unleashed to pretending that nothing had changed at all.

"Look, I cooked for *you* this time," he said through the screen, holding up the bag. "It was a lot of work."

Some of the dark lifted from her chest at seeing him there. This boy who drew her to stay close, even while she dreamed of escape. Who she would have left.

She walked over and opened the door. "You beat me to it. I was actually going to make us lunch today."

His eyes glinted, layers of dark browns, glints of gold. "What were you going to make?"

"Um, egg-salad sandwiches, spinach and strawberry salad, and double-chocolate brownies."

His expression turned stricken. "Please don't make me beg for lunch tomorrow. I promise I'll never think ahead again."

Marsden smiled. It surprised her that it felt real. How was he able to do that so easily? "You really messed up today, trying to be thoughtful." Suddenly, she felt the deep need to be away from the kitchen, from the boardinghouse altogether, her dismal future breathing down her neck.

And Jude with his careful arc of a grin was there to see her.

She stepped out onto the porch and instantly the sun began to sear her skin. She was very conscious of his gaze on her as she took the bag from him.

Ever see a forest fire when it's just on the cusp of really catching? Right before it takes on a life of its own, and it's beautiful to watch but also frightening?

Marsden kept her eyes on the food as she inspected what he'd brought. "Bottled lemonade, pizza wraps, and chocolate-banana waffle sandwiches."

"I wanted to bring you plain chocolate-chip waffles, but they didn't sell those."

"No," she had to laugh, "they wouldn't. I think it's a Wynn thing. Thanks for all this, really. It's perfect—e*specially* the chocolate-banana waffle sandwiches." She dared a glance upward at his face, and below the smug shyness, she saw a twinge of irrational regret at not being able to bring her the one thing he'd wanted to. Her pulse beat heavily at her wrists.

That was when she saw the wide strap of fabric looped over one of his shoulders. "What's that?" she asked, pointing.

Jude cleared his throat. The skin along his cheekbones turned a slight pink as he spoke. "A picnic blanket. It's hot out, but I was thinking we could eat outside, if we can find some shade somewhere. And I promise the idea seemed much more innocent when I left the house than what it feels like now."

The pink had spread to his ears by the time he was done, making Marsden laugh again, her nerves rewired to an edginess that felt good. "And what does it feel like now?"

He grinned. It was slightly lewd, and she knew he knew it. "I feel the question is a trap, and so I take the fifth."

He really did need to stop being so appealing. "Pretty forward, considering we haven't even gone out yet," she said, smiling in return. "Not even a matinee."

His grin softened even as his gaze turned hot, full of cryptic things that made her skin feel just as hot, but from the inside. "So if I ask you again, I might not get shot down this time?"

"Unfair." She kept her voice light, even as her skin kept tingling. "The town witch was waiting, remember?"

"I remember wishing we could have gone anyway. How disappearing with you for a bit in the middle of the day would have been pretty perfect."

Marsden's heart did a slow, tortuous flip, and she narrowed her eyes at him. Why couldn't he have flaws that made him unbearable? Like hating small animals. Rudeness. Zero sense of humor.

"I wish you *were* an asshole," she muttered. "It'd be a lot easier to not like you."

Jude laughed, low and quiet. "I like you, too. Even that whole 'gross candy instead of popcorn' thing. I can work with that."

"Commendable." She took a deep breath and stepped back, deciding to keep it—*them*, whatever they might even be—from going any further. If there was a time limit on their being together, she didn't want it close to being over yet. "So, lunch, to be eaten on a highly suggestive blanket—do you care where?"

He laughed again, and his cheeks went pink *again*, and Marsden could almost feel his heat beneath her fingertips. "Nope. Wherever you want."

"Even if there's no shade?" She knew where she wanted to go, but they would likely burn. Still, she'd already decided it was worth it, and she wanted him to think so, too.

"We'll handle it."

She led him to where the front drive met the highway. They waited for a gap between vehicles before crossing the road, and then they stepped off the shoulder into the embankment that dipped down toward the river.

At this end of the Indigo, dry land between the road and the river was at its widest, a good couple dozen meters. Weeds and crabgrass the color of pale hay brushed their ankles, and mud dried to a powdery dust crumbled even more beneath their shoes as they walked. The river gurgled and chattered in the distance, a low, constant non-quiet that reminded Marsden of how the covert sounded, how the wind blew through the trees like voices. The sun pounded down, baking their shadows into the ground.

"Here," she declared, coming to a stop.

They were standing on a particularly thick patch of grass, dense enough to cover up the mud beneath. From what she could see, they were equally distant from both the water and the highway, stranded between the two parallel arcs that cut into the earth. They could have been anywhere in the world, somewhere where neither of them was trying to bring the dead back to life, where they weren't who Glory said they were. Over a lunch, they could pretend.

Jude spread out the picnic blanket and sat down on it. "Finally. I was wondering if you were going to lead us straight into the river."

"Would you have kept going with me?" Marsden sat down next to him and began to take out the food.

"Depends on how deep it is." He lifted his gaze to the snaking current. "I wouldn't want us to drown."

Theola's words. "What if we could walk all the way across?"

"Still depends," he said with a quick grin. He glanced down at the waffle sandwiches spread out in front of them. "'I'll have to really think about it.' That answer sound familiar at all?"

She laughed, liking how he so easily remembered what she'd said about ever making him waffles again. She wasn't supposed to be able to laugh, given Nina's trap had just closed around her. And yet . . .

Jude pointed down the river, squinting in the sun. "If we followed that, we'd eventually end up in Idaho. Ever wonder what's in Idaho?"

"I don't know." The truth was, Marsden had always wondered *past* it, farther away. "Mountains and lakes. Camping. Lots of potatoes. Why?"

"I used to think we moved from there, because I only heard 'back East' growing up. Eventually figured out they meant the East *Coast*. Boston."

237

Boston. It made her think of baseball stadiums, clam chowder, mazes of concrete freeways—the very opposite of Glory. And now it would make her think of Jude. "Maybe you could go visit one day. You have family there, your mom's."

"Yeah. And they have good schools, for when I'm done here. I could always apply for student loans."

"What do you want to study?" The idea of Jude living elsewhere was strange, difficult to comprehend, lonely to think about. Glory was a place not many people seemed to leave, even though not many ever arrived, either. Townsfolk were layered deep here, most families going back generations.

"Leaning toward sciences, just because I suck less at those." He watched her. "You?"

She wasn't even going to bother to lie. "I can't leave Wynn."

"All your family is here?"

"Yes." Marsden found herself glancing in the direction of the covert. "We got a taste for gold a hundred years ago and decided to stay." Even this far away from it, she still sensed the presence of her family's land, the smothering weight of all it meant. She thought of never finding out more, of never being able to hear the dead, her father and Rigby forever questions, and her chest grew heavy.

"Too bad the gold didn't," Jude said. "Stay, I mean."

"I can't imagine how different Glory would be." She blamed the rush of cars hurtling down the highway—a swoosh of sound, what ran along with the wind, stirring up her blood—for suddenly feeling glib, nearly spontaneous. "What would you say to Rigby right now if he were here?"

"This very second?" Jude smiled. "To stay. But if that answer's too much like cheating, I'd ask him where exactly in the covert he'd buried that damn tin."

She had to smile back. "That would be one thought."

"No kidding." He reached for one of the waffle sandwiches and tore it open.

"Wait, that's supposed to be dessert."

"Coming from the person who made me breakfast for dinner."

Marsden began to unwrap the other sandwich and hoped she could make herself eat some of it. The morning had left her stomach in knots, tied by Nina's rose-tipped fingers, even as the wind kept her impulsive. "Jude?"

"Yeah?"

"Remember when we were in the covert and I told you I didn't want to talk about my dad? Right after I kind of did?"

He nodded.

"It was because I never wanted to believe what he said, all this time. But now I know the believing part isn't what's important—because it doesn't change what comes afterward."

He crumpled his wrapper. "And are you okay with that?"

"I'm not sure," she admitted. "How do you accept being the reason why something turns out terrible?"

"Does it help if I tell you half the time I think I'm wrong to be looking for Rig's tin?"

Marsden remembered him coming to ask, all his hope. "So why do you?"

"I don't know. Maybe I'm just hoping to fill in those parts of him I never understood but thought I did. If he kept secrets, did he keep them to protect me?"

"You're talking about guilt." She knew it too well.

He squinted at her in the sun. "So are you."

"I guess I am."

Jude slid closer and took her hand. His was hotter than the sun, larger than the world. "Then let's not drown."

thirty-one.

"KISMET."

"Say again?" Jude shut the shed door behind him, Rigby's metal detector in hand.

"Kismet," Marsden said again as they rounded the back of the boardinghouse on their way to the covert. "It means fate, or destiny— things being preordained. Your brother being the one to start all that wild ginger growing in the covert owned by my family, how that led to all of this."

"That kind of kismet means believing Rig was always going to kill himself, no matter what. I don't know if I can ever believe that."

And she didn't want to believe that she'd always been meant to drive her father away, that Shine was meant to be what she was, that her own path was never in doubt.

"Kismet about Rigby coming here to help him deal with your mom's dying, then," she said. "Because I really, really love the idea of that—the covert not always meaning something is ending. Or how something ending means something else is maybe beginning."

Jude's speckled eyes glimmered in the sun as he looked at her and then away again and Marsden thought of forest fires.

She swore he blushed.

As they walked along the fence, Marsden watched him examine all the carvings left on the splintery wood. Messages like *Think of your family* and *We'll miss you* and *God will save you*. Carvings of dates and names and crosses.

He touched one. The cross was particularly elaborate, his fingers tracing the carefully etched-out details. She wondered ruefully when the artist had managed to get it done, how fast he must have had to work to not be seen by anyone in the boardinghouse. Next, he touched a message about heaven. She knew he had Rigby on his mind, was so deep in thought that he seemed lost in himself, somewhere else. Marsden's throat ached for him and for the grief that came off him in waves.

"The part about heaven being easiest to reach from the covert, how you have to die there after touching its soil so you don't go to hell—do you believe it?" Jude's voice was jagged, as uneven as the Indigo.

She didn't know what to say. *Yes*, and it would settle him over Rigby's choice, however much her opinion could mean. *No*, and she could ask herself forever what her father must have seen in the river to have called him there instead.

Suddenly, he dropped the metal detector into the grass. He took out his truck key and began to carve into the wood of the fence, the biggest unmarked expanse he could find.

"What are you doing?" she asked.

"Changing things up. What's your favorite flower?"

She thought of his doodle for Wynn at lunch at the Burger Pit, his bouquet of tulips and lilies and daises, and smiled. People never just doodled on the covert's fence, they lamented, or wished, or mourned—but now it seemed Jude was doing just that. Doodling. On a fence that went back generations.

"Roses?" he asked.

Marsden laughed. "No."

"Too cheesy?"

"Kind of. And too . . . perfect, I think. How about—" She frowned. She didn't know flowers by heart, the way she knew spices, and salts, and sugars (death, even, she supposed). They had to be in front of her for her to name them. Her mind went back to yesterday. "How about sunflowers?"

It wasn't long before the blooms darted their way in between all the crosses and sayings about heaven. Jude stopped when he ran out of room, and he shook out his hand, its fingers gone tight from clutching his key. He'd added not just sunflowers, but also wavering lines of ivy, firework-like knots of dandelions gone to seed.

Finding a nail with the metal detector, Marsden had joined in, working on a different section of the fence. She'd scrawled nonsense—stick figures, tiny hearts, tic-tac-toe—and it was nearly cathartic how easy it'd been to mark up the covert that way. How she could almost forget how ancient the wood was, how heavy the years accumulated in it, the number of ghosts it'd seen into existence—it was just a fence, just a piece of a long-dead tree, and it had no real power.

"We might have just unleashed a monster, you know," she said, shaking her own hand out, leaving the nail on a post to be picked up on their way back out.

He laughed. "What, there's some kind of covert fence protector spirit? And I thought I'd heard all the stories."

She smiled. "Once Wynn sees this, she's going to want to do the same. We might be out here all summer, inscribing our way around the whole thing."

"I can't tell if you're happy about that or not."

She wasn't sure, either. To normalize the covert was dangerous, somehow almost disrespectful. But maybe she'd been wrong to never try to break down its odd legends, to try to lessen their grip. "Ask me this time next week. If you still need to be around."

Jude picked up the metal detector, brushed bits of grass from the sensor pad, and then looked at her. His expression was both amused and dead serious. "Like you said, this place is bigger than it looks. Sorry if I end up being here all summer."

"Well, there's shade in there, anyway." Marsden averted her eyes—she had no clue what he might see in them. That she really didn't mind so much, his coming by every day until the fall? That she also dreaded the idea of it, the proximity to his danger an abrasion on her nerves, working away at her heart? "Ready?"

They walked into the covert, and instantly the sunlight dimmed by degrees. The smell of ginger enveloped them as they headed to where they'd last left off in their search.

It didn't take long for Marsden to spot the thin white slash of kitchen twine in the half-light. It was tied around the trunk of a tree, and she'd gone back to mark off how much they'd covered the other day. She'd realized afterward how easy it would be for them to lose track, to simply end up going over old ground again and again. Jude never would be finished, then, forever caught in the covert's spell, its toy as much as she knew she was. It was a fact she couldn't change even if she wanted to—the place was in her bones, a part of her before she was even born. As tragic as Rigby's dying here was, it would eventually be crowded away by all the deaths still to come. And Jude could move on. He'd leave his grief behind. He'd go east, find somewhere else to belong, make a life. The covert would fade for him. But Marsden—she would continue to live it.

She was still teasing apart the knot in the string with her fingers when he called her name.

"What is it?" she called back, pulling at twine. "Hold on a second."

Silence.

"Jude?" She looked up to see how he'd gone just a bit ahead, that she could just see most of his dark hair, the jut of one shoulder, some of the wide plane of his back through the foliage of the trees.

"Marsden . . ."

He sounded farther away than she would have expected, his voice almost an echo of itself. As though the covert could bend space the way it could time, could stretch feet into miles the same way it made nights last nearly forever.

Her stomach lurched. She could still see him, but—

"Jude, wait up—this knot, I tied it way too tight . . ."

She trailed off as she watched him slowly back up. One step, then two. The metal detector was still in his hand, but forgotten, about to be dropped.

He turned to face her, and that was how she knew.

thirty-two.

SUCH LONG, BLOND HAIR.

The very first time she'd seen it on the newest girl to sign on with Nina, Marsden had thought of it as Alice hair, what the made-up girl from the made-up world of Wonderland had had. She'd been eleven when she'd thought that, but she hadn't ever really stopped thinking of it that way, despite finding out not long after that the quiet girl's actual name was Lucy. That she came from the very real place of Florida. That the Wonderland that had been her life was something she refused to talk about.

Such long, blond hair, worn in nearly the same kind of loose braid Marsden had woven for her with nervous fingers just yesterday morning.

But its crown had since been dusted with a generous handful of soil, its end now tipped with blood.

It was the first time in a long time the covert smelled of something more strongly than wild ginger.

She fell to her knees in front of Lucy's body and tried to keep the world of the covert from swaying. Lucy's wrists, the blackened soil at her sides, all still glistening with wet. Marsden swept the scene with eyes that moved jaggedly in their sockets, desperate to be wrong.

Lucy and all her sadness, the depths of which only she could see.

"Who was she?" Jude asked, his words faint. He was standing beside her, only inches away, but he might as well have been speaking to her from the other side of the forest, her shock a thick cocoon all around her.

"Her name was Lucy," she whispered. "She lived at the boardinghouse with us. She worked for Nina." Her chest hurt, an ache stinging her throat. She squeezed her eyes shut, trying so hard to hear her. She sent out her mind as though they were fingers, feeling the covert, touching all its trees, testing the wind. It hurt, how much she wanted to hear.

Lucy, you're still here, right? Please talk to me.

"I'm sorry." Jude's voice floated out from the darkness behind her lids, from the deep silence of the covert behind that darkness. "Was she your friend?"

Marsden nodded, opening her eyes. Though, she wasn't sure they had been, not really. Maybe at times, for moments and over the course of conversations, before Marsden hit reset. She knew no more about Lucy than she knew about any of Nina's girls, had never been able to ask, just as Lucy had never shown signs of wanting to share. Lucy, in her own way, had drifted through the rooms and halls of the boardinghouse, just as Rigby had lived yet not lived in his own home. As she and Wynn sometimes lived in the boardinghouse—hidden while in plain sight, their existence carefully portioned out between kitchen and covert and away from the whole place, time spent with Shine and Nina and all the rest spread out thin, easy to tuck away.

Ghosts, all of them.

Barely thinking, Marsden pulled her gardening gloves from the back pocket of her shorts and put them on. She reached out, her hand moving automatically like a dowsing rod over fresh and untouched land. She checked Lucy's clothing, saw the lack of pockets, saw how there was no purse or bag slung nearby. She turned the girl's hands over, pushed back the cuff of her sleeves—no rings, no bracelets, no watch.

Her necklace, though.

A dark silver chain that she'd worn for years, for as long as Marsden could remember.

She would have left it alone, the same way she always left jewelry alone. But because she knew the body, she knew the necklace—knew its meaning and significance. It was a match to the necklace Peaches wore all the time, the one piece of jewelry the other girl never seemed to tire of, for all the carefree ways she seemed to cycle through the rest of her belongings.

Marsden slipped the silver necklace from Lucy's neck and slowly placed it over her own, settling it beneath her long, black hair. She pictured soft, white, greedy hands gathering pies off a plate and shuddered. There was no way to prevent Hadley from the body—she would have to call as soon as she got back to the house—but she would not leave the necklace to him.

She pulled the hem of Lucy's dress lower over her legs and smoothed out the fabric.

She adjusted the dark framed glasses on her pale face so they weren't so askew.

She moved the thick woven braid so it draped over her shoulder again, the way she recalled Lucy wearing it.

Done, Marsden slowly stood up. Slipping off her gloves, she was momentarily startled to see Jude there. He was watching her, his eyes dark and hollow and shadowed with his brother.

Panic was a bow in her blood and strummed her pulse into racing. He had just seen her at work, the unfeeling way she'd flicked on autopilot. Who else but a skimmer could ever do what she just did without going insane? Had he imagined that day his brother had come? Saw it the way she knew it'd been, the day she'd found Rigby in the covert, and felt all of it like a blow? The way she'd bent over him and had calmly dug through his pockets, her face as blank as a fresh canvas even as Rigby's would have been blasted apart beyond recognition? How neither of them would have looked fully human?

She dropped her eyes as she shoved her gloves away. "I have to go back to the boardinghouse now." She heard the odd flatness of her voice, the cold void of her words, and didn't know how to sound different, better. Or had never learned, maybe, had always known what was required of her. "I have to call Hadley about the body. I have to tell Nina, Dany . . . Peaches."

Jude's expression was a slow migration of shock to confusion to a kind of quiet caution. Checking for bodies, skimming—she'd drawn the line between the two as fine as it could get. Only his being overwhelmed kept him from really seeing what she'd just done.

"Okay," he said. "Can I walk you over?"

"No, I'll be fine. I'll meet you here tomorrow, though. Right by the fence, same as always."

thirty-three.

SHE KEPT PEDALING, PUSHING THE HIGHWAY AND THE COVERT AND THE PRISON OF HER HOME BEHIND HER. The sun was getting lower, bouncing off the top of the river. She smelled the heat baking off the Indigo's muddy shores, smelled its damp, marshy, tinny contents.

Lucy had died with the covert all around her. She died knowing she would never get out of Glory, or see Florida again, or do anything different than work as one of Nina's girls.

Marsden pedaled faster, her legs burning. The echoes of Hadley's familiar questions rang in her ears, the dullness of her own robotic responses as she'd held the phone against her cheek and tried to not think about Lucy.

Did you hear anything in the covert before you saw the body, Marsden? Or right afterward?

No.

Were you alone?

Yes. I was checking, as I often do.

Did you touch anything?

I . . . Her dress. I pulled the hem down. I knew her, and I didn't think she would want . . .

I understand. Can you make a guess of how she might have done it?

A blade.

All right, I'll head over immediately.

I'll tell Nina to expect you.

And your mother, of course.

It was only after she hung up the phone that Marsden saw how she'd wound the cord so tightly around them that her fingers had gone purple. Behind her, the kitchen was empty, silent, chilled beneath the day's collected heat. Dany, upon being told the news, would keep Wynn at the market until the last possible moment. Shine, pale and pinch-eyed and unapproachable, had lit a cigarette with white-knuckled fingers and said nothing as she waited for Hadley's arrival. Peaches had barricaded herself in her bedroom. Nina was in the dining room with the rest of her girls, instructing them in hushed tones how business that night would go on as usual.

Marsden fumbled the cord away from her finger; the blood came back in a rush, and she wished it were as easy to sweep clean her mind. Those final images of Lucy—blue, bled-out, celery eyes forever shut— were embedded in her brain, splinters working their way in faster than she could pull them out.

She remembered that feeling, knew what it meant. As it was with Rigby, with Caleb Silas, she'd never be able to leave all of Lucy behind in the covert, would forever be marked with her tragedy.

Suddenly, she found the atmosphere of the boardinghouse absolutely smothering. She had to get away. She ran outside, grabbed her bike from the shed, and simply turned it onto the highway, almost dizzy with panic. The need for escape crawled over her, scraped at her insides.

Instinct, years worth of it, had her bike turning away from Glory, the front wheel wobbling as it sliced through the loose gravel on the road's shoulder. Glory was about feeling desperate and trapped. It was her parents and Nina and all the bodies in the covert. It was all her money gone.

But Glory was also Wynn, and her little sister still needed her.

And Glory, against all logic and anything that made any kind of sense, had also, somehow, become Jude.

Marsden swung her bike's front wheel free of gravel, turned onto the blistering pavement of the highway in the opposite direction, and began to pedal. The memory of his gaze as he'd watched her skim from Lucy, as she showed him just how mechanical she'd learned to be—sickness climbed her throat.

She got all the way downtown before realizing she didn't know where exactly Jude lived. Like everyone in Glory, he would live within blocks of the Indigo, situated somewhere along the river's curve like shingles along the line of a roof. He wouldn't be very close to her—the boardinghouse had the east end of that curve to itself, and only a handful of houses lay scattered between it and the rest of town. After Duncan Kirby's marking of the covert, Glory's townsfolk built outward from it, far from where disease first sparked.

Marsden biked to a gas station. It was the same one where Red and Coop's father worked the graveyard shift; the air hose on the side of the building was still out of order, his sons having broken it back in the spring. She saw the pay-phone booth on the side of the parking lot and peeked in through its dirty glass sides. There was a phone book hanging from a chain, and she went inside and found Jude's address.

It took her another twenty minutes to bike there.

A small house, one level, its beige paint age-stained. Poured gravel for a driveway, and weeds splitting open the yard. A wraparound deck that had seen better days years and years ago, its wood now weathered and gray. There was a wooden chair and table set looking so beaten she was sure the next windstorm would see all of it collapsed, nothing but a pile of kindling. She saw a stand-up telescope in the corner, gone beyond pale with pollen and dust. Its original color was a mystery.

Her heart sank a bit for Leo Ambrose. To have come from vast money out East, and an executive position in a powerful company, to this, on nothing much more than a bad turn of the economy. He'd moved his growing family out for a fresh start, even if that fresh start would have no cushion to fall back on, even if the first hints of a thirst for the bottle were starting to show more and more. And then his young wife had died, leaving him with two young sons to raise. Bottles became escape.

Marsden had already sensed it—the similarities between Leo and Shine, their shared terrible luck as parents, as individuals. But whatever sympathy she could still feel for her mother was only marginally greater than what she felt for Jude's father. Shine, like Leo, had become selective with her love for her kids—the amount of it, the price for it, the whens and hows and conditions of it.

The house had good bones, though, which still showed beneath the years. She imagined it with paint so pristine one couldn't find a scratch for searching. She pictured Isabel Ambrose on one of the wooden chairs, not dying. She saw Jude and Rigby beside her, playing, or hunched over the telescope. Nighttime, the sky clear, Rigby pointing out to his little brother all the constellations he'd memorized from a book.

Living at the boardinghouse, Marsden was sometimes still able to see past Nina's touches to the schoolhouse it'd once been: simple and uncomplicated—clean. Even Shine had her moments—when she sent Wynn to the store with a dollar for candy instead of a note and money and instructions to bring back cigarettes; when she asked Marsden to make Wynn's favorite dessert; when she didn't visibly flinch at being called *Mom* or *Mother*.

She leaned her bike against the front of the house and knocked at the door.

From inside, there was the muffled thump of footsteps. And then it was Karey standing at the door, his eyebrows lifting comically high in surprise at seeing her. But he was grinning within seconds, his long, blond hair shaggy around his face and his blue eyes warm. Marsden found herself smiling back despite her nerves.

"Hey, Marsden." He opened the door and motioned her inside.

"Jude's just in the kitchen. Me and Owen are helping him clean out his fridge."

Her mind scrambled, telling her she should reply even as she wanted a chance to look around the front room. This was Jude's home—how hard would she have to look to see the things he wished he could hide? What he was okay with his friends knowing?

She saw the dents in the lemon-yellow wallpaper right away, like shifts in the late afternoon light—they would match the shape of fists. That same traitorous light glanced off the top of the coffee table and revealed the raised, blurred damage of old moisture rings, kissed from the bottoms of too many wet beer bottles. A pair of old, nautical-themed canvas couches, their cream stripes for the beach, blue for the ocean, cigarette burns on the fabric like boats blistering their way to shore. The dark cherrywood floors Leo had once ordered for Isabel in an attempt to make her feel at home, gone splintered and scraped in spots.

"You guys are cleaning out the fridge?" Marsden looked up at Karey, knowing she'd only repeated him, wondering what she might have missed.

A sun-kissed grin. "Too many well-meaning casseroles from too many well-meaning ladies—they're going bad."

Of course. After Rigby's funeral and wake, the days immediately following would have been too full of difficulty and pain for his brother or father to even think about cooking. The town would have kept Jude and Leo fed out of the goodness of their hearts, because that's what people did; they would have also wanted to get a glimpse of the tragic Ambrose household for themselves, because that's also what people did. Glory brand kindness—it came with a price.

Karey motioned for her to follow him down a hall. "Ironically, Rigby hated casseroles. He'd be pitching in and helping us toss everything."

Marsden heard some of Jude and Owen's conversation as she and Karey neared the kitchen.

Jude first. "—talk about it. Not yet, anyway. It's . . . complicated."

"Isn't it always?" There was the sound of cutlery landing in the sink with a plunk and then Owen continued. "She's got a sweet face, but man, she sure does keep to herself."

"Can you blame her?"

"Not really. So, when are you going to ask her out for real?"

Someone shook out what sounded like a large trash bag. "Drop it."

"It's not like we can't already see it happening from a mile—"

Karey cleared his throat loudly as he stepped into the kitchen. Marsden followed, her face feeling like she'd just consumed an entire ball of fire.

"Marsden?" Jude held a casserole dish in one hand and rubbed his eyes with the other, as though he were just waking up or was seeing things. He blinked at her, his expression thoroughly confused. She thought he looked childlike, innocent, way too beguiling. "What are you doing here?"

"I'm sorry, I should have called first." She took in the mess that made up the room. Black garbage bags were strewn all over the floor, some of them lumpy with contents, some still completely flat. The kitchen counter was covered with tin-foil containers full of food, the table with a plate and fork and even more containers. "I was just . . . out for a bike ride. And thought I'd drop by. To say hi." She couldn't have thought of a flimsier excuse if she tried, and she stiffened with embarrassment.

"And we were just leaving." Owen, even more handsome than she remembered him, slid a pointed look in Karey's direction and smiled at her. It was a nice one, real and open, but she didn't think she was imagining the question there, the slight wariness that made her recall his twin's words: *Don't be someone else disappearing on him.* "Hey, sorry about this mess. Make sure Jude cleans it up on our behalf."

She waved, did her best to smile back. "Really, it's okay, you guys don't have to leave."

"Yes, they do," Jude said mildly, his gaze on her blatant and direct and making her stomach slowly curl up in a semi-painful knot. He threw the entire tin-foil dish he'd been holding into one of the garbage bags, moved on to do the same with the rest of the containers on the counter, and smirked. "But first, Owen, tell Karey what you found."

"Dude." Owen picked up the dirty plate from the table and placed it into the sink. "That bacon and zucchini melt you just inhaled half of? We found blue fuzz on what was left."

Karey snorted unconvincingly. Then he muffled a burp with the back of his hand and looked so queasy Marsden nearly laughed. "Seriously?"

"Like you wouldn't believe." Owen gathered all the garbage bags from the floor and finished clearing the table of tin-foiled sympathy. "How are you feeling? Want to go grab some air?"

"Air? I don't want air. I want to puke my guts out."

"Not in here, you're not." Jude shoved the now very full garbage bag at Karey. "Mind tossing this into one of the cans by the back door on your way out? Thanks."

Karey took it with an overly morose look. "Can I at least grab my basketball? I left it over by—"

Owen shoved him toward the front room. "Tomorrow."

Karey slung the bag over his shoulder and grinned at Marsden and then Jude as he headed into the short hallway. "Behave yourself, kids. And, please, Jude, keep my basketball safe until I can bring her home, where she belongs."

"If you don't stop," Owen said as he walked out after him, "they're going to give your basketball to the neighbor's kids. The scissor-happy ones."

Then the front door shut. Their voices faded through the open kitchen window. Other typical summer sounds trickled inward, breaking up the fresh silence that filled the kitchen—a dog barking in the distance, the faint shouts of kids running through a sprinkler, the low buzz of a neighbor's lawn mower.

But there was a quiet that went deeper than that now, and it was wrapped around Marsden and Jude. It was the quiet of a house forever changed, its makeup altered without repair. It was also the very opposite of the boardinghouse, a hive kept busy with meals, Wynn, Nina's girls, the push and pull of Marsden's schemes against those of Shine's and Nina's. Jude must have noticed it over their dinner of waffles and too-sweet lemonade, and she wondered what had gone through his brain. If it'd been close to pain, or simple grief—if he'd even been able to let himself care either way.

Small but sure signs of Leo's drinking also riddled the kitchen— missing panes of glass from the cabinet, a fist-size dent in the pantry door, a small, crescent-shaped gouge bitten into the outer corner of the wall that led to the hallway.

"A thrown beer bottle," Jude said. She'd felt him watch her as she'd looked around the room, had seen her notice the curved indentation, had then obviously felt the need to explain. "My father's way of asking Owen and Karey to leave. It'd been a long day at work."

Marsden peered more closely at the drywall, and her stomach flipped. "Good thing he has bad aim."

Jude touched the back of his head, the motion so practiced it seemed done without thought. Then he leaned against the kitchen counter, his hands sliding into his pockets. His face said he was still utterly surprised to see her in his house.

"Owen and Karey love thinking they're funny," he said, smiling, "but it's pretty pathetic, right?"

She smiled back. "They *are* funny."

"They wouldn't even try if they thought you weren't cool."

Marsden knew she had never been cool. "Sometimes I forget we've known one another since we were all kids."

His expression was neutral as he shrugged. "We all hung out in different circles."

He wasn't saying what they both knew—she hadn't hung out in *any* circles except the one she kept closed to everyone else at school but herself. It'd been too crowded already, with her mother, her sister, everything to do with the boardinghouse and the covert.

Longing swept her then, an acute ache that beat painfully at her wrists, in the back of her throat, as she dared again to imagine the upcoming fall. They would be strangers to each other. Jude might wave as he walked past, or he might not. She might meet his eyes, or she might not. He would be thinking about schools in the East, how to best put distance between himself and Glory; she would keep stealing from the dead and surviving life in a brothel. How could there be room for anything else?

"Your dad's at work?" Marsden guessed. Now that she saw first-hand how Jude lived, she wondered when Leo would be back. How long Jude could breathe freely each day.

"He works late on Mondays—catching up after the weekend."

Her shoulders relaxed a fraction. Still, the rest of her remained as tight as a wound spring. She hadn't pinpointed her reason for coming over until she was already here. And she still hadn't figured out how to wipe away the person he saw in the covert, the monster who could touch the dead so coldly. She recalled the weight of Lucy's blood-soaked braid and shuddered.

He moved from the counter to stand closer to her. Marsden smelled ginger and earth and him. "I didn't know if you wanted me to say anything earlier, with Owen and Karey here, but I'm really sorry again. About Lucy." Jude's eyes were dark as he held hers, soft with concern. She felt them like a touch. That kindness—it could almost make her cry again.

"They'll find out soon anyway," she said. "If they know to look for that column about the covert that's in the paper."

"I don't know if they do. Or they do, but they don't check it."

The idea of not checking was alien to her, but she also understood it. They didn't live with the covert as she did—it didn't shadow everything they did. Sometimes, she forgot that. How her land, as much as it colored and shaped Glory, was still only a single physical part of it. Why would two regular guys like Owen and Karey ever want to know what was happening in the covert unless they had no choice? They would have done it for Rigby, but that was all.

"Lucy . . . She and Peaches loved each other," Marsden told him. Nina had insisted on being the one to tell her, and Marsden—cowardly, the feel of Lucy's skin still on her hands—had let her. "And they were best friends."

"How is Peaches?"

Broken. Lost. "Not really here."

"I'm sorry." Jude sighed. "She could talk to someone."

Marsden knew he was remembering his own first days, after his brother. The way time must have stopped, even as it didn't. How it might have been like trying to find your way out of the dark, with your eyes shut. "Who did you talk to?"

"No one, really. I didn't want anyone but my friends. It hasn't changed." His gaze sharpened. "You, too. I want to talk to you."

She nearly smiled. "Do you think you might need someone later?" Glory had its share of doctors hoping to help people like Rigby before it was too late, to help people like Jude when it was. They left flyers all over town.

He shrugged, frowning. "I don't know. Maybe. I have the number for the school counselor if I need."

"That's really good." Marsden pictured the school counselor, how she would see him at assemblies and in the halls, his expression as overwhelmed as it was welcoming, and somehow helpless. She wondered about Peaches talking to someone like that. Peaches, who always used clients as much as they used her. Now that Lucy was gone, Marsden could imagine Peaches coping simply by developing more teeth.

But Marsden hadn't talked to anyone, either, after her father washed ashore. Or been made to talk to anyone, anyway, since she'd been a kid. She'd eventually gone to the covert, seeking answers there. Jude's anger with his father had been shattered by Rigby's death, and so he sought out his friends. He went to Theola, to *her*, to the covert to search.

Sometimes, Marsden felt the place *breathe*, made so alive by how much they needed it.

"Rig could have talked to me." Jude's voice was a harsh whisper. "Do you know how many times I've wished I'd been better at saying something to him when he'd been alive? How many times I said nothing at all when I knew?"

Marsden was the one who moved this time. She stood so closely, she could see each of his lashes. "I don't know, but I'm sorry." Had her mother sensed it in her husband? Had she, even as a kid, sensed it in her father in some small way?

"God, we're both so full of sorrys right now." His eyes crinkled just the slightest at the corners when he smiled, she saw. "I can't imagine how hard it must be to listen to us."

She had no choice but to smile back. "I'm counting on not having to say it much soon."

"Hey, so why did you come over? Is it about tomorrow? I totally get it if you want to stay away from the covert for a while. I just feel bad that you didn't call. You could have saved yourself a trip."

"No, tomorrow's fine. The covert—it's always there, and so am I. It's just . . . I was already out."

Slowly, Jude leaned his forehead down against hers. "Marsden, why are you *really* here?"

The light in the kitchen had gone weak, melting its way toward dusk. It let shadows dance over Jude's face and her head run wild with all the things she could not say but longed to.

What you saw today in the covert, I'm not the monster I might have looked like.

But when you find out what I'm hiding from you, I might as well be.

She fumbled for his hand and held on. "I felt like making you listen to some Shindiggs with me."

thirty-four.

"I KNOW HE'S JUST A FISH, BUT I THINK HE'S LONELY," MARSDEN SAID AS SHE PEERED THROUGH THE GLASS. The beta's blue-and-black fins flashed in the water, iridescent and hypnotic, a bruise come to life.

Jude tapped gently on the outside of the bowl. "Nah, Peeve's a fighting fish. It's safer for him to be alone."

"Poor guy. Unless a Mrs. Peeve comes along?"

"No can do. He's just going to have to be satisfied with seeing my pretty face from now on instead of Rig's. I was always the better-looking brother anyway."

The fish had been Rigby's, and now he was Jude's. Marsden leaned down and looked at Jude through the fish bowl. His dark waves became a blur, his features smears of burnished amber, someone familiar and yet not.

"So you know what you're doing as a responsible new pet owner, right?" She sat up again. In the background, his stereo played a Shin-diggs song. They'd gone to Rigby's room and found his *Burn Out* tape.

"Being a pet owner, I think I'm good with—it's the responsible part

I'm still working on." Jude slid the fish bowl farther along his desk, away from the edge. "I keep thinking I've forgotten to feed him, so I'll rush in here, sure he'll be belly-up, too late to save. If you dream more than once about a fear, does that make it a full-fledged phobia?"

"Technically?"

"Sure."

"No clue. But I don't think it really matters."

He looked at her. "Because the dream's still there."

She nodded.

Too many times she'd dreamed her fears, in all their different forms. The dead suddenly not so dead as they caught her skimming, as they buried her beneath heart-shaped leaves. Her father, stumbling from the river, soft and gray and still hating her. A teenage Wynn in Shine's clothes and makeup, telling Marsden she could leave Glory, there was no point in staying behind for her any longer.

A new restlessness filled her, as strong as a tide, and she walked away from Jude's desk, scanning his room to take it all in. She didn't even care if her curiosity bordered on nosiness, or that he would notice. She wanted him to notice, *wanted* him to be aware of exactly how much she longed to see, examine, not miss a single detail about him. That she could be selfish enough to no longer care what it might mean for him, being with her.

Want.

Was that what it was, then? To get close enough to someone that it would be hard to breathe, even as it also, somehow, got easier?

His desk at one side of the room, with Peeve in his bowl and papers and pens and one of his friendship bracelets on top of it. The bracelet courtesy of Abbot, Marsden still assumed, with her pixie hair and loud laugh and blazingly protective eyes.

A chest of drawers next to his closet, with textbooks from just that past school year piled on top—Jude had forgotten to return every single one before school let out for the summer.

A single framed photo sitting next to that pile of textbooks. In it, Isabel Ambrose, her eyes huge and luminous and not entirely happy, her brown skin shades richer and darker than her son's. Marsden thought it was Glory she could see in her gaze, doing its best to crowd out what she'd left behind, maybe making her feel as out of place in the town as Marsden still often did.

At her side was Rigby, a much smaller version of the teenage boy Marsden had seen that day in the library. Her being a witness suddenly felt fated, her memory of those moments what convinced her to let Jude into the covert, with the hopes of then hearing Rigby, to then hear her father. How else to explain where she was now, standing in Jude's room and looking at a photo of him as a baby sleeping in his mother's arms, and feeling not in the way at all?

"Wait, sorry." He grimaced, started scrambling to pick up dirty socks, an open bag of Pirate cookies, a damp towel from the floor. "This place is kind of a landmine, lately." He grabbed a plate with a half-eaten sandwich on it, then a jug of Tang, mouthed the word *sorry* again, and piled everything into one corner of the room.

She laughed. "It's fine. I'm no inspector."

"If you were an inspector, I'd be lighting up quality control with hits." He shoved his hands into his shorts pockets and watched her watching him.

He looked, Marsden decided, like someone thoroughly cornered, dissecting the best way to turn.

Guilt nibbled at her. She'd given him no warning about showing up, was clearly being nosy. "I'm so rude, I'm sorry."

"Why are you sorry, and how are you rude?"

"For intruding. I'm actually kind of wondering if I should leave."

"I was wondering how I could convince you to stay."

Her chest went achy with knots, and fire painted itself along her cheeks. "That was pretty smooth."

"Trying."

Marsden walked over to his bookshelf, trying to act casual. "You have a lot of books."

"Most of them are Rig's." He came over to stand next to her. "He usually gave them to me once he was done reading."

She ran her fingers down the spines, wishing she could have asked Rigby about his books. Why he'd chosen to read one over the other, why he kept the ones he did, how he decided which ones were then good enough for his brother. Horror, lots of sci-fi. "King, Adams, Butler—have you read any of them?"

"Most. Some of them—like those Gibson ones on the side—I got from one end to the other all right, but that's about all."

She pictured Jude lying on a couch with a book, his expression completely lost and close to furious, and laughed. "They're your books as much as they were Rigby's, you know. Not just because he gave them to you, either."

"What do you mean?"

You said are *Rigby's books, not* were. *When are you going to start feeling okay saying* were? "They're just . . . more Eddie Murphy movies that you guys saw together."

Jude's grin held a trace of sadness. "I like that. I bet Rig would have liked it, too."

Marsden moved along the shelf, saw piles of old Archie and Richie Rich comics nestled alongside the books. Bundles of hockey cards, a bright blue yo-yo.

"You've got as many toys on this bookshelf as you do books," she said.

"Hey, comics are books."

Then her eye caught on something that made her smile.

She wrestled out the Magic 8 Ball. The black sphere was covered with scratches and scrapes and dust, a hand-size planet with a liquid core. "For example."

"Wow. I'm ten years old, seeing that again."

"Now you can give Theola a run for her money." Marsden sat down on his bed, already flipping the toy.

"That was my plan all along." Jude sat down beside her, rumpling the already rumpled sheets, and she tried not to think about that fact and where they were and that they were alone in the house.

"I used to have one of these," she said, "but one day the die just stopped showing." The sloshing sound was deeply familiar as she tilted it, as was watching faces of the small die appear through the viewer window, the tiny blue bubbles that accompanied it like froth from a surf. Star had given it to her, too amused with such a thing to not bring it home from the store, she'd told her. Shine had given the Magic 8 Ball a look of disgruntlement but had otherwise left Marsden alone, refusing to say a single word.

Jude reached over and wiped off the dust from the small viewer window with a swipe of his thumb. She passed it to him, and he tilted it. The die inside slowly floated up through blue liquid. IT IS DECIDEDLY SO.

"What was your question?" she asked, realizing she wasn't even joking.

He flushed all the way to his hairline. "Uh, something about dinner."

She laughed, was aware all over again of that word *want*, how it'd infiltrated her brain, her blood, made her reckless. "You're an incredibly bad liar."

"I know." His gaze turned hot. She felt it on her skin.

Acting on absolutely nothing but instinct, Marsden moved to lie down on the bed. She turned on her side, inhaled his scent from his pillow, and tried not to think. "Come here." She touched the bedspread next to her.

He opened his mouth to say something but abruptly stopped. He shut his mouth again, then simply peered down at her on his bed.

Her pulse was a jackhammer, and she felt the first stirrings of a terrible and long-lived embarrassment.

"I asked if you being here was a good idea," Jude said quietly.

IT IS DECIDEDLY SO.

Marsden took the toy from his hand and placed it on the bed in front of her. "So come here. Magic 8 Ball orders."

"I can't." His voice was low, rough as fresh timber.

"Why not?"

"Because. I might never get up again."

She felt her own skin flush all the way from her toes to the top of her head. "There's something to be said about you going all out with the honesty thing."

Jude twisted over until he was lying down facing her, his face only inches away from hers on the pillow. Marsden knew, then, what it was like to have self-control slowly and definitively become untethered.

From the stereo, the Shindiggs song that had been playing suddenly surged into full chorus—*She likes the city but hates the maaaaan*—shattering the odd, delicious tension of the moment, and they both began laughing, hard.

"God, this song is *awful*," Jude finally choked out when he could speak again. "I don't know how Rig did it for all that time."

She wiped an eye. "Didn't you end up having to listen to them, too?"

"You're right, let me fix that. I don't know how *I* did it."

"Hey, they were big for a reason, you know."

"Well, it wasn't taste."

She grinned. "I like them. Don't make me challenge you."

He picked up the Magic 8 Ball. "Do the Shindiggs suck?" He flipped it. "MY REPLY IS NO."

It took them longer to calm down this time, to just let the music play without breaking out into fresh laughter. Marsden knew it had nothing to do with the Shindiggs and everything to do with the strain of the last few days, the covert having slid into their hearts like an uneven beat, into their minds like a nightmare for the day, the pain-pleasure question mark of whatever she and Jude were becoming. That moment of loosening their grip, just a bit—it was like coming up for air before the final plunge.

She cleared her throat and gestured to the Magic 8 Ball. "I have a real question for this thing now."

"Sure. Go."

"Ask how many days until we find your brother's time capsule."

Jude smiled, uncertain. "What?"

"I'm serious." And despite still being half-breathless from laughing, from lying so close to Jude she could feel his body heat, she now also felt a strange chill along her skin, the dance of skeletal fingers straight out of a graveyard. "Because even though it's just a toy, we're also in Glory. And Glory has its own rules."

He nodded, though his eyes remained hesitant. "Only yes or no questions, remember?"

"Oh, right. Okay, so ask if we'll find it."

"Will we find Rig's time capsule?" He flipped the Magic 8 Ball with one hand. "ASK AGAIN LATER."

Marsden frowned. "Ask again."

"I think later means *later* later."

"Humor me."

"Will we find Rig's time capsule?" Two flips. "CANNOT PREDICT NOW. See?"

"Stupid toy."

Jude snorted.

She shut her eyes. Her brain was on overdrive, fueled by the oddity of lying on his bed and needing to find some kind of truth from a toy. She saw the covert, the river, her father, each image seared into the back of her eyelids.

"Can you please ask if I'm ever going to hear the dead, so I can know for sure why my father left that day?" she whispered.

"It's a toy, Marsden." His voice was soft, infinitely understanding.

"I know," she said, still whispering, staying in the dark. In her head, she was running, hands out, soil flying beneath her shoes, ginger as thick as mist in the air. Her lungs hurt with exertion, her heart burst with her wishes—*I'm listening, I've always been listening!*

She heard him ask and then read out the answer. "REPLY HAZY, TRY AGAIN."

"Am I *meant* to hear the dead?"

"BETTER NOT TELL YOU NOW."

"*Now* I know what really happened to my Magic 8 Ball," she muttered. "It didn't stop working—I just threw it away because the thing refused to give me the right answers."

"At least you weren't a demanding kid?"

Marsden opened her eyes. She was staring at Jude's mouth, hovering so close to hers, and decided she wanted, more than anything else at that moment, to taste it. Him. Them, together.

She laid a hand on the side of his neck, let her fingers slide up and around to touch the back of his head, and stopped when she touched a curve of scar tissue.

"Stitches—the doctor never questioned Rig's story about my falling off my bike." His gaze was clear and unflinching. "My father never has bad aim."

She saw in her mind's eye the crescent of a dent in the kitchen wall, smashed in by a flying beer bottle, and knew she could hate Leo Ambrose forever. "Anyone ever tell you the scar's in the shape of a horseshoe? Which means it's a sign of luck."

Jude smiled. "I knew the shape, just never thought of it as a good-luck thing."

"Saving it. For one day."

"Today."

Marsden moved her hand to push his black hair out of his eyes, all thick waves between her fingers. "Ask if we're ever going to kiss."

The Magic 8 Ball slipped from his grip. It careened off the bed and smashed onto the floor behind him with a distinct crack.

He swore, loudly and without restraint.

She felt herself melt, felt her heart ache. "Well, now we'll never know."

Jude leaned up onto his elbow, wound one hand into her long, dark hair, and found her mouth.

thirty-five.

FROM WHERE SHE SAT ON PEACHES'S YELLOW PATCH OF BED THE NEXT MORNING, MARSDEN WATCHED NINA'S PROUDEST WORKER AND KNEW THEY'D BOTH CHANGED.

She wasn't supposed to be anything but happy to hear that Peaches was leaving. Peaches was Peaches. She'd always been abrasive, overly blunt, half enjoying Marsden's discomfort over the years. She had a hard heart, and only Lucy had been able to break it down.

But Lucy was gone, and Marsden never thought she'd see Peaches the way she was now—smaller, faded, beaten, made strangely vulnerable with brittleness. This Peaches, if Marsden squinted in just the wrong way, could easily remind her of her mother.

"Are you headed to Seattle, then, or just wherever?" She plucked at the blue pillow she held in her lap. On the bed next to her knee was Peaches's camera, returned.

Brom's photo was in her pocket. She'd tucked it there before coming to Peaches's room, thinking she would simply drop off the camera and then leave for Seconds. But then she saw Peaches packing, preparing to leave the boardinghouse and Glory. And because she didn't tell

Marsden to go away, Marsden had come inside and sat down, wanting to say goodbye but unsure how.

Also in her pocket was a letter addressed to Adam Lytton with a dollar bill inside, no return address. It was the name of the last man from the covert. She'd found it by flipping through the newspaper that morning. She would mail it that afternoon. One more absolution she would never earn.

Peaches fished in the depths of a worn duffel bag she'd placed on top of the bed. It seemed out of place with the rest of the room, and Marsden guessed it was the same bag she'd arrived in Glory with, hitching a ride into town with Lucy five years ago.

"Just wherever." Peaches tucked sneakers into the duffel. "But first, I'm going to Florida. There's someone there I have to see."

"Lucy was from Florida."

"Yes, I know."

She heard cool danger in those words. "Would she *want* you going to see this person in Florida?"

Peaches smiled, but it was hard and miserable, her eyes too shiny; Marsden couldn't help but think of Jude as he was when he first came to her. Standing at the fence to the covert, nothing but bleak anger in his eyes. Not the Jude who'd kissed her last night like he couldn't get enough, but the Jude who'd already seen too much and no longer cared.

"Ooh, no, probably not." Peaches's wink felt perfunctory, part of an old performance that was hard to shake. "But she always knew I had a hard time backing down from a fight."

"Who is it? Someone in her family?"

"There's a reason why Lucy never talked about her past."

"You know about it, though, don't you?"

Peaches nodded. "It only took about three years of being friends for her to finally tell me. But I'd kind of already guessed, putting together all the little things she'd let slip."

"She said when she got here, working for Nina seemed like her only option. So she couldn't go home, even if she wanted to?"

"There were no legal reasons why she couldn't go back. But she didn't leave home on a whim, the way I did. Lucy left because she no longer felt safe." Peaches carried over a plain jewelry box—like the duffel, it didn't match the room, and Marsden wondered if it'd been a gift from a john—and began to go through it. Her painted nails caught on earrings and flashed through paste gems. "Just because someone is blood doesn't mean they won't hurt you." Her voice was tired, desolate—Marsden heard the anguish of Lucy's absence in it. "Sometimes someone being blood means they think it's their *right* to hurt you."

The image of Jude as a little kid, damaged. Her own mother, begging Marsden to save her. "Lucy was beaten?"

Peaches said nothing, only looked harder at her. "You're sixteen now, right? And Wynn is eight?"

Marsden nodded.

"Well, Lucy was twelve and defenseless, and I guess I'm feeling the need to let a particular someone know exactly what happened to that little girl."

"So they can feel guilty?" Her stomach churned with growing awareness of what might have happened. And she thought of Wynn, who trusted way too much. How she was the one who'd kept her that way.

"No, because guilt means getting to feel sorry, and they don't get to have that. Straight-up shame is what I have in mind."

"Don't get hurt." Don't *be* hurt, Marsden wanted to say, wished could be true.

Peaches's laugh was flat, entirely humorless. "I'll be fine. And I might even be back—I've never hidden that I don't hate my work. I'll decide later, when this is done, when things might start feeling bearable again." Her gaze sharpened, turned knowing. "Has Nina asked you to work for her yet?"

The blue pillow shrank down within the sudden clench of Marsden's fingers. She said nothing. Couldn't.

Peaches moved over to her bedside table, pulled open the drawer, and took out a small handgun.

Marsden sat up straighter. In Glory, guns—real guns, not just the toy ones Red and Coop carried with them—were about as common as bad debts and hangovers, and she saw her share of them in the covert, left behind by their owners. But she'd never held one, was always careful to leave them untouched. "Have you always kept a gun in there?"

Intense grief crossed Peaches's face. "Lucy told me once that she thought she should get one, too, dealing with johns, but I convinced her not to. I was worried she wouldn't know how to use it, or she'd get in trouble if something went wrong. But I think another, smaller part of me also worried she'd use it for another reason, one that had nothing to do with protecting herself."

"She didn't use a gun, though," Marsden said quietly.

"I know. It doesn't change how I wish that that small part of me hadn't been so small." Peaches inspected the gun more closely. "If you decide to surprise the hell out of me by accepting Nina's offer, just know what you're getting into. And remember, aim to maim and go for pain."

"Seriously?"

"It'll be enough to stop them, and in the end, they'll probably still lose it. How very unfortunate."

"Who you're going to see in Florida—you're not going to take the gun, are you?" The possibility had hit Marsden like a slap. Imagining Peaches holding that gun with Lucy in her eyes.

"No." Peaches's lips curled into a scowl. "Though I considered it, because it felt good to. But if she wouldn't want me going in the first place, there's no way I can convince myself that she'd be okay with me killing him." She slid the gun back into the drawer, her shoulders seeming slumped with defeat. "And I only ever got it for work—it seems right that it stays here. I'll have to let Nina know about it before I leave."

Marsden slowly pulled Lucy's necklace from around her neck and off over her head. "I took this when I found her. I know she'd want you to have it."

Peaches reached out and took the thin silver chain. Her eyes narrowed. "You make it a regular habit to lift jewelry from bodies you find in the covert, Marsden Eldridge?"

"I didn't want it getting lost."

"That's not really an answer to my question, is it?" But Peaches slipped the necklace over her head, smoothing down her auburn hair—it looked right on her, just as right as it'd looked on Lucy. Her eyes were wet. "She bought this when she thought she'd finally escaped the past and could stop blaming herself. But I guess you don't really, not entirely. You can knit broken bones back together, but everyone knows they're still not the same. And Lucy felt those breaks more than she didn't. I should have been better about those times she didn't. I should have helped her make them last longer."

But Lucy had heard the call of the covert, Marsden knew, the one made powerful by the dark magic that ran in her family's blood, that twisted Glory into what it was. And whatever guilt Lucy hadn't been able to shake, it drew her to the land's promise of being saved.

It made Marsden hate the covert all over again, for being not just a place of tragedy, but also one of trickery. She hated her name and blood for having written that story, the town for not fighting harder against reading it. She hated herself for still needing the covert anyway.

thirty-six.

SHE SAID GOODBYE TO PEACHES AND LEFT THE BEDROOM.
Walking down the hall toward the lobby, Marsden shivered despite the
summer heat that simmered through the walls.

Since yesterday's discovery of Lucy's body in the covert, a kind of
uneasy edginess had burrowed its way into the boardinghouse. It was
as though whatever invisible boundary had kept the two places distinct was slowly falling away, letting both sides bleed into each other.
Nina's girls, normally a chatty, giggling group, went quiet and thoughtful. It'd been Lucy who had fallen prey to the covert, one of their own,
a reminder that living in the boardinghouse didn't mean they were any
safer from the woods' darker side than anyone else in Glory.

Reactions inside the house varied.

Peaches, of course, was leaving.

To keep Wynn from the covert, their mother signed her up for afternoon swimming camp. Wynn had barely reacted to the sudden loss
of freedom, she'd been so shocked about Lucy.

Aside from quietly serving last night's dinner after returning from
the market and then eventually emerging from her room that morning

to help serve breakfast, Dany claimed migraines and asked to be left alone.

And Marsden had gone to Jude's house and kissed him until he filled her mind and left her incapable of thought.

Only his father coming home had separated them.

The sound of the front door had barely swum through the haze in her brain, until she finally pulled away enough to say, "Someone's here."

"No, there isn't." His mouth was heated and everywhere.

Her skin was equally hot as she chased him back down, wanting to block out the world that existed outside his bedroom.

Then the louder slam of the front door, followed by the muffled sound of Leo's voice. *Jude? You home?*

They had hastily climbed off his bed, doing their best not to laugh, their hands smoothing down each other's clothes.

Jude's father's face was absolutely blank as they'd gone out to the front room to meet him, as Jude introduced her in a rough rasp of a voice that told her he would have given anything to be back in his bed with her, that he would have rather kept her from meeting Leo Ambrose entirely.

His father slowly set his briefcase down on the coffee table, rolled up the sleeves of his shirt, loosened his tie. She looked at his fists and winced inwardly for the little boys Jude and Rigby had been. Family bonds could be ugly. Sometimes they were chains.

"Hello, Marsden, it's nice to meet you."

She would never have guessed—Jude's father could have been talking about the weather, his tone was so indifferent.

"Nice to meet you, too," she lied. A partial lie, anyway. It *was* good to finally see him face-to-face, to finally be able to paint him as the mere human being he was instead of the nearly mythical power he'd grown to be in her head.

Still, she tried not to squirm as he glanced from his son to her, and then back again. Two minutes in his presence, and she longed for escape.

Did Jude feel as trapped living here as she did in the boarding-house?

But he was no longer a little kid. He was just as tall as Leo, his shoulders as broad. Rigby had waited for that. He'd waited until Jude could hold his own.

"It's a work night for me, Jude," his father said. "No one over in the evenings, remember?"

Jude's mouth twitched. "We were . . . reading."

Marsden coughed.

"Well, it's getting late now," Leo said.

She didn't miss the hint.

Before Jude could say anything that would likely make things harder for him later—that he would take her home, that she could stay for dinner, that he actually didn't give a crap if it was a work night—she strangled out an explanation about having to leave anyway, touched Jude's arm, and stumbled her way through the front door. She grabbed her bike from where she'd leaned it against the house, headed down the block, and turned onto the highway in the direction of the boardinghouse.

The just-about-cool evening air had washed over her as she'd biked along the river, calming her inflamed and wound-up nerves deep inside even as it tortured her still-tingling skin. She kept looping it over and over again in her mind—the press and feel of Jude's mouth on hers, his gently curious fingers.

He'd tasted like cinnamon.

She hadn't seemed able to get enough. And it had relieved her, that intense and delicious want. Living at the boardinghouse and knowing what Nina's girls did every night with their johns, a small part of her had always been unsure, full of questions. What if she'd come to hate kissing and being touched and just hadn't figured it out yet? What if having sex one day only disgusted her instead of being something she wanted?

The ache that filled her at having to stop kissing Jude—it was as good an answer as any.

It wasn't until she'd caught sight of the boardinghouse down the highway, its peaked roof sharp in the fuzzy evening light, that thoughts of Lucy began to creep back into her head, unraveling the thick knot of sadness in there so that it started to seep again. Marsden had barely known her, considering they'd lived in the same house for years, but Lucy's absence still loomed large, paving paths full of questions and regrets.

Once inside, she'd found Wynn watching television with their mother, the scene so rare Marsden had had to stare for several moments, processing it as real. Then she went to bed early, trying to forget about Nina's heartless ruthlessness in the name of business, how she didn't have long before she had to go to her mother's boss and admit she was hers. The gaping emptiness of both her boots left matching hollows inside her gut. By the time she'd fallen asleep, it'd been to thoughts of life and death in other ways—of a tall boy with a wicked slash for a grin and whose eyes contained a forest fire, of a girl with Alice in Wonderland hair whose wrists spilled blood onto heart-shaped leaves.

● ● ●

She'd spent longer talking with Peaches than she'd thought, and the lobby was already filling with guests waiting to check out by the time Marsden left the boardinghouse.

Brom's photo burned like a brand from inside her shorts pocket.

Seconds. The one question she intended to ask Fitz. And if his answer didn't bring her any closer to the answers she so wanted from her father—*Why did you leave? Was it me?*—then she told herself she would let it go. Just as Shine wanted. And then after Jude was gone, the covert would be simple again, even more so than before. No more trying to hear voices. No more wondering about her father. It would just be skimming from bodies and keeping Wynn away. There would be a new race to get away from Nina and their mother.

And she would be touched now. She would change and become someone different, someone she didn't want to know. She had no clue how to stop it from happening, and she could already feel a scream building up inside of her.

She'd gotten her bike from the shed and was headed down the front drive when she got a glimpse of Wynn just outside the covert. The top of her sister's head was a dot of black ink against the green of the forest.

"Mom's going to be so mad if you pull a no-show on your first day at camp, runt," she said as soon as she got close enough to be heard. "Aren't you looking forward to it?"

"You mean swimming lessons in a wading pool in Mrs. Clements's backyard?" Wynn made a face and swung her skipping rope harder at the ground. Shorn grass and dandelion bits littered the ground beneath her feet, a cascade of destruction. She was wearing her favorite blue terry shorts and a ThunderCats T-shirt—no hint of a swimsuit in sight. "No thanks."

A smile nearly escaped from Marsden. "It's not a wading pool—it's got real stand-up walls. And it's behind the school, not in Mrs. Clements's backyard. Just because she's a teacher there doesn't mean it's her backyard."

"Who wants to go swimming in the river, anyway? It's mostly mud."

"It's in case you fall in, to make sure you can swim out. Not everyone who goes in can come—" She thought of their father and let the warning peter away, unfinished.

"Mom just wants me to stay out of the covert." Wynn looked up, and Marsden was surprised to see a hint of tears in her eyes. "Even though it's not any more dangerous than it was before."

Lucy, on her sister's mind like a lingering nightmare. "She's just worried about you seeing something in there one day."

"She doesn't stop you from coming here."

"Because I'm older." Because Shine knew she'd do it anyway.

"Dead bodies can't hurt anyone. Besides, it's the house that feels more dangerous now, not the covert."

The hair on the back of Marsden's neck stood up. "What do you mean?"

Wynn whipped her skipping rope and decapitated dandelion heads flew everywhere. "Because no one killed Lucy. It was her own voice, in her own head." Now tears were streaming down her sister's face, coursing over the speck of grape jam clinging to Wynn's chin like a tiny bruise. "I wish she hadn't listened to it, Mars. I wish she'd asked for someone else to start talking over it so she couldn't hear it anymore."

"I really wish she had, too," Marsden said softly.

"Remember how I said I never wanted to live anywhere else in Glory but the boardinghouse? I changed my mind. Do you have enough saved up yet so we can move? We can share a bedroom again, if you want. I promise I won't be so messy."

Marsden's heart twisted and sank at the irony. She'd always been terrified, waiting for the day Wynn would fight her in earnest on the idea of leaving. Now that her sister was all for it, Marsden couldn't make it happen—not with Nina having taken all her money and no-where else in town to get a job. Even giving in and becoming one of her girls didn't mean Wynn would be going anywhere anytime soon.

They were stuck, tiny, awkward flies caught in a jeweled web.

"I don't have enough. I won't, not for a while." The words lodged in her throat, weak and bitter. "I think . . . we have to stay. For now."

Wynn stopped slashing at the dandelions, the carnage coming to a halt. "You were the one who wanted to go so badly. You even wanted to leave Glory altogether, remember? But then I said no so you said we'd just leave the boardinghouse. And now we're not even doing that?"

"I know I said that. But we can't go just yet. I'm really sorry."

"Is it because of Jude?" The corners of Wynn's mouth turned down as she lowered the skipping rope. Her dried paintbrush hair was wilder than ever that morning, and Marsden itched for a comb and barrettes—not so much to make it pretty but more to calm and soothe.

"Couldn't he just visit you, wherever we move? Besides, he's just a boy—they're always around."

"It's not because of Jude." Except that wasn't entirely true, either, Marsden realized, something in her chest twisting anew. She didn't know when exactly it happened, the idea of staying in Glory becoming acceptable as long as they didn't have to also live at the boardinghouse. But she had to admit a lot of that changing *did* have to do with Jude. And she didn't think it made her a bad sister as much as it made her human.

"We *have* to leave," Wynn said. "If we stay here, what if *you* end up sad? And dead? Like Lucy?"

"I don't know that kind of sadness, Wynn. It's more complicated than that."

"She always acted fine on the outside, but she wasn't, not deep down."

"She was really hurt, from a long time ago." Marsden touched the fence and felt the rough edges of carvings of well-meaning messages press against her palms. She saw the flowers and nonsense doodles she and Jude had put there just yesterday—in the bright early sun, they already seemed faded. "And she felt alone, I think, even when she wasn't."

Wynn flung the skipping rope aside and ran to throw her arms around Marsden's waist. "Don't be sad like that. Ever."

Marsden smoothed her sister's hair as best as she could with her hands, her heart now squeezing with worry, with the future, and lied:

"I'll think of something, okay?"

A muffled *okay* against her side.

"Keep away from Nina, and I won't tell Mom you're here hiding from swimming lessons."

And that was how, while Wynn disappeared into the covert to avoid being dragged to Mrs. Clements's wading pool—near the back, where she always insisted the wild ginger started growing in the first place; not because it was the thickest there, the leaves the largest and darkest that could be found, but "because that's where the roots fight me the hardest when I try to pull them out"—Marsden biked toward Seconds.

The wind pushed her along.

A photo in her pocket fanned into flame.

She biked faster.

● ● ●

Between Jude and their afternoons searching the covert, the work schedule that required her to be in the kitchen of the boardinghouse, and the times she spent with Wynn, Marsden supposed it wasn't entirely unforgiveable that it'd taken her this long to get back to Seconds.

The urgency she felt now made up for it. As though the past eight years hadn't even happened, as though her father could still be saved, as long as she finally got her answer.

Marsden opened the door and stepped inside.

It took her eyes five seconds to adjust to the dim lighting and make out Fitz behind the counter, leaning against the back wall. He was puffing away on a cigarette and reading that week's *TV Guide*. When he looked up and saw her, he waved her over.

"A photo, right?" He set the magazine down on the counter and blew out a stream of smoke. "To see if I remember that one guy back at Decks."

She nodded. "The one who knew my father." She could only hope that Fitz would remember one way or the other as soon as he saw the photo: *Yes, your mother's lover was there that night; no, never seen him before. Yes, he might be involved in your father's death; no, he couldn't have been, he wasn't even there.*

Marsden tugged the photo from her pocket. It came out half-creased, rumpled. But still, Brom's face was more than clear, even his oatmeal features made distinctive. She handed it over.

Fitz took the photo, stared at it through a cloud of cigarette smoke, and nodded. "It was him."

thirty-seven.

MARSDEN'S LEGS STAYED SHAKY AS SHE LEFT SECONDS AND HEADED TOWARD THE POST OFFICE.

She couldn't stop from making ugly connections, all the possible scenarios sprouting to life in her mind like bad spots on fruit.

Brom didn't look good in any of them.

He followed her father after Fitz and the others had already gone back inside, unnoticed. Had then robbed him. Had then left him for the river.

Or he'd followed him, saw him in danger from the river, and had done nothing.

Or he'd followed him, killed him, and the river had swallowed up the signs of murder.

Or he hadn't followed at all. Had stayed at Decks, or even gone elsewhere.

But whatever had happened, he'd stayed quiet to Shine about ever being there that night. He'd hidden it—and for eight years. And that, most of all, proved he was guilty. Of robbery, at the least. And maybe even of murder.

She'd wanted to leave his photo behind at Seconds for Fitz to throw away with the rest of the day's garbage. The idea of Brom's face swarming around her father's, and his money, and his night of luck—her stomach rolled.

Instead, Marsden had asked to see Seconds' phone book. She looked up Brom's address and scrawled it onto the photo—directly on his face, admittedly—before slipping it back into her pocket. She would mail Adam Lytton his cash and then she would bike over to Brom's. Shine had a hair appointment in the afternoon, and according to Nina, Brom was never at the boardinghouse without her. Marsden wanted to catch him at home, while he was still alone. She wanted to ask him what he remembered of a night eight years ago, when there had been a terrible spring storm, and as it'd been building up, how he'd been in Decks, watching her father have a winning night.

The mailbox was just up ahead, and she was already holding the envelope of cash in her hand when the sound of her name came from behind.

"Marsden?"

Her heart flew into her throat and she spun around to face him.

His eyes, lit with a smile that made her pulse go uneven, teasing her mind back to his bedroom and his bed and his hands. He held a take-out tray of coffee. Against the backdrop of the dusty road, the sun-beaten buildings and storefronts of Glory, he stood out like a beacon.

"Jude." She hurriedly stuffed the envelope back into the rear pocket of her shorts with fumbling fingers as he came to meet her.

Panic and heat danced a tango in her stomach. "What are you doing here? I thought you worked in the mornings."

He took her hand with his free one, tugged her closer. She smelled coffee and lavender, planting soil, the savory sting of rosemary. "I used to. I just quit. The coffee at Roadie's sucked too bad."

She laughed and he leaned in, kissing her until they both needed to breathe and still they kept going. It was impossible to melt from the inside out, as indisputable a fact as laws concerning gravity, combustion, the speed of light—but she might very well be the first to do so.

He eased away and said against her lips, "That thing you said once about kismet, remember?"

Marsden swam up from through the clouds. *Kismet.* Meaning things being preordained, things meant to be. Fate. "Is your being out here kismet?"

"How else do you explain the coffee machine in the staff room finally busting this morning? That sucker's been on the verge for *years.* Add in my being the only one around for Roadie to force on a volunteer caffeine run and"—another slow kiss that Marsden felt in her toes, the tips of her fingers—"kismet. The good kind."

The presence of the letter in her back pocket turned sharp, a nest of brambles against the denim that poked through to her skin, and she flushed against Jude's lips.

She could easily have been holding cash meant for Rigby instead of Adam Lytton. If not for her involvement with his brother, if she'd somehow been delayed over the weeks in sending it, maybe Jude would have gotten it in the mail that very morning on his way to work. Would have seen his dead brother's name on the envelope and been torn apart all over again.

Maybe it was the fate that simply hadn't happened yet.

Marsden sighed against Jude's neck and pretended that fate was also the wrong one.

"What are *you* doing out here?" He leaned back and peered at her more closely. "I thought you had to check the covert in the mornings."

She stiffened, then forced her shoulders to drop. "I already did. And now I have some errands."

"The post office, right? You were holding a letter."

Marsden shook her head so fast she got dizzy. "No, not—It was something else, actually. But I was just about to head home. I *did* promise someone lunch, if he wants to come over early."

"About yesterday, your friend . . . Well, are you sure you're still okay with my coming over in the afternoons? I can always look on my own, if you'd be okay with that. If you really don't want to be there."

She leaned against him, tried to believe allowing him to be in the covert was some kind of atonement. "The covert is the covert. I just have to deal with it."

Jude bent down and kissed the side of her neck. "Okay, now I seriously have to bring back coffee for Roadie or the guy is going to put me on manure duty again—last time, it took me over two days to stop smelling crap everywhere I went. Want to come over to say hi before you head home?"

"You want your boss to meet me?" she asked, sure she'd misheard.

Everyone in town had already met her, more or less. She had a label, a box in which to stay, making her easy to figure out.

He smiled. "Yeah, I *do* want that. Roadie's a good guy. And it feels wrong that you haven't met him yet."

So it bothered him, then—that she'd met Leo before Roadie. Marsden pictured the garden center from the last time she was there, its stretch of sun-washed display floor, the splashes of color and fragrance and everything that was somehow the opposite of Glory. She'd wondered if she'd see Roadie inside, if she'd get a glimpse of the man Jude thought of as a father. But instead, it'd been Leo who'd showed up, the last person she'd expected to see, his presence like an errant thorn.

"Did Roadie love your mom, you think?" she asked. What made a person love someone who wasn't theirs? Brom and her once-married mother. Her wanting Jude, when she already had the world working against her.

"Maybe, yeah." Jude didn't seem bothered by it at all. "I could never ask, but . . . maybe. When I was kid, I once asked him to be my dad. I was seven, and I remember his face and how I could tell he'd *wanted* to say yes, but couldn't. Seeing him so torn was almost harder than hearing the no."

She thought of her father, who'd said to her face he'd never wanted her. She thought of Shine, who couldn't seem to make up her mind between blaming and loving her.

Meanwhile, Roadie would have taken Jude for his own.

"Sure, I'll come say hi," Marsden said impulsively. "Should I prepare myself to hear really embarrassing kid stories about you?"

"He's going to say me and Rig were a couple of shits, that's for sure," he said, laughing.

"Well, were you?"

"Absolutely. Me crawling around eating garbage off the display floor and giving him heart attacks, Rig drowning out the inventory with too much water. Really, thinking about it, he *must* have loved my mom to have that kind of patience with kids who weren't his own."

And it'd been Roadie who'd given Isabel that first ginger plant, the very same one that Rigby would later save by bringing to the covert. Which still grew there now, so thickly and deeply she could never imagine the place without it.

Just how much did Roadie know about her family? Raised in Glory and as old as he was, he'd be no stranger to the history of the covert, the stories and legends that went with it. Jude had said as much when he'd told her Roadie still recalled the place without ginger, before it'd gained its signature spice, the scent that anointed its bodies. He would have read all about Grant Eldridge's tragic death, the reports about Nina buying the boardinghouse at the east end of the Indigo. And whether he chose to believe or not, he would have heard the rumors about Shine no longer working there as just a housekeeper.

What if he took one look at Marsden and assumed she was doing the same?

What if Jude read that in his eyes? Jude, who'd revealed everything to her in asking for her help?

Marsden was suddenly painfully aware of just how many secrets she was still keeping from him. Rigby's note. Being a skimmer. Trying to hear the dead. Her mother's plans for her.

"Jude." Nerves pulsed in her throat. She felt sick. "You know about my grandmother being able to hear the dead, right?" She didn't see how he couldn't. It was like Theola being a psychic: basic Glory knowledge.

He nodded.

"What do you know about my mother hearing the dead?"

"I assumed she couldn't, since I've never heard of anyone going to her for that."

She took a deep breath. "What else do you know about my mother?"

A second's pause. "She's a cleaner at the boardinghouse."

"You've heard nothing else about her work there?"

Jude looked, she saw with a sinking heart, distinctly uncomfortable. "I've heard the stories, Marsden."

"And if I said they were true?" Her words came out bitterly, pills being yanked back to the surface. A dread that bordered on fear danced on her tongue, pushed the dusty storefronts and dirty concrete pavement all around them further into the background. "How much would that bother you?"

"It doesn't. I admit it did at first. But now I know you, *really* know you, and it's like . . . You're you, and whatever your mom wants to do is just . . . everything else. The rest doesn't matter."

But you don't *know me. Not really.*

"Think of it this way." He shifted the take-out tray to his other hand. Marsden had the vague thought the coffees would be nearly cold by now, and wondered if it meant Roadie would stop asking Jude to go on food runs. "Does it bother you to hear stories about my father, or when people keep trying to guess why Rig killed himself?"

"It bothers me for *you*."

"So, okay, then."

"But what you hear about *me*—that doesn't bother you? How I'm not going to inherit a house or money, just the creepiest piece of land in all of Glory? That I'm destined to forever work at the boardinghouse in some way?" She thought about Nina's threat and shuddered. "I know everyone at school talks about it—about me, who I am, who I'm meant to be. A lot of it won't be wrong. A lot of it might eventually matter to you."

Jude narrowed his eyes a fraction, and when he didn't speak right away, Marsden's heart sank further.

"Going to see you at the covert that first time, all I could hear were those stories," he said quietly. "I didn't know you, so what everyone else said, I listened to all of it. And no, not all of it's wrong—your folks, the covert, those are a part of you, too. But you're also way more than just those things. You are outside of them. You are beyond them."

She blinked so the world didn't blur, but it blurred anyway. He was saying everything she wanted to hear, but he didn't know how she had no options left. How could she tell him the person he'd come to discover was going to change again? That the person he thought was better than all those terrible things was really nothing *but* those things?

Jude leaned close to kiss her, and Marsden let herself pretend again about that one kind of fate being wrong. "Now c'mon, before Roadie refuses to let me back into the shop."

thirty-eight.

"OKAY, WHAT'S THIS ONE?" Marsden held out the flower, unable to keep from laughing at Jude's blank expression as he struggled to come up with the name. "Seriously, shouldn't you know?"

He grinned at her. "But you don't know, either."

"I also don't work here."

His grin wasn't even a bit sheepish. "It's a daisy?"

"Jude!"

The bellow came from across the display floor, and Jude winced, laughing, as a man strode up to them. "Damn, guess that was the wrong answer."

She'd known what Roadie looked like, but only in the same way she knew what all the locals in town looked like when she'd never met them. Seen from across the street, while on her bike, through a store window.

Up close, he looked like he could run any business *except* a plant shop—personal bodyguard, home security, slick casino dealer.

Beard a broad smear of peppered stubble, head shaven clean as a whistle, build as solid as a truck. Tattoos peeked out from his T-shirt sleeves, dragons and hearts and women, all meandering about his arms in shades of smoke and teal and ruby. His eyes were a warm brown, his scowl full of bluster, and he was balancing a honey cruller on top of the coffee Jude had left for him on his desk in the staff room.

Marsden liked him immediately.

"You work in a garden center!" Roadie yelled, inches away from Jude's face. "With plants and flowers! You should at least know the items on the display floor!"

His voice was a sonic boom in volume, each word explosive, and she barely managed to keep from instinctively covering her ears.

"Sorry, I forgot to warn you about him going deaf," Jude said to her in an exaggerated whisper, smiling even as he pointed to his ear, cupping it with a hand. "He insists he just likes being so obnoxiously loud, but really it's because he's getting old. He can't hear so well anymore."

Roadie smacked him on the back of his head. The gesture was affectionate, careful not to hurt.

Jude rubbed the back of his head, turning to his boss with his own mock scowl. "Is that for the daisy answer or the deaf remark?"

"Both, kid. Didn't hear me coming, did you?"

"I was distracted."

"And if I can't hear, then how'd I know you messed up?" He took a bite of the cruller. "It's a gerbera, kid! *Gerbera*. Be a good boy, write it on a piece of paper, and put it under your pillow for tonight!" He took a sip of what had to be ice-cold coffee and nearly spit it out. "Jesus, how far did you have to go to get this? You cross state lines or something?"

"Or something. And daisy, got it." Jude grabbed Marsden by the hand and gently pulled her to stand right in front of him. Her face warmed as Roadie's expression turned scrutinizing, as Jude tugged her even closer, her back resting right against his chest. "Roadie, this is Marsden. I wanted you to meet her and see why I was distracted."

She watched Jude's boss's eyes flicker as he realized who she was—Marsden Eldridge, daughter of Shine, the boardinghouse's delightfully exotic prostitute, and Grant, the man who drowned under mysterious circumstances eight years ago. Even if her name hadn't given her away, her looks would have.

Roadie did a little bow that somehow wasn't absurd, given his size and that he was still carefully balancing his doughnut on top of his coffee. Neither was it, she sensed, condescending or scornful, given what he must have known about her family.

The vise that had been closing tighter and tighter around her chest ever since Jude asked her to meet Roadie loosened a bit.

"It's good to meet you, Marsden!" Roadie bellowed.

"Same here. Um, Jude talks about you a lot."

He barked out a laugh. "Too much, I bet. The kid never shuts up at work, either. Too bad it's usually him complaining about something."

Jude snorted. "Roadie knows I barely say jack at work. Because, catch his attention, he sends you out on food runs—he likes to call it 'volunteering.'"

Roadie smacked him on the back of the head again. Then he ruffled Jude's hair as though he were three years old. Marsden watched him turn serious, how he was full of love for the boy who'd once asked him to be his father. "I tell you, he's a pain in the ass, but it seems I'm stuck with him." His voice was at nearly normal volume—rock-concert level instead of an airplane taking off.

"So, all it took was coffee—and cold coffee at that—to make you quit trying to smash apart everyone's ear drums for a few moments?" Jude sighed. "Even shoveling manure wasn't good enough for you."

"No, it was the doughnuts that did it. And I had to order those in myself." Roadie crammed a huge bite of cruller into his mouth and started talking around it. "Okay, I sent Kelly out on delivery, the others are wheeling in inventory, and I can cover the floor. Why don't you take a few minutes and show Marsden the rest of the place?"

The "rest of the place" was the back entrance and the large, semi-secluded workroom off to the side. Jude told her it was where all the flowers and plants came through for inspection before hitting the display floor—domestic, imported, "whatever happened to catch Roadie's eye that he wanted for the center." Not the hard inventory, things like the giant potted trees and hedges and planters that came into the place on wheeled dollies, but the soft merchandise, what Roadie assumed a girl would like most. "Because deep down, the guy is a total romantic." Everything was already neatly labeled from the supplier, saving Jude from messing up that task. She drank in rockets of color, the feel of velvet against her fingertips: hydrangeas, orchids, and tulips; snapdragons and tea roses; catkin and cherry tree and magnolia cuttings.

"It's *incredible* in here." Unable to keep her hands to herself, she stroked open boxes of blooms, caressed fat stands of bouquets, all of it the very opposite of Glory's hidden prickliness, the town's layered darkness. "I think if I worked for Roadie, I'd never want to leave this room."

"You work with *food*, Marsden. Bacon. Cake. Cheeseburgers."

Jude's voice was surprisingly terse, and she looked over to see him shoving bunches of chrysanthemums across the long butcher's block of a table, making room to toss down bundles of wildflowers to be cut. He seemed set on not meeting her gaze, at concentrating on his hands and his work and being too busy to notice her.

And she wondered if it was because it was the same for him—what she couldn't ignore, had come to accept.

That despite the hundreds if not thousands of flowers in the room, all he could really smell was her.

She went to stand next to him and waited. Her skin felt too alive, overly sensitive, run through with an electric current, needing to be touched. It made her brave; it made her stupid. "Hey."

"Yeah?" He finally looked up, and Marsden thought of how much of himself he'd already entrusted to her, and she nearly pulled back.

Nearly.

"I . . . Thanks for bringing me here," she started. "For showing me this amazing room. And . . . for not freaking out about my mother, and all the things I haven't really been able to tell you yet." She knew it sounded more like a confession than anything to do with gratitude, and she knew that was right, too.

"Don't thank me." His voice bordered on ragged. "You don't need to. It's just baggage, what you're talking about, and I have that, too."

She nodded. Baggage. Together they both had ghosts, a paralyzing need for closure, guilt—what would he say when he saw she had lies on top of all that?

"Do two wrongs ever make a right?" She grasped for words to best shape the ache in her chest, to paint how she wanted him even as she knew she shouldn't. "When it comes to people?"

"Depends." His eyes were midnight, full of raw nerves, as he slowly set the flowers aside. "On whether or not they're making it worse by being together."

"Worse for others, or for themselves?"

"Either."

"And if it's neither?" Marsden slid her hand along the side of his face. Her heart drummed; she saw the echo of its beat in his pulse along his neck.

"Then it's right."

Jude drew her to him, and she pressed her mouth to his, letting herself slowly fracture into pieces.

thirty-nine.

BROM'S PLACE WAS ABOUT TEN BLOCKS FROM EVERGREEN.

She'd left Jude behind at the garden center, in that fragrant, semi-secret workroom, petals crushed onto his skin and fire still lit in his eyes as she made herself step away and out the door. The floor had been covered with a wild sprawl of flowers and stems, the layers of blossoms and leaves that they'd sent scattering across the room as they'd lost themselves in each other. Her lips still thrummed; she could still taste him there.

Later. She would let herself think about him again later.

Marsden jogged back to her bike, still in the alley behind Seconds. She wheeled it out to the sidewalk and turned it in the direction of the address she'd written on Brom's face. She rode past buildings bleached pale with sun and dust, and the heat burned its way into her brain until she was nearly light-headed.

Four grand.

The amount kept flashing behind her eyes, was nearly a visceral flavor in her mouth for how real it was beginning to seem. Four grand, when she'd always thought two would be enough to get her and Wynn away from Glory for good.

Was it also the price her father paid to end up in the cold, muddy waters of the Indigo?

When she reached the house, Marsden got off her bike and leaned it against the tree in the front yard. The place was a duplex, what might have been a cookie-cutter copy of her family's old place, except that it wasn't run-down at all and neither was it very old. The neighborhood was also one of Glory's better ones. Brom was doing well enough.

The outside of the building had been painted a putty shade, tasteful and discreet. A trail of small paved stones split the dandelion-dotted rectangular lawn in two. Brom's half needed a cut, but the whole thing was dried out and crispy from the sun. A pair of large picture windows faced the street—Brom's was covered with a plain blind from the inside, while the other had long patterned curtains.

Marsden walked up his front steps, her hands skimming the black painted banisters that lined them. She had the vague memory of her own house once having the same kind, but that they'd been splotched with rust. She looked at her hands and was almost surprised there was no powdery orange residue on them. Just as she was almost surprised they didn't smell of metal.

She knocked at the door, questions already on her tongue:

Did you follow my father that night?

What did you see?

What did you do?

But no one answered, and Marsden hesitated, uncertain what came next. If she waited even just a couple of hours, she would find

310

Brom at the boardinghouse. His reservation always lasted at least a couple of weeks, and she was sure he'd only checked in days ago.

But then Shine would be there, shielding him, picking him over her daughters again. Marsden would find out nothing—even worse, if Brom *were* involved, he would then know *she* knew. And then what?

Unable to just walk away now that she was here, she circled around until she was at the rear of the house.

The backyard was a wide swath of wheat-like grass, and Brom's half here needed a cut, too. The other side was strewn with water guns and overturned flip-flops and the occasional patch of grass burned even lighter by dog pee. An empty wading pool sat deflated and dejected near the center, a rawhide dog bone alongside it.

She went to Brom's back door and knocked. Silence from this end, too. Wherever he was, it wasn't here.

She turned to go and saw a little boy watching her from the side of the house. His thumb was in his mouth, and he had a bad sunburn.

"Hi," she said. "I guess you live here?"

He didn't move, and then a woman appeared around the corner. She was holding a baby in one arm, a bag of groceries in the other, and looked about done in for the day. A dog bounded onto the lawn, panting and running in circles, the tag on his collar jangling.

"Oh, hello," she said. "Who are you?"

"Um. I was looking for Brom. He lives here."

Her eyes got wide. "Oh, you must be his daughter! Funny, I always thought you'd be younger. Are you here for a visit?"

Marsden felt herself nodding along, even as her head spun. Brom had a daughter? Did her mother even know that?

"Yes," she said. "A surprise visit." Her own words shocked her. What was she thinking? What was she getting herself into?

"I thought he was out of town again, the place has been so quiet," the woman said.

"No, I'm here to see him. But, uh, I forgot my key."

The woman slung the baby over her shoulder, set her bag of groceries on the ground, and began to fish around in her purse. "Here—your dad asked me to hold on to one just in case. You can just give it back to him when he gets home."

"Thanks." Marsden took the proffered key. Well, now she'd done it, she thought as the woman watched her unlock the back door. She had no choice but to go inside.

Blinds all pulled—the walls glowed like a sunset, all ochres and oranges. The air smelled musty, unused and staid. So Brom wasn't even coming home during the days. The boardinghouse—and Shine—had become his life. Until his next week off from his bank job, anyhow, a couple of months from now.

She stood there for a moment, guilt leaving her unable to move. What was she doing? Could she slip away yet without the neighbor noticing?

Her curiosity grew as she debated, and soon she was walking around, inspecting, *gathering*. She didn't know what she was looking for, specifically, or that she was even really looking for anything. Just being there was the closest she'd come to dissecting this man, who now wanted in on her mother's life, without being protectively filtered through Shine's desperation.

The place was small, but tidy; not dull but not interesting, either—basic kitchen, front room, short hall leading to bedrooms and bathroom. Perfectly fine, just like Brom.

Would her mother be living here soon with Wynn? While Marsden stayed with Nina, paying down a debt passed on to her as much as the covert would be one day?

She went to the main bedroom—people slept close to what they most wanted to stay hidden. She would know. And if Brom had secrets going back eight years, he wouldn't let them stray.

The space was sparse and spare: a bed, a chest of drawers, a nightstand—nothing strange, nothing incriminating.

In the drawer of the nightstand, she found blank envelopes, some late bills, receipts. A Michener paperback, the kind sold on racks by the checkouts in grocery stores, reminding her of Jude and his admittance of struggling through Gibson, the mix of pride and sheepishness on his face. Her hand touched a box of condoms, which reminded her of Jude *again*, but this time of his mouth and fingers. With her pulse uneven and a slight flush climbing up her neck, she slid the box out of the way.

Tucked in the very back was a small pile of notebooks. All identical, the covers faux brown leather, the kind people carried around to jot down lists. She pulled one out and opened it.

Names and numbers, in neat columns down the page:

02/12/87–02/25/87

Rm3 0938174 Citi

Rm4 1370322 WM

Rm11 038611 Union

Rm13 275891 BoA

Confused, she took out another book from deeper in the pile. Flipped it open.

06/03/85–06/13/85

Rm4 127890 BoA

Rm5 788994 GWB

Rm6 241417 HSBC

Rm12 080411 WM

Marsden had no clue what any of it meant. She thought *Rm* might mean "room" and that some of the shorthand at the end of each row might have been banks—Brom was in banking, after all—but she wasn't sure.

She placed the notebooks back into the drawer, changed her mind a second later, and tucked one into her pocket. There were so many of them—one being misplaced wasn't impossible. And she felt better having it—as proof, or insurance, she supposed, in case she ever needed it.

There was one last thing inside the drawer. A small stack of photos, held together by a rubber band.

She slipped the band off with fingers suddenly gone shaky and began to flip through the stack.

And felt her heart go small and withered at what she saw. She recalled with a kind of dull, pathetic insistence that she'd always known Wynn had inherited Shine's jawline, cheekbones, nose, hair. How she would have gotten the shape of her eyes, her slightly clefted chin, her paler coloring from her father.

She'd been right.

But Wynn's father wasn't Grant Eldridge, as she'd assumed.

Because he was Brom Innes.

forty.

MARSDEN BIKED ALONG THE HIGHWAY SO FAST, HER TEARS
DRIED ON HER CHEEKS BEFORE THEY COULD FALL. She tasted
the mud of the river in her mouth with each gasp for air. Rocks flew
from beneath the wheels of her bike, bouncing back off the shoulder of
the road like loosed scattershot.

But she couldn't move fast enough. She could never outrace the
truth of Wynn and who her father was, what he might have done. It
shamed her, too, that so much of her *wanted* her father's death to be
on Brom's hands instead of hers, whatever that might mean for Wynn.
Shamed her to the core. Her mind stewed over the idea of bonds drawn
by blood, the supposed sanctity of those links. She and Shine, Jude and
his father, Lucy and her family—no wonder she questioned. Even her
connection with Wynn now felt strained and odd.

A honk from an approaching vehicle startled her, and she slowed
down a fraction. A truck passed her and pulled over to park crookedly
on the shoulder of the road. *Evergreen* emblazoned on the side, forest-
green paint on black, all of it sheened over with a fine layer of dirt.
Behind it, the river coursed brown and the sky blazed blue.

Her pulse leaped.

Jude.

They'd just been with each other, fingers driven into each other's hair, the crushed perfume of too many flowers adding to their lightheadedness. His skin had been searing, his mouth and tongue the hottest.

Marsden should have been scared to let him get that close. She knew he saw things in her that she'd always been so careful to hide before. She didn't have to ask to see the truth of that on his face, the way his eyes couldn't hide a single thing when he looked at her.

Forest fires.

Maybe, even, kismet.

And she wanted him.

Now, as she listened to him cut the motor of the truck, the need to tell him everything came in a flood. Her future at the boardinghouse, being a skimmer, that she'd taken a part of his brother from him—all of it. The relief of finally wanting to admit everything she was eased some of the tension in her gut, told her how wrong she'd been to not do it earlier.

Jude stepped out from the truck and headed toward her. She heard the sound of tiny river rocks crunching beneath his shoes, the dried-out weeds that had blown over from the riverbanks snapping and screaming.

There was an envelope in his hands, white and creased, as though it'd been worked over by disbelieving hands.

Marsden recognized it instantly. It must have fallen from her back pocket. She instantly felt sick. The expression on Jude's face was pure, miserable fury.

She recognized that look, too.

It was the Jude from before the covert. The one still reeling from damage, made raw from the people he needed, the same ones who kept falling short.

And she'd been the one to do that now.

"Adam Lytton," he said as soon as he reached her, staying an arm's length away. His voice was steel, pounded flat and sharp. "I recognized the name from the covert column in the paper. Why would you send a dead man money?"

"Where did you find that envelope?" Her own voice was dull. Delaying the burn.

"I found it on the floor at Evergreen. After you left. Why do you have this?"

"Why did you open it? It wasn't for you."

"I couldn't help it. Seeing his name on an envelope you were just holding made no sense at all, so I needed to—Marsden, why do you have this?"

"I was going to tell you." There was a ringing in her ears.

"I guess I beat you to it." Jude's gaze was unmoving from her face. "So tell me."

"I got the money from Adam Lytton's body when I found it in the covert." Each word was supposed to have come easily. She thought she'd been prepared, hadn't she? But she'd never been more wrong as each one slowly scraped itself to life, proving her horrible. She paused, her longing for time to stop so acute it nearly hurt. The quiet around them blistered; her next words crawled from her slowly and painfully. "I'm a skimmer. I've been one since I was nine."

He sucked in a breath. "For money?" His cold revulsion hung in the air, as thick as the tan silt that made up the river, the mud that birthed it. "Doing all of that just for money?"

"It was our way out of Glory—Wynn's and mine. I had to get us out of the boardinghouse. Watching her get older there, seeing what people did—I had to."

"I'd be the first to tell you that money only goes so far."

"I was running out of time. I still am." *I'm* already *out of time.*

"Why were you sending away money if you need it so badly?"

"It was my way of saying . . . sorry, I guess. Asking for forgiveness, in a way."

His face seemed to break. The wind came off the water and tossed the waves of his hair, dashing grit all around them. The warm breeze was cold against her skin.

"You lied right to my face," he said. "Back at the covert, when I asked you outright if you thought a skimmer could have gotten to Rig before you did. When all along it'd been you."

She said nothing. What could she say that would change that truth?

"Did you take something from Rig? When you found his body?"

"Money."

"That's all?"

Marsden closed her eyes. "A note. It was in his pocket. Four lines, handwritten." She opened them to see Jude's completely torn apart. The colors in them were wild, chaotic, dangerous.

"This whole time, you didn't tell me." His voice was molten. "You made me trust you and want you, and you kept that from me. You knew how badly I'd needed more from my brother. I would have taken *anything*."

"Not this," she whispered. "You wouldn't have wanted this."

"*Bullshit.* That was *never* your decision to make. You were just trying to hide how you had it in the first place, because then I would have known about you being a skimmer. You chose that over what you knew I was looking for."

"I didn't want you hurt, having to read it, seeing it for yourself. Doesn't that matter to you? That I cared?"

His expression darkened, became cutting and cruel. "Not nearly enough. *You* don't matter nearly enough. You barely matter at all."

A series of cars slung themselves along the highway, and Marsden heard a catcall from one driver's-side window. It meant nothing and the sun was useless and something in her chest felt splintered.

"Tell me what he wrote," he demanded bitingly. "The note."

She knew he would hate her, would never forget the sound of her voice saying Rigby's last words. "Jude—"

"Goddamn it, Marsden. *Please.*"

"Your brother . . . he wrote, 'I'm sorry, Jude, I never wanted you to know. I told myself it was Dad. I didn't want to stop. But I didn't mean to do it.'"

She watched his eyes absorb his brother's words, try madly to untangle the puzzle that they were and make sense of them. "What was he talking about? Do what?"

She remembered how she'd thought of violence, reading those words, and how she hadn't been sure what that meant. "Killing himself, what else could—"

"No, because he *did* mean to do that—he walked into your covert all on his own." Jude shook his head. "So he told himself *who* was Dad? He never wanted me to know *what*? It doesn't make sense."

Suddenly, his fury died away, and his expression turned uncertain, and Marsden felt it in her own bones—the other ways Rigby's words could be read, if you dared to. And the image that bloomed in her mind wasn't how he'd looked as she'd stood over his dead body in the covert, but how *he* might have looked standing over someone else's.

She watched that same image cross Jude's face like a shadow, linger there like a bruise. One dealt not by his father, but by his beloved brother.

"What else did he write?" His eyes, emptier than she'd ever seen them, utterly desperate. "*Those were not my brother's last words.*"

She shook her head slowly, unable to say a thing.

Marsden watched him be devastated, be buried beneath the depths of her and his brother's betrayals, and was absolutely numb as he got back in the truck and sped away.

forty-one.

SHE WAITED THERE FOR A FEW MOMENTS—HEART IN HER MOUTH, PULSE THICK AND PAINFUL IN HER VEINS—AND HEARD NOTHING BUT HER OWN SHALLOW BREATHING. The summer sun was a ball of flames, but she was so frozen, she wondered if she'd ever thaw out. Alongside her, the river gurgled and giggled and made her shiver.

When she'd read all the old fairy tales as a kid, she'd sometimes imagined herself as one of their princesses in trouble. Just waiting, sure she would be rescued by her special prince, whether it be from a dragon-guarded castle or moat-encircled tower or forest thick with poisonous trees. All she had to do was wait, and he'd come.

But no tale had ever covered being rescued from the shore of a river that was the color of mud. Or a covert stained with old blood. Or a town that was pitted with greed, made into a trap by its own people.

And Marsden especially couldn't think of a single story about someone being rescued when they were the ones who messed things up in the first place.

She was the dragon, the moat, the poison.

Jude wasn't coming back. His fury had been alive, absolute, his certainty of her guilt without a single doubt. He wasn't suddenly going to understand what she'd done, turn around on the road, and say *Marsden, you've been lying to me ever since I came to you for help, have just destroyed what I have left of my big brother, and made me think you were someone you weren't just so I wouldn't hate you, but I'm actually okay with all that. So you want to keep digging in the covert together?*

She got on her bike, swung it out onto the shoulder of the highway, and headed toward the center of Glory, moving as fast as she could.

To find him.

• • •

By the time she got downtown, road dust in her mouth and on her skin like a coating of ash, the sun had dropped past the midway point, shining down on the back of her neck instead of the top of her head.

Late afternoon. She should have been at the covert with Jude, dragging Rigby's old metal detector over the ground. Her chest pounded, was spiked with nerves as she biked along the streets and down the blocks, her eyes looking for him. She passed Evergreen, passed Seconds, and nearly rode right past the café, where his work truck was parked.

Theola.

Resentment for her grandmother's old friend rose in her, black and tidal. Wasn't it bad enough that Marsden had been born into a family with an ancestor so infamous that simply saying his name aloud gave people the chills, sure they'd just invited the devil into their homes? That her grandmother also had to be friends with a person who gazed at palms and read their secret lines? Someone who glanced at mushed-up dregs in the bottoms of cups and then claimed they spoke of the future?

She leaned her bike against the outer wall of the café and strode inside.

It was the business lull between lunch and the late-afternoon snack rush, and she was the only customer in the place. No sign of Jude at all.

Theola sat in her booth in the back, her ever-watchful eyes fixed on Marsden. As though she'd been waiting for her, had known she would return to hear what had been left unsaid in the presence of Jude. The thought came bitterly, her wondering how Theola kept it all straight, the desperation of the people who came to talk to her, how to best price their ghosts and guilts and tragedies.

The psychic beckoned to her—her hat was especially flashy today, gold and wide-brimmed, and the smoky black feathers on it bobbed deeply with the gesture—and Marsden, sure she was making a mistake, walked over.

"Phoenix feathers," Theola said, pointing at her hat as soon as Marsden sat down. "The man who made this hat for me—Lewis, who owns the costumer's shop a few blocks away? He still has such a crush on me, the old sweetie—said he did it after dreaming of the sun being set on fire, before it let itself be burned up so that it could glow even brighter. How coming from ashes only made it stronger."

"I'm not here to talk about the sun." Why *was* she there when she should be looking for Jude? He wasn't there—she should have turned right around and left already. Had she really wanted a reading but couldn't admit it to herself? Did she need to find out what was in store for her now? "Or about phoenix feathers." Or the ashes of her past.

In her smoker's rasp, Theola called to the order counter for banana smoothies. An old man emerged from the kitchen, cursing someone named Darby for calling in sick and griping about how the hell was he going to get any of the paperwork done if he was out there cutting up damn bananas.

The mysterious Oliver Finney, Marsden guessed, finally willed into existence in order to work the blender. She would have to remember to tell Jude about the rare sighting, then she realized he wouldn't want to hear anything from her at all.

Theola pushed aside her crossword puzzle—it was the same one she'd been working on last time, Marsden saw—so that only the elephant teapot and a set of cups sat between them. "You're looking for Jude."

"How did you know?" Her dark eyes already giving up her thoughts, when she'd always counted on them.

"His truck's parked right outside," Theola said.

"Oh."

"And you wouldn't ever come to see me on your own. I have come to be, thanks to your mother, somewhat of an enemy to you."

Marsden's face flamed as she wondered again just how much her eyes were revealing. Hadn't she just had hateful thoughts about the psychic before coming inside?

"Shine wouldn't approve of this visit," Theola said.

"I'm not my mother."

"No, you aren't. You're much more like Star."

"I am?" Because Marsden had never heard the dead, not even once in all her hours spent in the covert.

"You're sitting here, aren't you?"

The storm in Marsden's stomach churned. Could anyone ever really be ready to hear about the rest of their life? "I want to request a reading. Because I have something to ask you."

Theola moved the elephant teapot to the side. The white ceramic cups, too. "I don't need to do a technical reading to answer your question. And I can't ask you to pay—not for something so obvious to me."

More than uncomfortable now, it was all Marsden could do not to avert her eyes. Was Theola prying into her brain right that very second? Seeing through the tops of her hands right down to her palms and all their telltale signs? What did she think she was going to ask?

"I'm not asking about my father," she said. "You were hinting at him the last time I was in here, remember? Not with words, but I still knew."

"Of course I remember that. I also remember how on edge you were, skittish as a mouse. And you're that way now, but over something else altogether."

"I'm not . . . on edge."

Theola laughed, a rough tinkle of sound. "You might have your father's eyes, full of secrets you're too good at hiding away, but Jude Ambrose is written all over the rest of you."

The old woman's gaze was sharp, too aware, and Marsden couldn't meet it. She glanced out the window, saw a portion of Roadie's work truck, and considered again why she'd chosen to stay after she'd realized Jude was nowhere to be seen. From behind the front counter came the sound of the blender, the sweet scent of ripe fruit, a hint of what she recognized to be star anise.

She'd have to try that one day, she thought distractedly, however reluctant Wynn was at trying anything new. Maybe the next time she asked for homemade muffins.

Her little sister *had* to get used to trying new things. The realization came with a spurt of annoyance. When they left Glory, they'd be leaving everything behind, after all. They'd already talked about it, dozens of times once Marsden knew Wynn could keep her plans a secret.

It'd been hard to wait as long as she did, since she'd needed to spin her reasons to suit a little girl simply tired of too many rules. Having to eat hidden away. Not being able to stay inside. Living in a house where certain areas were off limits. Marsden guessed if she waited too long, Wynn would begin to poke holes in all those reasons and demand better ones before agreeing to leave. It would make Marsden have to tell her more about the boardinghouse and how Nina really ran it. She would have to consider telling her sister about their mother.

Wynn was still mostly excited about leaving. Marsden knew she thought of it as an adventure, and that she liked Marsden secretly planning with her. They spoke of how they would decorate their bedrooms, and how they would stay inside all day long if they wanted to. Wynn could finally have pets. And Marsden would cook Chinese food for her. She'd bake Wynn egg tarts, exactly how Star had showed her to make them.

"He's stronger than he thinks he is, you know."

She looked at Theola.

"Rigby dying the way he did is leaving him feeling about as helpless as a newborn deer stumbling along the highway. But Jude will get his footing and, eventually, walk away just fine. Same as how you've grown beyond Shine by refusing to be blind—by working with the covert instead of fighting it."

Marsden felt like she'd been fighting her family and its history her entire life. Because if she stopped, she would become her mother, and so would Wynn. If she stopped, she would have to let go of Jude for good, the ruined specter of Rigby forever between them.

"I wish we had nothing to do with the covert," she whispered. "Just like my mom wishes."

"Shine ran, has run from the very beginning, and will keep on running. You never have. So however much you hate the covert, you also accept it. Just as some people might always hate their scars, but without them, they'd be different people."

Marsden heard the echo of Peaches's words in Theola's. The idea that someone could fix pain and even settle scores, but it didn't mean the damage never happened.

Oliver Finney came over to their table, smoothies in tall glasses on a silver tray. His appearance said nothing of his unique ability to hide from a town with too many eyes. He wore a Seattle Mariners baseball cap, an annoyed frown on his face, and impatience in the line of his shoulders. But he'd thoughtfully topped the drinks with a sprinkling of crumbled banana chips, and a dab of almond butter anchored an oversize star anise to the lip of each glass. His eyes were full of affection for his wife as he set the tray down.

"Don't choke on the garnish," he grumbled. "Christ knows I can't run this place myself."

"I wouldn't do that to our customers, darling."

Marsden waited until he was gone before speaking again. She pulled her drink close, let its spice tickle her nose—not wild ginger, at least.

"What does Jude one day accepting Rigby being gone and my not being like my mom have to do with anything?" she asked. "What are you trying to tell me?"

Theola pulled off her star, shoved the sliver of almond butter into her glass with her straw, and stirred alive a milky, fragrant tornado. "I'm trying to tell you, Marsden Eldridge, that you and Jude Ambrose are far from done."

Marsden's eyes stung. "You already knew my question."

"*You* already knew my answer."

The taste of sugared fruit still lingered in her mouth as she left the café. She climbed onto her bike, turned it onto the road, and slowly began to pedal home. If Theola was right, she and Jude would meet again soon enough.

She knew choosing to believe the psychic even just a bit was the beginning of a slippery slope. After all, Theola never guaranteed anything, for anyone. She had no real way of knowing if Jude would forgive Marsden, or if they'd ever even be anything close to friends again. Just as there was no way of knowing if Theola was simply a fraud, through and through, and always had been.

But Marsden didn't think so.

She needed to believe.

And because the world had never been kind to her, she took in what she saw next, and humiliation washed over her, telling her she was still a fool.

Stopped on her bike at the light on the corner, Marsden watched Jude and Abbot in front of the Burger Pit, their faces close together as they held each other, and wanted to disappear.

forty-two.

MARSDEN ROUNDED THE CORNER OF THE FRONT DRIVE, SPED
TOWARD THE ENTRANCE OF THE BOARDINGHOUSE, AND
SWUNG OFF HER BIKE.

She left it leaning against the side of the building, the side that led
to the covert, not caring if guests saw it, not caring if their eyes followed the line from it to the covert and they wondered about the forest and its bloody soil. Nina would have a fit, too, that the bike wasn't
stored in the shed the way she liked it. She kept the landscaping as tidy
as she could, as though doing so kept the boardinghouse more distant
from the covert than it actually was.

Marsden simply didn't care. She wasn't scared of hearing the lec-
ture, would even invite the anger, actually, let it stir into a rage. It'd
give her the chance to yell back at someone. If that someone ended up
being Nina, then she'd probably enjoy the argument even more. If it
convinced her to think she could get her money back by simply breaking into Nina's room and tearing it apart to find it, she would overlook
how Nina had the whole boardinghouse in which to hide anything she
wanted.

The memory of Jude on the street corner ensnared her mind, shoved it toward places she didn't want it to be, made her map out the world's cruelest corners. Her pulse hurt.

A single argument between them and, minutes later, he was off with Abbot, needing to be consoled, soothed. The image of them wrapped around each other—his fingers knotted in her cool, carefree pixie hair, her arms around his neck, pressed so close they would have felt each other's heat—was a giant, livid tattoo smeared across Marsden's brain, behind her eyelids, everywhere she looked.

Asshole. He was an asshole to the nth degree.

Yet, whatever he'd been proven to lack, she knew she was just as much to blame for him needing to fill that void—for helping *create* that void. And it hadn't felt like just another argument, either, standing there with him as the Indigo raged and ran alongside them, his expression broken. It'd felt like . . . ruin.

She needed to keep moving. Keep going. Do her best to hate him when she knew, deep down, she never could. Abbot had been there from the very beginning, had built up a history with him and closeness to him that wasn't based entirely on misery. Jude had only come to Marsden out of necessity, needing to go through her to get to the covert. Maybe whatever she thought they'd built on top of that—above it, beside it, *other* than it—would have never been enough. Maybe it wouldn't have even come close.

She entered through the kitchen, as she always did. But instead of staying there to look over the menu for that night's dinner, or to check what Dany might have brought back from the market, she went upstairs and headed for her mother's room.

Marsden had questions for Shine—about Brom, about Wynn, about whether or not she'd known her husband had been with friends other than his best ones at Decks that night. She wanted to know why she'd told Nina about her daughter having a means to escape.

She knocked at the door, her heart thudding. Again.

No one there.

Then she remembered that her mother had had an appointment. The salon was downtown—she could have gone shopping or to eat afterward if she had no reason to rush back.

Marsden's mind raced as she backed away. Where next? Who to ask? Her questions were suffocating, and time, Nina, Shine—their demands pressed harder.

She started walking down the hall again, knowing then what had to be done.

Peaches's room wasn't locked. The scent of her perfume still lingered, much fainter than before. Most of her things had been left behind, and Marsden remembered how lightly she'd packed. It was hard to tell what it meant—that Peaches had left enough to quickly slip back into an old life when she returned or that it was easier to keep going the less weighing her down.

She moved over to the bedside table and opened the drawer. It would come down to whether Nina had been more efficient than Peaches had been forgetful, or if she'd been rushed.

Marsden wasn't entirely sure she wanted it to be there still.

It was.

She picked up the gun. Her hand trembled. The metal was strangely slick, almost oily—definitely unfriendly.

Could she really use it? She had no real idea how, only that if she went by books and movies, the recoil alone would be difficult to control. But she was not Grant Eldridge—she would likely need more than her poker face when it came to bluffing.

Peaches's closet was still nearly full—clothes, shoes, jewelry—so Marsden had no problem finding a purse.

She dropped the gun inside, slung the purse over her shoulder, and left the room.

The lobby was largely deserted, which was typical in the hours right before check-in. Nina was at the front desk, fussing with a fresh bouquet in a glass vase, releasing its fragrances into the room.

Marsden's throat went tight. The flowers had come from Evergreen. She recognized the hydrangea cuttings, the thin spires of quince, the puffs of pure color and scent. She wondered if Jude had put it together. Had delivered it. Had touched it. She again felt the echo of his skin on hers.

Her stomach twisted as she approached Nina, considering the last time they'd spoken it'd been over blackmail and raspberry crumble. Instinct told her to turn and go the other way, but she had no choice now.

"Are you here with good news?" Nina stroked a blue hydrangea blossom with an elegant finger. Her eyes were cool and probing and hard as diamonds.

"You said I had a few days."

"Well, I'll be here waiting—don't make me wonder if I should be worried."

"Nina." Marsden's voice was stiff, full of taut wires. "Someone's at the back entrance, wanting to talk to you about an advertising opportunity for the bed-and-breakfast."

Her mother's boss's mouth curled up into her moue of distaste. "You should have told them to come around front."

"I'll watch the desk for you while you talk to them."

Nina set aside the vase. Marsden got a whiff of deep, earthy sweetness, was instantly back at Evergreen—that back room, that sprawl of flowers on the floor, Jude's mouth—before mentally dragging herself back.

"Fine," Nina said with a huff. "As if I don't have better things to do. I'll be back in a minute."

As soon as she left, Marsden opened the guest log and flipped the pages until she found his name and room number. She shut the log, fished out the corresponding room key from the front drawer, and turned down the guest wing.

Ignoring the *Do Not Disturb* sign hanging from the doorknob, she made herself knock before she could think too hard about what she was doing. Did it count as a real plan when all she had were questions she didn't know how to ask and a gun she hoped she wouldn't have to use?

When there was no response, she unlocked the door and stepped inside.

It was decorated as the rest of the bedrooms in the boardinghouse: gray-flocked wallpaper, navy tiling with a faint fleur-de-lis pattern, pine-framed windows. There was also a television and an electric kettle on the desk, a clock radio and lamp on the bedside table—standard for all the guest rooms. One of Dany's welcome baskets still sat on the dresser, and Marsden knew that it would hold packaged mini soaps for use in one of the two communal baths down the wing, coupons for the local movie theater, and a package of the homemade rocky road brownies that Marsden baked and froze by the panful just for those baskets.

Already nervous, her breathing uneven and too loud in the room, she placed Peaches's purse on the bed and pulled out the drawer of the bedside table.

A notepad, a pen, a leather-bound Bible. More of the standard.

Marsden slammed the drawer shut, suddenly full of fresh doubt, despising her own desperation to finally be free of guilt.

What *was* she expecting to find? Her father's four grand from winning blackjack eight years ago? If Brom *had* taken it that night, it would be long gone, spent or saved or lent out—anywhere but there in the boardinghouse, she was sure. And even if she did find the money and could somehow prove it was her father's from that night, it *still* wouldn't mean Brom had anything to do with his actual drowning.

You know how sometimes you just feel it in your gut? That it's something way beyond logic and probability yet somehow just is?

Heat rose behind her eyes at the memory of Jude's words. She wondered where he was right then, what he was doing besides hating her.

She pulled out the drawer again, this time careful to look more thoroughly.

Gut feeling.

And humans were creatures of habit.

In the very back was another notebook, identical to the ones she'd found at his house. It was only half-full, the most-recent section dated just last week, with more rows of *Rm*s and what she felt more and more to be shorthand for names of banks.

And neatly printed in the far margin: *Nina's cut 30%*.

A rush filled her ears at seeing the name. Whatever Brom was doing, he was paying off Nina. She remembered her earlier guess of *Rm* meaning "room." Nina somehow being a part of it meant it would have to be rooms of the *boardinghouse*.

Those rooms came with guests. Guests who, unless they were paying up front with all cash—which almost never happened—had to provide some kind of bank info to secure their stay.

And Brom was in banking.

The rush in her ears grew louder as all the pieces tried to fall in place to become an answer.

Could Brom and Nina be working together to steal money from boardinghouse guests? Brom must have access to all kinds of accounts through his work, and it was Nina's policy to get that bank info so she could use it if a guest's payment didn't go through.

If the two had a system and were careful, Marsden could see how they might have been scamming people for years.

It was all still just a guess, she knew, even if most of it felt more right than wrong. And none of it explained what Brom might be hiding when it came to the night of her father's death.

But Marsden was no longer a stranger to blackmail.

forty-three.

BY THE TIME HE ENTERED THE ROOM, A BAG OF TAKEOUT IN HIS HAND, SHE WAS SITTING IN THE CHAIR AT THE DESK, HOLDING PEACHES'S GUN AND POINTING IT DIRECTLY AT HIS FACE.

"Shut the door, please." Her voice was smooth and cold and hid the fear that floated like ice in her veins. For an instant, his shocked eyes were Wynn's, and she nearly wavered. "Now."

A full second before he could speak. "Marsden? What's—?"

She dropped the gun until it was aimed at his crotch. "I said shut the door."

He pushed the door shut with his foot and dropped his lunch onto the bed. The bag, stained with grease, had come from the Finneys' café; the smells of chicken and balsamic vinegar and bread rose in the air. "Does your mother know you're here?"

"Considering where I have this gun pointed, you sure you want to bring up my mother right now? I really preferred her as a housekeeper."

His hands slowly lifted. "What do you want?"

"I'm going to ask you some questions, and you're going to answer them. That's all I want from you. Just simple yeses or nos." *I'm going to shake you like a Magic 8 Ball, Brom.*

"Questions?" Confusion pulled his features tight.

"You and Nina are working together to steal from the guests here. She gives you access to the bank information the boardinghouse collects from them and you then access their accounts through your own work." *Bluff, bluff, bluff.* "And don't bother denying it—I found your notebooks. The one here and the ones at your house."

Brom's eyes went narrow and knowing, his mouth clenched at the corners. Wynn's face, Marsden couldn't help thinking, how it would look once she saw too much, knew everything.

"It's true," he finally said.

"Unless you want Hadley coming around to talk to you, then I need to know one more thing."

He said nothing, only waited.

"You were there the night my father died. At Decks. You knew he won four grand. You followed him home." More bluffing. She prayed her poker face was as good as her father's had been. "You robbed him, didn't you?"

Being suddenly asked about Grant Eldridge, a long-faded memory from the long-ago past, disoriented Brom, left him fumbling.

"He was my friend," he managed. "For a long time. Of course I didn't. Rob him, I mean."

"But you knew he had that money."

"I did. But I didn't take it from him."

"Don't lie. And don't forget where I have my gun pointed." She heard her voice break, took a deep breath. "A friend told me to shoot to maim because it's more painful. That in the end, they still have to cut it off."

Brom swallowed so loudly she heard the click of it in his throat. "I . . . followed him for a bit. After he left his friends outside of Decks. Because, yeah, I was thinking about stealing it from him—it was so much money, and he was going home to Shine, and—I just couldn't do it in the end, all right? Believe me or not, but I didn't touch him. Last I saw, he was walking down the highway toward home. And I let him go. He was my friend, so I let him go."

That night came to life in her mind, what she could remember of it, how she'd imagined it as she struggled through the article in the local paper. She saw the Indigo, a wild, foaming curlicue. The sky, sooty with clouds, shot through with white lightning like veins on the back of a grizzled hand. The air would smell like something burning on the stove, hot and humid and brimming with electricity.

Marsden stared at Brom and noted the way he met her gaze, took in how she'd always be connected to him through Wynn. She felt her heart ache for her own father, the mystery of his mind. And knew she couldn't force a truth that didn't exist.

"And now you're sleeping with his wife, after chasing her for years," she said. "What kind of friend does that?"

Contempt scrawled itself across Brom's features in a fast-moving wave. It wiped away his fear.

"I've always been Shine's second choice—first with Grant and then with this damn boardinghouse," he snapped. Her question had broken open some kind of floodgate, she saw. "She'd rather have had him and all his failures than me. Even our own kid—she knew Wynn was mine, but still she wouldn't leave this place. Do you know how *infuriating* that is? She chose *any* paying guy over being with me. And *here*, in this town full of people who are never going to stop wondering if she *really* understands them when they talk to her. She's lucky I'm better than all of them."

His rage had her flinching, left her as cold as the Indigo in deep winter. Only the thinnest of lines separated the mess of what this man felt for her mother, the way both love and hate existed in his heart for her. What existed for her father, too.

"Still, she's kept me strung along for years, and now she's finally chosen me." Brom's eyes glittered, the pulse at his temple pounded, and Marsden tightened her grip on the gun. "Thinking I'm her way out, me and my money, now that she's realizing she won't stay young forever. Well, I'm just returning the favor while I can—my turn to string *her* along. I'll break her heart later, just when she thinks I'll never say no."

"You're pathetic."

"And your mother's a whore."

"She still chose my father over you, however weak or stupid he was. He's dead, and you're still nothing more than a last resort."

He made a forward motion, kind of a half leap, and Marsden's arms twitched, letting the gun jerk wildly for one single second before she steadied it. "Don't think I won't use this. The covert's my backyard, remember? Dead bodies mean nothing to me."

Brom fell back on his heels, suddenly beaten, his confession the draining of some pent-up poison from an old wound. "Are you done yet?" he muttered.

She tried to picture her father this defeated, how he must have been the instant he'd decided he would greet the terrible pull of the river, and instead she saw only the man who'd once smiled his way through drinking pretend tea with her.

Marsden lowered the gun. "I have one of your notebooks—show up here again and I'll pass it around for all the dinner guests to see. And stay away from my mother."

"Wynn. She's my kid. What about her?"

"Eight years, and you've never said a word. You really want to start being a dad now?"

His silence, woven through with resentment, was answer enough. Then he nodded, and Marsden got up. She dropped the gun back into Peaches's purse, pulled the strap back onto her shoulder, and left the room.

She found Nina less than a minute later, perched on the same love seat in the lobby where Shine and Brom had pretended to be people they weren't. She only had paperwork on the table in front of her, though, and for one giddy, delirious second, Marsden wondered if she should bring over a slice of raspberry crumble from the kitchen before breaking the news.

Nina glanced up as she sat down beside her. Her expression was cautiously triumphant, a gloat barely held in check.

It slid away like butter off a hot pan as Marsden spoke.

"I know you're helping Brom steal from the guests here," she said in a low whisper. From across the room, there was the ringing of the boardinghouse phone before one of the staff picked it up; from the kitchen she heard the muffled clatter of ceramic and water being run into the sink. "For a thirty-percent cut. I don't think even *you* could keep the boardinghouse going once word spreads about you being a thief. Don't you agree?"

Nina's rose-tipped nails—dug deep into her palms, like blades into fruit—went even deeper with each passing second, each uttered word. Her eyes tried to burn holes into Marsden's, invisible fingers gouging invisible holes. "Perhaps."

"Here's our new deal now: I'll keep quiet about it, and you give me back all the money you stole. The debts my family still owes you from taking us in are now paid off. And you won't ask me to work as one of your girls again—if it's all the same to you, I'll just keep working in the kitchen, and back to full wages."

A slow hiss from between her teeth, like that of a spent grenade. "Fine." Nina bit out the word as though she'd been close to choking on it. "Are you done yet?"

Exactly what Brom had asked her. She hadn't been done then but she was now, and she nodded. Without another word, Nina went back to her paperwork, and Marsden stood up, headed for the front entrance of the boardinghouse, and walked out.

forty-four.

THE COVERT.

Shine had said it was unhealthy, her being there as much as she was, and maybe that was true. But Marsden had been drawn to the woods as soon as she saw Caleb Silas hanging from the tree, by the knowledge that her father was buried in its soil. And right or wrong, Duncan Kirby's mad blood ran in her veins, as thickly as the wild ginger that grew in the place.

Still shaken from Nina and Brom, she turned from the boarding-house and headed for the dark heart of Glory.

She saw the truck from Evergreen before she got there. It was parked haphazardly along the shoulder of the highway, just beyond the entrance to the covert.

Then she saw Jude, and the earth pitched.

He was clutching the open door of the truck as though it were the only thing keeping him from falling. Raw and bruised and clenched white, his knuckles unfurled over the window frame, shattered, adrift. One eye was puffed completely shut, his lips split, his cheek slashed open along the bone. His dark hair looked wet from blood, freshly varnished with it. She tasted it—hot and coppery, battery in liquid form—in her own mouth as she ran up to him.

While she'd been holding a gun to the man she'd thought responsible for her father's death, Jude had met the drunken fists of his own father all over again.

Her eyes blurred, turning his face into streaks of garish color, pinks and reds and purples. She wanted to touch him, was deathly afraid to. "God, Jude, what happened?"

He shook his head, but just once, as though he hurt inside there, too. His eyes were absolutely hollow, their depths littered with shock. "You should have seen *him*." Then he attempted to smile, and his lips started to bleed again, and he swiped at them with his hand. "*Damn it.*"

She pulled his arm away. "No, you're being too rough." She tried to blot away the blood with her fingers and felt a fresh wave of disgust for his father. "How could he do this?"

Jude tugged at her hand, turned it over, and lifted it to his mouth. "What I said to you earlier, back at the river . . ." His voice was hoarse, as though it'd been beaten along with the rest of him. "I'm sorry. I was an ass. My anger—sometimes I can't control it. Sometimes I don't stop it from getting that way." He took a deep breath. "Sometimes it feels good."

In her mind, the images were ugly and raw: Adam Lytton's note in his hand, Rigby's last words spilling from her mouth as he faced all the lies she'd spun, Abbot in Jude's arms . . .

Marsden fell back a step, breaking his grip. Her heart pounded its way up along her throat, and the earth was still pitching.

"I did something terrible when I kept Rigby's note from you," she said. "I had no right to do that. So I'm sorry for that, too."

"That part about you not mattering. That wasn't okay to say."

"It was, if it was what you felt."

He narrowed the gap between them. Up close, his swollen eye was livid, awful, his father's nursed rage collected into a single explosion. His other eye was hot with guilt, what she recognized in too many forms. "It wasn't what I felt. Not even close, okay? You *matter*."

"And if I told you I can't stop being a skimmer? Wynn's getting older, and I can't hide everything from her forever." An image of her sister popped into her head—grin a mile wide, telling Marsden she was the best cook ever, pouring achingly sweet lemonade for the first guy who'd ever come to the boardinghouse who she hadn't been warned away from. "I can't hide *her* forever."

"She calls you Mars for a reason. And I know why you skim now. I do."

She felt his understanding reach out for her, try to tell her things could be all right again.

"I saw you with Abbot," she said softly, hating herself for still wanting everything, simply unable to stop. "Outside the Burger Pit. You literally went from me to her in minutes."

Jude shut his good eye, swore under his breath, and opened it again. "I was upset after leaving you at the river. I drove back into town, not thinking straight, and decided I'd go see Theola again, bug her some more about what Rig might have said that she'd forgotten. But then I ran into Abbot, and she was just— We're only friends. We've only ever been friends, and that's all we'll ever be."

"I'm never going to make friendship bracelets for you."

His brow wrinkled. "What?"

"You guys have this history, years and years of it. I'm not saying I want it, but I'm saying it's never going to be ours. Should I be worried about never being able to catch up? That I'll never be her?"

He made a sound like he was still being punched and his jaw went tight. "I don't want you to be Abbot. I don't want Abbot, period. I just want you."

She stared at him, heart like thunder in her chest. She'd never wanted to believe words so badly. But the smells of blood and ginger filled her head and left her confused. His fury when he'd left her along the river, his regret now—which was more real?

"You can't just do that," she said.

"Do what?"

"Say you hate me and then decide to take it away. Because whatever made you change your mind about hating me could easily change it back again."

"I won't change my mind."

"So what happened? What's going on?"

Jude opened his mouth, shut it, opened it again. His eyes were dazed, defeated looking, even as they flickered with heat. "I . . . I found out something. After I left you."

The air in the covert stirred, running through the trees, along her skin. "Tell me."

"Did you know that you being a skimmer has actually kept Rig safe in this town? You taking his note and hiding it—if anyone else had found it, everything would have come out. Hadley would have gotten involved, there might have been an investigation, and everyone in Glory would know."

"Know what?" She was completely bewildered. Rigby's note—the meaning of his words, what he'd really been saying—was still a mystery to her.

"What he'd done."

"What could your brother have done that would let you stop hating me?"

Jude swayed on his feet, pain written all over him. The sun glinted off his blood-streaked hair, and her stomach clenched.

"Marsden, I can't ever hate you, but the thing is—" His voice broke, then split wide open like he was just as injured inside as he was on the outside. Tears turned his eyes wet as he stared at her, his expression suddenly helpless. "The thing is, after I tell you, *you* might hate *me*."

• • •

She made him wait by the fence while she ran inside the boardinghouse for bandages. Not because she still didn't trust him alone in the covert, but because she didn't trust the covert alone with him. It was her woods, and she knew its trees and soil and concealed paths, could close her eyes and sketch out the entirety of the land. But hundreds of hours she'd waited for the dead to talk to her as they were supposed to, and still they never did.

The covert, sly and secretive the instant that Duncan Kirby's mind broke and he picked up a gun. Who knew what games it would play with Jude, alone?

And now he finally had a secret. One he was compelled to tell her. Whatever it was, it had to be bad enough to make her no longer so terrible. So many responses were immediately on the tip of her tongue when he said she would hate him: *What are you talking about? What do you mean? I could never hate you.* But something had kept her from saying any of them before she'd stumbled away, whispering that he needed something for all his cuts. How she would be back in just few moments.

His secret terrified her.

Marsden was grateful to find the kitchen deserted, though just. A crumpled napkin and a smattering of crumbs still littered the top of the table, there was a dirty plate and fork in the sink, and the last of her raspberry crumble was gone. She imagined Nina, raging over her lost business investment, trying to drown out her bitterness by finally indulging in more forbidden dessert, and was coldly glad.

Jude was sitting against the fence when she got back. At the sound of her approach, he straightened up to face her. Beneath the bruises and cuts, she watched his skin pale with the motion, all its umber and amber tones washing away.

"You need to move more slowly." She knew she sounded stiff,

but she couldn't help it. Her nerves rippled in preparation for what he might say. "Sorry, it'll take me a bit to use all this stuff on you." Unsure of what she needed, she'd grabbed towels, bandages, a bottle of water, and aspirin.

"This is all going to hurt, isn't it?" His voice was just as stiff as hers, but she also heard guilt there, etched all the way through, and it left her cold. He rinsed out his mouth, spat into the grass.

"Probably," she said, knowing he was stalling and not caring— she wanted to stall, too.

She poured water from the bottle onto one of the towels and began to carefully dab the blood off his face, from his lips. Her hands shook as she touched him.

He sucked in a breath, and she passed him the aspirin and the rest of the water. The smell of ginger wafted over them, spicy and barbed and dizzying. The sight of pretty heart-shaped leaves everywhere only turned Jude's injuries starker, more painful looking.

"Wynn always runs and hides when she cuts herself," Marsden said. "I end up having to chase her down."

Jude stared at her as she worked, his uninjured eye blinking at her like an inquisitive owl's, a blaze of brown flecked with amber. "You're comparing me to an eight-year-old?"

"You *did* ask." She poured antiseptic on the towel and touched it to his face gently. "I'm sorry."

He hissed through his teeth. "Damn, that stings. Tell Wynn she's smart to run."

Marsden smiled, and it felt about as hollow as her stomach. *She* wanted to run. She also wanted to stay, to be able to kiss him and keep him from telling her whatever he needed to tell.

He picked up her hand and wove his bruised fingers between hers, and she braced herself. "Rig's note and what it meant . . . Marsden, my brother killed someone."

She froze. The world swelled and receded in waves as she stared at Jude in shock.

But, deep down, she'd known, hadn't she? Had recognized in each of Rigby's last words the signs of a guilt so great it could only come from the ugliest of crimes? Had sensed shades of that same kind of guilt when she stole from the freshly dead in her covert, when she stood over her father's grave and wished not so much for him to come back but to be told she wasn't at fault for him being gone in the first place?

"How do you know?" she asked, feeling her heart ache for him as the loss of who his brother had been—was supposed to have been— turned his face bleak.

"My father finally told me." His good eye was far away; in it, she saw him replay the horrors of the day. "After I left Abbot, I went home. He was supposed to be at work; but as soon as I walked in, I could smell the booze. Turns out he knew the entire time what Rig had done and wasn't happy with the secret suddenly seeming close to being found out. He was waiting for me, wanting to tell me that." With his free hand, he gestured tiredly toward his swollen eye, his split lips, his raw cheek.

Marsden's thoughts ran rampant, entered Jude's house alongside him as it might have happened. She saw every detail, heard every sound, smelled each scent. Leo's temper an explosion and his elegant eyes gone a red-rimmed, galvanized blue. The reach of his huge, frustrated hands. The sound of knuckles against bones and flesh, the bright cascade of broken beer bottles, the smell of wet steel.

"You asked him what Rigby's note could have meant, and it scared him that you knew?" she asked. "And that's why he beat you?"

"No, I never got a chance to ask him about the note. It was seeing *you*, when you were over, that scared him all over again. You reminded him of how he'd been hiding my brother's secret for years, ever since science-fair night. How Rig's secret might not stay buried forever, no matter what he did."

Marsden was lost.

What did *she* have to do with Rigby while he'd been alive? Even after he'd died, she hadn't known anything about him, other than being the one to find his body. Even now, with this discovery that he'd actually killed someone, she didn't understand how she was connected. Rigby would have been thirteen to Jude's nine, big for his age but still a kid. And she would have been eight, and she was still living in their old duplex, and her father was still—

A single sliver of dread, sharp and cold in her throat, hammered out a steady pulse. She could taste it, thin and metallic and of the Indigo.

And she knew.

Jude's hand tightened around hers to the point of pain. His eye, ablaze and despairing as he watched her understand. "I'm so sorry. What happened to your dad—Rig killing him—it was an accident. Just listen."

forty-five.

THE COVERT SWELLED AND SWAM, AND MARSDEN THOUGHT SHE WAS GOING TO BE SICK.

"I wanted root beer floats that night, remember?" Jude's words came fast, like he was worried she'd run before he could finish. "But it was already late, and there was that storm, and my dad had already had too much to drink. But Rig insisted that we should celebrate because of my project. He said we could go on our own, he'd just take the truck and he'd be extra careful about driving. But my dad lost it, the way he always lost it back then, and Rig just grabbed me and the keys to the truck, and then we were driving on the highway, along the Indigo.

"He just drove and drove, wanting to run away with me and not come back. And the storm—it was bad that night. I remember the wipers going so fast, this wild kind of drumming. I'd already fallen asleep in the backseat when Rig saw the man walking along the shoulder of the road. And that's when he thought of money—if we were going to run away, we'd need money."

Marsden shut her eyes. Her stomach was heaving, just like that same storm. Her father, coming home from Decks.

"My dad used to keep a pocketknife in the glove compartment," Jude continued quietly. "For emergencies. Rig pulled over, got out of the truck, and told your dad if he didn't give him his wallet, he'd have to hurt him. He was bluffing, he had no clue how to use a knife, but he was desperate. Your dad saw how he was still just a kid despite his size, and he said no and began to walk away. Rig decided that he was already in too deep to go back. So then he *did* try to stab your dad."

She could see it. The thundering rain, the way it would have made the river roll and crash. A moonless night, a slippery road, a young boy's blind need for escape in order to save his little brother—all of it coming down to the single stranger who stood in his way. Would she not have done the same for Wynn?

"It was along a part of the highway where the Indigo nearly came right up to it, the shoulder was so thin," Jude said. "Your dad managed to wrestle the knife away, and then he tossed it into the river. He told Rig to go home or he'd call the cops, and then he turned to leave again. And Rig—he panicked. He'd just pulled a knife on someone who knew what his face looked like, and he just . . . panicked."

Jude's eye was a huge dark moon, and he was nine years old again, and Marsden saw him relive her father's death as Rigby would have witnessed it. Rigby, who had now joined them at the fence of the covert, his ghost sitting beside Jude, telling him about the wild summer storm of Glory eight years ago.

"But just as your dad couldn't have guessed how strong Rig was for a kid, neither did Rig. And when he pushed your dad to stop him from leaving, your dad's head hit the ground hard enough that he stopped moving. Stopped breathing. So my brother . . . he dragged your father's body over to the edge of the Indigo and waited until the river took it away.

"Then he drove home. He carried me into the house, and I kept sleeping. I kept dreaming about root beer floats and drumming windshield wipers and families who never fought. He told my dad, who was scared sober by the idea of anyone finding out—sober for a while, anyway. And then your dad's accident was in the local paper, and that's how everyone knew who was the latest to die."

Jude finished talking then, the last of it an echo that rolled throughout the covert, as thick and heavy as the ever-present scent of wild ginger. Silence fell between them, an invisible wedge of shock.

Her father, dead because of Rigby, the one person Jude had ever relied on—not possible. It needed to be a lie. Better that it'd been Brom, an old friend willing to murder for money, or Grant Eldridge himself, who was already drowning while on dry land. And if Marsden had any part in his decision—well, the worst of the town's madness circled back to her own blood, didn't it?

There was no way she and Jude could ever be okay with Rigby and her father between them. He would change his mind about not hating her, the same as Shine did, as her father had, as even Wynn might one day, tired of having her life controlled.

"You're wrong." Her denial burst from her like a dam breaking. She felt unwound somehow, all parts of her trying to escape the moment.

"They found his body. Washed up, drowned. They said it was clearly an accident. *They said.*"

"It *was* an accident."

"There were no signs of that kind of struggle. There was nothing."

"The rain, though. The storm. It would have washed everything away." He dared to move closer. "I wish it hadn't been Rig, either, but you need to know that whatever your father said to you before leaving, you had nothing to do with him dying."

She let out a shaky breath, then another, unable to speak. She'd been waiting for years to hear those words, except always from the dead, not from Jude. Closure was a dream, still. How were they going to shake the ghosts they carried like a disease? Marsden felt the pull of the covert, of Glory as a whole, promising her and Jude they would never escape. She heard her father, his voice nearly drowned out by the storm. She heard Rigby, calling out from the woods for his brother.

"I don't blame you if you hate Rig," Jude said. "If you hate *me* for it being him."

She shook her head, suddenly newly exhausted, all the way down to her bones. Rig had been made to live in a corner for most of his life, had only done his best to escape. And deciding to hate Jude would be like saying *he* killed her father—by always needing Rigby, by making his big brother think he had no other choice.

"He was just being your big brother," she finally said, "and he was thinking of you. How could I not understand that?"

"It doesn't change what he did. I'll always love him, and he didn't mean to do it, but it doesn't change what he did."

"I know." Just as her father hadn't meant to leave the way he actually did, hadn't meant his last words to be the ones he actually said. "If I could, I would tell him I forgive him."

Rigby, her father—she needed to forgive both.

And so she returned them—to her family's covert, to the Indigo, to the places they'd chosen to rest—and she let them go. Into the trees, into the tide—the weight of years slid free of her heart and she blinked away tears.

Jude let out a soft sigh, tugged her closer. "Don't do that."

"Don't do what?" She saw the way his gaze searched hers, as if trying to read her eyes the way Theola might have tried to read her thoughts.

"Make me no longer give a crap about moving carefully with you."

She slowly slid her arms around his neck. She'd lived with caution and fear and the darkness of the covert for most of her life. But for this boy, who looked at her as if none of that mattered, she was tired of being careful.

Still, he was hurt, his mouth cut and bruised, and she hesitated.

Jude pulled her close and kissed her. She tasted the singing rawness of his lips, the taste of him beneath that, and didn't want to stop. Couldn't. So she didn't, and neither did he, not for the longest time, and—

"Hello!"

From within his arms, Marsden jumped. She tugged her mouth free and looked up. "Wynn!"

"Hi, Mars." Her little sister was smiling, frank curiosity all over her face. "Hi, Jude," she said to his still-turned back. "Does this mean you guys are going out now?"

"Hi, Wynn," Jude said mildly, his gaze remaining unmoving from Marsden's face. "Come back later, okay?"

"But why? I just got here," she said, laughing.

Marsden heard the affection for Jude in her sister's laugh, liked how safe it sounded, and peered more closely at her. It was her first time seeing Wynn since finding out about Brom, and she couldn't help but notice now. That where she and Wynn looked the same hadn't changed, but where they'd always been different stood out more clearly now, more obviously. She wondered if, over time, she'd forget to notice, would unconsciously smooth out the fresh jaggedness of those differences until they blurred, became soft once again.

The corner of Jude's mouth twitched as he continued to watch Marsden. "Just because."

Aware of her little sister's intense scrutiny, she gave Jude a fast kiss and got to her feet, adjusting her shirt while hoping her face looked nothing but calm. The whole time, his good eye continued to burn her skin, and she flushed at the unspoken words inside that flame—*That's not enough, not nearly.*

Wynn was holding Rigby's old metal detector.

Marsden frowned. The metal detector had come to represent too much of the covert—seeing it in her sister's hands looked wrong.

"Where did you get that?" she asked.

Jude got to his feet beside her, swept aside her hair, and kissed the back of her neck. "It's okay, Rig wouldn't have minded. It's meant to be used."

Flushed again, Marsden looked over and saw Wynn, in no rush to answer the question, staring at Jude. She hadn't seen his face with all its cuts and bruises yet. Her expression was a mix of surprise and awe.

"You got beat up!" she exclaimed loudly.

He grimaced as he reached up to touch his face. "Oh, yeah, this. Uh, I fell. Playing basketball."

"So you aren't very good?"

"Sure I am."

"But you fell. And pretty badly, from the way you look."

He laughed, and Marsden's heartbeat did a little flip at seeing him so at ease with Wynn, when he could have chosen to merely tolerate her. "The pavement won," he said. "But it's okay to fall once in a while—just makes you tougher."

"Did you need stitches?"

"Nope."

"That's good. I heard getting them hurts. Once, I cut my knee and I cried for hours because I was so worried I would need them. You know, if Nina had seen you and Mars kissing like that inside the house, she probably wouldn't have liked it."

"We thought ahead," he said, smiling. His bruises and cuts rippled, the surface of a lake with a strong wind on it.

"Actually, if you'd even walked into the house looking like that, she would have asked you to leave. Mom, too—you really do look kind of scary."

The mention of Shine reminded Marsden about Wynn's new afternoon schedule, which her sister had obviously chosen to ignore.

"You're supposed to be at swimming camp," she said. "You already missed the first class. Maybe you should just tell Mom you really don't want to go. I bet she's looking for you right now."

Her sister shrugged. She mimed sweeping the metal detector over the mix of ginger and grass at her feet. "I was in the covert, but then I got hungry and went to eat. I told Dany to tell her."

She wondered how long Wynn had been sneaking the metal detector to use on her own—it was clear she'd been practicing for a while. *How long do you stay in the covert on your own? What have you found? Who have you heard?* "How often do you use the detector?"

"I don't know. Just once in a while." Her sister clicked it on and started scanning around her. Marsden saw the way she held it perfectly, neither too high or too low, and her unease grew, a kind of buzzing in her veins that matched the low hum of the thing's motor.

"It was my brother's," Jude said. "His name was Rigby."

Wynn glanced up, her expression suddenly fearful as she remembered just who Rigby was. "I'm sorry, I didn't know it was his," she half whispered. "I just thought it was yours."

"It's okay. He would have been happy to see you use it. He used to try to find coins with it, most of all. Every summer for a few years, he talked about trying to save enough for something big."

Wynn nodded, concentrating. The motor hummed, ginger swirled, the sun shone clear and sharp. "I like finding coins, too, and old buttons. I even found an old bullet once—"

Marsden sighed. "Oh, Wynn."

"—stuck in the base of a tree. Oh, and an old metal tin."

Her nerves went taut and tense, and a current ran along Marsden's spine—her pulse flew. Beside her, Jude froze.

"What kind of tin?" he asked Wynn, his voice tight.

"A cookie tin. Blue. You know, those round tins of butter cookies that everyone buys at Christmas. They're not even that good, you know. Mars's are way better." She glanced up from the ground to search Marsden's face and then Jude's. "Is that what you guys have been looking for? I knew there had to be something since you were using this."

"Something like that, yeah," Jude said.

"I left it in there, if you want to go see."

"You didn't open it?"

"I couldn't." Wynn shrugged. "I was going to ask you or Mars to try later."

Suddenly, Marsden was cold. "Where did you find it in the covert?"

"Near the back. You know, where the ginger started growing in the first place." *Where the roots fight me the hardest when I try to pull them out.* Wynn wandered off around the fence, still waving the detector.

As her small form disappeared, Marsden imagined Rigby as a little kid walking beside her, holding dying ginger in his arms, telling her it needed planting deep in the covert.

Jude touched her arm, and she turned to look at him, already dreading the question, knowing she couldn't protect him from it anymore.

"The area Wynn's talking about." His eye was steady on hers, as dark as the Indigo at midnight. "It's where you found Rig's body, isn't it?"

Marsden took his hand, careful of the cuts there. "Yes."

forty-six.

EVEN IF SHE'D DOUBTED THE EXISTENCE OF THE TIME CAPSULE, SHE SHOULDN'T HAVE DOUBTED ITS LOCATION.

She should have known right from the start.

Rigby had never been about fear, even as a kid. He'd protected Jude from their father. He risked and lost everything over root beer floats. He'd biked across town to go to a place filled with ghosts and perceived sins of all kinds.

She should have known it wouldn't have been fear on his mind when he came into the covert with his mother's plant. He would have found the best place for it, even if it meant walking all the way through. To the very back, where it was darkest, the shade deepest. Why wouldn't he do it again with something he buried as a treasure? And then when he was saying goodbye for good?

Marsden pushed aside branches as she walked.

"I can practically hear you beating yourself up still," Jude said. "You couldn't have guessed where he would have buried it."

"Even if I never would have guessed he'd go to the very back, it being where he shot himself should have been a clue."

"That's like trying to connect the dots when the dots don't even exist yet. Rig buried that tin sometime when he was a kid. He probably didn't even remember where it was when he came back."

Whatever trail Wynn had taken earlier had already filled in again, disappearing entirely. Wild ginger swallowed Marsden's and Jude's sneakered feet as they continued to cut through, gave them glossy green shoes with a heart-shaped leaf pattern, reeking as it rolled off their skin.

The sun peeled back and away, taking degrees of warmth and light with it. It could have been sunrise in the covert, or sunset, October or April. It was nothing like the late afternoon of the broiling July day that actually existed just beyond the fence.

She heard Jude mutter under his breath. She caught the words *creepy* and *goddamn it* and *stupid Rig.* It was almost enough to make her grin.

Almost. Because she pushed aside a final handful of branches—filigreed, delicate, a gentle protest to their presence in this least-navigated and most-untouched part of the covert—and knew they'd reached where they'd been meant to go.

It was the only part of the covert not burst through with trees and bushes. Negative space, a gap between the trees, a mini meadow of wild ginger. Out in the open, it would have called for picnics and dozing beneath the hot sun. Here, walking beneath the shade and nearly cool dampness, Marsden could almost believe someone would sink in and never come back out.

Rigby had shot himself through the temple. The results had

been devastating and destructive—she'd shut her eyes at seeing his body and had to steel herself to approach. She hadn't fully looked at what was left of his face, and now she wondered if she would have seen some of Jude there. How much had they looked alike? How much of Jude had Rigby taken with him? How much of Rigby did Jude keep?

Then the covert spoke, and she *felt* it through her feet, in her hands. It was like a rumbling of the ground, even as the earth didn't shift an inch, and her entire body seemed to tingle.

Was this—?

"Do you hear that?" she asked. Her mouth was dry. "The covert. It's . . ." Her words trailed away. She couldn't explain it. It was like trying to describe a color only she could see, a flavor only she could taste. How could she define something she didn't hear with her ears but felt along her skin, in her teeth, that was a quiver in her veins? She thought wildly of stories of animals that sensed earthquakes long before they came.

Jude was confused, staring at her with dark, startled eyes. "No, there's nothing."

"I think—"

The echo came again—a trembling of the air, an unseen ripple that ran throughout the wood—and she hugged herself, chilled.

She was listening to all the covert's *bones.* All its blood. All its sins and guilt. From Duncan Kirby to his wife and kids and all the others who'd ever taken the passage of the covert—she was finally hearing the dead.

Telling her what, though?

"You're hearing them." Jude's whisper was half-frightened, half-awed. He took her hand. "The dead. Their voices."

"I think so."

"What are they saying?"

Marsden shook her head. "I can't tell. I'm not—" She took a deep breath, closed her eyes, and focused, trying to grab on to the invisible fingers she now sensed reaching out from the covert. A meeting of the minds.

There were no words, but she heard them still. They washed over like water, like the wind, and she read them the way she might read the weather, a fever, a face.

We speak now only in echoes, in traces of what once was—ash and dust and salt, from blood and bone and tears. And you hear us now because you've let us go. Because you know no answer will change us back from being that ash and dust and salt.

Why can I hear you, if you have nothing to say?

You hear what you are ready to hear.

She opened her eyes when the covert's fingers danced away from her brain. "No less cryptic than a Magic 8 Ball, really," she muttered.

Jude's fingers squeezed. "Tell me."

"They're saying whatever answers we might find in here, it doesn't change what's already happened. How finally figuring out how to be okay with that *is* a kind of answer."

He glanced around as though expecting ghosts to show themselves from within the trees, out of the air. "So they're really here in the covert with us?"

"No. More like"—Marsden laid a hand on his cheek—"I'm touching you, there's no mark on your skin, but you feeling it is absolutely real, right?"

"Why can you suddenly hear them now?"

"Because I finally let the dead be free."

He tugged her close, kissed her. "I prefer the living, too."

They saw it a moment later, just a few feet away.

The edge of a round blue tin poked out from the thick mat of ginger on the forest floor.

They approached it as though it were alive, a skittish creature that would up and leave at one wrong move. Wynn's squirrel came to mind, that first day at the fence outside the covert. When she'd shoved buttered toast into Jude's hand and asked him to feed a wild animal, and he'd done it without hesitation. He'd been so lost, his face battered in invisible ways as he asked her for permission with a plea in his eyes. And then he'd grinned with that overly generous mouth of his, and she'd forgotten how he was supposed to be a stranger.

They fell to their knees.

"Holy shit." He picked up the tin and slowly rubbed dirt from the rounded edge of it with his hand, a blue of velvety, glossy night skies gleaming through. "Can you believe it? I owe your sister *big*-time."

"Don't tell her that, or you'll never hear the end of it." Then Marsden opened her mind to that tremble and *felt* for Rigby's voice. Filled her head with her own message: *Jude is okay. He loved you. You didn't fail him.*

A single frisson that raced along her spine before it was gone. The sensation it left behind was like cobwebs on her hands, more unreal than real, almost impossible to gather back together and form into words.

But she did, and that they left her almost cheered meant something, too.

Jude was waiting, his hope reluctant and careful but still there, written all over his face. "Well?"

"Rigby just . . . wants you to be fine. He knows you thought he was the best brother."

His eyes filled. "I miss him."

"He knows that, too. I could tell he knew even before I heard him."

Jude swiped at the flat surface of the lid. There were drawings of butter cookies on it—some with sugar on top, some iced, some twisted into knots. A strip of masking tape slowly appeared from beneath the veneer of old soil. Scrawled on it in faded childish handwriting was *Property of Rigby Ambrose. Top Secret!* For a single second, Marsden saw four scrawled lines echoing with desperation, of being haunted.

"Should we take bets on what's inside?" Jude asked. "I really have no clue what he might have put in here. I remember this tin now—our mom used it to hold her sewing supplies. After she died, he kept it for storing toys and stuff. But I don't think we're going to find baseball cards or marbles." He shook it gently. There was little to no sound. "Definitely not marbles."

"It depends on when he buried it, what was important to him at the time. So it *could* just be baseball cards."

"But you don't think so."

"I don't think so." Rigby's life had been a landscape of deep hurts and sharp terrors, with only his love for his little brother keeping him from being buried beneath the two—he wouldn't choose to leave behind anything that wasn't equal in terms of feeling. She didn't think he could, even if he wanted to. Feeling would have been all he knew, even the slow dying of that feeling as he got older, as his guilt begun to overshadow everything else.

She touched the tin. The circumference of it was no bigger than a side plate, the kind Dany would set out in the dining room for dessert. But looking at it there in the deepest shade of the covert, the way Jude held it as though it were made of glass, it seemed much larger, oversize with significance.

He pulled at the lid, but it didn't budge at all. She watched as he kept trying to loosen it with no success and remembered how Wynn had also been unable to open it.

After Jude swore loudly again, she held out her hand. "Here, let me take a turn before you start shouting at it."

She'd expected to struggle just as he and Wynn had, but the lid twisted loose from the tin nearly as soon as she touched it. The thought came and went, fleeting and disturbing: that the tin had *wanted* her to be the one to open it first. Not Wynn, and not even Jude. *Oh, Rigby, what* is *this?*

"You got it," Jude murmured. His eyes were wide as he stared down at the still-covered tin.

Marsden nodded. Then because she was scared and because it was Jude, she placed it between them. "Open it with me?"

"Together?"

"Together."

The lid hit the ginger-covered ground with a soft rustle. The hollow seep of stale air being released emerged from the tin, the final gasp of something dying.

And time reeled back. Years disappeared. Rigby was alive with a knife and a bluff; Jude was nine and sleeping in the back of a truck; Marsden was eight and crying while her parents hated each other in the front room, while her father told her he'd had enough.

Jude's face was completely unreadable as she reached inside.

A letter.

And four thousand dollars cash.

• • •

I don't know if this will ever be found. A part of me hopes it won't be, because then I can keep telling myself none of it happened. Maybe I'll even believe it one day. I'd wanted it for me and my brother, but not this way. The money feels full of bad luck, like there's magic in it but none of the good kind. It tells me if we try using it anyway, we're doomed. So that's why another part of me does want someone to find it, especially if they can really use the money. Because I know it's only cursed for us.

I can't keep it in my room anymore. Sometimes it feels alive. I see his face all the time, everywhere. I hear the knife splashing into the river. His skull when it hits the ground. I feel the water pulling at my shoes. It's not just when I'm sleeping that I have nightmares.

It happened so fast that I can't remember much of it. I know I was supposed to walk away after he gave the money to me, that's what I promised him. But then I couldn't do it. It was like someone else was inside of me, telling me to not let him go. The same way I found myself lying about just accidentally hitting him with our truck. No one knows anything about this money either. Just like how no one knows that when I pushed that guy down, I had been thinking about Dad. That if he were somehow gone, life would be so much easier for me and my brother.

I wish I could take it back, more than anything. That if I said I was sorry enough, it would change the past. Most days, I want to be dead, so it'll stop replaying it in my head, except that I can't leave my brother alone. Dad says he's never going to drink again, and I want so badly to believe him. And he hasn't broken his promise yet. So maybe this time he really means it.

I saw a movie once about blood money. The idea is that a victim's family gets repaid for their loss by the person who hurt them, or by the *person's family. So while this money isn't really blood money, because it was his in the first place, maybe somehow it will still make it back to his family. It's why I'm burying it here on their property, in the deepest, darkest part of the covert.*

forty-seven.

THERE WAS A SOUND AT THE BEDROOM WINDOW.

"Mars!" Wynn's voice, sounding panicked from across the room.

Again. A series of small, dull thumps.

Something was being thrown at the window screen.

"What *is* that, Mars?"

Marsden opened her eyes to see Wynn sitting up in her bed. Moonlight shot in through the window and everything was tinted grays and blacks, smears of smoke. The outline of her sister's bed hair was again the wild bristles of an oversize paintbrush.

The sound came once more, still soft and now more than insistent.

Marsden climbed out of bed, kicking aside the blankets she'd been using despite the heat of the day lingering in the night air, turning it soggy and full. Her pulse raced, her heart crept into her throat. She supposed it should have been caused by fear, but she knew it wasn't.

Jude. It could be no one else.

She peered out through the mesh of the screen.

He was standing out there just below the window, a mere blur against pale moonlight. His face was nearly hidden in the dark.

Still, she would have known him anywhere.

He must have seen her move behind the mesh, because he lifted his arm in a wave.

Marsden pushed open the screen and leaned outward, letting the slightly cooler night air wash over her skin. The moon had left a thin silvery sheen on everything, wiping away the hot, dry dust of day. Farther beyond him, she could see the swaying treetops and scraggly brush of the covert, the shadowed line of the fence that encircled it. It was just hours ago that they'd walked through it, holding a tin full of cash and with the knowledge they could finally stop listening for the dead.

"What are you doing?" she called down in a loud whisper.

"I was trying to be goddamn romantic." There was embarrassed, disgruntled laughter in his voice. "I wanted to wake you up by tossing pebbles at your window."

The corners of her mouth twitched. "You were aiming wide—you kept hitting the screen."

"Crap, sorry. I have a good arm, I swear—I blame only having one eye. Anyway, I couldn't sleep—I forgot that Karey *and* Langston snore like hell when I said I'd stay over. And . . . I wanted to see you."

Heat rose along her cheeks. "It's the middle of the night." She tried to sound like boys coming to her window after midnight was an ordinary occurrence.

"I like nights. Plus, chocolate-chip waffles, if you're up for it?"

She laughed. "Come to the kitchen door."

"Okay."

She pulled the screen shut and turned around. "Go back to sleep," she said to Wynn. "I won't be long."

"I wasn't sleeping—and neither were you. I could tell by the way you were breathing."

No, she hadn't been remotely close to sleeping. Thoughts of Jude and the day had crept into her brain and wouldn't leave.

Her father's winnings were in an envelope, folded into an old winter scarf tucked into the highest shelf in her closet. She could have stuck the bills into her boots as she'd done with cash from the covert since she was nine, but it felt wrong. Like going backward. Even the money that Nina had already returned—silently, coldly, her mouth set in her familiar moue of displeasure as she handed it over—was now stored elsewhere, a coffee container Marsden had taken from the pantry that she'd emptied of its fragrant contents.

After finding Rigby's tin, Marsden had led Jude to where her father was buried in the covert and listened for him. Eight years, and she'd never guessed the truth of his dying—she wanted him to know she would no longer wonder about him, all her questions had been answered. *I don't hate you. I've never hated you. I'm sorry you're no longer here.* His voice had rolled in like soft thunder, so that for a handful of seconds, the woods blurred and the air felt full of echoes. She'd cried at his understanding, at finally accepting what was.

A part of her still hurt to think that he'd died for that money—that in a way, his life hadn't even been worth the four grand, since Rigby had panicked anyway and still ended up killing him. But she understood panic, too, understood desperation and how it could make someone do things that could lead to the unthinkable. When she thought about her father from now on, she wouldn't always automatically think of the river or of rainstorms at night. Instead, she'd think about how he liked the radio loud and his pretend tea spiked with pretend sugar.

She grabbed a T-shirt from the closet to wear over her tank top. "I *know* you were sleeping, Wynn, because of the state of your hair."

"It's Jude outside, isn't it?" In the half-light, her sister resembled their mother more than Brom, more Marsden than a stranger of a father. "Do you like him?"

"Yes, I do. Is it okay if I do?"

"He's nice—and he likes your waffles. But he sure gets into lots of fights. I guess because he looks like he *wants* to fight a lot of the time."

Marsden grinned and pulled on the shirt. "He doesn't really want to fight all the time."

"Was the cookie tin his brother's?"

"Yes. Now go back to sleep."

Wynn slid back beneath her covers. Marsden noticed she hadn't bothered to change out of her clothes from the day, as was typical.

"He killed himself, just like Lucy did," her sister said.

Images of Rigby and Lucy, each covered in blood, a boy named for a song, a girl with Alice in Wonderland hair.

Marsden sat on the edge of Wynn's bed, unsure of what to say. Until Lucy, her sister had never known any of those who died in the covert. And until Rigby, she supposed, simply because he'd been Jude's brother. "He did, yes."

"He listened to that voice in his head, then—just like Lucy listened to hers. If he'd been like Grandma, he might have had someone else to listen to, since he was in the covert." Wynn drew the covers to her chin, sounded sleepy again already. "Sometimes, lately, I hear them. I wonder how close it is to what she used to hear."

A chill ran through Marsden's blood. "You can hear the dead?"

"Not words or anything. But a really strong feeling that tells me something."

"Finding Rigby's tin out there today"—Marsden shivered, remembering how she'd heard the dead with her bones, with her *teeth*—"was it not because of the detector?"

"It was. But it also wasn't. I just . . . knew where to go. And then it was there."

"Wynn, I can hear them now, too."

Her sister sat up like a shot. "Really?"

Marsden nodded. She wasn't sure if she *wanted* Wynn being able to hear the dead—not that it was up to her—but she felt better that neither of them was alone in it. "Let's keep this our secret—you know Mom doesn't like you in the covert anyway."

"Have you talked to her?"

Marsden had not seen Shine since Brom and his confession about his stealing, the admittance of his strange and twisted love for her and her dead husband. The topic of why she'd told Nina about the money remained untouched and was an eruption in the making. Now, Marsden was no longer sure she *wanted* it to erupt. What could she say that wouldn't just be making things worse between her and Shine? She didn't know if she could trust her mother to ever pick her or Wynn over Nina—worse, she didn't know if she cared that it didn't really matter anymore. "Talk to her about what?"

"About us moving from the boardinghouse, remember? We still need more money."

"Actually, Nina's going to give me a raise, so that'll help a lot." *And we also have an extra four thousand dollars. That'll help a lot, too.*

Shine would still fight them leaving, Marsden knew. Maybe she would even threaten to turn her back to them if they didn't stay, her love for her daughters as volatile as a storm over the Indigo.

But things had changed. Brom was over, no longer her mother's prince. And Nina would be more than happy to see them gone from the house, considering what Marsden knew about her. Which meant except for her daughters, Shine would be alone. How far would she go to prove her desperation was greater than theirs?

That was something Marsden didn't know. But she was no longer going to pay for her parents' decisions—or be the excuse for their failures.

Wynn went to lie down again. "And Jude can still be your boyfriend, wherever we end up living in Glory."

In the shadows, Marsden had to smile. It was hearing it stated so naturally, how Jude Ambrose was very much her boyfriend. She liked how it sounded, those words put together in just that way. She liked it a lot.

"Okay, I should go, or Jude's going to start throwing more rocks at the window." She slid off the bed and stood up. "Don't tell anyone about him showing up here so late, all right?"

"Only if you make waffles for breakfast."

"With chocolate chips, I know. Hey, we should try something new next time, okay?"

"Like what?" Wynn said through a yawn.

"I don't know. Banana anise muffins." Marsden shook her sister's foot through the blanket. "Rice porridge. Steamed buns."

"What's all *that*?"

"You'll see, runt. Now, good night."

Downstairs, she flicked on the light above the stove before quietly opening the back door.

Jude closed the gap within seconds. His mouth was hot, the thrill of his tongue against hers both primal and sweet. He still tasted like cinnamon. She didn't give an inch, pushing back even as she felt she was barely holding on.

Then his stomach growled, and they both laughed, their lips still tangled together.

He pressed his mouth to her neck, making her ache. "Christ, it's late, but I'm not sorry at all for coming over."

She pulled back and did a onceover of his injuries.

Beneath the porch light, he was a palette of colors, from pink to red to purple, his bad eye at the dark end of the spectrum. Cuts everywhere that were properly scabbing now. She thought he looked like he'd challenged an entire gang—a gang made up of his father, his fists, and bottles of alcohol—to a fight and was lucky to have walked away in the end. She had a hard time connecting the image of that man to the one she'd met, the one with the cool blue eyes and cultured accent who barely looked at her as she stood in his kitchen beside his son.

Marsden held the door open, and Jude was about to step inside when he suddenly stopped.

"Wait a second, I almost forgot him out there." He stepped back out and lifted something from the floor of the porch.

Him?

He held a water-filled glass bowl, and inside, Peeve swam in circles. In the half-lit kitchen, the beta's fins were minute flashes of deep color, glowing and winking.

"I was thinking your sister could adopt Peeve." Jude shut the door with his foot. His cheeks had taken on a hint of blush. "You said she's always wanted a pet, and he'll just be sitting in a bowl in her room, so she can't get into trouble for that."

"But Peeve was Rigby's." Her pulse in her throat hurt. She knew how much it all meant, him bringing Peeve.

"I keep worrying I'm going to forget to feed the poor sucker." He placed the fish bowl on the table. "I'd feel guilty forever. And Rig—I bet he would have gotten a kick out of Wynn. I was going to give her all his Shindiggs tapes, too, but I figured you guys already had that covered."

He said all of this with a new kind of ease, the acceptance of his brother being gone, of Rigby being an imperfect person. Jude had been anger that had nowhere to go, a bird smashing its own wings as it battered at an unbreakable cage. But even the worst of cages had its weak spots, bars that could be bent away to lead to escape.

Marsden had escaped with him. She could never leave the covert entirely behind, but it was no longer all she saw ahead. She'd bent bars of her own.

She leaned up and kissed him, more gently this time, thinking of his cuts and bruises. "She'll love Peeve. Thank you."

Jude pulled her close. "More." The word was soft, rough, and desperate against her mouth. "I won't break."

"But you're hurt."

His eyes said he thought *she* was, with everything they now had between them that would never be simple or go away completely. "You'd tell me if you weren't okay, wouldn't you?"

Marsden ran her hands through his hair, touched his lucky scar. "I won't break."

"So, then, more. Please."

Acknowledgments

I wrote the book, but *Along the Indigo* wouldn't exist without every single person on this page. My thanks to all of you.

My brilliant, passionate, and tireless agent, Victoria Marini. I'm so very lucky to have you in my corner, and I wouldn't be here doing any of this without you.

My wonderful editor, Anne Heltzel, who believed in this book from the start. You saw all the things I couldn't, and that's why you're a genius.

The rest of my team at Abrams—my copy editors, proofreaders, and publicists—and your endless enthusiasm and support for this book. I will always be grateful.

Author and writer friends Ellen Oh, Mindy McGinnis, Caroline Tung Richmond, Dhonielle Clayton, Mark O'Brien, Bethany Morrow, and Camryn Garrett. For helping me get this book on track and for sharing with me all your talent and wisdom. I owe you guys so very much.

Bak and Hing, Wendy, Ray and Peggy, Heather and Terry, Ashley and Steven, Dallas. Your constant encouragement means the world.

And, of course, Jesse, Matthew, and Gillian. I once thought dedications were a kind of thank you. But I was mistaken, because I can never say it enough. So thank you, for every single thing.